For All Our Tomorrows

FREDA LIGHTFOOT

For All
Our Tomorrows

Typeset in Plantin Light by Hewer Text Ltd, Edinburgh

Printed in Great Britain by
Clays Ltd, St Ives plc

ACKNOWLEDGEMENTS

This novel is set in Fowey in Cornwall, a place that is close to my heart having lived there for thirteen years, but the story is entirely fiction. The place is real, but the people are not.

My sincere thanks to Arthur and Janet Baker, Maureen Waller, Edna Kenny, May Poulton and John Libby for the invaluable information they gave me on life in Fowey during the war.

I dedicate this book, with great affection, to all my friends living in this most delightful of towns.

I

The oranges rolled across the narrow street, bouncing on the cobbles and bumping seductively against the feet of the two young women. Children were running helter-skelter in the Cornish sunshine, giggling with excitement, eager to catch one of these glorious golden orbs as they were tossed and rolled with such reckless generosity.

Gasping in amazement, the younger of the two women snatched one up, to sink her pretty white teeth into the flesh.

'This is wonderful!'

Juice spurted, running down her chin to leave little orange blobs on the bodice of her print frock as she greedily stuffed segments of fruit into her mouth. Not that she appeared to care one bit, nor that her expertly coiled, soft auburn hair had shaken loose from its pins as she'd run down the steep hill of Lostwithiel Street. All she wanted was to keep pace with the trucks, jeeps, gun carriers and goodness knows what else which were parading through Fowey town, and catch another of these glorious fruits.

So she lifted her face to the grinning man high above her in his vehicle, and laughed.

Her sister too was laughing as she chased one orange, clearly heading for the town quay, while tossing a second to the child running excitedly beside her.

Other women were doing exactly the same. After four years of war, many of the children had never seen such a thing in their lives before and their mothers had almost forgotten the delicious, bitter-sweet taste.

Nor had they ever seen men like these.

These men didn't carry the weariness of war on their shoulders, nor were they dressed in utilitarian battle dress that didn't quite fit. Even their vehicles were blazoned with stars and nicknames such as 'Just Jane', 'Lucky Lucy' and 'Cannonball'. These men were fresh and smart and young, bristling with sexual energy which not a girl or woman in the crowd didn't recognise as such.

Bette Tredinnick certainly did. Her hazel eyes were teasingly provocative as she tore the skin off the fruit with her teeth. 'More please. Give me more!'

'What's it worth, honey?' the marine mischievously asked her.

'Name your price,' Bette shouted back.

'Hon, the captain would kill me with his own bare hands if he heard me make such a suggestion in a public place.'

Bette made a show of innocence as she shielded her eyes against the sun and gazed back along Fore Street in the direction of the jeep that was leading the parade. 'Take a chance. He isn't listening and I'm open to all reasonable offers.'

'See you later then, sweetheart, down by the quay.'

'I'll be there,' she called, just as his vehicle swept away to be swamped by the crowd.

Sara Marrack, having made sure that both her children were each provided with the delicious treat, began to delicately peel her own orange, for once making no comment about her younger sister's bold flirtatiousness but laughing with her, enjoying this unexpected holiday along with the rest of the flag-waving townsfolk.

Bette should be in their mother's hairdresser's shop, cutting and styling, and herself doing chores at The Ship Inn. But women in curlers were openly joining in the fun and the pub was fortunately closed till lunch time, so here they were, along with everyone else, stealing time off work to witness the arrival of these American marines.

They'd come by train only days ago, arriving at Fowey station in the pouring rain on a gloomy autumn day. Now the sun was shining and everyone had turned out to give them a hearty welcome.

There had been times when no one had quite believed that this moment would ever come, in spite of the preparations made in recent months by the Construction Battalion, the Sea Bees as they were called, whose task it was to prepare quarters for the expected friendly invasion. They'd erected rows and rows of Nissen huts up at Windmill, a field high above town, cleared one or two beaches of mines and coils of barbed wire so that training for some operation or other could safely take place.

No one quite knew what that might be, but it had something to do with all this talk of the Second Front.

Sara didn't care that there were jobs she should be doing, floors to scrub, beer pumps to flush out, or that when Hugh returned from his regular weekly trip to the brewery he would take her to task for neglecting them. What did it matter if she got a bit behind for once? This was an historic day for the town. Even the teachers recognised it as such, and had honoured it by closing the school and allowing their pupils to run down the hill to meet these new arrivals who had come to help win the war.

None of the other businesses in town were doing much trade either. The women who, moments before, had been queuing with their empty shopping baskets outside the green-grocer's, hoping for half a cabbage or a turnip or two for the stock pot, were now revelling in the acquisition of much choicer fruit. Children no longer had their noses pressed against Herbie Skinner's ice-cream shop window.

Even an elderly man in the process of being fitted for a new suit at Williams the tailor's, stood grinning on the pavement, uncaring of the pins holding it in place.

The townsfolk of Fowey had long since grown accustomed to disruption, to anti-aircraft guns, to the boom across the mouth of the River Fowey which had to be negotiated to allow for the passage of friendly shipping. They no longer paid any heed to pillboxes and searchlights, and took for granted the activities of the river patrol on constant lookout for spies and saboteurs. They accepted the need for muster points and fire wardens, the ARP and all manner of other defence measures deemed necessary in case the posters plastered all over town warning of the threat of invasion, proved to be correct.

IF THE INVADER COMES, screamed the headline. WHAT TO DO – AND HOW TO DO IT. STAY PUT was the chief message, instructing civilians not to block the narrow Cornish lanes which would need to be kept clear for military movement, for OUR OWN BOYS TO COME TO YOUR AID.

But it was the American marines who had come with their amphibious craft, rolling into their small town as if they owned the place. They were now the occupying force and the people of Fowey couldn't believe their luck.

As the last of the trucks disappeared along Fore Street, teachers began the difficult task of shepherding reluctant children back to their desks, shops opened their doors for business again and normal life resumed, at least momentarily.

Bette returned to the salon and a frustrated Nora Snell, her small round head still tethered to the permanent waving machine which was in turn fixed to the ceiling.

'Did you miss them?' Bette mischievously enquired, recognising the expression of frustration in the woman's inquisitive little eyes. 'What a pity.'

'Not so's you'd notice,' said Nora, as ever determined to have the last word. 'I could see everything through your window here, though a good clean would do it no harm at all. If you can find the time midst all your gallivanting.'

'I'll do my best, Nora, to be a model citizen, as you and the town council expect, though I can't promise. My talents lie in other directions, rather than on the domestic front. Isn't that right, Mam?' Bette added, as her mother breezed in and reached for her pink, floral overall from its hook behind the door, before getting back to work.

Sadie gazed upon her daughter with a jaundiced eye. 'I'd say the day you willingly lift a finger to do a bit of cooking or cleaning, or any sort of hard work for that matter, will be the day pigs start to fly and it rains pink elephants.'

'There you are, what did I tell you?' said Bette, apparently well satisfied with this damning opinion upon her character.

Sara too was hurrying back to work. It was as she ran across Trafalgar Square that she slipped. A final vehicle, an army jeep had unexpectedly rounded the corner just as she approached the front door of the pub. Sara took a step back, attempting to avoid it but her foot skidded on a piece of orange peel left carelessly about, and she went flying, falling with an uncomfortable and embarrassing bump onto her backside.

She lay winded for a second, half aware that the vehicle had stopped and the driver was rushing across to her. She put up a hand and managed a smile. 'I'm all right. Nothing broken. Don't panic.'

'Here, let me help you. I didn't see you there. Jeez, I nearly ran you down. You'd have been Spam, for sure.'

Sara couldn't help but laugh and then winced as a pain shot through her behind. 'Oh dear, perhaps I spoke too soon. I do feel a bit sore. Bruised on fragile portions of my anatomy, I should think.'

'And it's all my fault.'

'Well, you were driving rather fast for these narrow streets,' she gently scolded him.

'Right. You're absolutely right, ma'am.'

With his assistance, Sara managed to get to her feet, saying she could manage very well now, thank you, but he insisted on taking her right to the door, taking her keys to unlock it for her and helping her inside.

He seemed pleasant enough, for all he was a reckless driver, an officer too, judging by the two stripes and star on his uniform, and earnestly anxious to put things right. He brought her a glass of water, even started to dust down the skirt of her dress but then stopped himself, flushing slightly with embarrassment.

'Sorry, sorry,' he kept saying, over and over. 'Hey, I'm so sorry.'

'If you were late before for the parade, you must be even more so now. Hadn't you better report to your unit?'

'I guess so, but I hate to leave you like this.'

'Don't be silly, I'll be fine. Really!' when still he showed no sign of moving.

He had the kind of physique one would expect of a soldier, rather broad and robust, not at all in keeping with the fuss he was making. His hair was dark brown with a slight tendency to curl, dampened slightly from beads of anxious moisture forming on a high brow.

'You sure?'

'Positive.' She desperately wanted him to go before Hugh arrived. It simply wouldn't do for her husband to find her here, with this man, yet she kept on sitting there, just gazing into his face. It was a very nice face, strong and square, and he had the gentlest brown eyes she'd ever seen.

'You're OK then?' Still he made no move to go.

'I'm fine, truly I am.'

'I can't imagine what I was thinking of to be driving so fast. I didn't even see you.'

'You can see me now, and that I'm perfectly all right.'

His wide mouth lifted into a slow smile, as if to say she was more than all right. 'I'd best go then.'

'Yes, you had.'

With great reluctance he took his leave, his parting words warning her to take things easy for a while. Sara smiled and nodded and waved him away but then the minute he'd gone, and despite her aches and pains, she ignored his advice completely and flew about, desperately trying to catch up on tasks that should have been done hours ago.

For once, The Ship was late in opening and an impatient queue had formed outside, a sternly frowning Hugh turning up just as she unlocked the door to let them all in. He cast a furious glance in Sara's direction then gave his full attention to offering humble apologies to his regulars. Her silver fair hair was still untidy and windblown, her normally pale cheeks flushed with a betraying pink but she smoothed down her skirt, pinned a smile of welcome on her face and calmly prepared herself for the expected lecture.

2

For the next hour or more, husband and wife were far too busy pulling pints and selling pasties to have time to think, let alone talk.

Sara loved being part of a tightly knit community, considered herself fortunate to live in this ancient inn right in the heart of town. She might well have long since have grown oblivious to the constant cry of seagulls, but she adored the smell of the sea, customers breezing in and out, the feeling that she was caught up in their lives.

Today there was a particular buzz in the air, following the excitement of the morning.

'About time they showed up, that's what I say,' said Ethel Penhale.

'Aye, they nearly missed all the fun,' agreed her husband, Sid.

'They slouch,' said Nora Snell, setting her lips primly. 'And chew far too much of that dreadful gum.'

Sara enjoyed chatting to the regulars, listening to their gossip, the men happily leaning against the bar and the womenfolk nodding their heads together over a port and lemon on the window seats, so that they were able to keep half an eye on what was happening outside in the square. She didn't even mind hearing for the hundredth time how Hamil Charke caught a shark, even if it was of the basking variety and barely had any teeth, and she'd learned to ignore Nora Snell's sharp tongue.

Only when the last straggler had reluctantly left at closing time and Hugh locked up for the rest of the afternoon, did he turn to her, his expression grim.

'I can't believe you did that.'

Sara started, a beat of alarm fluttering in the pit of her stomach. 'Did what?' Surely he hadn't heard about the incident already? She hoped it had gone largely unnoticed as most people were still chasing after the parade.

'Abandoned your duties to gawp at those dreadful men.'

'Oh!' She half turned away to collect up beer-soaked glass cloths, desperate to compose herself; a part of her wondering if she could get away with not telling him at all as he'd only make a scene. 'Don't be silly, Hugh, I wasn't gawping and why do you call them dreadful? They're here to help us win the war, to fight against Hitler. Aren't you glad to see them? Everyone else is.'

'Everyone else doesn't have my standards of moral decency. Even you can't be unaware of their reputation for bigamy, divorce and unspeakable diseases I wouldn't care to mention. Besides, I'll not have you making an exhibition of yourself. I suppose your flighty sister was there too, behaving even worse. Didn't I say there'd be trouble, the minute I heard they were coming?'

Sara hid a smile. This clearly wasn't the moment to mention that Bette had already caught the eye of a GI, and made a date for the evening which she would undoubtedly keep. And why shouldn't she, being twenty years old and fancy free? Life was for living and who knew what tomorrow might bring?

'There was no trouble, Hugh, none that I saw. I don't see why you were expecting any. They seem perfectly nice, respectable boys to me. A tribute to Uncle Sam.'

'They are well known for rudeness and inconsiderate behaviour, for throwing their weight about where it isn't needed. Well, no GI is setting foot in my pub, I'll tell you that for certain. I won't have them in here chatting up the girls and throwing their money about.'

By 'girls' he meant herself, his wife, of course. Sara understood the implication even though she didn't comment on it. God knows what he would say if he knew that one of these 'dreadful men' had been in the pub already, alone with her, after having very nearly knocked her down.

'We need their money, Hugh, don't forget.'

'I believe I am still entitled to refuse to serve troublemakers in my own bar.'

Sara stifled a sigh. 'Let's wait and see if they are troublemakers first, before you start banning them.'

It was rare for her to criticise him, or even disagree, since she'd discovered the fruitlessness of this exercise quite early on in their marriage. He was a man with firmly fixed views and generally found a means to have his own way in most things.

'Put the takings in the safe will you, while I give the bar a quick wipe over, then we're done for now.' She smiled, to soften the fact that she'd given him an instruction but he briskly responded that he'd been about to do just that, and would she please hurry up.

Sara had been little more than eighteen when she'd married Hugh Marrack, flattered by his interest and charmed by his maturity and good looks. He rowed on the gigs, sailed, swam, was athletic and strong, a risk taker and, at thirty, had seemed like a god to her. She had loved his tall leanness, that shock of blond hair he would sweep back from a high forehead with the flick of one hand; the classically straight nose, the blue-grey eyes and the way they would gaze at her in a slightly perplexed fashion, as if not quite able to believe his good fortune. She'd adored his patient, old-fashioned courtship of her, and had been impressed by the good solid future that he'd planned for them by taking on the management of the inn.

She'd become pregnant with Jenny within months of their

marriage, quickly followed by Drew. Two children was enough, Hugh had decided, and there'd been no more since.

Some of the fizz had gone out of their sex life as a result, certainly so far as Sara was concerned. Hugh too seemed less interested, since he instigated love-making less often these days, which she thought rather sad. But then they both worked long hours and if sometimes she felt a tinge of disappointment with her lot, that she'd perhaps been a mite hasty in marrying so young, and that life hadn't turned out quite as she'd hoped, Sara blamed herself for having too many romantic notions.

Or she blamed the war, which had dominated their lives for so long and seemed to go on for ever. But what could she do about that? Nothing, except endure, like everyone else.

Hugh was a member of the lifeboat crew, and also carried responsibilities with regard to the coastguard service, so was very often unavailable when there was work to be done. Even when he wasn't out on training and doing 'his missions' as he liked to call them, he was busy with paperwork in the little office up in the eaves. His time, he told her, was far too important to waste on mundane tasks, which she supposed was true.

So here she was, seven years later, still only in her mid-twenties, minding her children, feeding her husband and doing a hundred and one jobs each and every day. She served behind the bar, baked the pasties, did the cleaning, the endless washing and ironing, as well as catering for occasional bed and breakfast guests. Sara even cleaned out the beer pipes, as she'd done this morning, although not very well.

Not that she ever complained. Hugh was a very private man, liable to sulks and dark moods if she should ever object to the workload or claim that he was neglecting her.

And he was a good husband in other ways, caring and solicitous, perhaps too much so at times, almost suffocating. Sara frowned as she wiped down the bar counter, filled with a rush of guilt for viewing his assiduous attention in such a light.

Perhaps she craved a little too much freedom. Maybe the fault was hers. After all, as he repeatedly informed her, he always had her best interests at heart.

As he was telling her now.

'You've got that glazed expression in your eyes again, Sara. I do hope you're paying attention. I can't stand about here all day explaining things your own commonsense should tell you. I have more serious work to do. Do you understand?'

'Yes, Hugh. Of course, darling.'

She saw him soften, as he so often did when she addressed him thus. He came to her then and slid an arm about her slender waist. 'My God, no wonder I'm jealous of anyone else coming near you. Have you any idea how ravishing you look with that silver haze of soft curls framing your enchanting little face, and those large, adorable green eyes.'

Sara giggled. 'Don't exaggerate, they're more grey than green, and my hair is a mess.'

He slid one hand down the length of her thigh and, pulling up her skirt, slid it between her legs to fondle her possessively. She pushed him gently away, laughing as she half glanced over her shoulder to the windows that looked out over the street. 'Be careful, someone might see. If Nora Snell walks by, she'll have a heart attack.'

'We could slip upstairs for half an hour.'

Chuckling softly, she dismissed his optimism with a kiss on his nose, then turned away to search for her purse. 'I have to go and collect the children, and they'll be bursting to tell you all about their exciting day so do try to be patient with them.'

'Make them damn well wait for once. I'd forgotten how much I fancy you,' he said, his voice urgent now, thickening with need. He pushed her back against the bar but Sara easily evaded his grasp.

'It's good to know that you do still fancy me, but I really don't have time right now.'

The smile instantly faded and his tone turned peevish, like a spoiled child deprived of a treat. 'You never do have time these days, or else you complain you're too tired.'

She was stung by the accusation, which Sara felt to be largely unjust. Hugh seemed to avoid intimacy far more than she did. 'I'm sorry if you think so, but I do work hard, Hugh.'

'Is that some sort of dig at me?'

'No, of course it isn't. We *both* work hard,' she added hastily. 'Perhaps we should both try harder to inject some romance back into our marriage.'

'You're saying I don't do enough in that direction, are you? You want me to bring you flowers every day?'

'No, no, of course I don't. Look, this is a stupid argument. I was simply agreeing with you that we should find more time for each other, for romance.'

'Did you see someone you fancied on those trucks then?'

Sara shook her head at him in a gesture of despair, even as she felt her cheeks grow warm. 'Don't be silly.'

'Oh, silly is it, to want to protect my wife from those louts? I've told you, Sara, I'm not having those Yanks in The Ship.'

She was already on her way through the back door that led out onto the church path. 'Look, I must go. We can talk about this some other time and perhaps later I will be able to convince you that there is no other man for me but you, my lovely husband.' Blowing him a kiss, she hurried away, still smiling. Hugh remained where he was, scowling at the closed door.

The Yanks came in their dozens, noisy and happy, raucous and loud, complaining about the beer, the accommodation they'd been allotted, the black-out, even the food, and Hugh was helpless to stop them. He could do little to prevent them leaning on his bar and ordering service, not without creating a scene which could easily turn nasty.

Hugh kept a close eye on them, scowling while they happily played darts or dominoes, joked and teased each other in big loud voices, chewed their gum and even burst into song now and then. They'd call a pack of cards a deck, demand checkers when they wanted to play draughts, and ask for potato chips when really they meant crisps.

And they constantly chatted to his lovely wife. They told her how pretty she was, asked if she'd care for a stroll by the river later, if she was free for dinner tomorrow, if she liked sailing by moonlight. Sara laughingly countered all offers but after a while, unable to bear it any longer, Hugh ordered her upstairs.

'Go to bed, Sara, I can manage.'

'How can you manage? The place is heaving. What will it be, sir? Well, if you don't care for the beer, have you tried our local cider?'

'I'd fancy a bourbon but you ain't gonna have such a thing, right?'

'Sorry, there is a war on, you know. I could let you have a small shot of Irish whiskey, which we happened to come by the other day. Only a small one, mind, and expensive.'

Hugh snatched the bottle from her grasp. 'Go on, get upstairs. I'll deal with this lot.'

'Don't be silly,' Sara hissed at him under her breath. 'You need me here.' She'd been half thankful, half regretful that the young officer who had almost knocked her down had not made an appearance, although she'd kept an eye out for him all evening.

'Upstairs. Now!'

Sara recognised the tone as one which must be obeyed. To defy him would put him in a sulk for days, make him more peevish and bossier than ever. He used to take out his ill temper on poor Valda, his long-suffering mother but since she'd passed away a couple of years ago, it was Sara who now suffered the brunt of his moods. Sighing softly, she slid quietly out from behind the bar and reluctantly pushed her way through the crowd.

'Hey, you ain't leaving us, are you, babe?'

'I must go and check on my children,' Sara excused herself with a smiling apology.

One young man pulled her into his arms. 'Say you'll be back, honey, or I'll die on the spot from a broken heart.'

She couldn't help but giggle at the outrageousness of their flirting. These boys were such fun. She slapped playfully at the GI, urging him to let her go. 'Behave yourself, I'm a respectable married woman.'

'Now that's a big disappointment, 'cos I sure do like the other sort better.'

Seeing Hugh's glowering expression darken even further, Sara prised herself free and escaped. She could see that life wasn't going to be easy with these newcomers around.

As well as the marines, the place was humming with local girls, all of whom had been tempted in to meet these demigods at closer quarters, these Government Issue as the Americans had dubbed them.

Bette hadn't shown her face in the bar all evening, but then she already had a date, didn't she?

Oh dear, Sara thought as she made her way up the stairs to their private quarters on the top floor, leaving her husband to cope with the chaos alone, this long anticipated 'friendly invasion' was going to create havoc, not only to the town but to their own little world within it. That much was obvious already.

3

Bette Tredinnick was only too aware that she had the kind of looks that would turn any man's head. She brightened her mouse brown curls with just a touch of henna and, as she said herself, if Sara was silver fair, her own charms were pure gold. She was also quite proud of her eyes, which some might call call hazel but Bette described as a translucent green shot with flecks of gold. Add to that a small nose, prettily pointed chin and a mouth which lifted easily into an impishly tilted smile, not forgetting a petite and shapely figure, Bette held no illusions about her charms. She was a stunner, didn't everyone tell her so?

She'd certainly never had any difficulty in attracting the local boys, uncouth as most of them were, although much of the time she didn't even bother as they really weren't worth the effort. Love them and leave them, that was Bette's motto.

She dreamed of escape from the suffocation of small-town living, of meeting someone handsome, rich and romantic who would whisk her away to a new, exciting life. She constantly kept a lookout for new arrivals from the yachts and other craft which occasionally came up river; Londoners mostly, seeking respite from the war, retreating to their holiday cottages in Polruan or Bodinnick and lived in hope that one day Mr Right would be on board one of them.

There was no sign of him so far, but how could there be when all decent young men were serving their country?

Besides, the trickle of escapees from the city had dried up long since and she was left with the likes of Tommy Kinver, too young and far too stupid to be allowed to fight. Or Dan Roskelly who worked on the docks and wouldn't leave her alone for a minute, pest that he was.

The thought made her grimace as she tucked a stray curl in place and smoothed down the short skirt of her best frock, a leaf green crêpe de Chine with a daring V-neck. Bette rather approved of utility fashions which fitted close to her neat figure and allowed her to show off her shapely calves.

'And where do you think you're going, all dolled up like a dog's dinner?' Sadie stood, hands on hips, regarding her younger daughter preening herself before the living-room mirror with something approaching envy. Daughters were the very devil and she'd had two to blight her life. Both had been blessed with good looks, not surprisingly, since she'd been a stunner herself in her day, but somehow it was hard to adjust to the fact that her own beauty was beginning to fade just as both daughters were blooming. 'Up to no good, I'll be bound?'

'Why do you always think the worst of me, Mam? I've told you a million times, I won't be put upon by anyone, nor be so accommodating and trusting as soft Sara, fool that she is doing everything that domineering husband of hers tells her. Jump off the headland, she would, if he told her to.'

'Don't you speak ill of your sister and that fine man she married. You should be so lucky, miss.' Fortunately, she'd managed to marry Sara off quite young, and she'd married well. Quite a catch was Hugh Marrack, but this little madam was another matter.

Cory, Sadie's ever patient husband, ambled over and, as he reached for his windcheater from behind the door with one hand, chucked Bette under the chin with the other. 'How's my little maid? You off out for a good time? Proper job.'

'Don't you take her side,' Sadie retorted, turning on him fiercely and wagging a finger in his round, placid face.

'Why not? Someone has to,' he said in his gentle Cornish burr. 'Now, don't you get in a lather, me handsome, does no good at all. Our Bette is a good little bird. Her won't do nothing wrong, I'm sure.'

'I wish I could share your confidence. She took hours off work today, just to ogle those boys, and now she's got a date with one, a perfect stranger I'll have you know.' It occurred to Sadie that, as usual, Cory wasn't paying her the slightest attention or listening to a word she said, being thoroughly absorbed finding his pipe and pouch and matches. 'And where might you be off to then, playing on the river with your cronies, is it?'

'We'm off on our patrol, as we allus are, doing our duty to make sure them Germans don't slip in shore when our back is turned.'

'God help Cornwall, if her defence depends upon the likes of you and Hamil Charke.'

'There's others on board besides me and Hamil, the whole blame crew of us, led by Scobey as you do know, my lover.'

Sadie let out a snort which amply expressed her opinion of Scobey Snell as leader of this lively band. 'Nora was swanking about him today when she came in to have her hair permed, talking a lot of nonsense about how he was a born sailor and used to climb the rigging like a cat when he was a lad working on the Hockens boats. Scobey's never been to Australia in his life, I told her, and he wouldn't know how to furl sails if you paid him. Hasn't got a brain bigger'n a pea, and would be a liability on any boat. She wasn't best pleased with my opinion, said as how he'd done his stint already for Kitchener's army, and I'd no right to criticise.'

'Well, she do have a point,' commented Cory in his mildest tones, tucking the ends of his scarf into his windcheater. 'He might be getting on, as are we all, but he's still handy with his fist. Box the ears of any Jerry stupid enough to try and land on these shores. And he don't miss much, don't Scobey, even if he is cross-eyed.'

Bette stifled a giggle and tried to squeeze past her mother's ample form to reach the kitchen, too accustomed to this bandying of words between her parents to take it too seriously. 'Want a cuppa, Dad, before you go? Or I could make you up a thermos to take with you.'

'Warm the cockles nicely that would. Gets cold out on the water at night, it do.'

'Mam?'

Sadie tightened her lips and shook her head fiercely, even though her throat was dry as a bone. 'I'm warning you, madam, if you bring shame on this house, I'll . . .'

'Aw, put the plug in, Sadie,' Cory groaned, reaching the end of his patience at last. 'She'm happy as a duck, so let her be, why don't you? You and me had us bit of fun too, in our day.'

Sadie flushed scarlet. 'Are you accusing me of being a woman of easy virtue, because if you are, Cory Tredinnick, I'll . . .'

'No, course I'm not. You're getting in a proper boil over this nonsense. I'm only trying to say as how she ain't likely to get into no trouble, so far as I can see, so long as her keeps her wits about her.'

'Well, you tell her how to do that then. She might listen to you. Tell her what they're after, these soldiers.'

Cory sighed, then addressed his daughter with a deeply apologetic expression on his kindly face, as if regretting that he must carry out this unpleasant duty. 'Now you do listen to your ma and keep yourself pure, girl, if'n you tek my meaning? And don't you go believing everything you're told by these GI blokes. Promises are as easy broken as a pie crust, and a pretty little maid like yourself do need to bear that in mind.'

Bette went and kissed him on his plump, soft cheek, assuring her father that she understood everything he was telling her. She tried to do the same with Sadie, but her mother turned her face away at the last moment.

If there was one thing Sadie hated, it was to hear Cory call either of his daughters pretty. It might well be true, but, in her opinion, it did no good at all to flatter them by telling them so, and this little madam was vain enough already. Apart from which, it might make her feel better if, just occasionally, her husband noticed that she was still a handsome woman herself, and paid her more attention. He might call her 'my handsome' in that typically Cornish way of his, but the words were meaningless. Sadie was bleakly aware that she'd put on weight during the long years of her marriage and that her once lovely face was weathered and wrinkled; that both her daughters now left her standing in the beauty stakes. And she hated them for it.

Her ill temper deepening, while her younger daughter banged about in the kitchen boiling kettles and making tea, Sadie continued to berate her unassuming husband, needing to prove her superiority, making it plain what she thought of him and all of his sex.

'I'll be off then,' Bette said, the minute she'd handed over the filled thermos, edging out of the door before her mother started to nag her about taking a coat, which she certainly didn't need on this lovely autumn evening and would only be an encumbrance.

'I'll walk along with you,' Cory hurriedly added. 'Since I'm going that way meself.'

'Then you do look him over, this soldier, and give him a piece of your mind,' ordered Sadie, then stood at the door and continued to issue instructions in increasingly loud and stentorian tones as her husband and daughter hurried off along Passage Street, ever quickening their pace, desperate to be out of earshot.

As they approached the slipway by the Riverside Hotel,

Cory made his excuses to Bette. 'You don't need your old dad playing Peeping Tom, now do you? I'll nip in here for a swift half with old Hamil afore we go out on the water. But you do mind what your ma tells you, d'you hear?'

'I will, don't worry.'

And having satisfied himself that he'd done his duty, Cory disappeared inside to 'wet his whistle' with his mates, before going off on patrol.

He looked gorgeous in his smart uniform, even taller and broader than when he was high above her on the vehicle; so big and handsome with his hair cut short and his cap set at a dashing angle; the shirt and trousers neatly pressed, showing all his muscles and a fascinating bulge in the latter. Bette averted her eyes, feeling herself start to blush at her own daring thoughts.

Oh, but she wasn't for giving up on her dream, even if her mother's had gone sour. As luck would have it, the war seemed to have offered her a new opportunity to pursue it. A chance to escape had fallen right into her lap, and she wasn't going to waste it.

'Hey, there you are. I wasn't sure you'd come. I've been standing here watching sweethearts come and go, feeling kinda lonely. And the smell of those French fries are sure making me hungry. Fancy some?'

'I certainly would, but they're called fish and chips.'

'OK, fish and chips it is,' he said, trying out the new phrase, and they both laughed.

Chad Jackson, as this brawny American introduced himself, might not exactly be the answer to a maiden's prayer, but he certainly had everything required in the looks department. Even so, Bette was determined to choose carefully, to be astute enough to vet him carefully before things went too far. She sought status, good manners, and that vital and all-important ingredient of life, money, which counted most in the end. Bette meant to go places, not spend her life working flat out, as her soft sister did.

This particular marine had made a good impression so far. Unlike the British Tommy, who generally expected a girl to pay for her own supper, Chad happily paid up without demur, and they sat on a bench to enjoy a bag of cod and chips each, relishing every delicious mouthful.

'How you all manage to live on wartime rations, I can't imagine. We had something called brown Windsor soup for lunch, followed by tasteless sausage, lumpy mash and horrible little green balls with some foreign name or other.'

Bette giggled. 'Brussels sprouts. It's true there'd be very little meat in the sausage but you have to appreciate how long we've been suffering this war. And I love sprouts. They're good for you.'

'You're sure welcome to them, honey. Hey, I do understand that you must be starved of stuff after all you've had to endure. What you're in need of is some of my momma's home-made apple pie. Failing that, you'll have to settle for a little tender loving care. Pretty little thing like you shouldn't be all on her lonesome.'

'Oh, yes?' The accent might be different but the chat-up lines were much the same.

Yet his gaze was openly admiring, sending little shivers of excitement running down her spine, and Bette did so love to be admired.

'Now why don't you show me this little old town of yours, and maybe I've got something in my pocket that you might like?'

Bette managed to look shocked, firmly informing him that she was a decent girl and what did he take her for?

'Hey, don't take offence, I only meant these,' and he handed her a packet of silk stockings.

'Oh, Chad. Oh, how wonderful! I can't remember the last time I wore a pair of stockings, and real silk.' She never had worn stockings, silk or otherwise, never in all her life since she'd been only sixteen when war began and such treats quite beyond her.

'Maybe you'll wear them for me some time, huh?'

Bette hastily changed the subject, feeling perhaps this was all going rather fast. 'Where do you live then, in America? San Francisco? New York?' These were the only two places she knew of.

He laughed. 'Naw, a little place somewheres in the Appalachian Mountains, way south of New York, and Washington DC where President Roosevelt lives, ya know? Jest in a ways from what we call the Eastern Seaboard. Me and Barney, we both hail from that neck of the woods. We joined up together and managed to stay in the same unit. I'll introduce you some time, you'll like Barney. Real screwball but the best friend a guy could have. Been together right through school in a two-bit town nobody's ever heard of. I guess you wouldn't have heard of it either, so ain't no use in telling you no names.'

'No, of course not, sorry.' She was dazzled by the thought of anyone living so close to the president, bemused by the strange names he'd mentioned, and Bette didn't understand what he meant by two-bit, assuming it to be meaningless American slang. 'I've heard about Times Square and the Empire State Building.'

'Hey, you're well informed, honey.'

'I've seen it at the pictures. I love going to the pictures, do you?'

'Aw, the movies, I love 'em. If you ever come to America, I'd love to take you to New York, up the Empire State, and to Hollywood, then you could see where movies get made.'

'Would you really?' Bette looked into his eyes, entranced, and Chad felt his throat tighten as he gazed back down at her.

She was even lovelier close to than she'd appeared that morning from the truck, when he'd fallen for her hook, line and sinker, at first sight. But what was he thinking of making such promises? How could a dumb country boy like him ever hope to take her to those fancy places? He'd never had much luck with girls in the past as they generally fell for Barney's dark, Italian looking charms, giving his own more homely features scarcely a glance. Not that he minded, he was real proud to be Barney's best buddy and there never was any animosity between them.

Maybe he was doing better with this chick because he was spinning her a bit of a yarn, not lying exactly, more stretching the truth somewhat, taking a leaf from his friend's book. Barney was usually the one to shoot his mouth off but it generally won him the girl, so where was the harm? She was cute as a bug's ears, this one and he just needed to *be* someone for once, instead of a nobody. Still, best not to get too carried away and overdo it.

'Not that I live anywhere near Hollywood, you understand, but it sure is pretty. We got mountains and lakes, woods and deep ravines, hot springs and gushing falls, Indian reservations and real fine houses that were built way back before the civil war. Ante-bellum, we call 'em. Hey, we got it all.'

Bette's sense of history was scant, but she shivered delightedly at the prospect of Indians, captivated by the romance of his descriptions. 'And that's where you live is it, in one of these fine houses? How wonderful!'

Chad gazed into her enchanting, golden-green eyes and couldn't bring himself to disappoint her. 'Well, it sure ain't a bad house, nor small neither. My family has lived there for a generation or two, that's fer sure.' He slid an arm around her waist, anxious to stop all this chat and get down to business.

Bette slid away, further along the bench, teasing him with her smile as she sucked salt and vinegar from her fingers, determined to make every effort to be sensible and practical and concentrate on essential details, as she'd promised herself that she would. 'So what is it you did, exactly, before you joined the marines?'

Chad got up, collected the used chip papers and went to stuff them in a nearby waste bin, his thoughts racing. He'd worked on the family farm before the war, like many another southern boy, though that had never impressed a gal yet, so why take the risk of being too honest with this one when he was doing so well?

'I guess you could say that I've got me some land in Carolina. You ever been to North Carolina? No, course you ain't. Like I say, prettiest place on God's earth, just like you're the prettiest woman I ever did see.'

'Land, but I thought you said that you lived in a fine big house in town?'

He was growing confused by his own lies now and mumbled that there surely was a town close by, but Bette was persistent.

'And is it a big town, where you live, with cinemas and big fancy shops and such like?'

'We live a ways out of town,' Chad reluctantly admitted, carefully avoiding answering her question in too much detail, wishing that he'd kept quiet and not tried to impress her at all. 'I'd love to show you Athens and Charleston and Savannah. Real fancy towns, they are, but some ways off.' He didn't say just how far and rushed on, eager to see her smile once more. 'Then Hollywood here we come, huh? Boy, I love those eyes of yours. Are they gold or green, I jest can't make up my mind.'

He snuggled closer and Bette giggled some more. He really was sweet and the names sounded magical, very much like something out of a movie. 'Oh, that would be marvellous. I'd so love to travel.'

'Jest as soon as this little old war is over, honey, we'll see the world together, meanwhile . . . how about that tour you promised me, huh?' He offered her his arm with sweet, old-fashioned courtesy.

They strolled together along to Whitehouse, Bette feeling very special and important to be out with such a gorgeous guy, one who lived in such an exciting place, not too far from the President of the United States himself, and a land owner at that, just like the Cornish gentry. If that didn't prove he was rich, she really didn't know what would.

Having reached the tiny little beach, they sat huddled in among the rocks, while they had a bit of a kiss and cuddle. Admittedly there was a pillbox nearby, and ships in the river, but Readymoney beach was too far away and embroiled in barbed wire, so this would have to do.

If they kept their heads down, nobody would spot them in the darkness, and with the silk stockings safely stowed away in her bag, how could she refuse?

He was certainly bold, cheekily fondling her breast without the slightest invitation, and never had she known such an expert kisser. Bette was growing dazed with emotion and quite breathless, beginning to worry about how far she should let him go when suddenly there came a great bang out on the water and she nearly jumped out of her skin with shock.

'What's that? Oh, my God, have the Germans attacked? Are they bombing us?' She was ready to run, instantly trying to decide whether it was quicker to dash to the shelter on Lostwithiel Street, or down to the Butter Market. Or maybe Porphyry Hall would be safer if she could get there in time.

Chad was on his feet in a second, peering into the black dark that blanketed the wide river. 'Hey, don't fret. That wasn't big enough for a bomb. Just a stray shell going off, I reckon. There's a boat out there though, quite a small one.'

'It's the river patrol. Oh lord, that's my dad's boat. He's dead. I know it. Oh, my God, no!'

4

Cory Tredinnick and his crew had set out in their boat as soon as they'd downed a few pints, ready to carry out their role on the water rather as their comrades, the Local Defence Volunteers, or Dad's Army as they were more popularly known, did on land.

'Do'ee remember when the Home Guard sank the boat that was towing the target upriver, that time they were practising shooting?' Cory remarked with a chuckle.

The river valley and creeks of Fowey were well defended, as they provided a relatively secure place to hide munitions which the enemy would more likely expect to find in Plymouth, surely never thinking to look in this secret, wooded hideaway.

'Daft clucks, the lot of 'em,' agreed Sid Penhale. 'Our river patrol is much more skilled.'

The docks, from where the ammunition was shipped and the china clay dispatched, were guarded around the clock, with nobody allowed in without a pass. There were guards stationed in the pillbox at Whitehouse, and Albert Quay had tank traps across the centre with barbed wire along the seaward edge, as did many of the beaches. In addition, at St Catherine's, closer to the mouth of the river, there was a gun point, and one on the opposite side at Polruan.

'And better prepared for the invasion,' put in Hamil Charke.

They all solemnly nodded in agreement.

Temperatures had dropped considerably after a warm day,

and a slight mist rose from the water, glowing with an eerie ghostliness in the light from a pale moon. Scobey, as usual, was on the tiller and the rest of the crew dipped in their oars and rowed with a rhythm which spoke of long practice. All were expected to keep a lookout for unwanted intruders, and for any stray mines. At least that was the general idea but, as usual, it was Scobey who spotted it first. It was floating in the water, but, instead of calling out and warning everyone, he leaned right over and picked it up.

'What you got there, m'boy?' asked Sid, the more alert of the crew.

'I do reckon it be a shell,' said Scobey, holding the offending article in his hand.

'What sort of a shell would that be, 'xactly? Mussel or scallop?'

'The sort that goes boom,' said Scobey, giving his gap-toothed grin.

The silence in the boat following this statement was palpable, and had anyone dropped a pin, they'd have heard it for sure across the water in Polruan. Though as things turned out, the calm and quiet was perhaps a good thing since it gave Scobey time to think on what he'd just said, and every drop of blood seemed to drain from his face, leaving it as waxy and pale as the moon.

'I do reckon,' said Hamil, in a carefully composed tone of voice, 'That you should put that back, d'rekly.'

'I think 'ee might be right there, m'boy.'

And so he did, except that instead of setting it gently back where he found it, in the water, Scobey flung it with all his might at some nearby rocks that jutted out into the river. The explosion broke the largest rock in two, sending the major portion of it catapulting into the water which, coupled with the force of the blast, created such a wash that it rocked and near overturned them.

The men clung to each other, and the boat, with grim and terrified determination; Hamil and Cory having a few choice words to say in the process. Even as they roared their disapproval at Scobey's hare-brained stupidity, they suddenly became aware of a strange phenomenon.

'What's this? I do believe it be raining fish,' said Cory, as a mullet dropped into his lap.

'Will you look at that! Scobey must've hit a shoal.'

He had indeed, and a good one at that, judging by the number of monkfish, sea-bass and sea-trout that flopped into the little boat.

'Well, it do save us the trouble of going fishing in the morn.'

'Aye, and saves on coupons too, that's for sure,' said Scobey, well pleased with their catch. Their stroke of good fortune would be sufficient to feed all their families, friends and neighbours, for days to come.

It was Nora Snell's idea that some of the fish be used to hold a welcome party for the newcomers. Nora wasn't particularly well known for her generosity but even she couldn't cope with this bounty, and she always enjoyed showing off her husband's prowess, considering the stick he got just because of his misfortune to have a slight squint. Nora, however, did not want the bother of organising the event herself but was past-master at organising people, and since she naturally needed a venue in which to hold it, who better to ask than Sara Marrack?

She cornered her the very next morning outside Varco's wet fish shop, the proprietor of which wasn't best pleased by this competition, even though he'd agreed to take a few off her hands.

Sara was startled. 'Goodness, I'm not sure I'm the right person to ask. Besides, I don't think there'd be room at The Ship, do you, Nora? We'd need somewhere much bigger.'

Nora wasn't for letting Sara off the hook quite so easily and chewed over this problem in silence for a moment or two. 'You could always ask the mayor if we could use the Town Hall. I'd do it meself only I have enough on my plate, d'you see, cooking the fish. And we'd have to do it quick, afore they go off. Tomorrow, at the latest. Besides, those boys do deserve something special to show they'm welcome.'

Sara lapsed into deep thought. Nora was right for once. It would be good to offer some sort of welcome party. And if, at the back of her mind, she felt a twinge of hope that it might also offer her the opportunity to see a certain lieutenant again, she pushed the thought firmly aside.

'It could make us some money for Weapons Week.' Nora added, by way of enticement. 'This is the biggest catch in living memory, at least since the pilchards used to run by these shores early in the nineteenth century.'

'I suppose so, and worthy of celebration on its own account, let alone putting out the welcome mat to our visitors,' Sara said, and found herself agreeing, although in her heart she knew that Hugh would be furious at the very idea of her being involved. But how could she possibly refuse? The whole town was talking about the catch. It was a phenomenon. She put this point to Hugh, hoping to sway him, but he wasn't fooled.

'You must think I'm mad. This shindig will cost me money, I'll be bound.'

'Don't be silly, Hugh, you might actually make some. Everyone is going to want to come so we thought we'd hire the Town Hall, get Hamil to play his fiddle and we could have a bit of a dance, followed by the fish supper. But since it's only a step away across the square, they'll no doubt wear a path to your bar for constant lubrication.'

'These men have come to fight a war, not dance or go to parties.'

Hugh did not believe that Sara took the war seriously. How could she, being merely a woman? Yet ever since the start, Fowey had played an important role in operations. The river was deep enough to allow passage of ships up to 15,000 tons to berth, and the town already possessed working docks and a railway, all safely cloaked by hills and woods.

The navy had come first with their minesweepers and Z boats, armed trawlers and motor gunboats, swiftly followed by the RAF, the Royal Army Ordnance Corps, plus many units doing jobs nobody quite understood or dared question. Situated as the town was, relatively close to the Channel Islands and to France, the movement of the French fishing fleet within these waters was commonplace, and who knew what they were up to half the time?

Hush-hush boats, they called them. Hugh was highly curious about their activities but had more sense than to ask. Should he ever chance to see strangers being disembarked, slipping away into the narrow streets of the town, he averted his gaze and forgot about it instantly.

'Be like Dad and keep Mum', was advice to be taken seriously in these parts. Not volunteering, was another of his maxims.

But the prospect of profit always appealed and Hugh was sorely tempted to agree to Sara's request, wondering if perhaps he'd been a touch hasty. Of course, it would mean that his own wife wouldn't be available to help so he'd have to hire it for the evening, which galled him somewhat. He hated to fork out money unnecessarily.

'You should be here in the bar with me, as my wife.'

'It's only for one night. Iris Logan would come and help, I'm sure. I've heard she's courting a sailor and saving up to get married. She'll be glad of the money.'

This gave Hugh further pause for thought, since she was quite a tasty number was Iris, not that he allowed Sara to see his interest. 'Anyway, why would they ask you? What do you know about running a dance?'

'It can't be all that difficult. Nora and Isobel are organising the food, so all I have to do is to ask Hamil to play his fiddle, and perhaps find a gramophone and borrow a few dance records.'

'Don't be stupid. There's much more to organising an event than that. You'd need to advertise, make and sell tickets, keep proper accounts of money paid. And what would you do with the profits?'

'Give it to the war effort, of course, what else? Nora already has that all organised, and word will soon spread, like wildfire I should think. And we don't intend to charge much.'

'I still can't see you managing all of that on your own. You'd make a complete hash of it, for sure. Then we'd all be wasting our time.'

Sara swallowed and was suddenly filled with uncertainty, as so often happened when he doubted her ability. Perhaps he was right. Had she been a touch hasty in agreeing to take on the task? It had seemed perfectly straightforward when Nora first suggested the idea, now she viewed it as a mountain to climb. There probably was much more to organising a dance than she'd imagined, and, as Hugh said, she'd get in a muddle and make a hash of it.

Look how furious he'd been with her when he'd discovered how badly she'd flushed out the beer pipes the other day. Incandescent with rage, calling her useless and a liability because she'd ruined perfectly good beer. Ruined or not, he'd continued to serve it. Even so, Sara clung tenaciously to her rapidly evaporating self-esteem.

'At least I'd know that the drinks were well organised, by you dear, and you could offer me advice, couldn't you, from behind the scenes, as it were?'

Hugh was mollified somewhat by her apparent need of him,

and, in spite of his disapproval of what he deemed to be trivialities, thought again about the likely profits he'd make, which at least would come *his* way rather than to the war effort. He needn't pay Iris too much, she'd be glad of the work if she really was courting.

'If I do agree for you to be involved with this event, and to host the bar myself, I shall want an assurance that your role will be purely administrative.'

Sara frowned her puzzlement. 'I'm not quite sure what you mean.'

'I mean, I don't want you hobnobbing with those Yanks, Sara. You must keep well in the background.'

'I might be asked to help pour the tea, Hugh,' she said, keeping her face very straight.

He glared at her, not sure whether to take her comment seriously or not, although surely Sara didn't have the wit to be sarcastic. 'I believe there are many women in this town far more capable of this task than you. However, as you say, at least I can keep an eye on things, if *you* do it. But I will not allow you to slave away over a hot stove, frying fish all night long. And you absolutely will *not* fraternise with those marines. So long as that is quite clear, I will grant my permission.'

Sara mentally counted to ten before kissing him quickly on the cheek and saying how very much she appreciated his generosity. 'I'm sure I shall manage perfectly well and not have to bother you at all.'

5

It was to be a night to remember. Tea and biscuits were laid out on long tables, and, in honour of the occasion, coffee had somehow been acquired to please the Americans, though nobody quite liked to ask how this miracle had come about. Plates, knives and forks had been borrowed and were laid out ready and waiting. Nora and her happy band of helpers were cooking the fish in a big skillet in Isobel Wynne's kitchen. Hamil was tuning up his fiddle and even before the church clock sounded the hour of seven, the place was humming with locals and marines alike, with naval officers, sailors, ARP wardens and various members of the auxiliary forces, not forgetting any number of bright-eyed girls.

A lively, if not particularly sparkling rendition of 'What Shall We Do With the Drunken Sailor', got the evening off to a good start, with Hamil sawing away for all he was worth on his fiddle and Sid Penhale battering the life out of an old drum.

At what seemed an appropriate juncture, Sara relieved them and offered to put on some records. The pair went happily off for refreshments at The Ship while the notes of 'We'll Meet Again' brought couples to their feet once more.

Sara could hear one of the marines telling a girl that he was this size because he'd been brought up on a cattle ranch and ate beef all the time. Another claimed that he owned a huge apartment block in New York. She couldn't help smiling, wondering how much truth there was in any of this, and then glanced across at Bette, held tightly in Chad's arms, where she'd been for much of the evening. What had he told her, and would it be true? Who could judge? These boys were out to impress the local girls in a foreign country.

The song ended and Bette came over to request another slow number.

Sara protested. 'I thought we'd have "Woodchopper's Ball".'

'Oh, for goodness sake, can't you see everyone wants to hold each other close? Where is your sense of romance, sister dear? Here, let's find "Moonlight Serenade". It must be here somewhere,' and she began rifling through the records.

Sara took the opportunity to whisper a quick word of caution to her younger sister. 'Take care, Bette. You know nothing about him, he could be married, spinning you a yarn, anything. I don't want you to get hurt.'

'You sound as bad as Mam. I'm a big girl and can look after myself, thanks very much.'

'I'm sure you can in lots of ways, but I just want you to take care, to be aware that you've no means of checking him out. All this about him owning land could be nothing more than a tale, one big fairy story. He can say what he likes and you wouldn't know any different. You wouldn't believe the bragging I've heard this evening alone.'

'Are you implying Chad is a liar? Charming, you don't even know the man and already you're condemning him.'

'No, I'm not, but . . .'

'Yes, you are. You just said that he was spinning me a yarn.'

'I said that he might be.'

While they were arguing, Sara's job as record changer was taken over by one of the marines, probably because everyone was tired of waiting for the next record. He put on a bebop and within seconds, the men had grabbed partners and the room was jumping, pulsating with energy. Chad came and whisked Bette away and the conversation abruptly ended.

Sara stood watching and laughing, despite her reservations about her sister's behaviour, dazzled by the display of energy, as well as the show of stocking tops, as girls were lifted and whirled and spun with crazy abandon. Never had she seen the like in all of her life.

'Care to try it for yourself?' A voice at her elbow politely enquired, and Sara laughingly shook her head without even looking to see who spoke.

'No, thanks. I'd make a complete fool of myself.'

'I very much doubt that could be possible.'

Something in the tone made her look up and there he was: the tall, rather earnest lieutenant with short, curly dark hair and the so familiar face smiling down at her. 'Oh, it's you. Hello again!'

He held up both hands in a gesture of surrender. 'I left the jeep back at base this time. Are you OK?'

'Quite recovered, thank you. Still a little bruised on the – er – um . . .'

'On your butt,' and they both laughed.

'I expect I'll live.' She felt a rush of embarrassment and begged to be excused, mumbling something about having to check whether the fish supper was ready, and scurried away. Even as she ran, Sara kicked herself for a fool. Why had she fled? Not because he'd used that word, surely. Was it because of Hugh? Because she didn't want it to get back to her husband that she'd been talking with a GI who'd asked her to dance the jitterbug with him? How very silly.

'What was the chat about? Looked like you two were having a real spat.' Chad shouted over the din as he spun Bette around.

'Oh, take no notice. She's just my sister, being bossy as usual.'

When the dance was ended, he took her over to meet Barney. 'He's my best buddy, so I expect you two to be pals.'

Barney was every bit as big and cheerful as Chad, and even better looking. Bette was instantly fascinated by him. Where Chad's hair was an indeterminate brown, Barney's was so dark it was almost black, what you could see of it since it was cut so close to the head. In contrast to the pale, insipid complexion of a regular British Tommy, his olive skin glowed with a honey tan, as if he'd spent the summer lying on a beach somewhere in the sun, or out at sea perhaps. His eyes were his most striking feature, a pale grey with a darker rim around the iris, and the eyelashes so lush and long they seemed to curl up at the tip. He looked almost Italian but as soon as he spoke, it was in very much the same southern drawl as Chad. He stuck out a hand for her to shake.

'Good to meet ya, Bette. Chad tells me you and he are getting on real fine, and I can see why. You sure are a looker. Pity I didn't get to you first.' And he flashed her a grin, showing perfect white teeth.

Chad slapped him on the back. 'Well, I beat you to it this time, you old rascal, and won me the best girl in town.'

'You sure did, though now she's met me, she might change her mind.' Barney's gaze upon her was steady and Bette felt her cheeks grow warm beneath its scrutiny, understanding why Chad liked him so much. He seemed easy-going and relaxed, if a bit full of himself.

When the next slow number came on, Barney asked her for a dance. 'You don't mind?' he asked of his buddy, already leading her out onto the floor, and Chad shrugged his shoulders.

'Hey, I know we share most things, but not girls, right? One dance, that's all.'

'OK!'

They grinned at each other, with much slapping of shoulders and then Barney swung her away, holding her so close that Bette judged it wise to strike up a little conversation, so that things didn't get too smoochy between them. He was a nice guy but she already had her date for this evening. However, who knew what might happen tomorrow, or any other night? Bette was all in favour of a little variety in life.

'Chad has been trying to explain the size of things in America. It sounds such a *big* country.'

'Sure is. You got such small towns here. Small houses, small cars, narrow roads. Back home we got space, and lots of it.'

'He tells me that you and he have been friends for years.'

'Aw, Chad and me go way back. Went to the same school, church, everything. Our folks are neighbours, both in the same line of business, friendly rivals as you might say.'

'What sort of business? Doesn't Chad's family own an estate in North Carolina?'

Barney tripped over his own feet and bumped into another couple sashaying by. It was a moment before he caught his balance and they were back on course. 'Sorry, no Fred Astaire, me. Hey, old Chad been telling you his life story then?'

'Only that his family owns land.'

Barney half glanced across at Chad anxiously watching them, then spun Bette expertly around, steering her well away from his friend. She was such a pretty little thing, no wonder Chad had stretched the truth somewhat, left out a few details like the fact that the landlord owned the land and the Jackson family only rented it. Well, he was much better at this game than his old buddy would ever be. 'Sure thing. Got himself a fine stretch. My family too, matter of fact. You could ride all day and not reach the end of it. That's America for you.'

'Goodness!' Bette couldn't begin to imagine quite how much land that might mean, but it sounded a great deal. 'So what's all this about business?'

He chuckled softly against her ear, nestling her close so that she couldn't see his face while he worked on his answer, with the added benefit that he could enjoy the softness of her breasts pressed against his chest while he did so. Telling her that both families were little more than dirt-poor farmers producing poultry and vegetables wouldn't help either Chad's, or his own suit, one little bit. 'Ya might say we're in the food industry.'

'Oh, you own restaurants?'

Barney half choked on his laughter, but managed to stifle it just in time. 'We Americans call them diners.'

'And how many do you have?'

He just couldn't resist those eyes, so big and trusting. 'A couple. Hey, no, a whole string.'

'Goodness, where?'

Barney snatched at the first town that came to mind. 'Savannah. That's in Georgia. Got pretty-bitty squares, fountains and fretwork you'd never believe, and great Gothic villas and fine Georgian mansions set in tree-lined avenues. It's some fine town is Savannah, built on the back of cotton.'

'Oh,' Bette gasped, wide-eyed with wonder. 'But I thought Chad said you lived in North Carolina?'

Barney didn't flinch over his mistake. 'Ain't so far away, jest over the border. Chad and me got together, left home to seek our fortune, as ya might say.'

Smiling happily, Bette relaxed, slid her hand up around his neck and pressed herself ever closer. Barney had shoulders worth hanging to. 'I just knew my sister was wrong and that Chad was telling the truth. He's told me all about his house too, built after the American civil war, ante something or other.'

He had one hand on her pert little butt and Barney's mouth had suddenly gone very dry. God, he wanted this woman. She was some chick. He wanted to take her outside and give her one right this minute, but she was still patiently waiting for an answer. He cleared his throat. 'The houses in the South are called ante-bellum. They're the big plantation houses that used to keep slaves to do all the work in the house and on the land. Now they have servants and fancy butlers, land managers and the like. Course, Chad and me, we don't live in one of those.'

'You don't?'

'Naw.' She looked so cast-down and disappointed that Barney swiftly revised what he'd been about to say. What was he thinking of? He'd never told the truth in his life, and this wasn't the moment to start. Where did truth every get you where women were concerned? Not even past first base. He sure did hope that this one would soon grow tired of his dumb pal and move on. And he'd be waiting. ''S'matter of fact, we built us each a fancy new place on the edge of town.'

'In Savannah?'

'Right.' He'd stopped caring what lies he told her. One place was as good as another in Barney's view. He'd slid the hand beneath the edge of her little jumper and she didn't seem to mind. Her skin was soft as silk. 'Hey, you and Barney, you're not stuck on each other, right? I mean, you're open to other invitations?'

'Oh, I don't know!' Bette gazed up at him, mesmerised. The rim around the iris in his eyes was violet, and they were sparkling most seductively at her. As for the hand, she didn't care to think what that was doing, but it was making her feel all weak and funny inside. If she moved her head just one more inch, his mouth would be within kissing distance.

'Jeez, what we doing talking about houses and history? That's some heady perfume you're wearing. What's it called, sugar?'

Bette flushed, giving a little pointed wriggle of the hips to shake herself free of the wandering hand. 'Only Lily-of-the-Valley. Now don't you dare flirt with me, or I'll tell Chad.'

Breathing rather rapidly she pursed her lips and attempted to look cross, sternly reminding herself she should be sensible and check out details properly. But America being such a big country it surely must be rich, as must the men who lived and worked there, so what he'd said made perfect sense. 'Tell me more about this diner of yours.'

Barney was no longer listening. 'You wouldn't sneak on me, would you, sugar? You wouldn't tell my old buddy how I think you're the sweetest gal I ever did see? Jest gazing into those golden-green eyes of yours turns my insides to mush.'

He was smiling seductively down at her, a crooked, wicked smile that spoke of danger, and his hands were off on their wandering yet again, smoothing her hips, circling her waist so that Bette began to feel quite weak at the knees. He was so gorgeous, she almost wished that she'd met Barney first. Still, there was always another day. Bette sent him a tantalising glance up through her lashes, just to let him know that she wasn't really cross, and was rewarded by a tightening of his arm about her that sent a little bolt of excitement shooting somewhere it shouldn't.

'I think you could be a bad man to know, Barney.'

'I think you might be right, sugar, and don't you just love the thought.'

Chad appeared suddenly at her elbow, having pushed his way through the crowd. 'I've decided that best buddy or no, you've had long enough with my gal.'

Bette was disappointed to be interrupted, yet thrilled that Chad appeared so keen, that he wanted her all to himself, and gave Barney a smile of pure triumph.

Barney's words had reassured her though, that Chad wasn't spinning her a yarn, as Sara had suggested. It must all be true. Why would they both lie? Not that she hadn't trusted Chad absolutely, and even if she had any more questions, they very soon vanished clean out of her head, just the moment he started kissing her.

6

The fish supper was a great success and everyone came back for second helpings, declaring they were being fed like kings. Sara noted that several of the men did indeed slip across to The Ship for a cider or beer, though no one got too drunk, so far as she could tell. She and Sadie poured tea while Isobel Wynne and Edith Penhale helped Nora serve the fish.

Once Sara was sure that everyone had been fed and the music had started up again, Hamil back on his fiddle playing a lively barn dance to get everyone going again, she slipped outside to look for Bette.

Her sister was nowhere in sight, but the fresh air was a welcome relief after the heat of the hall. Sara escaped to the quay to breathe in the sweetness of the night. Despite it being black dark with not a light showing, she was only too acutely aware of work still going on, of ships standing at anchor in the docks further up river, perhaps being loaded with munitions or supplies of china clay as this work still continued, war or no war.

From behind her came the strains of 'You Made Me Love You', and below her, the slap of water against the quay walls as the tide came in. Comforting sounds which could change in a instant.

Out there, at sea, the enemy might be searching for a target, perhaps hovering even now over Plymouth, their nearest city, which had suffered badly in the blitz. And then out of the darkness would come the drone of the enemy planes, blotting out all other sounds, stopping hearts from beating, filling them instantly with fear.

'This is my favourite time of year. Back home in Boston, it would be fall and the colours of the trees would be magnificent.'

Sara was startled, having believed herself to be quite alone. For all the comment seemed to indicate that he was homesick, she couldn't find any words of comfort to offer, couldn't even bring herself to turn around and smile at him. Simply knowing he was standing there beside her, made her feel gauche and unnerved. She half glanced over her shoulder, not at the officer but across the quay, as if to make sure they were unobserved. People were standing about outside The Kings Hotel, chatting and drinking. The music was still playing. There was no sign of Hugh.

'I hope you don't mind my following you. It got kinda hot in there.'

'Yes, I thought so too.' Finally she plucked up the courage to risk looking at him, offering a polite little smile, and saw that he'd stuck out a hand for her to shake.

'Charles Denham, ma'am, at your service.'

She acknowledged his introduction with a shy nod as she slid her hand into his, and felt the firm warmth of his grasp. Somehow it filled her with new strength and she was sorry when he let it go. 'Sara Marrack.'

She had the sudden urge to tell him that she was married to the landlord of The Ship Inn, but thought better of it, knowing it would sound silly and inappropriate.

'You've got a fine town here, ma'am, and you certainly know how to make folks welcome. Our boys are having a real swell time.'

'Thank you. That was the general idea. I hope you enjoyed your fish supper.' Sara stopped, thinking how trite she sounded, almost patronising, and bit down on her lip, wondering what to say next. He seemed equally tongue-tied and they stood for some time gazing into the darkness, seeing nothing but the glint of moonlight on the rippling water. After a long moment, Sara stirred herself. 'I really should get back. They'll need help with the tea, I expect.'

'Everyone seemed to have finished with tea by the time I left, but I'd be glad to lead you out in a waltz, if that's allowed.'

Sara felt flustered by the question, innocuous though it might be. What could she say? That her husband would object, that he'd accuse her of being a loose woman, of betraying him, or some equally melodramatic nonsense. But he could come out of The Ship at any moment, and catch her talking to a Yank, smiling up into his eyes. She shook her head and moved quickly away. She didn't even to pause to check if he followed, yet somehow she sensed that he watched her every step of the way.

'Where've you been? I've been hunting for you high and low.' Hugh was waiting for her on the steps of the Town Hall, a scowl on his face which made him look almost ugly.

Sara smiled as she took his arm, knowing he was always prone to exaggeration and turned him towards the pub, away from the quay. 'I went for a breath of fresh air. It's been pretty hectic in there. How did it go for you? Have you had a profitable night?' Little point in asking if he'd enjoyed the event.

Hugh grudgingly admitted that it had indeed been most profitable, yet managed to turn it into a complaint. 'Iris and I have been run off our feet.'

'Did she cope OK?'

'Don't use Americanisms,' he reprimanded her. 'Yes, Iris did fine. She's really a very capable girl and quite popular with the customers.'

'Good. Everyone seems to have had a marvellous time,

made lots of new friends, which was the point of it, as well as eating up every morsel of the fish.' Sara giggled. 'At least the food didn't cost us anything. Only Scobey could do something so stupid.'

'He's fortunate he didn't blow the entire crew to kingdom come, and half the town along with him. Look what happened with HMS *Gloucester City* early in the war. She might have been fortunate enough to escape being hit, and thank God, considering she was fully loaded with munitions at the time, but there was hardly a window in town that wasn't broken by the blast.'

'Oh, I don't think this was a big bomb or anything of that sort. Not like the *Gloucester* at all.' Some instinct made Sara turn and look back, just in time to see Charles Denham pause at the door of the hall, meeting her gaze across the small square with a quiet smile as if they shared a secret, before slipping inside.

'That man is a liability,' he said, and Sara jumped.

'Which man?'

'Can't you focus your mind on anything for more than half a minute. What a scatterbrain you are turning into. Even worse than usual.' Hugh finally registered the direction of her gaze and frowned at the now empty doorway. 'Who are you looking for? You weren't wanting to go back in there, were you? I've locked up now. Time we were in bed.'

'No, no, of course not. The dance is over, everyone will be off back to base. I was simply looking for Bette, to say good-night, but it doesn't matter.'

The moment she slid between the covers Hugh pulled her to him and began to kiss her with an urgency she hadn't known in months.

'Hey, not so fast. Give me a chance to catch up.'

'You don't have to do anything. You're no doubt too tired, anyway, after all your *hard work*, but I need to know that I do still have a wife.' The spiteful tone in his voice was stronger than ever, and, pushing her back against the pillows he thrust hard into her. Sara held him close and wished with all her heart that she could feel something more than compassion.

Over the next few days The Ship was inundated with GIs coming in especially to thank her.

'Gee, is it right that you were the gal who organised the dance? Can't thank you enough. Had the best time ever.'

'Changed my life,' said his mate, while another wailed something about meeting the love of his life but then losing sight of her and not even managing to get her name. His comrades, however, treated this as a huge joke, pummelling and thumping him, laughing at his earnestness and telling him that she probably did give him her name but he was too drunk to remember.

'If I describe her to you,' he said sadly to Sara, 'Do you reckon you could pick her out and tell her I really do love her and want to see her again.'

Sara did her best, listening with patience to his muddled description which might have fitted any one of a dozen girls in Fowey. He was not the only one to come to her with such problems. So many dates had been made that night, was it any wonder if some details such as names or addresses were lost or muddled in the confusion.

Then there were the dates that did take place but went wrong, perhaps because in the sober light of day, one or other of the couple concerned looked less enchanting than memory, and the dim lighting in the hall had led them to believe. Or perhaps the poor marine simply got lost driving the narrow country roads trying to find her. Then there were the guys who were stood up because the girl had come to her senses, or got a better offer. And the girls who'd been left waiting in vain because the GI in question had suddenly remembered that he had a wife already, back home.

Sara became their agony aunt, the one they all turned to with their troubles. Local girls too would come sneaking into her kitchen through the back door to say much the same sort of thing.

And those whose parents had not allowed them to attend were asking when there was to be another dance, and if they could have a soldier next time.

None of this pleased Hugh one little bit. 'Why are they pestering *you*? Why won't they leave you alone? You've done your duty, now it's over. What happens next in their sordid little lives is not your responsibility.'

'They're not bad boys, and many of them are homesick. I'm only trying to help.'

Bunches of flowers started arriving, a box of chocolates, and on one occasion, a whole crate of apples together with several bags of sugar. 'Next time,' said the note enclosed, 'please make some apple pies. That's what we miss the most.'

'Look at this,' she laughed, holding out the note to show Hugh. 'They think I'm their momma.'

He went quite red in the face. 'They do not. Haven't I told you, Sara, to take care. I will not have you being used. These men are nothing but trouble.'

Night after night the marines, and their adoring fan club, continued to pour into The Ship and it was Sara, not Hugh, who they wanted to serve them.

'You've got a national treasure here, man,' they told him. 'I hope you appreciate her.'

'What a doll!'

'She sure does know how to make a guy happy.'

'And this is the best apple pie I ever did taste.'

'Aw gee, you can cook up a storm for me any time, sweetheart.'

Hugh endured all of this for a couple of weeks or more, and then made his announcement. 'I believe it would be for the best if you ceased to work in the bar.'

'What?'

'I've arranged for Iris to take over your job on a permanent basis. I will not have my wife make an exhibition of herself, or have these Yanks flirt and harass you in this way. Nor do I enjoy being made the butt of their jokes.'

'They aren't laughing at you, or flirting with me. I've told you, they are simply homesick and want to show their appreciation for the fact that the townsfolk have made them feel welcome.' Sara might like to have added, everyone except you, that is, but managed to hold back.

Hugh wasn't listening. 'I've made my decision, Sara, and I will be obeyed. I mean to have my way in this. Understood? You may continue to work upstairs, dealing with any guests, and in the kitchen making the pasties, of course, that sort of thing. You can clean the place, flush the pumps and pipes through and so on: all the usual chores, but I will not have you present behind the bar when it is open for business. Is that clear?'

And all she could do was to bite her tongue and agree.

7

Bette and Chad were secreted in what had already become their favourite spot, tucked in the rocks on Whitehouse beach, and Bette had almost made up her mind that she was in love. But was this a good enough reason to allow him to 'go all the way'? Much as she ached to let him, she really didn't think she should. Sara had lectured her yet again about taking care not to trust too easily and what if she was right? What if he did have another girl back in North Carolina, or Savannah, or one in every port for all she knew?

'Maybe this isn't such a good idea,' she said, panting for breath and pushing him reluctantly away. 'It's too soon. We've hardly known each other any time at all.'

'Aw, hon, I feel as if I've known you for a lifetime, even if it is only a few weeks.'

'You'll go back to America next month, next year, whenever the war ends, and forget all about me. You haven't even told me if you're married.'

Chad looked deeply offended. 'Hey, what a thing to say! I've no one back home, no wife, no girlfriend, only my momma and poppa, a young brother, and my sister Mary-Lou. I could never forget you, hon. Boy, you're a gal in a million.'

Betta tugged down the skirt of her dress, which had somehow got all rucked up, and slapped his exploring hand away. 'Then why don't you behave like a guy in a million and slow down.' But she was smiling as she spoke, in order to soften her words and show that she wasn't too cross, holding out the hint of a promise that she might even change her mind one day. 'You never told me about the restaurants.'

'Restaurants?' He frowned, looking puzzled, as well he might.

'Diners, then. Barney told me all about the business you run together in Savannah.'

Chad paled. 'Hey, what's he been saying?'

'He explained that your families were in the food business, and that you and he, the younger generation, got together to make your fortune and now own a string of restaurants, sorry – diners. Why didn't you tell me?'

Gazing into her trusting eyes, Chad guessed what had happened. Barney had been shooting his mouth off, as usual, and this little gal would swallow just about anything. She was so innocent and knew so little about the reality of America, that big old country of his across the pond, that she'd believe whatever they told her. But he was equally to blame. He'd never meant to mislead her, only to impress. Now Barney had evidently made the situation a whole lot worse. Maybe he should confess that he'd exaggerated and tell her the truth. 'Hey, you shouldn't believe everything he tells you. Barney sure does love to brag.'

'Are you saying that you've both lied to me, because if so, Chad Jackson . . .' and she began to get to her feet, her mouth going all tight and prim.

'Naw, hon, I'd never do that. Why would I lie?' Now he was in a worse mess. He surely didn't want to risk losing her. 'You can trust me, absolutely. It's not exactly a string, that's all I mean. A couple, mebbe.'

'A couple?'

Those glorious golden-green eyes regarded him with cool appraisal and Chad felt sick inside at the thought of losing her. 'Three maybe, and hey, Barney might have his eye on another, even as we speak.' Why hadn't he just shut his mouth when he had the chance? Chad offered a shaky smile, wishing he could think of some way to change the subject and get out of this hole he was digging for himself.

Bette saw his misery and misunderstood, her soft heart swelling with fresh love for him as she kissed his cheek. 'Don't be jealous. It's you I fancy, not Barney. You're so kind and gentle, you're the type I go for, not his brash sort.' Who was she kidding? Bette shut from her mind the dreams she'd had since that oh-so-dangerous dance with Barney. He was far too exciting for his own good, that one, and Bette had every intention of being sensible. Barney was the sort who would bring nothing but trouble. Chad, on the other hand, was indeed sweet and kind, and putty in her hands. 'You're the man for me, so long as you understand that.'

'Aw, hon.' Chad felt choked with emotion. He couldn't remember a gal ever choosing him over Barney before.

'I'm beginning to understand how it is with you Americans. Everything in your own country is so big, so wonderful, while we seem small and shabby by comparison. Our houses, our cars. Barney told me all about that, too.'

He laughed with relief. 'And you drive on the wrong side of the road.' The awkward moment had passed and he relaxed, reaching for her again.

Bette sat up and began to tidy her hair. At least that was ostensibly her ploy, although she was well aware that this particular angle provided him with a tantalisingly perfect profile of her breasts. She heard his soft groan.

'Don't do this to me, hon. How's a guy supposed to resist you?'

'Take a cold shower?' Bette giggled, and cast him another mischievous, sideways smile before leaping to her feet and laughing down at him. 'I'd suggest you take a skinny dip in the river, only with the kind of shells and mines that blow up even the fish, best not to, eh? Come on, you can walk me back to work. My lunch-hour is over and you shouldn't even be here.'

'Aw no, you're not leaving me already, so soon?'

'You don't want the military police after you, do you?'

'The Snowdrops? Jeez, you say the sweetest things. Just give me one more kiss, then I'll go back to base like a lamb. Just one, honey?'

And somehow he was pulling her down to him again, kissing her stomach, her breasts, her throat, all the way up until he reached her lips when he captured her completely in a breath-taking kiss that never seemed to end. Chad was certainly a good kisser.

By the time it was over and they'd walked the long way back, Bette arrived at the salon all rumpled and flushed, to much teasing and joking from the customers, and a sour look from her mother. Sara too, was sitting there, looking unusually glum, while little Jenny was playing with curling pins and Drew scrabbling about the floor among the cut hair, playing with his Dinky cars.

'Where've you been till this time?' Sadie demanded. 'Up to no good, I'll be bound.'

Sara put out a hand to hush her mother but Bette only tossed her head and reached for her overall, tying the strings very tightly around her slender waist. Oh, she'd definitely made up her mind. She loved Chad Jackson all right, and maybe next time, she'd show him just how much. If Mam believed her to be a bad girl anyway, she might as well have the pleasures that went with the reputation.

'Take no notice,' Sara said to her, the minute Sadie went off for her midday break. 'She cares about you, that's all.'

Bette snorted with disbelief and picking up a comb began to tidy her disordered curls back into place before her next customer came in. 'Pigs might fly. She cares only for herself, as you well know. She can't be bothered with either of us. Sees us as rivals, not daughters to cherish. Nothing would give her greater pleasure than to see me come a cropper. Well, it isn't going to happen. Chad loves me.'

Sara instantly looked concerned. 'Has he told you so?'

'Not in so many words, no, not yet. But I can tell. He's absolutely besotted. Talks all the time about showing me his home in America, and a wonderful home it is too by the sound of it. This could be a marvellous opportunity for me, and all Mam wants to do is spoil it.'

'Give her time, she'll come round.'

'Why do you always have to see the best in people? Sickening.'

Sara looked startled. 'I don't. I'm not. Is that how you see me? How awful. Maybe I just try harder than you, to be understanding of other people's problems, I mean.'

'Too understanding by half.' Bette stopped titivating her hair long enough to glance across at her sister, then looked more closely. 'Hey, what is it? Have you been crying? Not that bloody husband of yours again? Hugh hasn't left you, has he? Or better still, you've left him. Tell me that it's suddenly dawned on you what a useless bugger he is.'

Tears spurted in Sara's eyes and Bette was instantly contrite. 'Oh, lord, I didn't mean that. I'm sorry. Look, I was just upset over Mam.'

'Why are you crying, Mummy?'

Sara instantly turned to her children, recognising the anxiety in their little faces as they saw their mother upset. 'It's all right darlings, Mummy has a bit of a cold, that's all.' Then she gave them each a penny and told them they could go and buy themselves a lollipop. When they'd run off, giggling excitedly, she turned back to Bette. 'He's given me the sack.'

'What?' This was the last thing Bette had expected to hear. 'What are you talking about? How can he sack you, his own wife?'

Sara sighed. 'I mean, he's told me that he doesn't want me to work behind the bar any more. He's going to employ Iris instead.'

'For heaven's sake, why? No, don't tell me, I can guess. He was against your helping with the fish supper, wasn't he?'

Sara was aware that her husband and sister had never been exactly bosom pals, yet it troubled her that Bette could be so hard on Hugh, who was nowhere near as bad as she made out. 'He's concerned that I not be taken advantage of. And if he's overreacted, well, he's tired and overworked, that's all.'

'As we all are. He's jealous as hell that you are popular and he isn't. That's the real reason. So he denies you the most sociable and liveliest part of the job, the part you most enjoy, and puts that fancy piece, Iris Logan, in your place.'

'She's very good at the job, actually. And she's glad of the money since rumour has it she's saving up to marry a sailor.'

'No doubt you'll still be expected to do all the cooking and cleaning, as per usual?'

'Of course.'

'Bastard!'

'Bette!' Sara was shocked.

'I'm sorry, but he really does take the biscuit. So damned selfish, and you just stand back and let him walk all over you.'

Sara started at her sister. 'Is that how you see me, as a door mat?'

'So prove to me that you aren't. You've danced to his tune ever since you stupidly walked up that aisle, far too young to know your own mind. It's time to do something *you* want for a change, without asking the wonderful Hugh's permission first.'

Seeing the distress in her sister's face, Bette put her arms about Sara and hugged her close. 'Go on, why don't you be brave and start thinking for yourself, for once. Now's your chance, lovey. View this decision as a blow for freedom, as the moment for you to strike out and do something off your own bat at last. What do you fancy, then? What have you always yearned to do with your life but never been able to do because you were always too busy?'

Sara scrubbed at her eyes. 'I haven't the first idea.'

'Then you'd best start thinking about it, start making some decisions of your own. Be yourself at last.'

Sara looked at her sister and half laughed at the earnestness of her expression. 'You might well be right, love. Perhaps it's long past time that I did.'

8

The Americans were made most welcome in Fowey. They might object to the moist Cornish weather but the hospitality of the natives was greatly appreciated and the Yanks loved the green hillsides, the woods and secret creeks, Cornish pasties, and, of course, Cornish girls. They'd whistle at anything in a skirt, and were particularly impressed by bus conductresses, land-girls, in fact any female in a uniform.

People opened up their homes to them, invited them in to supper to enjoy some home cooking, not that they always appreciated such dishes as bubble and squeak or Woolton pie.

'Where's the meat in this pie?'

'There isn't any, actually.'

'You call this coffee?'

'Camp coffee. The bottled variety.

'Why is it called camp?'

'No idea. Perhaps you'd prefer tea?'

'You got any Coca-Cola?

A shake of the head. 'Sorry.'

But they accepted it all in good spirit. If they thought that wartime rations were sparse and tasteless, the patched-up clothes people wore drab and colourless, and the tiny cottages with their smoky coal fires a bit cramped, they never said as much. They happily joined in family sing-songs around the piano or listened to the wireless, laughing along at ITMA.

In return, the GIs provided tinned goods the like of which Fowey folk hadn't seen in years. Peaches and pineapples and

Spam. And for the children there were candy bars, chewing gum and peanut butter, and the inevitable Coca-Cola.

The next dance was held in the Armoury, which was situated at the top of the town above Place, the ancestral home of the Treffrys. Thankfully, Sara was not responsible for running it this time. It was simply one of the normal, run-of-the-mill dances that were held regularly for the entertainment of the soldiers, sailors and marines who were stationed in Fowey. And very popular they were too, the small hut so packed with people that many were compelled to dance outside or were forced to climb out of the window just to get some air.

Bette went with Chad, of course, but, as a married woman, it would have been quite inappropriate for Sara to go with her sister. Not that she had any wish to do so, much as she might love dancing.

She'd thought a good deal about what Bette had said, and deep down agreed with every word. She did need to be more independent and not give in to everything Hugh told her to do. Putting this decision into effect, however, was quite another matter.

Yet when she listened to Bette telling of the fun she'd had, Sara experienced a strange sort of heartache. She couldn't remember the last time she and Hugh had had fun, or enjoyed any sort of relaxation. There was certainly no point in asking him to come to the Armoury with her, or to take her to any other dance for that matter. He was far too occupied with running the inn and with his more important 'missions', whatever they might be.

Only the other night he'd stayed out till the early hours, apologising for waking her as he slipped between the sheets.

'It's all right, I wasn't properly asleep. But I'm glad you're home safe.'

Sara had put an arm around him to warm him up and kiss

his cheek before sleepily asking where he'd been all night to get so cold. She instantly sensed a tension in him and felt a burst of regret that she'd said the wrong thing yet again.

He pulled away and switched on the small lamp by the bed to look down at her so fiercely that he seemed quite unlike himself. 'Don't you realise how dangerous it is to ask questions? Haven't you learned that much by now?'

Sara quailed, almost as if she were confronting a stranger. 'Sorry, I was simply trying to show an interest. I wasn't expecting details. I thought at least you could say whether you were with the lifeboat or on patrol with the coastguard, or whatever.'

'If I were to tell you I was out on the lifeboat, and let drop where we'd gone, let alone what rescue operation we'd been involved with, who knows how far the information might spread, or who might pick up useful knowledge about the British fleet.'

Sara felt herself flushing with embarrassment for his point was a fair one. She'd simply jumped to the conclusion that Hugh was yet again trying to make his war-work sound important, rather as Cory did, and that more than likely he'd been involved in nothing more than a training exercise which had gone on too long, or ended up in the Lugger and stayed on drinking with his cronies. 'Sorry, but you know that I wouldn't breathe a word. You don't imagine I would talk to a German, do you? Or even exchange gossip with Nora Snell?'

'Careless talk costs lives,' he sanctimoniously reminded her, and, sighing, Sara was forced to agree that, hurtful as his lack of trust in her might appear, in theory at least, he was probably correct.

'Sorry, I didn't mean to upset you. Do lie down, darling. You'll catch cold, if you haven't already.'

Reluctantly, he switched off the light again and lay stiffly beside her, saying nothing.

Sarah tried again, whispering softly in loving tones. 'My reason for asking was entirely selfish, I will admit. I thought maybe some night when you are not called out, or on some training exercise or other, we could perhaps ask Iris to look after the bar on her own, which would give us some time to go out by ourselves for once.'

She could sense him looking at her, even in the semi-darkness, just as if she'd suggested they fly to the moon. 'Take time off? There is a war on, Sara.'

'Other people still manage to have fun, dance, go to the pictures, or simply enjoy a walk together, or have a picnic. It would be so nice.'

'You can walk with your sister, picnic with the children, though it's November and I never liked picnics at the best of times, let alone in winter. You know that.'

'I don't care what we do, I just want to be with you, my lovely husband, not just with my sister or the children,' and she kissed him affectionately. 'You need to relax too, darling. It's not good for you to be working all the time. Not good for either of us.' Sara snuggled up to him in the bed, tried kissing the profile of his cheek, since he still hadn't responded. 'Will you at least think about it? I do love you, you know.'

He turned to her then, moved by her words at last, almost contrite, and agreed that he would think on the matter. When he made love to her this time, it was with a greater tenderness, making a little more effort to please her by not rushing things quite so much. Even so she would have liked more in the way of kisses and caresses, and when he was done and lifted himself off her to fall instantly asleep, Sara was again left with a strange sense of dissatisfaction; the feeling that he hadn't really been aware who he'd been making love to at all.

Today was one of those mellow autumn days which Cornwall did so well. It felt as warm as summer and the two sisters were

walking over the headland from where there was a grand view
of the river. Not that the view was quite what it had once been.
At one time in Fowey's past the river would have been filled
with tall ships and fishing boats. Before the war, the small
harbour had bristled with the masts of pleasure yachts and was
a highway for the great ships that sailed upriver to the docks to
be loaded with china clay. These last remained, but the
pleasure craft were all gone.

The two sisters tried to look beyond the views of barbed wire
and Nissen huts and see the wider vista, although even the
shine of blue sea was blotted by minesweepers, gunboats, tugs
and ammunition barges. Even the trawlers were armed and the
sky sulked with grey cloud, as if to echo the mood.

But the weather was mild and dry, and Bette had a free
afternoon as the salon closed at lunch-time on a Saturday.
Sara had rather too much free time on her hands these days
and was feeling very much at a loose end, so was grateful for
the company. And she was absolutely determined to at least
give the children a little fun.

They couldn't traverse the headland with quite the freedom
they'd enjoyed before the war, since severe restrictions were in
place, but they slipped up through the woods behind the ruins
of St Catherine's castle, and keeping low between the gorse
bushes, enjoyed a decent enough walk over the headland,
revisiting old haunts.

Jenny and Drew were eager to fly their kites, while Sara
carried a basket with a flask of tea, bottles of fizzy lemonade
and fish paste sandwiches, plus some Cornish splits which
she'd made just that morning and a small jar of home-made
strawberry jam.

They were aiming for a spot overlooking Combe Bay, a tiny
cove where they'd used to swim and picnic often before the
war, though they wouldn't risk going right down into it now,
because of the possibility of mines.

Sara was still thinking about her conversation with Hugh, remembering how there'd once been a time when they would often go off together on a Sunday for the whole day, to walk and swim and relax. They'd regularly go as far as Polridmouth Bay close to the woods by Menabilly, or further still and visit The Rashleigh Arms for lunch.

Once, quite early in their marriage, they'd enjoyed a few days away in Torquay, and after Drew was born, a whole week in the Isles of Scilly. The war had changed everything, for some more than others.

As if reading her thoughts, Bette said, 'Why doesn't Hugh take you out any more? He's such an old misery boots these days.'

'He's working hard in the pub, and he has his other duties several nights a week, training and such like. It isn't easy for him to get time off.'

'Nothing is easy at the moment, with the war, but other people manage to enjoy life along the way. Why doesn't he?'

'There are always those who seem able to carry on regardless, dancing, drinking, having fun; those who become completely reckless in their pursuit of pleasure because tomorrow they might go out on their ship or aircraft and not come back. You should bear that in mind, Bette, when you're out with your marine.'

Bette rolled her eyes, as if to say, here we go again on another lecture.

'Others retreat more into themselves and can't be quite so heedless, that's all I'm saying. It isn't always possible to judge how people really feel, or to say how anyone should cope with this kind of trauma. We all do the best we can. For Hugh it involves working extra hard to do his bit, so who am I to criticise, or expect more from him than he can give?'

'Why shouldn't you expect more? He's quick enough to criticise you if he thinks *you* haven't come up to scratch, and yet expects you, even now, to carry on doing the brunt of the work behind the scenes, without any fun whatsoever.'

'You're far too hard on him.'

'On the contrary, not hard enough. And you're far too soft.'

Sara was saved from defending herself as Jenny came up and wanted the string on her kite untangling. 'Can we fly it now, Mummy? Drew says his will go higher and I've bet him mine will.'

'Of course you can, darling, but you must keep a tight hold on the string.'

Bette continued to make her point as the pair of them attempted to sort out the kite. 'The marines who regularly come to the pub every night are already asking where you are. They say you explain the money to them better, which they never can understand, and they miss your sweet smile. Don't you miss it, too?'

Sara looked suddenly sad. 'Surprisingly enough, I do.'

The two sisters spread out their mackintoshes and made themselves comfortable on a hump of grass while Jenny and Drew set about flying their kites; putting on their head scarves and fastening their cardigans against a breeze that had sprung up. 'I used to complain that I had too much work to do, now the opposite is the case. I don't have nearly enough.'

'So what are you going to do about it? You surely don't want to work at the salon with Mam and me? She drives *me* mad, don't *you* get involved for goodness' sake.'

Sara laughed. 'Certainly not, I don't have your skills with hair for one thing. Actually, I don't have skills of any sort to speak of.' She was frowning, looking quite doleful. 'I mean, what can I do besides cook, clean, pull pints and mind children? Good for nothing, that's me.'

'Don't be daft, there must be something, lots of things you could do. If you like children, why not help out at the school? You could dig for victory on Fred Pullen's market garden, collect salvage, raise money for War Weapons Week, or join the WVS. They are always in need of help.'

Sara's eyes widened. 'Oh, I never thought of that. Do you think they'd have me?'

'Of course they would. Nora Snell is always complaining to Mam how she needs someone to sort clothes, pull back old knitting so she can hand out balls of wool for the children to knit scarves or whatever.'

'I'm not sure I'd be any good at knitting but I could certainly sort clothes and things, or perhaps provide transport for people, if and when needed, assuming the WVS can supply the extra petrol coupons.' Sara was beginning to get quite excited at all the possibilities. Perhaps she wasn't so useless, after all. 'And there's to be a Salute the Soldier Week next year, I believe, so I could perhaps help fund-raise for that, organise a concert or something.'

'That's the ticket. There you are, loads of things you can do. Hugh will be proud of you.'

It was as if a balloon had burst. 'Oh dear, he might object to my borrowing the car, or getting too involved with war work.'

'For goodness' sake, why on earth should he? He does his bit, why shouldn't you do yours?'

'You're right, of course.' But Sara still looked doubtful.

Bette put her arms about her. 'You deserve better, Sis. I've said it before but it bears repeating. It does no good at all to have a husband telling you what to do all the time. It worries me how he bosses you about, but he isn't always in the right, you know. You said he was out the other night till the early hours, well the rest of the lifeboat crew were in Safe Harbour, having a knees-up.'

Sara thought about this for a moment before answering. 'It must have been the coastguard patrol he was on then, or one of his other jobs. Like I say, he works hard and is involved in so many things. And I can't ask questions, can I? It's not allowed.'

Bette sighed with exasperation. 'Whatever he gets up to, he keeps you tied at home on a very short lead, won't even let you talk to a few lonely soldiers. It's ridiculous.'

'Now who's over-reacting? He may be a bit of a fuss-pot but Hugh is a caring, considerate husband who wants only the best for me. All right, so he's over-protective but he can't help being a bit jealous, it's in his nature, and I *do* adore him.'

'Yeah, yeah. Say it often enough and you might come to believe it.'

Sara ignored the jibe. 'What's more, he's your brother-in-law don't forget, so do try to be nice to him, for my sake.' She playfully tweaked her sister's nose.

Bette pulled away, irritated by her sister's lack of confidence in herself and not wishing to have her comments so lightly dismissed. 'You're always ready enough with advice to me, so let me hand some out for a change. Give yourself a chance, that's all I'm saying. Who knows what you might be capable of, if you don't try.'

They were different in so many ways. Sara so quiet and sensible, a caring mum who always put her husband and children first, with no thought for herself, while Bette as the younger, unattached sister was, according to Hugh, a complete scatterbrain whose only object in life was to enjoy herself.

Maybe his judgement of her was correct, but Bette knew that she also possessed a fierce determination to explore and experience life to the full, and not to be put upon by anyone. Least of all a man. She only wished Sara would show the same sort of spirit.

Sara interrupted her thoughts. 'What about this Chad, then? Is he *the* one?'

Bette gave a casual shrug, tossing her auburn curls with a studied air of nonchalance. 'He might be. Then again, he might not. We'll have to see, won't we?' and she giggled. 'There are so many fanciable men around, it's hard to choose. His mate is cute, too. Barney Willert, he's called. Maybe I'll try him next.'

'Oh, Bette, what am I to do with you? You're man-mad.'

'I am, aren't I?' said Bette with a grin. 'Now why don't Chad and I sit with the children tonight, and you and Hugh go out for a romantic supper, just the two of you. Do you good.'

The suggestion quite perked Sara up. 'That does sound rather nice. Would you mind?'

'Of course not. What are aunts for but to indulge their niece and nephew with a bit of spoiling once in a while. We'll play Ludo with them, or Snakes and Ladders. What do you say? And you can go out and enjoy a candlelight supper, somewhere grand like the Fowey Hotel, just the two of you.'

Sara's face was alight with hope. 'It does sound a lovely idea. I'll speak to Hugh.'

9

Hugh dismissed the idea as quite impossible. 'I have training tonight.'

'Tomorrow then, I shouldn't think it makes any difference to Bette, though I'm not sure about Chad.'

'Chad? That marine? No, Sara. Absolutely not! I'm not having a Yank in my house, not at any time. Your stupid sister is bad enough, utterly irresponsible. The last time she sat with the children, they got so over-excited they hardly slept a wink and she let them make some sort of liquorice juice which they spilled all over the sofa.'

Sara giggled. 'It's a very old sofa, and it washed off quite easily.'

'That's not the point. Anyway, I'm out tomorrow night, too.'

'Oh.' Sara was deeply disappointed. 'But how will Iris manage on her own?'

'She can't, so Sid Penhale is going to lend a hand. He's helped out at the Lugger and various other pubs in the town, so he'll slip into the job quite easily.'

'I assume by that, you are still against my doing a stint behind the bar then?'

'Absolutely, Sara, on that point I am adamant.' But then he softened slightly, as was his wont. 'But you're right, we do need more time alone. I'll take you to the Fowey Hotel for lunch on Sunday.'

But even that was denied her, as they discovered that the

hotel had been taken over by the military and was being used as a galley and mess hall and goodness knows what else besides.

Sara was welcomed by the WVS with open arms and Nora Snell soon put her in the picture. 'Collecting is what we are renowned for, dear. Newspapers and cardboard, aluminium and all kinds of scrap metal from milk bottle tops to saucepans and kettles, used to build ships, don't you know. Then there's waste food for the pigs, rose hips for the vitamin C, black-berries for the jam-making and any piece of second-hand clothing we can lay our hands on.'

'Goodness, that sounds like a great deal of work. What could I do?'

Nora considered. 'Well, I expect you are already saving food scraps and the like. Can you knit? Women and children are always needed to knit socks, scarves, helmets and mittens.'

Sara admitted that she couldn't, but offered to do a stint at pulling back old pullovers so the wool could be recycled. She also sorted clothes for a while, and came across a rather good overcoat that had been donated by Mrs Glynn, who lived in one of the big houses on the Esplanade.

'Do you think she'd mind if I kept it for Hugh?' Sara asked Nora. 'I could put one of his old ones in its place.'

'Not at all, dear. One overcoat is very much the same as another so far as I am concerned.'

Hugh was of a different opinion entirely and raged at her when she made the suggestion. 'You certainly will not give away my old overcoat.'

'But it's very worn, and the one Mrs Glynn has sent was made by a London tailor in very fine worsted. They are quite wealthy, you know.'

'I will not wear their cast-offs,' Hugh briskly responded, going quite pink with anger. 'I'm surprised you even ask. This work you are doing is utterly demeaning. I will not have it. I shall have to speak to Nora Snell and demand she find you something more respectable.'

'No, no, it's all right. I'm sorry I even thought of it. Forget the overcoat. It was a silly idea, obviously, but I never meant to insult you.'

Hugh did indeed speak to Nora and sorting second-hand clothes was banned from that moment on.

Nora was almost apologetic as she promised to find some other, more appropriate job for her to do. 'Can you drive, dear?'

When it was discovered that Sara could, and had use of a vehicle occasionally, she was moved on to collecting salvage, which Sara gladly agreed to. Newspapers were surely safe and the total collected was published each week as there was fierce competition between the villages.

Driving between Par, Lanlivery, Gollant and Fowey, it was amazing how often she passed American army vehicles. She would find herself checking on the driver to see if it was First Lieutenant Charles Denham, then chide herself for being foolish. On one occasion she thought she'd spotted him and almost waved, but then thought better of it. It could have been anybody, and it wasn't at all the thing for a married woman to be seen waving at American marines.

Most of her time was spent making up parcels to be dispatched to the local Cornish boys serving in HM forces. As well as the knitted items there were tins of food, home-baked cakes and preserves, provided mainly by the ladies of Fowey who were veritable experts at pickling, salting and baking.

Sara also went round the shops, begging for unsold stock or small treats which might be suitable and the shopkeepers were, without fail, generous to a fault.

She kept looking for Charles there, too. She sometimes left

off his full title, whenever she thought of him these days. Perhaps because the only private place she had, was in her head. And then one morning, on her way into the chandler's, there he was on his way out, just as if she'd conjured him out of her thoughts.

'Oh, hello.' She could feel her cheeks growing pink, and hated herself for this weakness.

His face lit up into a delighted smile. 'It's good to see you again. We do so miss seeing your cheery face behind the bar, and hearing your merry laugh,' which made Sara's cheeks turn an even brighter crimson. 'What are you doing with yourself these days that's so much more important than serving beer to tired soldiers?'

He'd taken her by the elbow and was leading her away from the shop, much to the curiosity of the group of men waiting to be served, not to mention the woman who ran the draper's next door.

I really must be careful, Sara thought, though she didn't quite know which scared her the most, local gossip reaching Hugh, or her own vulnerability.

'How about a cup of your wonderful tea? I've got an hour to kill before I have to get back. No, don't even think of refusing. I absolutely insist.'

He led her firmly to the Odd Spot, a tiny café so called because it was on the very edge of town, catering mainly for dockers; their great shovels, which they used for loading the clay, leaning up against the wall outside.

He took off his cap and placed it on the table, his hair ruffled and untidy, refusing to be slicked down as it really should be. She resisted an urge to smooth it and folded her hands into her lap, to make sure they behaved.

Tea was brought, and Charles ordered two toasted tea cakes as well. These were utterly delicious, for all they carried only a scraping of margarine rather than butter, and the jam was rather tart. Strangely, even though this was indeed an odd spot for her to be sitting in the midst of all these dockers taking tea with an American GI, Sara felt perfectly relaxed and at ease, starting to really quite enjoy herself.

All the while they ate, he chattered away, telling her about Boston, and the fall, his work up at the base.

Sara told him about the WVS, the children, collecting salvage, the removal of gates and railings, small details of town life, of folk doing their bit. How she missed being able to go up to St Catherine's Castle, sit on the old stone walls to watch the ships coming in, now that it was covered in camouflage nets and gun batteries. Even how to make powdered egg taste good, and the fact the pasties she made weren't as good as before the war, because of the lack of decent meat. 'More of Fred Pullen's home-grown vegetables from his allotment than good steak, but I do my best, and people seem to enjoy them.'

'I'm sure they do.'

What am I saying? Sara thought, yet they were talking so easily, as if they'd been friends for years. 'That was wonderful but I really should be going. It was most generous of you. Thank you.'

'It was worth it to see you look so relaxed and smile. You still haven't fully explained though, why we've been deprived of your delightful presence in the bar.'

Not for the world would she tell him of Hugh's absolute ban. Far too disloyal. 'Actually,' Sara said, trying to make light of it, 'I don't have time any more. I'm far too busy driving all around the countryside collecting newspapers and bottle tops to turn into battleships.'

He was considering her expression with intense scrutiny, as if trying to read the truth behind her words. 'Ah, I see, and this battleship will be made of such rubbish presumably?'

'Got it in one.' Sara leaned towards him, her voice suddenly eager. 'I'm doing my best to be useful but, oh, I do envy the women who do *real* work: are despatch riders for the military, work in factories, on the land, or have joined the WRNS, ready and willing to fight the enemy in any way they can. My own efforts seem insignificant by comparison.'

He didn't laugh or pooh-pooh her feelings but considered them quite seriously. 'I'm sure that is not the case at all. I was only teasing when I suggested the battleship would be made out of rubbish. Fund-raising, salvage, all of that stuff is an essential part of the war effort, too. I've heard how many thousands of pounds the folk of Fowey have raised this last year or so, and I'm deeply impressed. Enough to build two battleships, I shouldn't wonder.'

'Several torpedoes, I believe.' Sara giggled. 'You should have seen Fore Street and Trafalgar Square when it all first began. Everyone emptied their lofts and cellars and the streets were awash with tins and boxes, old iron bedsteads and battered frying pans. It was hilarious. The council didn't know where to put it all. Poor Nora had to organise dozens of trucks to clear it all away. It's getting harder to find so much now, although we have to keep trying, apparently. That's what I'm doing today, begging for treats and comforts to send to sailors. Anyway, I'd like to think that it's all worth while, and that I'm doing something useful.'

She was talking too much, Sara knew it, but couldn't seem to stop, couldn't bring herself to get up and walk away.

There was something in the sympathetic tone of his voice, in his steady gaze that made her feelings come bubbling out, almost as if she had no control over them. 'I do *miss* working in the pub and chatting to you all. I wish I was still allowed to . . .' She stopped, appalled by what she'd been about to say.

He pretended not to notice. 'If anyone can prise stuff out of folk, you can. That's what you were doing the other day, when I saw you driving from Lanlivery?'

'Oh, I wasn't sure that it was you.'

'I'll wave next time, to make sure you do.'

'Yes.'

Again silence, their gaze locked. He had the gentlest eyes she'd ever seen, a dark, chocolate brown.

'I really should be going.'

'Me, too.'

Sara looked down at their hands resting on the table, almost side by side. His were tanned and square, the fingernails long and smooth and very clean. She saw the muscles twitch slightly, as if he wanted to reach out and grasp hers within them, and she quickly began to pull on her gloves, to gather up her bag.

'I hoped to visit all the shops in this part of town today, and then I must pick up the children. Do you have children? Oh, I'm so sorry. How extraordinarily rude of me.' Sara was flooded with embarrassment at her own forwardness. 'Thanks again for the tea and toast,' and she fled before ever he had chance to answer. Which was a pity, because she would like to have known what the answer was.

10

One day, Jenny's teacher asked if she would help organise the school children into collecting bagfuls of seaweed. This was a special commodity which the coastal towns of Cornwall could provide, being a variety known as gonothyraea, used in the making of penicillin. 'Someone needs to be with them, and I'm so short-staffed.'

Sara gladly accepted the challenge.

'The seaweed helps our injured soldiers get well again,' she told them, whenever they complained about the cold or the wet, or the slippy rocks. 'Be brave, children, and think about those brave men.'

'And at least we're missing arithmetic,' piped up one small voice.

Sara laughed. 'Yes, I suppose you are.'

This appealed to such an extent that volunteers doubled overnight.

By December she had been co-opted onto the War Weapons Week committee where plans were indeed in progress for a major fund-raising event the following year. Having done so well in the past the town meant to do even better this year, perhaps sufficient to buy boats or equipment for whatever operation was currently being planned and carried out right here in Cornwall, before their very eyes.

'Perhaps you'll have some new ideas, dear,' said Nora Snell, when the idea was broached at one of their regular meetings. 'After all, it is well known how very friendly you are with the GIs.'

'I wouldn't say so,' Sara protested, thinking of what Hugh's reaction would be to such a statement. 'No more than anyone else.'

'Come dear, don't be modest. We all know how much they miss you at The Ship, but you could perhaps organise some sort of event for us, Sara dear, since you did the dance so well. Perhaps a whist drive or concert?'

'I would need to ask my husband.'

'Would you really?' Nora clearly would never dream of asking Scobey's permission to do anything.

'Yes, I believe I should.'

'Well, I suppose *you* would dear, in the circumstances. We all perfectly understand why he has banned you from the bar, poor man. All the local men are so jealous of the GIs, and is it any wonder? Overpaid and oversexed, isn't that what they call them? They're like wild beasts, or so I'm told.' She tittered rather foolishly, delighted by her own outrageousness.

Sara was determined not to rise to the woman's vindictiveness. Nevertheless, in view of Hugh's strong objections to her involvement with the fish supper, it would be wise to check with him first before committing herself to anything further.

'If you must, you must, dear, only we'd really like to get this matter settled then we can get on with other business. So run along and ask him now, if you please.'

And Sara had no alternative but to comply, just as if she were a small child needing to ask permission from a parent or headmaster.

She couldn't find him behind the bar, nor was there any sight of Iris. Only Sid stood there, happily wiping glasses and pontificating on his favourite subject of fishing. 'Have you seen Hugh anywhere, Sid? I'm really in the middle of a meeting at the Town Hall but I'd just like a quick word.'

'Upstairs, I reckon,' and he jerked his chin towards the ceiling.

Sara spun about and raced up the wide staircase, two at a time. She'd just reached the first floor when Hugh suddenly appeared on the staircase which led from their own quarters above, rushing to meet her looking all flushed and flustered. 'Sarah, I thought it sounded like you. What are you doing here? You're supposed to be at a meeting. Has something happened?'

'No, no, of course not. Only Nora wants me to get involved with the War Weapons Week, to help organise a jumble sale, whist drive or some such. Or maybe something more ambitious like a concert. I just wanted to be sure that you had no objection before I committed myself.'

He pulled her into his arms. 'Darling, how sweet of you to ask.'

'Well, I know how you reacted that time over the dance, and I don't want us to be at odds over this. I want to make you proud of me.'

'I am proud of you. I think you're a marvellous wife and mother, a little lacking in the brains department, sweetheart, but we can't all be bright, and you can safely leave all of the difficult stuff to me.'

He kissed her then, so the instinctive protest which rose in her throat never got uttered. It was quite a passionate kiss which went on for a surprisingly long time and during it she had the strangest sensation that they were not alone, as if someone had brushed past them on the stairs. Sara ignored it as the feeling was not so unusual. The Ship Inn was rife with stories of ghosts and hauntings. She'd once or twice seen a grey lady on the stairs who seemed quite friendly and benign, and it really was lovely to be held so close and embraced with such passion. When the kiss finally ended, Sara was quite out of breath.

'I have to go. They'll all be waiting for my answer.'

'Of course. We can't have them thinking you dilatory, and

we can carry on where we left off once your meeting is over, can't we?' Hugh suggested with a sly wink.

Sara smiled. He could be so sweet, so exciting when he put his mind to it. 'So I can say yes?'

'I really have no objection to your little activities, why should I? Everyone should do their bit, however small and insignificant it might be, and it's good to see that you are finding something to keep yourself amused, darling. So long as it doesn't get too much for you, or intrude upon our life too much.'

Embarrassed now over holding up the meeting for so long, as well as seeming to be very much under her husband's thumb, Sara brushed the patronising remark aside as of no consequence. It was so typical of Hugh to need to see himself as the best at everything. She popped a swift kiss on his nose by way of thanks, then turned and flew down the stairs, her heart still singing with her husband's praises and his passionate kisses. Consequently, she failed to notice that Iris had seemingly appeared out of nowhere to join Sid behind the bar.

One afternoon, a week or two later, Charles slipped into her kitchen to ask if she was willing to help him organise a Christmas party for the children. Sara didn't hesitate for a moment, feeling safe now that Hugh would not object. Hadn't he made it clear that his attitude had softened considerably since those first awkward days? Besides, the end of the year was surely in sight and a Christmas party would be lovely. She couldn't remember the last time the children of Fowey had enjoyed such a treat.

'I'd be delighted.'

'Excellent! We can supply the food, don't worry about that, and lemonade, balloons, all that stuff.'

'And paper hats. There must be paper hats. Oh, but we can't get any crêpe paper. I know, we could get the children to make some out of old newspapers. Miss Ross, Jenny and Drew's teacher, will organise that, I'm sure. They can paint them lovely colours. Oh dear, will they have any paint, I wonder.'

'If they don't, we'll get them some. We must have something other than battleship grey. And we can supply presents, one for each kid. What I want to know from you is how many children we would be catering for. How many boys? How many girls? What ages? We want to get it right. And will you organise the games? Hell, we're hopeless at your English party games.'

Sara laughed. 'No problem. On children, I'm an expert.'

There was a moment's silence while she waited to see if he would take this opportunity to volunteer an answer to the question she'd unwittingly asked in the tea rooms about whether or not he had children of his own, but he didn't. Perhaps he'd forgotten it.

'That's great. I'll be in touch. At least we've got the ball rolling. What I need next is a Santa Claus, which shouldn't be too difficult to arrange. See you,' And with a wave of his hand he jumped down the step to stride away up the church path.

As she watched him go, Sara's heart was beating unnaturally fast, but that was only because she was excited by this new challenge, and had at last found a purpose to her life. Nothing at all to do with the prospect of working alongside Charles Denham.

The party took more organising and planning than Sara had bargained for and she was keen to get it right. As well as the party hats there were crackers which needed to be made, and she found herself roped in by Miss Ross to help with this particularly messy task.

Then there were the games to plan and music to organise. Lists of necessary food supplies had to be drawn up; jellies made, bread ordered, cakes baked. Last, but by no means least, there were all the presents, generously paid for out of the marines' own pockets, to be wrapped and labelled, clearly stating what age of child would most appreciate this gift.

And all of this necessitated numerous meetings between Sara and Charles Denham, and as a result their friendship grew. Sara made a point of always holding these meetings at the primary school with Miss Ross present. It wouldn't do to appear to fraternise, or for Hugh to start thinking she was getting too 'cosy' with Charles.

When the meeting was over, they would often walk back to town together, as Charles always insisted on seeing her home.

Sara would laugh. 'It's very kind of you but I shan't be in any danger. This is my town. I shall be perfectly safe.'

'Where I come from, no man would ever let a girl walk home alone, no matter how safe. It simply isn't done.'

'How does your wife manage then, with you away? Oh dear, there I go again, being nosy. Sorry, it's really none of my business.'

'She copes, as we all do.'

For some stupid reason the thought of him having a wife brought a lump to her throat. But then, why shouldn't he have a wife? Didn't she have a husband? What difference did it make? 'You never did tell me how many children you have. You must miss them terribly.'

'We hadn't got around to starting a family but I do miss Yvonne, I guess. We were childhood sweethearts so we've never been apart before.'

'It must be difficult. I'm fortunate that Hugh can do his bit for the war effort at home, and has managed to avoid being called up. But I worry when he's out on exercise with the lifeboat or coastguard, all the same.'

He looked at her for a moment. 'Sure you do.'

'So you married the girl next door?'

He frowned. 'Almost. Next block, anyway.'

'How romantic.'

'One of those things, you know. Didn't come as a big surprise to anyone. How about you and – Hugh?'

'Swept me off my feet.' Sara laughed. 'I'm a sucker for a bunch of roses.'

They smiled into each other's eyes and then both quickly looked away again. They'd reached the end of Hanson Drive by this time and Sara stopped.

'This will do fine. I've only down the hill to go now. Really, I'll be all right from here.'

'OK, I wouldn't want to upset your husband by seeming to hog too much of your time. Thanks for helping. It's appreciated.'

He stood and watched her walk away until she was quite out of sight.

Surprisingly, Hugh had been amazingly calm about the whole business. But then the party was in a good cause, and he clearly thought it quite safe to have his wife work with children. Sara was careful to be equally generous in her praise of his own war work. When she got back home on this occasion he was up in his office and she went straight to him and kissed the top of his head as he bent over his desk. 'Hello, I'm back.'

He gave a little start of surprise. 'I didn't hear you come in. You seem to be making a habit of sneaking in quietly these days.'

Sara laughed as she put her arms about his neck to give him a hug. 'Why, what are you doing that's so secret? Writing to your mistress?'

He scowled, then his brow cleared and he laughed with her. 'Can't you ever take a joke, darling? I wasn't really complaining, though some of us do have serious work to do.'

'I know, there *is* a war on. Well, whatever it is you're

engaged in, I promise I won't breathe a word. My lips are sealed. But am I allowed to sit on your knee for a quick kiss and cuddle or would that break the official secrets act, do you think? I mean, have we time for a little passion, or should I just go and make tea?'

Hugh did not respond to her teasing banter but took the question at face value and answered with all due seriousness, as if surprised she should ask. 'Tea, I should think. The children will be home soon and I really don't have time for your silly games today, Sara.'

She tried not to feel rebuffed. 'Right. I shall jump to it, then. Whatever you say.' He'd already turned away from her so didn't see her mocking salute, all meant in light-hearted fun, of course, but his indifference left her feeling rather flat and silly.

Sara couldn't even see what it was he was working on with such earnestness, because he'd slid one hand over it, covering the writing. Always one for secrets, was Hugh. It was probably nothing more than his regular stock list for the brewery. What else could it be? But he had to make out that he was the only one who could understand such things, so that he felt in charge, even if she was the one to remind him when they were running low on beer or sherry, or whatever.

'Anyway, I think this party is going to be absolutely splendid. Thank you for letting me help, darling.'

Hugh gave a noncommittal grunt. 'The war will be over by next Christmas, so it's unlikely ever to happen again. You can concentrate on being a proper wife and mother once we finally achieve peace.'

'Aren't I one already?'

'You know what I mean, darling.'

Sara wasn't sure that she did. 'Are you saying that once the war is over, I shall not be allowed to work in the pub even then?'

'Goodness, I shall make that decision when the time comes. Tea, darling. Have you forgotten?'

For some reason Hugh's assumption that he would decide made Sara feel uncomfortable, as if her future was being mapped out without her consent, as if she had no control over her own life, no say over what she might decide to do.

Perhaps it had been a mistake, after all, to ask his permission. He seemed to be doing his best to belittle her efforts, yet Sara's resolve to heed her sister's advice and take control of her own life, as Bette did, as even Nora Snell did, was growing ever stronger.

Why did she always obey him? Perhaps because she wasn't entirely sure that his feelings for her had any depth? Because she wanted to see some sign of emotion, some evidence that he truly cared? There were times when she felt that her husband merely saw her as a possession, like a pet dog, or his favourite mahogany clock.

'Besides,' he continued, his head still over the stock sheets or whatever the dratted papers were. 'The children's teacher, what is she called . . .?'

'Miss Ross.'

'Yes, Miss Ross, she is surely the one bearing the brunt of the work with the children, not you. You are only helping. You'd never be able to manage on your own.'

Sara stood silently watching him, feeling her new-found confidence drain away, her smile becoming more fixed as she struggled to remain calm.

He glanced up at her. 'Tea! Run along and see to it. You've gone into one of your silly day-dreams again.'

Swallowing a lump which blocked all hope of a response, Sara turned to do as she was bid.

II

Sara's efforts were certainly appreciated by the children. Just to look at their shining faces was reward enough for it turned out to be a real slap-up party. There were piles of food, huge stacks of sandwiches: corned beef, cheese and pickle and something called peanut butter which went down a treat. Then there were miniature Cornish pasties; heaps of sausages; iced buns and great bowls of jelly and ice cream. And there wasn't a child in the room who didn't have a great brown moustache above their upper lip from all the Coca-Cola they'd drunk.

All the children, including Jenny and Drew, had a marvellous time, collecting a stack of American comics in addition to the other goodies.

Santa Claus arrived in an army truck loaded with sacks full of presents, one for each child. There were dolls and books, Dinky cars and footballs, skipping ropes and kites, candy and gum, and after the children had near worn themselves out from playing such games as Musical Chairs, Blind Man's Bluff and Pin the Tail on the Donkey, they were given rides in the jeeps, queuing up excitedly to be taken all around town.

It turned out to be the best party the town could ever remember, a most wonderful day in their young lives, one they would never forget.

Nor would Sara forget it in a hurry either. She felt conscious the entire time of Charles Denham's presence, aware when he crossed the room, when he glanced in her direction. She found herself actively avoiding him, not even caring if he thought her rude, so fearful was she that perhaps Nora Snell or Isobel Wynne, who of course had insisted on coming along to help serve the tea, might make more of what was nothing other than mere friendship.

Wasn't it?

If that was true, why did she feel as tremulous as a young girl whenever she caught a glimpse of him, even at a distance? Why could she not speak to him without blushing? And why didn't she trust herself to go anywhere near him when others were around?

Because they might read the feelings printed so clearly in her adoring eyes? Nonsense! He was just a nice man, nothing more. A nice, *married* man, Sara reminded herself. Just as she was a respectable, happily married woman.

Christmas passed in its usual whirl of activity, with a gathering of friends and family at the pub to enjoy goose with all the trimmings: sausages and bread sauce, roast potatoes and artichokes as a special treat, and Sadie's home-made Christmas pudding with no fat, since there was none to be had. It tasted wonderful all the same.

The children got very excited over opening their presents. They all went to church of course, then after lunch gathered around the fire in the old inn to sing carols while Sara accompanied them on the piano.

'I'm not very good,' she protested, but everyone seemed quite happy until Hugh told her to stop because she'd accidentally played a wrong note.

'That's enough, darling. Don't make a fool of yourself.'

'Don't be cross with Mummy,' said little Jenny, ever-protective. 'I like it when she plays "Away in a Manger".'

'Time you were in bed, child,' snapped Hugh.

For one awful moment, Sara thought it was all going to go

wrong, he had so little patience with the children. 'It is Christmas, Hugh, no need for them to go to bed early.'

He turned on her, eyes blazing at her temerity to argue with him but Cory saved the day by starting to sing a jolly sailor song to the strains of Hamil's fiddle.

Then Bette persuaded Hamil to liven up the tempo even more, pushing back the rugs so that they could dance. They all had a marvellous time, save for Hugh, who went off upstairs, and Sadie snoring happily in the corner, rather the worse for wear after a glass or two of Hugh's finest sherry.

To Sara it was a relief to have the pub closed for the day, and her family gathered about her. Yet a part of her mind wondered how Charles and the other GIs were managing, so far from home.

The moment the festivities were over, Charles Denham was back in her kitchen to thank Sara for all her effort. He felt that all their hard work had been worthwhile, giving the children a Christmas to remember.

'And you were splendid.'

Sara chuckled. 'The problem is that I think I did rather too well. I'm now in charge of fund-raising for War Weapons Week, or Salute the Soldier, as it is to be called this year? What have I let myself in for?'

'Excellent! I'm delighted, because it means I'll see much more of you. I'm sure we can find some way for me to be involved with all of that too.'

They looked at each other and Sara could think of no reply to this. What was he implying? She didn't dare to think. She turned abruptly away to slide a fresh tray of pasties out of the oven.

'Those smell delicious.'

'Do have one.'

'No, no, I wasn't begging . . .'

'Of course you were. Here, take one. I shall have one too, since it's lunch-time. Plonk yourself on that stool and I'll put the kettle on.'

'What about – your husband? Won't he mind?'

'He's at one of his brewery meetings, or else one of his training sessions, of which there have been quite a lot lately. Iris and Sid are running the bar. Go on, make yourself comfortable. I'll be glad of the company.'

In the event they sat on the doorstep, enjoying the pale winter sunshine while they munched their pasties and sipped hot, strong tea. There was no conversation, simply a feeling of mutual contentment. When they were finished, he turned to her with a smile, brushing away a few crumbs.

'I can't remember when I last enjoyed a meal so much.'

'It was only plain, home cooking.'

'That's what was so good about it.' He was looking down at her but with no hint of his usual smile. 'I really should be going, and I'm sure you have better things to do than feed hungry soldiers.' He got to his feet, but, as was often the case, seemed reluctant to actually go.

'You miss your wife, don't you?' Sara felt she should say something, try to show sympathy and encourage him to talk in case he was feeling homesick. Besides, it was occasionally necessary to remind herself that the woman existed, but he dropped his gaze, avoiding her eyes.

'Not quite so much as I should, perhaps. She was always there, you know, always a part of my life and yet . . .' He sat down again, cleared his throat. 'May I ask you a very personal question, Sara. I can call you Sara, can't I? I mean we're buddies now that we've both packed presents for Santa together, right?'

Sara smiled. 'Of course.'

'And you must call me Charles, or Charlie, as my friends back home call me.'

'Oh, I don't think I could do that.' She found herself blushing at the very idea. It was true that they'd become friends through working together, yet she still felt strangely shy with him.

'Try it. I'm just an ordinary guy underneath all this fancy uniform, these buttons and ribbons and spit and polish. I'd just like to hear someone call me by my given name, instead of addressing me by rank or number, Sir or Lieutenant. Then I'd know that I was still a real person.'

She looked at him consideringly. 'I can understand that.'

'Charlie. You can understand that, *Charlie*.' He was grinning now, teasing and challenging her to do as he asked.

She smiled in response. 'All right, I can understand that, Charlie! Now do try to be serious, please. What did you want to ask me?'

The grin faded and his gaze fell to his boots. They both watched in silence as he kicked a small stone off the step. 'You know, it's been real fun working with you. I've enjoyed your company. You're one fine lady, Sara. I hope you don't mind my saying that.'

'No, no, of course not. Not at all.' She felt flustered and could feel her cheeks start to burn like fire.

'So I hope you don't mind my taking advantage of our newfound friendship, only I'd be interested in your opinion, as a woman. Do you think, that if one party doesn't find a marriage truly happy, that they should stick with it for the sake of the other party?'

He glanced up, looking keenly at her now, waiting for her answer but Sara could think of nothing sensible to say. She was astounded by the question, this being the last thing she'd expected to hear and her brain simply refused to come up with the right platitudes.

He doesn't love his wife was the single thought running through her head and with it came such a burst of joy, it left her utterly stunned.

Yet even in this state of blissful realisation, Sara knew she really mustn't reveal the slightest hint of her reaction. It would be crazy, mad, over-emotional, absolutely uncalled for and desperately dangerous. She struggled valiantly beneath the intensity of his gaze to somehow keep her expression studiously bland, while her useless brain searched for some innocuous, innocent response, failing utterly.

He was on his feet in an instant. 'Hell, I must be out of my mind asking you such a question, and you a happily married lady. Forget it. I apologise for the intrusion. I must waste no more of your valuable time. Thanks again for the pasty.'

And then he was gone, striding away up the church path. Only when he'd disappeared from view, did she answer his question. 'No, actually, I don't.'

As winter wore on, the nation became increasingly obsessed by the need for secrecy. Yet despite all the care and the warnings, news did leak out from time to time. The talk now was very much concerned with 'Operation Overlord'. This was to be the master plan for an Allied invasion of Europe. Everyone agreed that something was going on, but nobody dared speak of what they saw or knew, or thought they knew, in anything but hushed voices to their nearest and dearest.

Party time was over and normally quiet roads were massed with vehicles as the infantry were taken to training grounds often far distant from their billet, and the skies were filled with aircraft. Some planes were spotted flying with bomb doors hanging open and undercarriages dangling as they returned from night raids or from training flights, others fell into the sea or crashed into cliffs before managing to land safely. And those who went to their rescue were likewise in danger, sometimes becoming trapped by the tide or caught up in a wreck.

Sid Penhale, who also worked as an ARP warden when not

serving beer behind some bar or other, was responsible for making sure not a glimmer of light showed anywhere.

'The last thing we want is to have them bloody Jerries chasing our pilots up our river,' he'd roar, at anyone foolish enough as to ignore blackout regulations. Yet out on the moors where Sid, or any other ARP warden for that matter wasn't allowed to go, lights would blink on and off at all hours; buildings would magically appear overnight and a day or two later vanish, only to spring up in another place entirely.

'Decoys, that's what they be,' Sid would tell anyone who questioned why this was permitted, yet they'd been fined five shilling for not properly shielding a bicycle lamp. 'Keep old Hitler guessing. Mum's the word!'

Every family in the neighbourhood became aware of the training exercises as houses would shake while the blasting went on and on, but they might all have turned deaf, dumb and blind, judging by their silence on the subject.

Reconnaissance parties were sent out, local beaches selected for training on small boats and landing craft, and boatyards were kept working flat out to keep up the necessary supply of equipment.

Fowey folk thought these amphibious vehicles resembled floating cattle trucks since they had ridged ramps that let down to allow the men to walk on shore. Some were called DUKWS, designed to be driven straight off the larger boats through the surf and up the beaches.

The likes of Cory Tredinnick, Scobey Snell and Hamil Charke predicted drowning for anyone daft enough to embark in such vessels.

'And proper ducks they do look. They'll weigh the ships down and not survive the crossing. Even if they ever get to France, they'll sink soon as they hit the water. Goes against nature,' Cory declared with much shaking of his head.

'And all the rules of seamanship,' Scobey agreed.

'I reckon they be dafter than even you, boy, to try it,' put in Hamil Charke. 'Utterly brainless, but that's Yanks for you.'

If the Americans had arrived in Cornwall as young men with very little combat experience, they were certainly doing everything they could to make themselves better prepared.

Barney and Chad were sent, along with their comrades, on long route marches, or out on Bodmin Moor where it was cold and damp, swathed in mist or with a bitter wind blowing which was particularly tough for guys like them, used to a warmer climate. They would crawl under barbed wire weighed down with a full backpack of combat gear, learn how to set and detect booby traps and the inevitable mines, plus an assortment of stringent endurance tests and drills for basic fitness.

They were drilled in target practice, often using the old Cornish engine houses, and out on the open moorland were involved in carefully planned and extensive manoeuvres, sometimes with live ammunition, which meant that they must keep their wits about them as things could all too easily go horribly wrong, as Chad soon discovered.

12

It went wrong for Chad one day when he somehow became separated from his squad. He didn't seem to have his compass, grew confused and then thoroughly lost in the mist; finding himself ankle-deep in bogs and swamps with not a clue which way to go. It was over an hour before he rejoined his comrades, and was forced to explain about the lost compass.

'Didn't you check your kit, soldier?' roared the sergeant.

'Yessir!'

The sergeant came closer to whisper with a dangerous quietness in Chad's ear. 'Next time, try to keep your mind on the job in hand and not lose valuable equipment. Think you can manage that?'

'Yessir! Can't think what happened to it, Sarge.'

'You're not expected to think, soldier, only to obey orders. Learning to check your kit correctly is one of them. Check and check and check again. Got that?'

'Yessir!'

'What did I tell you to do, soldier?'

'Check and check and check again.'

Only the way Barney was smirking behind his hand told Chad what had really happened. 'You nicked it, you god-damned-son-of-a-bitch.'

'You gotta keep your wits about you in this business,' Barney responded with airy unconcern.

*　　*　　*

The first time Chad had ever set sail was when he'd crossed the Atlantic. He hadn't enjoyed that experience one bit. They'd crossed on a banana boat meant to carry 80 passengers but packed with 300 soldiers. Some had slept under tables in the mess hall, others on piles of ropes on the decks, freezing cold and frequently soaked through from the pounding waves. They'd been fed largely on slops of rice, powdered eggs and chopped liver, most of which had ended up in the ocean, one way or another. The stink was awful as most of the men had suffered from sea-sickness and many actually prayed for death to come there and then, Chad among them. They'd suffered fifteen days of hell at sea in a dirty, stinking vessel.

But if he'd thought that was bad, the training he was undergoing now, was a whole lot worse.

And when it was finally over and they got around to crossing the Channel, the boats would be smaller and even more crowded. Word had it that for all it was only a short distance in terms of miles to France, the crossing could be rough.

As if that wasn't bad enough, they would be loaded down with a full quota of heavy equipment and be under enemy fire. In these impossible conditions they were expected to disembark and wade through the water to reach the shore so they could claim the beach.

'Doesn't sound like a whole lot of fun to me,' he dryly remarked.

Barney agreed. 'I never wanted to be in this goddamned war in the first place. What in tarnation has it got to do with us, anyway? But now we're here, let's beat the ass off Hitler and finish it for good, then we can all go home.'

They attended lectures, held at the base classroom on Windmill Field, to study maps and plans. There could be as many as 700 men packed into the hut at any one time, all striving to listen and understand, to make sure they gave themselves the best possible chance to survive. Then there was first-aid drill and learning how to evacuate casualties. Last but by no means least, hand-to-hand combat and bayonet practice.

None of it seemed as much fun to Chad as he'd imagined it would be when he'd first enlisted.

Today they were practising climbing down ropes and nets, and transferring from the transporter ships to the smaller landing craft out at sea in waves that made Chad throw up time and time again. He couldn't remember ever feeling so ill in all his life, not even on the banana boat. Barney made it worse by shaking the netting just as he was gingerly making his way down it, so that he lost his footing on the slippery rope and tumbled to the deck where he lay flat on his back, thoroughly winded.

'Get the hell off your butt, soldier. Do you think we're on a cruise here? Jump to it,' yelled the sergeant.

'Yessir,' and Chad scrambled to his feet, cursing his old buddy under his breath. 'This isn't the time for your sodding practical jokes.'

'It's just one long vacation, huh? Come to sunny Cornwall. Where's your sense of humour gone, matey?'

'Cut the crap, Barney. We're all in this together, so let's not fight amongst ourselves, right?'

'At least you got the girl this time.'

'I sure did. Is that what this is all about, because I got her and you didn't? Let me tell you it's sweet little Bette who's keeping me sane.'

By the time this particular day was finally over, Chad was bone weary and couldn't wait to see her. Bette was always sympathetic and although he told her very little in the way of hard facts about what he did, or even how he felt, she always understood when he was suffering and was ready to kiss his wounds and soothe him any way she could.

But he was feeling a bit apprehensive about meeting her tonight. He was to meet her folks, which scared the pants off him.

In the tiny cottage on Passage Street, nerves were stretched even tighter.

'You'd no right to invite him without asking our permission first.' Sadie banged a few pans about in her minuscule kitchen to show the extent of her annoyance.

'How can you be so unfriendly? He's risking his life for us all here and you aren't even prepared to give him supper. He's a lovely guy. Give him a chance.'

'Guy? Listen to yourself, talking like an American. You put a guy on a bonfire and maybe that's where this Yank deserves to be.'

'Mam! What a dreadful thing to say, and you know you don't mean it. You're just in a mood. What have you got against him? Why are you being so horrid?'

'Because he's a foreigner. I've told you a dozen times, you know nothing about him. He could have a wife and six children back home. What's wrong with one of the local lads like Tommy Kinver or Dan Roskelly?'

'If even the armed forces won't have Tommy Kinver, why should I? As for Dan, he's younger than me, very dull, and boring. Besides, he's been called up too now and leaves to join the Merchant Navy next week.'

'Well, there's John Penhale and . . .'

'Stop it, Mam. I'll choose who I go out with, not you. Chad is coming tonight because I want you to meet him, to see for yourself that he's a decent bloke, so be nice to him please, for my sake. Tell her, Dad, for goodness' sake.'

Cory stirred in the depths of his comfy chair and took the pipe from his mouth long enough to say, 'Is this the chap who helped rescue our crew when we were hit by the shell?'

'Yes, of course it is. Who else would it be?'

'Well, my lover . . .' His face was unusually serious as he faced his wife. 'Had he not called out the lifeboat, we might well have sunk and lost all o' them fish. We were holed, you know, by that shell. Proper job he made of it, getting us out of there without losing a single fish.'

Sadie turned on him in a red-hot rage. 'That's all you ever think about. Bloody fish!'

'No, my lover, I enjoy all of it, even the rowing up and down the river all night long. I don't mind it in the least, fish or no fish.' And having said his piece, stuck his pipe back in and continued reading the paper.

'Oh, I despair of both of you, I do really.' Sadie flounced to the mirror that hung over the fireplace, her scarlet lips in a sulky pout as she patted her stiff, tight curls into place and struggled to calm herself. Temper did nothing at all for the complexion, so she really should be careful. 'And what he'll think of us, I can't imagine. No doubt he's used to big fancy houses in America, if he's as rich as you say he is.'

Realisation dawned, and Bette went to put her hands on her mother's shoulders, plump and soft, they were made even wider by the shoulder pads she'd stuffed into her dress.

'Is that what's really bothering you? That he'll look down on us because our house is small and we aren't well off. Well, he isn't like that. He's very polite and kind, not like some of the others, always showing off. Not like his mate, Barney.' Bette slipped her arms further round the cushiony warmth of her mother and laid her cheek against her shoulder. 'Stop fretting, Mam. You'll like him, really you will.'

Sadie pushed her off. 'We'll see,' she said, flouncing into the kitchen. 'In any case, I shall make no extra fuss just because we're having a visitor. He can take us as he finds us. We're only having fish pie, so if he doesn't like it, that's his hard luck.'

Bette smiled to herself, knowing that it would be delicious, filled with scallops and shrimps and fresh ling, the best of the catch, topped off with creamy mashed potato. If there was one thing Sadie excelled at, it was cooking. And there was also a chocolate cake tucked away in the cupboard, which her mother had made just that morning, no doubt having bribed Mr Whitting with extra coupons in order to get the fat for it. Bette felt a nub of excitement deep inside. It was going to be a lovely evening, she was sure of it.

Barney and Chad strolled down into town from Windmill, exhausted from their training and in dire need of a beer and some relaxation. There was still a tension bristling between them, hovering beneath the surface, but they'd been friends so long, it didn't prevent them enjoying a pint together.

'Come on, let's grab that beer before you go play with your gal. We deserve it.'

Chad was not against the idea. It had been a long, hard day, a long, hard week in fact. They'd been soaked through to the skin and some of the ammunition they'd used on the exercise had been live. Things were getting much more serious, he could tell. No date had been fixed for the invasion, so far as he was aware, but word had it that it would be soon, once Eisenhower and Churchill had stopped arguing and come to an agreement. Any opportunity for a bit of pleasure must be made the most of. Even so, he didn't want to get involved in a long session.

Beer and broads, that's all some of his buddies ever thought about. 'I can't be late. I promised Bette. I'm supposed to be meeting her at Whitehouse first, then she'll take me home for supper. It's an important night for her. I gotta get it right.'

'Don't worry, she'll wait. They always do.'

They went into The Kings Hotel and the place was humming with GIs and servicemen. Barney fought his way to the bar and ordered a couple of pints. He downed his in one long swallow, ordered another round and did the same again. Barney had polished off a couple more by the time a group of sailors came in, and he shouted over to them. 'Hey, you Limeys, can you afford to come in such a smart place? How much d'you make in a day, huh?'

'Three and sixpence,' said the youngest among them.

'Shucks, that's too bad! Here, let me give you a dime,' and he tossed them a few coins.

'You watch yer bleedin' mouth, buster. Don't you try throwing your weight about in here.'

It was clear that the sailors were not amused and, worried about possible consequences, Chad quickly stepped forward. 'Hey, take no notice of my buddy here, he's a bit the worse for wear. Slow down, Barney. There's a chippy round the corner, why don't you get some decent food inside you to soak up the alcohol?'

'Get the hell off of me. This gal turned you into a plaster saint, or what? Drink your damned beer and live a little, for Chrissake.' And Barney gave him an almighty shove that sent Chad sprawling back against the bar.

The barman was quick to intervene. 'If there's any trouble, you lot are out of here.'

Chad slammed down his glass. 'I'm off now. Like I say, I don't want to keep Bette and her family waiting.'

'Told her any more fairy stories lately about your big estate with the ante-bellum mansion?'

'OK, I made a big mistake there but you made things a million times worse with all that bragging about a string of restaurants. Shooting your mouth off, as usual. Dumbhead!'

'Who you calling dumb?' Barney roared back, his face turning ugly with anger.

Chad flapped a hand, warning him to keep his voice down as the sailors and the barman continued to glower across at them. Stepping close, he spoke quietly, adopting gentle, calming tones. 'Look, old buddy, this one is serious, right? So I don't want it messed up by your bragging. You keep your big mouth shut. I'll put things right in my own way, in my own time, when the moment's right. You've done enough damage.' So saying, he marched out the door.

Barney strode after him, flinging himself down the steps and dragging Chad to a halt as soon as they reached the quay. 'Whoa, that's no way to talk to an old friend. I thought you and me were buddies. What's mine is yours, what yours is . . .'

'Naw. You're not sharing my gal.'

'You've been happy enough to take *my* leavings in the past, when I'm done with them. So now it's my turn to take *yours*.'

'No way. I already said, Bette is special.'

'Only because you got there first. You have got there, I suppose?'

Chad ignored the jibe but shook himself free and kept on walking. The sooner he got to their little beach and found Bette, the better. 'I've had enough of listening to this crap. You've really got on my nerves lately with your damned practical jokes and clever quips. You never let up for a minute. Always showing off, bragging that you know best, that you always get the girl.'

Barney shouted after him in his lazy drawl. 'Well it's true, I generally do. Never failed so far. So, has she opened her legs for you yet, chum, or not? Come on, own up. She sure would have if I'd been in charge. Maybe she has already, for all you know.'

Without pausing to think of the wisdom of his action, Chad swung back and socked his best friend right in the jaw. Barney didn't see it coming, didn't even have time to duck as his knees buckled and he staggered backwards, nearly keeling over. Swearing profoundly, he launched himself at Chad, flooring him with a tackle which would have raised a roar of approval from his local football team, of which he was a star player.

Having pinned him to the ground, Barney found a use for his fists while Chad did his utmost to counter the blows with several of his own.

Within seconds, sailors and marines were pouring out of the pub, punching and kicking and generally joining in the fracas, glad of the excuse to express their jealous hatred of Yanks.

And then out of nowhere came the sound of running feet.

'Chad! Barney! What the hell are you doing? Have you gone mad? What are you fighting for?'

Bette, tired of waiting in the dark loneliness of the little beach, had come looking for him. Now she desperately struggled to pull the pair apart. But when it looked as if she might get caught up in the blows herself, hands grabbed at her and dragged her out of the way.

'Back off, Bette. This could be dangerous.'

It was Hugh, who seemed to have emerged out of nowhere. Iris Logan was there too, and Dan Roskelly who always loved a fight, plus several others: Ethel Penhale, Isobel Wynne and Hamil Charke among them. And of course the ubiquitous Nora Snell, standing there in her old coat and hat, arms folded, greedily absorbing every detail so she could spread the tale far and wide. The whole dratted neighbourhood seemed to have turned out to watch.

Ignoring them, Bette yelled at the two men. 'Stop it! Stop it this minute.'

They paid not the slightest attention. Whatever had upset them, they were clearly not going to be pacified by the screams of any helpless female or a set of gawping townsfolk.

'Let them fight it out,' Hugh said. 'Damned hooligans.'

The battle raged on with admittedly more punches missing than actually connecting but violent enough for Bette to keep on begging them to stop, and others too were becoming concerned.

There came the screech of brakes and police whistles, and

the thud of boots on cobbles. The Snowdrops had arrived. Seconds later the punch-up was brought to an abrupt end, and any hopes Bette had nursed of introducing Chad to her family were rudely dashed. The battling twosome would be spending the night in the glasshouse instead.

'And serves you right,' she shouted after them, tears rolling down her cheeks. 'Men!'

'Did you see that fight?' Hugh demanded of Sara, when he got back to The Ship. 'I saved your stupid sister from being permanently injured, although why she'd put herself in danger by getting involved in the first place with those louts, I cannot imagine. I hope I've made my point, though. Can you see now what troublemakers these Yanks are? Grown men fighting over one hare-brained girl. Ridiculous. Makes one wonder what idiots we've got fighting on our side.'

Sara had gone quite pale. 'Is Bette all right? She wasn't hurt?'

'By a miracle, no she wasn't.'

'I thought Chad was supposed to be meeting Mam and Dad tonight?'

'Clearly he felt the need for some Dutch courage first. Can't say I blame him, with your mother.'

'But how come you saw it all? What were you doing on the quay?'

'Looking after your sister's interests, obviously. I was the one who called in the MPs. Well, somebody had to,' he said, when he saw her shocked expression. 'The situation was serious.'

'I expect you're right.' Sara was reaching for her coat.

'Where are you off to now? You can't just run out on me, there's work to be done.'

'You don't need me when you've got Iris to serve behind the bar. You won't let me anywhere near.'

'But there's the cleaning to be done, we need more pickled onions, and we're running out of pasties.'

'They'll have to wait. I need to see for myself that Bette is all right.' She almost ran out of the door. Hugh charged after her.

'Sara, come back here this minute, this minute I say. *Sara, are you listening to me?*'

Sara evidently wasn't. She didn't even stop to apologise for her disobedience. People in the street turned to see who Hugh Marrack was shouting at, and when they saw Sara hurrying away up Lostwithiel Street, smiled quietly to themselves.

'Maybe the worm has turned at last,' wondered Nora Snell, watching events from the window of her little flat overlooking the square.

13

'Are you all right?' Sara found her sister back at the salon, seated in one of the chairs beneath a hair dryer, sobbing her heart out.

'They've arrested him. What will they do to him? Will they send him to jail, or transfer him to some other unit? Oh, lord, I couldn't bear it if they did.'

Sara put her arms about Bette and rocked her gently. 'Come on, love, pull yourself together. I'm sure it's not the first time this sort of thing has happened. All men get drunk now and then.'

'He wasn't drunk, I swear it. He wouldn't. He promised me. If he was, it would be that Barney who put him up to it. That man is so full of himself.'

'I thought you quite liked Barney? Isn't he the good-looking one you said you might try out next time?'

'He's all right, I suppose, but I don't feel the same way about him as I do about my Chad.'

'*My* Chad, is it now? Well, they apparently showed those cocky sailors a thing or two about American type football tackles.' Sara was smiling, trying to persuade her sister to see the funny side, but Bette wasn't in the mood.

'Chad is special. He's gentle and kind, and fun to be with. I really like him, Sara.'

'I can see that. And he makes you happy?'

Bette's eyes suddenly shone. 'Oh, yes, he makes me very happy. I think I'm falling in love with him. Would that be very terrible?'

Sara hugged her tight. 'Why should it be?'

'Mam doesn't like him, and this business won't help. She'll be furious. She'd taken such trouble, made a cake specially.'

Sighing, Sara pulled a face. 'Then I'd better come home with you. You might be in need of someone to act as referee.'

Hugh was furious. He stormed back inside and slammed shut the pub door, swearing profoundly. Fortunately, the place was still deserted, it not quite being opening time. Iris looked up with a half smile, having been thoroughly entertained by the entire performance. She sidled over to him and smoothed a hand over his chest, fiddling with one of the buttons on his waistcoat with her long, painted fingernails. 'Has she guessed you were with me on the quay, do you think?'

'Of course not, but we'll have to be more careful in future. She's not entirely stupid.'

Iris twiddled some more with the button. 'There's still half an hour before opening. Plenty of time to get rid of all that surplus energy.'

Hugh had only to look at her to be filled with lust. Maybe it was the lushness of her breasts, clearly visible above the low-cut blouse she wore; the pout of her full, pink lips; the provocative swing of her walk; or simply the way she had of looking at him that made him feel as if he were the only man in the world who was important. He'd never experienced anything like this in his life before.

He'd thought himself fortunate to win Sara but this was entirely different. This was nothing like the clean, honest adoration that he felt for his wife. There were things Iris was prepared to do, and let him do to her, that he wouldn't dream of trying with Sara. He quailed at even mentioning such matters to her. But with Iris he could say and do what he liked.

He grabbed hold of her and pushed her into the stock room

where he had her French knickers off within seconds and was inside her in a flash, thumping into her as hard as he could. Not that she objected. On the contrary, Iris was game for anything. Sometimes, as now, she gave a little startled cry as he first entered her, but mainly she just giggled and always egged him on for more.

'You can have me again later, if you want,' she said, on a breathless little gasp after he'd expelled himself and all of his anger into her. 'We could meet on your boat and – talk – some more. There's a little scheme I want to put to you.'

'I'm not sure if that's a good idea. Someone might see us. Your place is better.'

'Don't be silly. Deaf, blind and dumb they are round here. We've been seeing each other for weeks now, and who's noticed? Not a bleeding soul. Too wrapped up in worrying about whether the butcher has any sausages.'

He was wanting her again right now, even as she smoothed her stockings and adjusted her suspenders, pulling her skirt high as she did so to reveal a tantalising length of pale thigh. God, what risks wouldn't he take to be with her?

But would he risk his marriage, Sara, his unblemished reputation?

He didn't care to say, not right at this moment. What he did know was that he wanted to drag her down to the floor and ravish her all over again among the beer slops.

Hugh half glanced at his watch and sadly admitted that there simply wasn't time. Customers were probably even now lining up at the door. He swiftly buttoned up his trousers and straightened his tie.

'What little scheme is this, that you want to talk to me about then? Tell me now, quickly, before Sara gets back.'

Iris tapped his nose with the tip of one pink nail. 'Not now. Later. It's a very sensitive subject. Anyway, you've managed to give her the slip so far. One more night won't make any difference, will it? And I'll make it worth your while.'

Iris sat in the cramped quarters of Hugh's small boat and explained in a quiet, firm voice, quite different from the flirtatious one she used with the Yanks in the bar, how he could be of use to his country.

'Airmen and POWs get trapped behind enemy lines and need to be shipped back to Britain, and agents selected for operations overseas are taken out under cover of darkness in small boats such as yours to rendezvous with the French fishing fleet.'

Hugh was astounded, bemused. His mind fixed on stripping her naked and having her just as many times as he could manage, was not in the mood for a lecture on warfare. 'Hold it, I'm not taking this in. What on earth are you talking about?'

Iris continued as if he had not interrupted. 'The folk of Cornwall are experts at secret operations at sea. In the past there have always been innocent-looking boats slipping in and out of quiet creeks and estuaries, brandy and silks being brought ashore right under the noses of the customs men. So why not follow the same routine, only this time with people. It happens all the time.'

'What does?' She seemed to be changing before his eyes, no longer the empty-headed, luscious Iris he knew at all, but a coldly calculating operator.

'We take them out and when they've done their intelligence work, we bring them back. We also ship out people used for sabotage and disruption in German-held territory, and get people out in a hurry, if needs be.'

'What the hell is all this? What are you saying?'

'That you've been chosen as a possible candidate for seeing these men make their rendezvous. The Free French operate from creeks further down the coast, there's no need for you to know exactly where, but it would demand some coastal runs, or short trips out to sea to meet up with the fleet. A boat such as yours can do that quite easily, so long as you're careful.'

Not for a moment had he ever imagined her like this. Hugh was completely taken aback by this new side to Iris Logan. Yet he found himself flattered that he should be selected for such an important mission, entranced by the whole idea.

His work with the lifeboat and the coast guard was genuine enough but nothing like so dangerous as an operation of this nature. He had, in any case, often exaggerated the risks in order to justify his avoidance of call-up and of course in recent weeks he'd lied a good deal to Sara, making out he was on a call when really he'd been snuggled up with Iris in her little boat loft. This would not only give him even more opportunities to be alone with his young barmaid, but make him into a true hero and not simply an imagined one.

'Who chose me?' he wanted to know, preening himself a little.

'I did. I was instructed to find a boat. Yours is sound, which is more than you can say for some, a decent size for sea journeys at twenty-four, twenty-six feet and you seem like the sort of chap who can be trusted. A man not afraid of taking risks.'

Iris regarded him with a steady gaze, to give the impression that she meant more by this than his willingness to cheat on his wife. She'd chosen him because he was a man with weaknesses, and had made sure he was entirely besotted with her so that she was able to control him, before making an approach. When the true nature of her work finally emerged, she needed to be absolutely certain that Hugh wouldn't back out, or spill the beans to someone he shouldn't. 'You'll be told very little and be expected to obey orders. Can you do that?'

Hugh nodded, excitement and fear warring for supremacy inside him. 'How will they check me out? Will there be a test run?'

'You might be called in for a little chat, just to look you over, but no test run. You are either in, or not, as the case may be. Well?'

'I'm not sure.'

'You should be honoured that they trust you enough to let me tell you all of this.' She was already beginning to lose patience with him. The sex was good certainly, even imaginative, but in every other way she found Hugh Marrack slow and lazy and entirely selfish. Totally wrapped up in himself.

She still had her sailor boyfriend but mainly as cover, for when she needed an alibi for whatever reason.

'Your boat will be requisitioned in any case, so either you are the one to operate it, or you'll be expected to keep your nose out of it and your mouth shut about what's been said tonight. That goes without saying. Your silence can be guaranteed – if necessary. But once you've joined our operation, then that's it, there's no going back. If you don't come up to scratch, or you become a danger to other members in the operation, you'll be eliminated.'

'Eliminated?'

This time Iris remained silent while he worked that one out for himself. Then she crossed her long legs and leaned back while she waited for his decision.

Even in dungarees, far more suited to an open boat than the jumper and short skirt she usually wore, Hugh's eyes were riveted upon the turn of a trim ankle, her shapely calves, the soft curve of her stomach, savouring the enticing knowledge that he was privy to the secrets hidden beneath the rough fabric.

The thought brought a rush of blood to his head and a strange tightening in his chest. God, but he wanted her, and somehow the threat of danger made the sex all the more exciting. It would add extra zest to the proceedings. Besides, he could see the reports in the newspaper even now, once the war was over and all of this came out. *Local hero saves countless lives*. He cleared his throat and finally found his voice. 'Right. I'm your man. When do we start?'

'Right now, at least in about . . .' Iris glanced at her watch . . . 'an hour. Time for your reward first. Shall I take off the dungarees, or will you?'

Hugh couldn't believe the buzz it gave him. Their coupling on this occasion was even more savage than usual. So violently did he take her, that she banged her head against the cabin door. He heard the crack like a gun shot in the tiny space but she didn't even whimper. He'd underestimated his little barmaid. Iris Logan was made of strong stuff.

A week later, when Bette saw Chad again, she flew into his arms with a gasp of relief. 'Oh, was it dreadful? What did they do to you?'

'Hey, I'm OK. Don't you worry none about little ol' Chad. Ain't the first time I've been in the glasshouse for a bit of fisticuffs. What about your folks, though? They won't want to have anything to do with me now, I reckon.'

Bette wouldn't care to repeat Sadie's reaction to the news that all her time and trouble over the fish pie, not to mention bribing the grocer for extra marg in order to make the cake, had been for nothing. It was all most embarrassing. Even Sara had failed to persuade Sadie that it wasn't all a Yankee plot to do her down. And Bette was under stern instructions never to ask him again.

'Aw Mam, don't say such a thing,' she'd pleaded. 'I like him. I like him a lot. Chad is a real nice guy.'

'Listen to you, child, sounding more and more American every day. You'll not see him again, do you hear me? I don't want that Yank ever to set foot in my house.'

'Don't say such a thing. I love him.'

'Love!' Sadie gave a mocking laugh of disbelief. 'You don't

know the meaning of the word, young girl like you. Forget him. There are plenty more fish in the sea, Cornish ones at that.'

Bette gave no indication of this battle as she turned to him with a confident smile. 'Don't be silly, of course you're welcome to come any time. We'll fix something up next week maybe, but give me a kiss for goodness' sake before I expire from frustration. I can't tell you how much I've missed you.'

She'd work on Sadie, make her change her mind.

Chad didn't need asking twice and because Bette felt so sorry for him, had missed him so much this last week and perhaps because her mother disapproved so strongly, somehow her feelings seemed more intense than usual. Consequently she allowed him to venture a little further along the exciting path of passion than perhaps she'd intended. She certainly made no protest when he removed her blouse, beyond a tiny whimper of need, so he swiftly unhooked her pink brassière as well.

It felt wonderful to feel his warm hands caressing her. Even the coolness of the breeze on her bare flesh seemed to excite her and when he teased her with his fingers in more intimate places it brought her to such heights of ecstasy, she really couldn't think straight.

She was begging him to take her in the end, all resistance gone. She loved him. She wanted him. What more was there to even consider? Tomorrow he might sail away and be blown up.

Next came a warm, pulsing sensation deep inside her, overwhelming her with emotion, making her cry out loud for more. He took her to the limits, lifting and carrying her with him to undreamed of heights as he loved her with all the skill he possessed, as if she were the most precious person in the whole world.

This was no quick coupling, no hasty fumble among the

rocks. Bette could feel him trembling with emotion, desperately wanting to make her happy, moved by her trust and need of him, and he did not disappoint.

Never had Bette felt this way before and when it was over she lay in his arms quietly weeping as he kissed her and told her how very much he loved her and just as soon as he could, he would make her his wife. It was the most exquisite moment in her life.

'That's if you'll have me, hon.'

'If I'll have you? Oh, Chad,' and she burst into tears all over again.

Later, in the quiet calm of her own bed, Bette felt no shame at having given him her virginity. What else could she give him half so precious? She couldn't rightly find words to describe how she felt, all sort of churned up inside, excited and oddly fearful and deeply, deeply in love.

And if tomorrow she should discover that he'd got her pregnant, what did it matter? He was going to marry her. He'd said so. Besides, tomorrow might never come.

14

Having been granted the nod of approval by the Special Operations Executive, which controlled British agents in France, Hugh was put straight into training. There were the rigours of carrying loaded packs on long runs to build up stamina; a good deal of silent rowing both in boats and in canoes; learning to walk a shingle beach without making a noise; instruction in the use of radios and S phones; compass work, mapping and navigation. Hugh didn't mind the discomfort, or the agonising pain of unused muscles. He welcomed it, revelling in the excitement, the thrill of it all.

It was essential that he be able to find his way in the dark without the use of lights, and not get lost. People's lives, not least his own, depended upon it, as he was sternly and repeatedly informed. Most interesting of all, he was instructed in how to defend himself, both armed and unarmed, were he ever to get caught.

When the time came for him to go out on his first 'op', Iris issued instructions and Hugh calmly obeyed. He didn't object because he was keen to prove his skills and be taken on.

'Start the engine, we'll proceed slowly.'

'Someone might hear.'

'Leave me to worry about that. Once we're out of the river mouth, we may manage to catch a breeze then we can rig the sail. No lights, hold her steady.'

They ventured right out into the Channel, making what Iris called a trial run. Nothing untoward occurred and although there was indeed plenty of shipping about: French fishing boats, a passing German convoy, minesweepers and the usual motor gunboats, they elicited no attention from any of them.

On his second trip they repeated the same procedure but this time made it a much longer trip, anchoring just off the Cherbourg peninsula where Iris brought out a camera and took some photos of the shore, then told him to return home.

'Aren't we picking anyone up?'

'Not on this trip.'

After that, a routine was established which soon became second nature to him and he started taking it all for granted. In fact, Hugh found it quite titillating to be given orders by a woman, and a young attractive one at that, with whom he was enjoying carnal relations. And as with the sex, so it was with the ops, Iris seemed to push him a little further on each occasion.

The trips routinely involved going far out to sea, putting them in real danger of being spotted by submarines, although the coast was no safer with the E-patrol boats keeping a close eye on activities there. Generally Hugh would rendezvous with the French fishing vessels which then sailed on to the Breton coast where they would disembark their special cargo either on shore or by handing them over to the tunny fleet.

Sometimes it might occur to Hugh to wonder what might happen to these brave souls as they climbed up a rope ladder on to a fishing trawler and vanished into the darkness.

In what part of France would they end up? What dangers would they have to contend with?

Some claimed to be journalists, others freely admitted to being agents, generally being young and unattached. In the main they remained grimly silent, giving no indication at all of the work they were about to undertake.

Sometimes it might not be men at all he was carrying, but boxes of equipment, metal containers or mysterious parcels wrapped in waterproof silk. He was never told anything, either about their contents or their purpose, which he thought just as well. Hugh was content to keep his involvement in the enterprise to the very minimum.

Iris didn't tell him much either but did once mention that some of the boats might look French, but actually weren't. 'Many are British but have been painted in French colours and rusted over to make them look older, somewhat less well maintained like the French fishing fleet. And with the crew dressed in canvas trousers and smocks, and the right flags on board, no one would spot the difference.'

'But why?'

'Don't ask questions, Hugh. Just do as you're told.'

'Sorry.' He hated to find himself in the wrong, and whenever she slapped him down in this way, he took his revenge by punishing her with even more violent love-play later, sometimes tying her up and plunging into her just as hard as he could. Or he would tease her and refuse to have sex with her at all, making her pleasure him instead. How else could he make it clear that he only did as she told him because he wished to, that he was still the one in control?

But however much training he might do, however diligent and brave he was, it did little to ease the sensation of terror that curdled in the pit of his stomach on each and every mission. There were many trips when he would be gone for days, his crew comprised of strangers, while she stayed behind to run the pub. He liked those the least. It was always much more fun with Iris on board.

Once she asked him to row a dinghy ashore and place a parcel on a railway line. 'Someone will pick it up later,' she explained.

Never had he known such terror, sweat slicking his brow, making his palms slippy so that he almost dropped the damned thing. Only then did it occur to him that it might be a bomb, to blow up the railway.

A light flashed and he flung himself to the ground, wishing it would open up and swallow him as two Germans strolled by, swinging their torches this way and that. His relief when they'd passed by and he could deposit the parcel, as instructed, and make a speedy return to the dinghy, which he swiftly and silently rowed back to the yacht, was enormous.

Later, as they quietly crossed the Channel, he heard the explosion, loud and clear. The railway line had indeed blown up.

'Well done,' Iris said with a smile. 'That will halt their progress for a while.'

It seemed such a small thing to do, yet Hugh longed to shout his success to the heavens, to tell everyone of his part in the action, but he could not.

'God, Iris, it surely can't get any more dangerous than that.'

She took him to her little loft above the boathouse to dry off, giving him a shot of whisky and the kind of intimate attention only she could offer, in order to reassure him that it couldn't. But of course she lied.

It was during another day of training a week or two later, that Chad suffered yet another mysterious accident. For some reason a rope he was climbing gave way and he fell twelve or fifteen feet. Not a great height but he landed clumsily, hit his head on a projecting pole and was knocked clean out.

By the time he came round, the orderlies had him all tucked up in bed and nothing he said would make the dragon of a nurse allow him out of it.

'You're to be kept under observation overnight.'

'Hey, but I've got a hot date this evening, with my gal.'

The woman had a frosty look in her eye and the shadow of a moustache above the tightly pressed lips. Even as she apologised, Chad knew she wasn't in the least bit sorry. 'You aren't going anywhere until we're sure there are no repercussions from that blow to the head.'

Chad tried to persuade her but soon realised he was wasting his time. She looked far too ferocious.

The doctor was even less accommodating. 'You're staying put, mate. We've some big ops coming up and can't afford to carry passengers.' With his stocky build and substantial chest, so like the typical British bulldog, further argument seemed pointless.

'Trust me to get Grandmother Grim for a nurse and Father Grizzly for a doctor,' he complained to Barney when his buddy popped round later to see how he was.

'I'll let Bette know what's happened, shall I?'

'Tell her I'm real sorry, and I'll see her tomorrow.'

'Sure thing. Don't you worry about her. I'll take good care of little Bette.'

'Hey, you keep your groping hands off her. She's mine, remember?'

Barney held up his lily white palms in a picture of innocence. 'OK, OK. Don't worry. She's safe in my hands. I'll wear kid gloves and be the perfect gentleman. Promise.'

Bette was instantly concerned. 'Fallen and banged his head? Oh, no, poor Chad! It seems to be one thing after the other at the moment. I do hope he's better soon.'

'Sure he will. He's being fussed over by a gaggle of gorgeous nurses.'

'Oh, I see.' Bette wasn't sure she cared for that idea. She knew what nurses were like, chase anything in a pair of trousers. 'We were going to the pictures to see *Forever and a Day*. I was so looking forward to it.'

'No need for you to be disappointed, sugar. I'll take you.'

Bette considered this carefully for a moment. Would Chad mind if she went to the flicks with his mate? She wasn't sure. 'I don't know, Chad might object.'

'Naw! He's told me to take real good care of you, and I sure will sugar, don't you worry none. I'll be the perfect Southern gentleman.'

Bette started to giggle as he exaggerated his accent. Where was the harm, after all? Going out was always a thrill and demanded a great deal of preparation. She didn't have the coupons to buy many new clothes so she'd become accomplished at making over old ones, although some were beyond redemption. What had suited a sixteen-year-old girl before the war did little to enhance the glamorous image of a twenty-year-old.

It had taken all her skills with a needle to fashion something decent for her date with Chad tonight, shortening skirts, lowering a boringly high neckline, but she knew that she looked good, wanting to look special for him. It would be a pity to waste all that effort.

Besides, accepting Barney's offer was surely better than going back home and have Sadie say that Chad had let her down yet again.

'OK, let's go.'

Later, when she took off her coat to reveal a flirty little blue frock which gave no indication of its age, Barney whistled softly through his teeth, proving that it had been worth all the trouble.

'Boy, I wish Chad could be laid up more often.'

Bette thoroughly enjoyed the movie, as Barney insisted she call it. She particularly enjoyed Charles Laughton as the comic butler and Buster Keaton as a crazy plumber. Yet there were some sad bits in it too. Barney had been somewhat appalled by the size of the cinema, small by his standards, and with a tin roof. Nevertheless, he had indeed behaved like the perfect gentleman, not even attempting to hold her hand.

'That was a lovely evening, thanks.'

'Don't mention it. How about a little stroll before I take you home?'

'I nearly am home. I live only a little further along Passage Street, beyond the ferry slip, close to the water by the pill.' She still felt shy with him, so kept on talking as they walked. 'Did you know that three-masted schooners used to moor alongside Berill's Wharf here, now it's used for coal, which they load straight on to the ships.'

Bette's experience was with local boys who idolised her for her prettiness, not with mature men, and foreigners at that. Apart from Chad, of course. But he was different. She felt safe with Chad. He was so adoring of her, so sweet and caring.

Barney wasn't like that at all but he was handsome and exciting, a little dangerous in a way which secretly appealed. And he was so handsome, almost Continental. It momentarily crossed her mind that maybe she'd chosen the wrong GI. If she truly was a girl who liked fun, then maybe Chad would become dull and boring after a while, whereas Barney surely never would.

'You fond of this place, then?'

'I'd leave tomorrow, given half a chance. Just because I was born in Fowey doesn't mean I have to spend my entire life here. They say there used to be a pirate queen who once sailed these waters. I'd like to have been her. I don't think I was meant to sit by the hearth, as my sister does. The sea is in my blood and I want to see the world, to travel.' She flung out her arms and laughed, as if she could indeed capture the whole world in her embrace. Barney laughed with her.

'A girl after my own heart. Here, what's this?' They'd been strolling contentedly along but had reached an alleyway and he stopped. Still laughing, he caught hold of her hand and Bette happily allowed him to pull her along it.

'It's called an ope way, perhaps because it doesn't go anywhere but opens out to the river.' She shivered. 'Come on, Barney, it's cold down here, dark and damp. I don't like it.'

She turned to go back to the street but his arms came about her.

'Here, let me warm you up.' He pulled her into a corner, out of the wind, took off his uniform jacket and slipped it about her shoulders, then held her close with her back pressed up against his solid chest. Bette didn't protest because there was a cold off-shore breeze and he was warming her nicely.

They could see nothing of the river in the blackout, with not a glimmer of a moon, even though they were both aware of vessels moored, of clandestine movement of shipping, and unseen eyes watching for danger lurking in the shadows.

But here, cocooned in his arms, she felt quite safe from all of that, from the war, from the unseen enemy, even from the elements. His arms were tight about her waist, strong and firm, rubbing her hips and stomach gently to warm her some more. Americans, she decided, were so considerate and polite. Bette leant her head back against his shoulder and began to relax.

'I do hope Chad will be better soon. I worry about him. He's had so many problems lately.'

'He's accident-prone. Always was a clumsy great oaf.'

'Don't say such things. He's lovely and I miss him.'

'Hey, you're out with me tonight, sugar. Are you saying you'd rather be with him, than me?'

Bette giggled. 'Sorry. That didn't sound very polite, did it?'

His caresses were becoming more daring, his hands sliding up towards her breasts and Bette felt a stir of excitement in the pit of her stomach. What was she playing at, letting him cuddle her like this? What would Chad say?

He put his mouth to the curve of her neck and kissed her softly. Bette felt the tip of his tongue flicker out, and her eyelids fluttered closed. She'd been right. Barney was exciting and indeed very dangerous. She'd tell him so and make him take her home in a minute. Just as soon as she could catch her breath. Oh, God, she thought, tilting her head further back so she could savour the pleasure more sweetly. Give me the strength to stop him, please.

'How about a proper kiss, huh? Just a little one. Surely I deserve that much at least, for giving you such a nice evening, an' all.'

Bette hesitated. 'Cheeky.'

'Naw. I'm a little old pussy-cat, me. Come on, one little kiss. Where's the harm in a little old kiss between friends? We're both adults having a good time, war or no war.' He was turning her gently in his arms so he could kiss her cheek, her throat, her closed eyelids.

Oh God, what was she doing?

Bette turned her face away but knew in her heart that she was only playing hard to get. His fingers were teasing the peak of one nipple, sending wild sensations of pleasure coursing through her, her stomach all knotted up and her breathing becoming increasingly difficult. 'You're the kind of guy my mother is always warning me about.'

He seemed to find this amusing and chuckled softly into her neck, nuzzling his mouth in the hollow of her throat. Bette knew she really ought to stop him before he went any further, but all she wanted was for him to get on with it and kiss her properly, on the mouth. Desire was running through her like liquid fire and for the life of her she couldn't resist. She needed him to devour her, to make this pain go away. He was so good-looking and she'd really no quarrel with his behaviour this evening. He hadn't even done any bragging about how marvellous he was, or how much money he earned, oh but she wanted him to kiss her, she really did.

She lifted her lips to his. 'Just a quick one mind.'

She didn't mean that of course, and he knew it. His smile was one of pure triumph as he brought his mouth down to hers.

The kiss shook her to the core, his tongue invading and

exploring, nothing like the kind of kisses Chad gave her. His mouth was all enveloping, demanding and forceful, his hands everywhere, touching, caressing, teasing, insisting she ride with him on this rising tide of desire.

He pushed her back against the wall, pressing up hard against her and, to her shame, paying no heed to the danger she might be in, Bette could do nothing but respond. Whatever it was he had awakened in her, could not be stopped now. It was too exhilarating, too thrilling, too treacherously irresistible; tumultuous emotions churning inside of her which she could do nothing to quench.

And it was all happening so fast she could scarcely think. There was an urgency about him now, that hadn't been there before. She could feel his cold hands searching under her skirt, his fingers exploring her most intimate place which, shockingly, excited her all the more. Only when there was a piercing pain did she realise how far he'd gone. He had her pinned against the rough, wet wall, pounding into her as he grunted with pleasure.

Bette gasped, let out a little cry, but he either didn't hear her above the screech of the gulls and the slap of water on stone or he paid her no heed. Even when she started to sob he didn't pause until he'd expelled himself completely and sagged against her. Maybe he believed that she cried out of emotion, or from pure pleasure. Maybe a part of her did.

15

With the increasing number of bombing raids over Europe, the number of airmen needing to be brought to safety increased and Hugh was kept fully occupied. He'd discovered that rescue boats also came from a base near Helford, operated by men who, like himself, willingly left the relative calm of a peaceful river to face hostility and possible death in the tense operations close to the western shores of Brittany. Sometimes, the risks they took would all be for nothing, if they were unable to rendezvous with the fishing fleet or make contact with their special 'cargo'.

Once he saw a small boat rather like his own burst into flames having hit a mine, which made him only too aware of the risks he took on each and every trip.

On that occasion he'd hurried over as fast as he could to search for survivors but found only one young boy, badly burned. The rest of the crew were lost and had to be reported as missing.

Hugh was declared a hero by his comrades and he loved the kudos that gave him. But he would have been a fool not to be worried and scared for his own safety.

It irritated him if an op was unexpectedly cancelled because an airdrop had been made instead. Somehow this left him feeling unappreciated and not properly valued.

Hugh's least favourite trip was to bring back a group of American airmen who were travelling back from Paris. He really thought that his time could be much better employed.

The fact that they claimed to be protecting a scientist carrying important papers containing vital information about some weapons factory or other, was quite by the way. He didn't believe a word of it. Everyone knew that GIs liked to brag about their prowess.

Just as if he would never dream of doing such a thing.

In fact, one of the aspects of this work he found the most difficult was the need for secrecy. He'd always believed himself to be quite good at that, because of the necessity of not giving Sara any inkling of what he got up to with Iris, but somehow this was different. Hugh would love to have told her, to at least drop a hint about the dangers he was involved in week in and week out.

What he did was undoubtedly dangerous and he wanted his wife, wanted everyone to appreciate that fact and applaud him for it. Where was the point in being a hero if nobody recognised him as such? One day, perhaps when the war was over, he could reveal everything, and how he would savour their surprise and approbation, but for now, frustratingly, he must keep it to himself.

He took to creeping up to the children's room when he returned from one of these missions, telling himself that he needed to check they were all right, although he'd never been a doting father and in reality he simply felt the need to talk, and who better than a child who didn't understand a word he said?

Drew could easily be nudged awake although Jenny would sleep on soundly. He was barely five years old and as silly and innocent as all little boys of that age, in Hugh's opinion, but quite ready to idolise his father. Hugh told him how he was engaged in something very dangerous. How the French fishing fleet did much more than catch fish.

'As does your old Dad. I've saved countless lives, young pilots trapped in France, agents sent out there on special missions. It's my job to rescue them. I meet up with the French fishing fleet and bring the men safely home.'

The little boy looked at him with round eyes. 'Gosh, Daddy, are you a spy, like in my William book?'

Hugh smirked and puffed out his chest a little. 'There's a war on, son. We all have to be brave and do our bit as best we can.'

'Wouldn't the Germans shoot you, if they caught you?'

'They won't catch me, I'm far too clever. See this telescope, I use it to keep watch at sea, and when I return from a mission I usually go out on to the headland and check no one has followed me.'

'Gosh! Can I come with you next time?'

'Maybe, if you're very good. But you must never tell. This is a sworn secret between us, understand? Don't breathe a word, not to Jenny, or to Mummy or anyone.'

'Oh no, Daddy, I shan't tell. Cut my throat if I tell a lie.'

Hugh smiled at the childish oath, patted his son's head fondly and told him to go back to sleep.

He never did take the boy up on the headland. Children could be such a nuisance, a responsibility best left to women who had nothing better to do with their time.

But often, after that, he would find Drew waiting at the top of the stairs and they would sit and talk about the dangers he'd endured that night. It felt good to express his feelings, to relate it all out loud and see his son drink in every word, hugely impressed by his father's courage. Hugh felt quite safe in the knowledge that not only would the boy never tell, but that he didn't even fully understand. He was merely a child, after all. So if Hugh couldn't revel in his wife's approbation, at least he could enjoy his son's.

And there was also Iris of course.

Hugh liked it best when Iris came on the operation with him, though she rarely did so these days, maintaining that it would look far too suspicious for her to be spotted too often on his boat, and, in any case, she had to work in the bar. But there were occasions, usually late at night, long after the pub was closed, when she would sometimes sneak out with him, just for the hell of it, or if it was a special operation and her presence was required.

Generally they had to navigate without lights, on this particular occasion as far as Brittany, a trip which took a couple of days, negotiating the rocks in the L'Aber Wrac'h Channel on quiet engines, a wing and a prayer. He had no idea why they were going but with Iris by his side, he didn't care so long as they all got back safely.

The weather was terrible with a strong wind blowing up, getting worse by the minute. As if that wasn't bad enough, there were patrolling Heinkels overhead. An armed convoy steamed by on their north side, then half a dozen German corvettes heading directly towards them and Hugh's heart was in his mouth, afraid that at any moment they might spot his innocuous looking yacht, which really shouldn't be there at all. Fortunately they went on by, not even noticing him among the billowing waves, but by then he had dropped his sail and turned off the engine.

Hugh was vastly relieved when he finally recognised an approaching trawler tacking back and forth but definitely coming in his direction. Possibly not an innocent Breton boat but more likely one operated by British Intelligence, men perhaps who had once been fishermen in civilian life, men who understood the sea and knew what they were about.

He made fast on its starboard side and kept a sharp eye all around while a procession of people clambered on deck, helped by hands anxious for them to be swiftly dispatched so that they could all get safely on their way.

There were six passengers altogether, four men and two women, looking bedraggled and very much the worse for wear. There was luggage too, boxes and mailbags, all of which had to be bundled aboard, taking up precious time. Hugh was sweating, despite the cold and the lashing rain, by the time they were finally ready to leave.

Down in the cramped cabin quarters, the refugees sat huddled together sipping rum or hot tea, nibbling on Spam sandwiches, although the bucket was also frequently being passed round. Hugh cast them a disparaging glance and hurried back on deck.

The crossing was growing rougher by the minute, with no let up in the weather and it was as they were approaching the Cornish coast, with dawn breaking, that out of nowhere came the sound: that all too familiar drone of an enemy plane. It emerged as a dark shadow from a pink and saffron sky, like a vengeful vulture inspecting likely prey. And then came a second plane, circling low, one minute the pair flying close, the next separating, swooping around and over the boat again.

'Dear God, what the hell do we do now?'

For once, even Iris had no answer. The vessel was armed, but they had nothing that would touch two Heinkels.

Hugh was beginning to panic. 'This is madness for us to be stuck here in the middle of the bloody sea with no navy escort.'

He looked up and saw that the Heinkels had been joined by two others, that there were now four planes circling overhead, but the newcomers were ours. Beaufighters had been sent out from Cornwall to escort and protect them from possible U-boat attacks.

They quickly engaged the enemy in a dog-fight which took place right over their heads, Hugh and Iris watching the performance awestruck, even as they struggled with engine and sails, frantically urging the little boat to catch the right wind and tack away as fast as it could. One of the Heinkels performed an acrobatic dive, firing at them and spraying the water all around with bullets. But it flew too near and the tip of one wing hit the water and it catapulted out of control, crashing into the sea. A loud cheer went up and the two Beaufighters had no difficulty after that in chasing the second Heinkel away.

Much later, a motor gunboat arrived to take the passengers on to a different destination, the Scillys perhaps, and Hugh gladly handed them over, thankful to have survived.

'I must have been mad to agree to this,' he said to Iris as they finally slipped safely into harbour, but she only laughed and teased him all the more.

'You love it.'

And the awful thing was, he did, so if he found an antidote to fear in the warmth of her willing arms and luscious body, didn't he deserve it, he told himself?

Bette and Chad met by the rocks in their favourite place and he gathered her close and kissed her. 'Did you miss me?'

'Of course I missed you.' It felt so good to be held safe and warm in his arms. Bette couldn't ever remember feeling so cherished. She felt overwhelmed with love for him.

She hadn't set eyes on Barney since their night at the pictures and had done her utmost to shut their encounter out of her mind. What had come over her that night, she really couldn't imagine. Barney Willert was wicked, appealing to the wickedness in her, yet the blithe way he'd walked her home afterwards and kissed her a polite goodnight, you'd have thought that nothing untoward had taken place between them at all. They'd both agreed, however, to make no mention of it to Chad.

'He's a bit of a puritan, is old Chad. Best we keep this little matter just between the two of us, OK?' and Bette had been more than ready to agree.

So now as she smiled up into Chad's adorable eyes and told him how much she loved him, she said nothing of her betrayal.

'I love you too, hon. I've asked the major if we can marry

and he says it could take a while to get all the necessary paperwork done, and for permission to come through. Months maybe. The army isn't too keen on this sort of commitment, apparently. They believe marriage takes our minds off the job, that this isn't the time for us to be taking on new responsibilities and personal obligations. Load of baloney. I love you, Bette. I adore you and want you to be my wife. There's a war on, OK, and who knows what tomorrow might bring, so why the hell shouldn't we enjoy what little time we've got left together?'

Bette was in tears by the time Chad had finished his rant, hugging and kissing him for all she was worth; guilt playing no small part in her emotion. Oh, but she did love him, she really did. She couldn't seem to get enough of him, but then he grasped her by the shoulders and held her away from him.

'What about Barney? He dated you when I was laid up. He did behave himself, didn't he? He promised me faithfully that he'd not lay a finger on you. If he did anything to hurt you, I'll strangle him with my own bare hands and . . .'

Bette put her fingers to his lips. 'He kept his word. Nothing happened, I swear.'

Would she go to hell for telling such lies? Surely not. But what choice did she have? Bette believed Chad when he said what he would do to Barney if he'd so much as touched her, and she really didn't want a more serious fight between them on her conscience. She would have to view her lie as a way of saving a long-standing friendship.

Chad drew in a deep breath. 'He's the best buddy a guy could have. Come on, hon, give me another of those wonderful kisses. I hope you still want to marry me.'

'Of course I do, more than ever.'

Gaining permission to marry turned into a tougher job than either of them had anticipated. Chad's commander refused and said they would need to wait for a couple of months, to be sure of their feelings, then he could apply again.

'I'm sure of mine.'

'Me too, hon.'

'You might go off me.'

'No way. I love you, babe. He'll agree in the end but for now, he insists we go through all the proper channels, deal with all the policies and regulations, the dratted bureaucracy.'

Bette was beginning to get worried. She didn't feel sure enough of him to wait too long. 'You might meet somebody else you like better.'

'Aw, Bette honey, what a thing to say. We could just do it, if you like, and not tell anyone. Hell, what could they do about it then?'

'I'm not yet twenty-one, not till June. I'd need Mam and Dad's permission. Dad would give it, together with his blessing, but Mam never would. She doesn't approve, for some stupid reason.'

They decided that they needed help. Chad tried the Red Cross who handed him the necessary forms and explained that they could help only with his moral welfare. They could do nothing to speed up the paperwork.

The chaplain told Chad in no uncertain terms that wartime marriages should be firmly discouraged, that a foreign bride wouldn't necessarily be granted American citizenship, that she might not even get transport to take her to the US, such ships as were available being needed for shipping the wounded back home.

Stubbornly, Chad persisted. 'Yeah, but she'd get citizenship eventually, and we'll work on the transport problem. This goddamned war can't last forever. Tell me who to write to. General Eisenhower, if necessary.'

'Your lady friend isn't pregnant, is she, son?'

'She sure as hell is not.'

'Forgive me for asking but it is often the case that some of these girls think it would be an easy way out of the war, to get themselves pregnant by a GI. They're attracted by the lure of American freedom and money, and are prepared to use any tricks at their disposal in order to secure themselves a husband.'

At which point, Chad marched out of the chaplain's office, slamming the door behind him.

Their disappointment was bitter, their love-making that night holding a kind of desperation which intensified the pleasure each found in the other. Bette wanted to become a part of him, to capture the very essence of him, to put a stop on time and hold this moment forever in her heart. Afterwards, they huddled together in a crevice in the rocks, trying to keep warm against a cold off-shore breeze yet reluctant to leave this small sanctuary simply to find warmth.

They didn't talk much but held each other tight, as if they could build a barrier against all the evils in the world with the absolute power of their love.

The following Friday evening when again Bette went to meet him as usual, it was Barney waiting by the rocks, not Chad.

'It's OK, don't panic, sugar. He's just been transferred,' Barney said as she ran towards him with fear in her eyes. 'To some place in Devon called Slapton Sands.'

16

If anything, Hugh became more brazen in the affair, spending far more time with Iris than was strictly necessary, certainly so far as operations were concerned, yet savouring every moment.

On one never-to-be-forgotten occasion he did take one risk too many, openly kissing her behind the bar when really they should have been preparing to open.

He had Iris pressed up against the beer pump, his mouth to her breast and his hand up her skirt, when he heard the latch click. He hadn't realised Sara was actually in the building and certainly didn't expect her to suddenly walk in upon them.

Fortunately he managed to leap away in time, and Iris too was quick to snatch up a dish towel and pretend to be polishing glasses. But he felt ruffled and slightly disturbed at being very nearly caught in embarrassing circumstances by his dear wife.

Iris, however, maintained her habitual calm. She didn't have a nerve in her body, that woman.

Sara too seemed entirely oblivious of anything untoward. 'Oh, Hugh, there you are. I just popped in to let you know that I'm going out for a while. Committee work.'

He scowled. 'Seems to me that damned committee is taking over your life.'

'Really, Hugh, don't be childish. You're the one who never seems to be in these days. I never realised the lifeboat was kept so busy, assuming that's what is keeping you so occupied,' and she tilted her chin slightly as she thoughtfully considered Iris's innocent face.

Sara couldn't exactly swear that she'd seen anything going on between them, and she might well be imagining the frisson of tension in the air, but there was something about the girl's expression which troubled her: a kind of smug triumph.

Hugh suddenly became very busy wiping shelves, which, to Sara's recollection, she'd never seen him do in his life before, and his neck had turned an almost ruddy crimson.

'I mean,' Sara continued, having got the bit between her teeth and seemed quite unable to let go. 'I never see you these days. I'm not allowed to serve behind the bar so we no longer work together as a couple, and you rarely seem to even occupy my bed, since you're out half the night on these so-called ops of yours.'

'For God's sake, Sara!'

'Shall I go?' Iris smoothly offered.

'No, you damn well won't. This is neither the time nor the place to air your private grievances, Sara. There's a queue outside, if you haven't noticed, and we're all just trying to do our bit, after all.'

'As am I, in my committee work, which you seem to despise so much.'

Sara felt close to tears. What had possessed her to admit so blatantly to her loneliness, and in front of Iris too, who was still wearing that self-satisfied smirk. She never used to argue with him, why was she doing so now? Sara met the girl's amused gaze with defiance in her own. 'In fact, they've been asking me to take complete charge of the fund-raising instead of simply one event, and I might just do that.'

'You couldn't possibly. What about the children?'

'Mam would gladly come in to baby-sit. You won't be troubled. She's with them now, as a matter of fact. Not that you would care, since you haven't bothered to come up and see them all day.' Sara was breathing hard, desperately trying to calm herself, wanting to ignore the challenge in the girl's eyes and believe in her husband's innocence. Unable to bear it another minute, she turned abruptly on her heel. 'I must go.'

Hugh hurried out from behind the bar and took Sara gently by the shoulders, as he was apt to do when he thought she was being unnecessarily stubborn and needed a good talking to.

'You see what a state you've got yourself into, over absolutely nothing. Doesn't that prove my point that you are doing far too much? I'm only concerned for your sake, darling, that this dratted committee doesn't ruthlessly take advantage of you. Far from taking on more work, I really think you should give it up altogether. As for my own affairs, er – work, it is vitally important, but you know that I really can't tell you anything about it.'

'Of course not. Bye, darling. Bye, Iris.'

Hugh followed her out, determined to continue with the argument, and win it. Iris quickly dashed into the stock room and pulled out an attaché case from the back of a cupboard where she hid it. Within seconds she'd made contact and was speaking in soft, hushed tones, quite unaware that a small boy, who saw himself as William Brown, had crept downstairs to see what all the row was about and quietly watched her through a crack in the door.

Later, when Hugh returned, the brown leather case safely stowed away back in its cupboard, Iris turned to him with a face tight with anger. 'You didn't handle that at all well. It doesn't do to alienate your wife or have her get suspicious about what you do, so why drop great big hints like that? "*I really can't tell you anything.*" What sort of damn fool remark is that? You really must take more care.'

Hugh hated it when she was angry with him, or displeased in any way. He was the hero, wasn't he? He was the one taking the most risks, not her. All she had to do was pull pints and smile at people. What right did she have to criticise? Women could be so dratted difficult.

'*I* must take care? What about *you*? I didn't see you fighting off my advances just now. It takes two to tango.'

Iris had the grace to blush. 'All right, perhaps it would be more accurate to say that *we* must, but do please be careful, Hugh. No broad hints, not a breath that you might be involved in anything untoward or secret. You must maintain an air of complete innocence the whole time. The last thing we want is to arouse Sara's suspicions, on any front. This arrangement suits us both very well. I wouldn't like anything to spoil it.'

'Neither would I, so we're going to have to gird our impatience, I suppose and wait for later.' He was smiling down at her, trying to make light of the incident but his eyes were greedy with need as they traced the outline of her full breasts, which he no longer dared to touch.

He saw her relax slightly and cast him a teasing glance up through the sweep of her lashes, a smile curving her scarlet lips.

'I can see why you fell for her, though. She really is lovely, particularly when she's in a paddy. I feel so fortunate that you're even prepared to look in my direction.' Iris was playing her little girl act now, which always turned him on, knowing how tough she really was. It suited her purpose to do so, although this never seemed to occur to Hugh.

'Your wife doesn't know how lucky she is, to have you for a husband. I'd certainly appreciate you more than she seems to do, nor would I complain all the time about being neglected, or bombard you with inappropriate questions.'

He had to take her in the stock room after that piece of flattery and give her a quick one before tidying himself and pulling back the bolt to allow the usual rabble of GIs in.

Somehow, Iris had a way of always saying, and doing, the right thing. She made him feel wanted and special, and it gave him pause for thought as to why Sara didn't appreciate him more. If, in fact, he hadn't married the wrong woman after all.

It proved to be a busy night in the pub and afterwards he took a big risk and walked Iris home. He'd seen Sara come in and slip upstairs to bed. Guessed that she'd be asleep as soon as her head touched the pillow, never dreaming that her husband was anywhere but where he should be, either behind the bar serving late customers, on patrol with the coastguard or called out for service with the lifeboat. Hugh was arrogantly confident that she certainly wouldn't imagine for one moment that he was lying naked in Iris's bed, nibbling the rosy tips of her breasts.

He crept into bed sometime around two and Sara automatically turned to snuggle up against him. 'Oh, your pyjamas are cold. Where have you been? No, sorry, I shouldn't ask. Hugh, I'm sorry. I didn't mean to sound so petty before. I'd no right to quarrel with you. I was in a mood, I expect. It's just that I miss you so, miss what we had, before the war, when we worked together. Well, I don't mind so much for myself, it's the children I'm thinking of. They rarely see you these days. I do love you and think you're terribly brave, in case I haven't said so already.'

'Of course you do, darling.' Hugh wasn't listening, he was very nearly asleep.

'You're not involved in anything terribly dangerous, are you? Just tell me that, at least.'

She sounded so contrite, so sweetly concerned, and Hugh experienced such a rush of pride that he forgot all Iris's words of warning and arrogantly informed her that he could say nothing, thereby making it perfectly plain that he was.

But then he wanted Sara to know how very important he really was, instead of regarding him with that faintly amused expression which somehow managed to make him feel foolish. She'd always been a quiet, self-contained sort of person, and despite him being so much older than she, and having won her, he was never certain that he fully understood her, or that he had her complete respect. It had been exactly the same with his mother, who hadn't seemed to care for him very much either. So cold, so clinical, and so very distant.

He wanted his wife to appreciate what a fine man he was. Perhaps if Sara saw that the danger was real, his work vital, she might view him differently.

Tonight, Iris had told him that more information was needed on German defences of the Channel coast, that if he was able to supply it, she might have even more important work for him in the future.

'It will be dangerous, of course,' she'd explained. 'The kind of risk which makes what you've done so far look like a Sunday school picnic.'

'Can I ask what sort of operation it would be?'

'Not yet, sweetie. You just carry on being a good boy. You'll be told when the time is right.'

They'd enjoyed several hours of pleasure in her bed after he'd locked up, drunk some rather good wine and now he felt drowsy and sated. Even so, her words made his heart pound every time he thought about what she might have in store for him next.

Could he take it? Could he deal with yet more danger?

Although he felt a chilling fear deep inside, Hugh knew that he thrived on excitement, that whatever the challenge, he would accept it. He was gaining a reputation for being tough and reliable and rather hoped that one day he might be mentioned in dispatches, or awarded a medal for his services.

Therefore he felt more than prepared to do whatever Iris asked of him, was almost burning up with curiosity to learn what it might be.

Overwhelmed suddenly by tiredness he lightly kissed Sara's cheek, desperate for sleep. Burning the candle at both ends, not to mention the physical gymnastics between himself and Iris, was beginning to take its toll. More sleep was essential.

Seeing how tired he was, Sara felt a stir of guilty compassion that she'd ever suspected he was doing anything but what he claimed: his duty.

She couldn't claim that her marriage was perfect but Sara believed that she'd been reasonably content, hopeful that once the war was over, things would improve between them. Hugh was her husband, after all, and she did miss working with him, lazy and inconsiderate though he might be, and wanted to do so again.

What had possessed her to feel that awful burst of jealousy over Iris, she really couldn't imagine. Surely nothing but an over-vivid imagination, or her own sense of guilt.

Had she reacted so badly to Hugh's close proximity to the barmaid, which was no doubt entirely innocent, simply because she needed an excuse to dally with an American officer, one whom she really should try to avoid.

Every day when she drove around, doing her collections, there he would be, driving along in his jeep. He only had to catch a glimpse of her and he would flash his lights, encourage her to stop so they could have a chat, or pass the time of day for a moment. Worse, Sara was perfectly capable of flagging him down too, if only to remark upon the weather, or how busy she was, anything to spend a little time together. Not that either of them admitted as much, but the need was there, unspoken between them.

And if she didn't see him, she found herself looking out for him, a small ache of disappointment nestling between her breast bone.

Often they would both attend the same meeting to discuss some fund-raising issue that they were involved with. On these occasions, Sara would sternly remind herself that she was unmoved by his presence, that it was strictly business if, afterwards, they slipped along to the Odd Spot for a quick cup of tea together.

Charles Denham was simply a friend, nothing more.

Hugh was her darling husband whom she'd been badly neglecting of late, so what right did she have to complain of his neglect of her? Perhaps if they could get their sex life back on track, Sara thought, she would stop having fantasies about what it would feel like if Charlie kissed her.

Sara snuggled closer, swallowing her pride, these strange aches of longing. 'Is that why you don't want me quite so much these days? Because you're too exhausted from these secret missions you're involved with? I thought we might try again, some time soon. Now, if you like.'

Hugh almost laughed out loud. What would she say if he told her the very opposite was the case: that he was getting more than enough sex, thank you very much. That it acted like a drug to dull his senses but that he certainly couldn't find the right sort of buzz with her. Nor did he have either the energy or the inclination to even attempt to make love to her, certainly not tonight. He felt drained, replete.

He patted Sara fondly, as if she were a child, lightly caressing the silver pale curls. 'Go to sleep, darling. I'm rather tired tonight, and don't worry your pretty little head over what doesn't concern you. We can't expect things to be normal right now but it will be worth all the sacrifice once the war is won.'

'Of course it will, and I'm so grateful that you no longer mind my getting involved in the war effort.'

Hugh was happily indulging in his favourite Iris fantasy where she was standing on the deck of his boat stark naked and he was licking the salt from her wet skin. 'No, of course I don't mind. Not in the least.' His wife's little efforts with jumble sales and children's parties seemed very small fry indeed, by comparison. He really didn't care what she did so long as she didn't attempt to interfere with him. He was having far too good a time.

17

Bette couldn't believe that Chad was gone. Only a few weeks ago they'd made love for the first time, and the last occasion was the most wonderful of all but had now turned out to have been a poignant farewell. Chad wrote every day of course, at least at first, and Bette would eagerly rip open the envelope to read his loving words. 'If only we could be married, then you could ship out to the States and stay safely with my mom.'

The idea appealed and took root. Hadn't she always wanted to escape from the close confines of Fowey? It would be far more exciting to wait for him in his lovely home than in this boring old town, knowing she was a GI bride. She'd even filled in all the necessary forms, which she'd personally collected from a frosty-faced girl who'd looked at her as if she were dirt.

'Snatched the first GI who stepped off the boat, did you?'

Bette could have socked her one but had managed to remain icily polite and bite her tongue. The important thing was to get the right papers signed, not engage in a slanging match with a toffee-nosed girl who thought she could treat all potential GI brides as loose women on the make.

He sent her a photo of himself which she kissed every night before she went to sleep. It wasn't the same though. You couldn't cuddle up with a piece of paper. Bette felt cold and lonely inside and then nearly a week went by when she didn't hear from him at all.

A letter did come eventually, apologising for his silence, explaining how he'd been away at sea on a training exercise and couldn't write; that he wanted her to know he still loved her. It happened again and another week slipped by, then another after that with not a word from him.

Doubt began to creep in. Could she believe in his love, Bette wondered? Was his story that he wasn't allowed to write genuine, or was he simply making excuses? What if she got Stateside, as he called it, and he never joined her there, if he'd gone off the idea of marriage altogether. Perhaps he couldn't be bothered to go through all these official channels and had found someone else to amuse him instead.

Oh, she really mustn't think such dreadful thoughts. He loved her, didn't he say so in every letter? She must simply be patient.

But Bette didn't have a patient soul. Even if Chad did stay true and came back for her eventually, that could take months, and what was she supposed to do in the meantime? Sit at home alone and twiddle her thumbs? Weep into her pillow?

Neither of these held much appeal so when Barney turned up at the cottage one evening, bunch of daffodils in hand and asked her out, Bette knew she should refuse but his expression was so endearing, so humble and contrite as he shuffled his feet on her doorstep, that she was soon having second thoughts. She glanced up and down the street, to make sure they were not overheard.

'If I agree to go out with you, there must be no repeat of what happened last time. That was a mistake. I want to make that perfectly clear.'

'Sure, no problem. Our emotions got the better of us. We were overcome by the heat of moment. You have my word, sugar, that I won't do anything you don't want me to. OK?'

Still Bette hesitated, perhaps because of the way he was smiling so wickedly at her. 'Behave yourself. I'm absolutely serious.' She was hissing at him under her breath, trying to sound cross, yet Bette knew that she couldn't put all the blame onto him. She hadn't been exactly unwilling in succumbing to his charms, more's the pity. 'The perfect gentleman, right?'

'Got it.'

Barney behaved with absolute propriety, and did his utmost to cheer her up. After that first evening, in which Bette thought that he'd redeemed himself somewhat, he called regularly and was always anxious to take her wishes into account. 'Where do you want to go tonight, sugar? To the dancing, the flicks, or maybe a walk by moonlight?'

She didn't care, so long as she got out of the house, if only to escape her mother's nagging. Chad's letters were now bemoaning the fact that he couldn't get leave at all, though he didn't say why, or even where he was stationed as this wasn't allowed by the censor, but he did say that he appreciated the fact that his best buddy was looking after her and treating her with proper respect.

He certainly was. Too much respect, almost. Barney would take her to the pictures, or to the dances at the Armoury and if he held her a little closer than perhaps he should, or told her how drop-dead gorgeous she looked, Bette didn't protest. It was a great boost to her flagging confidence to have a man find her attractive again, to give her that sideways glance which seemed to say, 'I know you fancy me, why not admit it?' Yet he made no move to take advantage, still behaving like the perfect gent she herself had insisted upon.

Deep down, Bette began to find this just a trifle disappointing. What was wrong with her that he didn't ever try anything on? She'd never had any difficulty getting boys interested in the past, so why didn't he try to kiss her again, or at least hold her hand?

Barney was a handsome guy and she felt very slightly piqued that he should lose interest in her quite so quickly. It wasn't as if she wanted an affair or anything of that sort, dear me no. Not for a moment would she let Chad down, but where was the harm in a little mild flirtation? After all, Chad wasn't here and Barney was. All right, they'd gone a bit too far last time but she'd keep better control in future. They were both young and needed to have fun and live a little. Where was the wrong in that?

And at night when she lay in her bed, the pictures in her mind were confused. One minute it would be Chad kissing her, the next Barney, and she couldn't any longer tell the difference. Oh, why couldn't Chad get leave? If it was true what Barney said, that he was only in Devon, why couldn't he pop over and see her? It was only a few miles down the road, for goodness' sake. Sadie took great pleasure in pointing out Chad's failures and, as his letters grew ever more erratic, preening herself at having been right. 'Didn't I say he'd up and leave you?'

'He hasn't chosen to go, he's simply been transferred. He'll come back one day. He does still love me.'

'Huh, if you believe that, you'll believe anything, girl. He's been gone weeks, so why doesn't he come to see you?'

Why indeed? If only she knew. 'He's on special training. Away at sea. I don't know. Perhaps all leave has been cancelled.'

'More likely he's got himself another woman tucked away somewhere, who he's now spinning his yarns to. You wouldn't know that either, would you?'

'Don't say such dreadful things. You're determined to see only the worst in him, which isn't fair. You don't know Chad. You wouldn't even let him in the house.'

But she let Barney in. He would frequently arrive early, bringing Sadie flowers or chocolates. He would patiently listen to her moans and groans about the inadequacy of the doctor at diagnosing her aches and pains, at her husband's uselessness, or how hard she worked at the salon. And when she constantly pointed out the failures of his erstwhile friend, Barney never contradicted her, or defended Chad in any way. He would nod sympathetically and tell Sadie how he understood her feelings.

'It's true, he's an individual sort of guy, is Chad. Not to everyone's taste. Bit dull, ya know? Yet unpredictable. No one can be sure what he really thinks, or what he might do next. I hate to say this, him being my best buddy an' all, but he's got quite a temper on him, like the time he got into that fracas on the quay. Blew up over absolutely nothing.'

'Just what I said,' Sadie agreed. 'Then there were all those accidents. The question is, were they genuine or was he trying to get out of a difficult situation?'

Barney shrugged and looked sorrowful. 'Didn't surprise me none that the major decided to transfer him some place else. He'd become a real liability. Always was that way, ever since he was a boy in school.' It pleased him to see how Sadie swallowed everything he told her, but then his facility for lying had always intrigued him. He did it because he could, because no one ever challenged him. And it was satisfying to see how Bette grew increasingly confused and desperate for his attention. But then, he had long resented the fact that Chad had found himself the best-looking girl around. Not the done thing at all.

Bette closed her ears to all of this as she frantically ran around, desperately trying to get ready, but at the back of her mind lurked the traitorous thought that perhaps what her mother said might be right. Was Chad unreliable? Had he really manufactured those accidents so he could get out of a difficult and dangerous operation? It was all rather coincidental, and just a little suspicious. Wherever he'd been sent, she knew what US marines were like. He might well find himself another girl, as her mam was always saying, and look what an idiot she'd look then.

'Stop gossiping you two. I'm ready now, so let's go.'

'Hey, look at you, all shining and perty. You sure do look swell, sugar. But then you always do. Chad doesn't know what he's missing. He's a fool, that guy.'

'Why do you say such awful things about him? It's not fair when he isn't here to defend himself. He can't help being transferred.'

'I'm sorry, sugar. I didn't mean to upset you none.'

'I'm sure he only speaks as he finds,' said Sadie, a grim smile of satisfaction on her plump face. 'Mark my words, you've heard the last of that one.'

Time passed and still Chad didn't get leave, and then finally his letters stopped altogether, and Sadie's words began to take on an awful reality. It looked as if Chad had indeed let her down. She was heartbroken. If it hadn't been for Barney's unfailing support, Bette didn't know how she would have coped. Night after night she cried herself to sleep. Why had he abandoned her? Why couldn't he send her a postcard at least?

Sara would hug her and soothe her, trying to convince Bette that some dreadful fate had probably befallen the letters, rather than him.

'Such as what?'

'They might have been censored, or lost on a train somewhere. Things go astray all the time in wartime. Or Chad may be at sea on another exercise. How can we know, but surely no news is good news.'

Bette clung on to the hope that her sister was right. Sara meant well, unlike Sadie, but the words offered little in the way of genuine comfort. Perhaps the answer was that he simply didn't love her after all.

Perhaps Sadie was right and he'd only been using her. He'd got what he wanted, made love to her, taken her virginity, then gone on his way looking for the next chick, as they all did.

What a confused, silly young fool she'd been, bowled over

not simply by one glamorous Yank, but two. They just had different ways of taking advantage of her weakness and naivety, that's all. At least Barney hadn't spun her along with promises of marriage. He was completely unfront that all he wanted was a good time. It salved her conscience, as well as her pride, to stir disappointment into anger, but it didn't make her feel any better.

Yet why should she sit about at home with a broken heart? There were other pebbles on the beach, as the saying went. If Chad wasn't interested in her, then maybe *she* didn't really love *him*. Maybe he wasn't really the man for her either, not at all the man she wanted to marry but merely a passing fancy.

In her heart Bette knew that if he were here beside her now, holding her close, she would be perfectly certain that she did still love him, but as the days and weeks slipped by with still no word, loneliness and doubt welled up inside her and her dates out with Barney were all that kept her sane.

'Where is he? Have you heard from him?' she would constantly ask, only to see Barney sorrowfully shake his head.

If only she could be certain. One word, that was all she needed, one word to end this dreadful torment. She felt bereft, abandoned, unsure of herself, and of Chad, and at the back of her mind was quite another worry altogether.

18

Nora Snell just happened to mention at one of their regular fund-raising meetings that Scobey had seen Hugh's boat heading out to sea and he was quite sure that Iris Logan had been on board. 'That can't be right, can it dear?'

Sara was at a loss to know what to say.

Nora had no such problems. 'Why would that flighty little barmaid be in Mr Marrack's boat? Don't make no sense, I told Scobey. Your squint must be getting worse than ever and you'm seeing things that aren't there. But he would have it that it was her. Saw her plain as day, sitting in the bow in the moonlight.'

Sara made some excuse or other and could hardly wait for the meeting to be over so she could run to Hugh and ask him to put her fears to rest. She tried to make light of it, relating what Nora had said as if it were all very amusing, giving a soft little chuckle and waiting for him to laugh with her and agree that Scobey had indeed been mistaken.

Instead, Hugh coldly retorted, 'It seems you are determined to pursue this stupid suspicion of yours and presumably listen to every bit of tittle-tattle and gossip which comes your way in order to prove your point. Really Sara, I had thought you above all that sort of nonsense. I did hope that you might actually believe what I've told you, if only because I'm your husband and I love you. It's desperately sad to realise that you don't trust me at all.'

'Of course I trust you, that's not what I meant. I was simply telling you what Nora Snell had said and . . .'

'Nora Snell's opinion, or Scobey's cross-eyed visions, cut no ice with me, though I'm quite sure you must have encouraged the gossip.'

'What?'

'I shall have to punish you for this. I've no wish to, Sara, not in the least, but I really can't have you spreading gossip about me, telling people I go out to sea at night, with or without Iris.'

'But I'm not spreading gossip, I'm merely sharing a piece of amusing tittle-tattle with you. We all know that Nora is an old busybody, though she works hard enough for the town. There's talk of her being mayor next year. But nobody listens to her malice, or takes her gossip seriously, so why should you?'

'Because you obviously do.'

'I don't. I knew, of course, that Iris couldn't possibly be with you. And what on earth do you mean by punish me? I'm not a naughty schoolgirl,' and she gave a little laugh.

'I won't have the likes of Nora Snell sharpening her claws on me, or you allowing her to. Perhaps if you are deprived of transport for a week or two, then in future you'll make more effort to nip such nastiness in the bud.'

Sara sat down, her knees suddenly feeling very weak. 'Deprived of transport? You're going to stop me using the car because of what Nora Snell said?'

'I cannot control Nora Snell's tongue. But I can control yours because you are my wife. You cannot use the car for two weeks – no, a month. Perhaps then you'll learn to be more circumspect.'

'Don't be ridiculous, Hugh. I've done nothing wrong.'

'I will be obeyed in this.'

'You can't do that. I need the car if I'm to properly organise Salute the Soldier Week. And I'm still involved in collecting salvage and wool for the WVS. You know that they depend upon me.'

'Then they'll be disappointed and will be forced to make other arrangements. In fact I think it would be for the best if you handed in your resignation. That will show Nora Snell where her nastiness has got her, and how very unreliable you are, and she'll then have to find someone else to do her dirty work.'

'But I'm not. Unreliable, I mean. And I really don't mind helping her. I've no wish to resign. Hugh, this is all getting completely out of hand.'

But he only turned and walked away into the stock room, the discussion closed. 'You spend far too much time doing things for other people, and you haven't even begun to make supper. The children are out playing God knows where. Your place is here, looking after me and being a proper mother. One minute you complain that you have too much work to do, the next not enough, and all because I won't allow you behind the bar. I really don't understand you.'

Sara was almost weeping by this time, appalled by where her lack of faith in him had led. 'Perhaps I am a little jealous of Iris because she gets all the fun bits, working with you, and talking to people in the pub, while I just get the cleaning and cooking.'

He rounded on her, his eyes dark and angry. 'Oh, we're back to that complaint are we, that you get no fun? I believe it was you doing the flirting, with those dratted Yanks. I was entirely justified in my suspicions, and in banning you from the bar, while yours are not.'

Sara couldn't allow him to get away with that. She had to protest. 'But Iris is so often away from the bar on the same nights as you, sometimes for days at a time, also like you. Are you trying to tell me that you're not together during those periods?'

She thought that she detected a flicker of panic behind the cold eyes, but then it was gone in an instant, as if she'd imagined it. When had Hugh ever panicked or felt in the least bit insecure?

'I thought I'd made it clear that what I do is not open for discussion.'

'Yes but, Iris . . .'

'Is a work colleague. If Nora Snell has seen her in my boat, so be it. Unfortunate perhaps but it was for an entirely innocent reason. You'll have to trust me on that.'

'Are you saying Iris is involved with the coastguard service too?'

His patience finally ran out and he snapped at her. 'Questions, questions, endless bloody questions. Haven't I told you that the kind of work I do is not your concern. Leave it at that, Sara.'

Sara flew about the small kitchen finding frying pan, sausages and tomatoes, frantically peeling potatoes, flushed with embarrassment as Hugh droned on and on, listing her faults and inadequacies. All about how she was becoming utterly paranoiac, and seeing problems everywhere. Was this true? Was she paranoiac, imagining problems where there were none?

Or was this all hot air and Hugh really was having an affair?

It certainly seemed an unlikely coupling, a flighty young barmaid and a mature man with precious little in the way of a sense of humour. Sara stifled a small hysterical giggle at the thought. Yet how could she be certain? Could she trust him? Could one trust any man confronted night after night by the likes of pretty, curvaceous Iris Logan.

It was all very puzzling. First he claimed Nora Snell is nothing but a nasty old gossip, now he is practically admitting that yes, Iris may well have been with him on the boat, but that they were *working*! Presumably for the coastguard. Then why hadn't he told her this before?

Surely it was perfectly understandable if she was just the tiniest bit anxious?

Later, as Hugh tucked into sausage and mash, a dribble of brown sauce on his chin, he told her in forbidding tones, 'You will resign from the committee, forthwith. You can safely leave winning the war to we men. It's not women's business at all.'

Sara knew she should meekly agree and accept what he said. This had been the worst quarrel she could ever remember them having, and he expected her to apologise and agree to his terms. It's what she would have done in the past, but somehow she kept thinking of Charlie telling her what a fine woman she was; how gifted and clever she was to manage things so well, so that somehow she couldn't quite manage it. She had to speak out.

'Oh, but women *are* involved in this war, Hugh. You can't deny that.'

Hugh glared at her and almost laughed out loud. He certainly couldn't deny it. Just watching Iris issuing orders to French fishermen, secret agents, and undercover men from the Royal Navy made him breathless with excitement. He'd never realised that female power could be such a turn on. But Iris was different.

'No dear, not women like you, with no brains in their heads. Now run along and find the children, then get on with baking pasties, mopping the floor, or whatever little tasks you have to do before opening time, and let me eat my dinner in peace.'

Sadie had taken Barney to her heart. 'Such a nice boy,' she kept saying. 'Not like that other one.' And it didn't matter how many times Bette reminded her that she'd never even met Chad, Sadie was completely smitten and there was an end to the matter.

So was Bette. Despite a strong sense of disloyalty towards Chad, she was very attracted to him. Barney was fun. Exciting. Dangerous!

She never took him to Whitehouse, that had been special for

her and Chad; a daft place to have a cuddle anyway, so near to the pillbox. They'd go for a walk or to the flicks of course, but on a cold evening he was content to sit happily by the fire and then join the family for supper.

Cory loved to talk to him about fishing and one evening, her father proudly showed off his prize rabbits. 'I started keeping them for the war effort, do you see? You get one shilling and sixpence a pound for the meat.'

'You sell them to the butcher, do you?' Barney asked with interest.

Cory sucked thoughtfully on his pipe. 'Not yet, I haven't, but I could if I wanted. If I needed the money.'

'Aren't they expensive to keep?'

'No, they'm happy with potato peelings, soaked bread crusts and cabbage leaves. Proper job. Costs us next to nothing.' He was tickling one under its ear as he explained all of this. 'Bit of grass they do like, or hay. Cheap enough to feed.'

Barney nodded. 'And in return you get rabbit pie whenever you feel like it.'

A slight panic came into Cory's eyes and Bette put a hand to her mouth to hide a smile. To her certain knowledge not one rabbit had been killed and skinned, nor ever would be. 'Not yet, we haven't. But it's a possibility, if we ever got really hungry.'

To his credit, Barney's mouth didn't twitch a muscle as he answered with all seriousness, 'Good thinking.'

Barney Willert had turned out to be a far more interesting and perceptive person than he'd seemed at first sight. But he still couldn't resist bragging that American rabbits were bigger but then, that was Barney.

19

Barney and Bette were dancing cheek to cheek. He was breathing softly against her ear, stroking her back as they swayed together and Bette found herself nestling closer. She loved their Friday nights out at the Armoury best of all their times together, looked forward to them all week. This was where she most liked to be, in his arms.

The music ended and he let her go quite abruptly, looking around with a dazed expression in his eyes, as if he didn't wish to be seen anywhere near her, or as if he could hardly bear to touch her. Why was that, she wondered?

'What's wrong?' she asked. 'Something is, I can tell.'

'Let's go outside. We need to talk.'

They strolled down the lane, the scent of damp earth and new grass strong in their nostrils and somewhere in the distance, the thin whistle of a train and a hiss of steam as it drew out of the station.

'You've been cool with me all evening. What is it? Don't you like me any more?'

'Sure I do, but you ain't my girl and I have to keep reminding myself of that fact. I really don't think I can go on like this, Bette. I can't see you any more.'

Bette was appalled. She couldn't begin to imagine what her week, her life, would be like without him. Ever since Chad's letters had stopped Barney had become the entire focus of her existence. 'Not see me any more? But why? I'm sure Chad wouldn't object to us keeping each other company while he's away. Anyway, he won't have to mind, will he? If he truly cared, he'd find some way to write to me, censor or no censor.'

There were tears in her eyes, in her voice, though quite why she couldn't exactly be sure. Did she weep for Chad or at the thought of losing Barney? He slipped an arm about her shoulders and drew her close.

'Hey, don't take on. Chad is a lucky guy to have you waiting for him when he comes home. He'll be the one smooching you then and I'm gonna have to pretend I don't care, when really I do. You have a funny sort of effect on me, Bette.'

He was holding her much closer than he usually did, and she could feel the urgency of his need. Bette was young and lonely enough to feel some of his excitement transmit itself to her. 'Do I? What sort of effect?'

In truth, Barney's patience was wearing thin. He was a soldier, after all, and she was a pretty girl. He didn't believe in platonic friendships. That had never been part of his plan. He wanted her, and he meant to have her.

He was kissing her brow, her eyes, nipping her mouth with soft, teasing kisses, making her feel all giddy and slightly breathless.

'I dunno, can't seem to get you out of my head.'

Bette giggled, rather tickled by this. 'That sounds like a song title.'

'I'm serious. England is a cold, wet place, so small you could lose it in North Carolina. You have funny money, you queue for sausages which taste of sawdust and you pull a chain when you go to the john. I'd hate it, if it weren't for you, sugar. When I'm with you I find I'm kinda different – maybe even better than the real me, ya know?'

'Oh yes, I do see that.'

'You make me behave like this, all decent and respectable.'

'Goodness,' gasped Bette, her expression mock serious. 'How very remiss of me.'

'Don't tease, I can't handle it. If you were any other girl, I wouldn't be able to keep my hands off of you. I'd be after getting you in the sack, Chad or no Chad.'

His hands seemed quite unable to let go of her right now. One was slipping under her blouse, smoothing her bare skin, sending little shivers of excitement racing down her spine.

'But you're Chad's girl and therefore untouchable. I made a big mistake that first time because I really didn't care then. Now I do. I care a lot about you, Bette.'

'Do you?' It was the first time she'd heard him use her name.

'Sure. I couldn't be so selfish and arrogant with you now. But you want me too, I know you do, deep down.'

His mouth had found her throat and Bette let out a small groan of pleasure. 'Oh, Barney, it's true. I like you too. I've even found myself wishing that I wasn't Chad's girl, that I was yours. I'm never quite sure which of you I'm dreaming about. What are we going to do?'

There was a moment's silence, then his arms tightened about her as he buried his face in her hair, half of him transfixed by the sweet scent of her, the other part wondering where he might find a dry patch of grass. 'Maybe we'll get lucky and Chad will find himself another gal while he's in Devon, huh?'

'Oh, do you think that's likely?' Bette wasn't certain that this thought pleased her, yet as Barney led her into the woods, still kissing her, nibbling her ear and his hands doing things they really oughtn't, she felt half dazed with longing and hoped he might nod or say that yes, he had already. At least then she'd know where she stood. 'He hasn't written and said so, has he? Because if you know something I don't, I'd much rather you told me the truth, the whole truth.'

Barney was pushing her down into the long grass. 'I've heard nothing more than you. Wish I had. I don't know what's happened to him. It's a mystery.'

Bette felt a draught of cool air on her breasts, and then the warmth of his hands, which made her gasp. When did he unbutton her blouse? She really shouldn't be doing this but it was far too late to stop him now. The blood was pounding in her ears. She was young, hot with need and surrender seemed somehow inevitable.

The following week, when next she saw Barney she could tell at once that he had news. 'You've heard something, haven't you? He's back, isn't he? He's written you a letter saying he's coming home. We'll have to stop seeing each other, is that it?'

Barney's eyes didn't quite meet hers. 'Right after we'd talked last week, I gotta letter from his mom.'

'Saying what? That he's married, got himself a new girl, what?' She was frantic to know, impatient with his slowness to explain. Still he didn't answer and something about his silence chilled her. 'He is OK, isn't he? What have you heard? For God's sake, tell me.'

Barney rubbed a hand over his chin. 'I don't know how. It ain't easy.'

'Get on with it, please.' Bette felt as if every muscle were turning to liquid fire and yet she felt terribly, dreadfully cold.

'His mom was wanting news, as we all are, so I asked to see the major, just to see if maybe he could find something out. This afternoon, he sent for me and told me that Chad Jackson has been reported as missing in action, presumed killed. I'm sorry, sugar, but that's how it is.'

Somebody screamed, shouting that it couldn't be true, that it was all a lie, that Chad would be safe home next week, next month. Only when Bette struck out at him and Barney grabbed her by the wrists to stop her from hitting him, desperately trying to calm her, did she realise that the terrible sounds were coming out of her own mouth. Only then did the all-consuming anger leave her, as abruptly as it had come, and she fell into his arms in tears.

She'd known of course, that it would come to this. In her heart she'd known all along that he was dead. How could he not be? If Chad had been alive anywhere in the world, he'd have found some way to contact her. 'And do you know the worst thing of all?' Bette said, as she sat under the trees in Station woods, huddled in Barney's arms, trying to warm herself and stop this dreadful shaking as she struggled to digest the awful truth that Chad was gone.

'What?'

'I grieve for him, of course I do, but not as much as I would if I didn't have you. I love you both. Isn't that terrible?'

He seemed to go very still, then he gripped her hard by the arms, gave her a little shake, so that Bette was certain there'd be bruises there tomorrow. 'What the hell are you saying, girl? That you love me?'

'Yes. Of course I do. I do, I do.'

They fell back into the long grass and made love this time with a wild passion, a frantic, desperate need as if to prove that life still pulsated through their veins, at least. To Bette, it meant that she could endorse her words with every touch, every kiss, and in a burst of emotional tears at her climax.

To Barney it was a physical necessity, the needs of a soldier on the eve of war.

Afterwards, Bette lay in his arms and wept again, this time for Chad. 'I did love him once. He was sweet and kind, a bit awkward and shy, but so caring.'

'Best buddy a guy could have. I'll miss him.'

A small silence and then, 'There is just one other small problem that perhaps I should mention.'

He was stroking her hair as she lay with her head on his chest, surreptitiously glancing at his watch as he did so, to check if there was time for another round. 'What's that, sugar?'

'I'm pregnant, and the awful thing is, I don't know which of you is the father.'

'It's very good of you to give me a lift,' Sara said as Charles Denham pulled up in his jeep. 'I'm on one of my missions to collect prizes and stuff for the fête. I've pestered everyone in Fowey enough, so thought I'd try Golant, Lostwithiel and Lerryn. They often like to join up with our events. Good job I'm not collecting salvage. You certainly wouldn't want a load of old newspapers or bottles in an army vehicle.'

'Maybe I wouldn't mind so much, if you came along with them.' They smiled at each other, a smile which carried rather more meaning than it should. 'How come you've no car? Not that I mind, you understand. I'm just curious.'

Sara was silent, and he glanced curiously at her.

'Hugh is using the car this morning, so I would have had to catch the bus, which takes so much longer. I'm most grateful.'

'But if he knew you had to collect stuff . . .' His attention was taken by a herd of cows who were ambling along the lane right in front of them and he had to slow right down and then stop the jeep to wait for them all to be ushered through a gate. 'So why did Hugh take the car?'

'Oh, he has these moods now and then. All very silly. Male ego, I suppose.'

Silence again while he thought about this. One cow had made a break for freedom and the farmer was cursing and sending a dog after it. 'Anything to do with us?'

'Us?'

'Don't pretend, Sara. I don't think I could bear that. You know how it is between us, these feelings we're trying to pretend don't exist.'

A small silence and then a sigh. 'They mustn't exist. We can't let them exist. I'm married.'

'I note you've left off the happily this time. So am I married. Unfortunately, that doesn't make one immune to falling in love.'

They both sat watching the pantomime antics of the dog and the cow, not daring to even glance at each other. 'Is that what we've done? Fallen in love? Oh, I do hope not. That would be quite dreadful.'

'Why would it? OK, you already said why. We're both married. Blast it, they've caught the renegade, now we'll have to drive on.'

They said nothing more as he drove along the winding lane up to Fowey Cross and then on to Lostwithiel, but Sara's mind was churning. It was true, what he said. It might be frightening, terrifying even, to hear the words spoken out loud, but it was no revelation to her. She did love him, and in her heart she'd known all along that he loved her too.

He parked by the river but neither of them made any effort to get out of the vehicle, and still Sara hadn't cast a single glance in his direction.

'Look at me, Sara.'

'I can't.'

'I'm not going to do anything. I'm not going to embarrass you by kissing you in public, for all I might long to do so. I have too much respect for you for that, but I want you to know how I feel about you. I want you to see it in my eyes, to know that it's not anything to do with my being homesick or missing my wife. The sad fact is I don't miss her at all. We should never have got married, Yvonne and I. Both our families hustled us into it, and it was a mistake. I think she may have found herself another guy, someone to keep her company now that I'm not there. Soon as I get home, I'll be filing for divorce. I know this doesn't help much, not right now, but I wanted you to know all of that.'

'Thank you.' Then Sara got out of the jeep and walked away, spine rigid, without a single backward glance. Only when she reached the bridge, quite out of sight did she lean on the parapet and sob as if her heart would break. Charlie might well be able to break free from his marriage, but there was no way she could ever escape from Hugh.

20

'Whatever happens, Mam must never know.' Bette and Sara were on the Polruan ferry, ostensibly taking the children out for one of their regular Saturday afternoon jaunts while the two sisters caught up on each other's news. The kind which would take some explaining on all sides.

Sara had said nothing yet about her own situation, being far too stunned by Bette's news.

The sun was shining on this clear April day, and the picturesque village of Polruan just across the water from Fowey, with its huddle of cottages that clung to the hillside, bore its usual bustle of activity. The navy was much in evidence, as usual, along with the US marines, the boatyard awash with work, men crawling over half-finished vessels like dozens of busy ants. And around the corner of the harbour wall, in Pont Pill, a warship stood at anchor, perhaps suffering some repairs or resting beside the calm wooded banks before returning refreshed to its duties. A Dutch salvage tug stood not far away, a couple of drifters, and the usual clutch of motor gunboats, auxiliary patrol boats and minesweepers moored cheek by jowl in the river.

A fishing trawler, French, by the look of it, hit the only incongruous note in this armoury of fighting vessels. Frightening as the reality was behind this erroneously idyllic scene, Sara felt proud to be a part of it.

Yet sadness was a part of her emotion on this day.

'I can't believe poor Chad is dead. Or that you could so

quickly forget him. Are you certain that you know what you're doing, Bette? I thought you didn't really care for Barney.'

'I haven't forgotten him. I still love Chad but I love Barney too.'

'How can you love two men? That's not possible.'

'I don't know but somehow I do. Oh, Barney has his faults, I don't deny it. He loves to brag about how marvellous he is, how big and wonderful America is, and how small and shabby England is, but there's another side to him altogether. One I've seen a lot of recently. He can be fun, a dreamy dancer, and surprisingly home loving. There's nothing he likes better than to share our simple suppers, and you should have seen him with Dad and those rabbits. Hilarious!'

'And you say he's offered to marry you, even though . . .' Sara dropped her voice, making sure that Jenny and Drew were out of earshot, happily helping the ferryman to steer. 'Even though the child isn't his?'

'He *wants* to marry me. He *loves* me!'

Barney had been utterly stunned when she'd confessed her pregnancy to him, his face had gone so white and shocked that she'd thought for a moment he might turn tail and run, but that was men for you. Never did consider the consequences of their actions.

'We don't know for certain that the child isn't his. It could be.'

'Bette!'

The expression on her sister's face compelled her to add, 'Don't look so accusing. We had a mad moment of passion, that's all. He's behaved himself since. The perfect Southern gentleman. Well, mostly. It's different now that we're engaged, of course.'

'Engaged? He's given you a ring already, with Chad only just . . .?'

'No, no, no ring yet, but he will, as soon as it seems right.'

'Oh, Bette, I do worry about you, I really do. You're so impulsive, flitting from one man to the other. That's no way to carry on.'

'And what about you? Miss Goody-Two-Shoes. You should have heard what Nora Snell was saying about you when she was under the dryer the other day. It's just as well it was me who was doing her hair on that occasion, and not Mam.'

'Oh, lord, what's she been saying now? Whatever it is, don't believe a word of it.'

Bette laughed. 'So you weren't in Charles Denham's jeep then? And your cheeks aren't bright pink with guilt?'

'Look, we've arrived. Come on children. Take care as you get out of the boat. Don't forget your fishing net, Drew.'

'You carry it for me, Mummy.'

'I certainly will not. You know very well I told you not to bring it. You'll be lucky if we get near enough to any rock pools today. Jenny, look where you're putting your feet or you'll fall into the sea. There we are, safe and sound on dry land. Right children, race you to the top of the hill.'

'You've got to be joking,' Bette laughed. 'It's a hard slog up there. I think we'll take it slowly, and save our breath for the climb. Once we've got Lantic Bay in our sights, we'll have this out good and proper.'

They felt as if they'd walked for miles. Along West Street with its panoramic view of Fowey, looking even more beautiful somehow from this side of the river. Then on past the block-house, now a ruin but once used for coastal defences back in the fifteenth century when a heavy chain was slung across the harbour entrance to a similar blockhouse on the Fowey side, intended to keep out the French.

'It's strange that the French are welcomed as allies now, when you think how we used to fight them once. Hugh has even started to learn the language. Most odd, but I heard him practising some phrases the other day.'

'Maybe he's going to take you to Paris for a second honeymoon.'

Sara frowned, wondering if that could be true, and if she would enjoy it if it were.

As they walked on past the coastguard station, Sara wondered if he was away on coastguard service today, and if Iris was with him. She certainly wasn't at The Ship, as Sid was managing on his own, with Sara doing the meals upstairs, of course. He'd been gone for a few days on this, his latest mission and she knew he wasn't with the lifeboat, as the familiar dark blue vessel was standing anchored in the river, ever ready for service. Where he went, or what he did on these trips, she hadn't the first idea, nor dare she risk any further questions on the subject but simply sent up a silent prayer each time that he would come back safe and sound.

She did once try to break the rules while he was away, and sneaked behind the bar to help, as the pub was so busy, but Sid wouldn't have it. 'Lose my job, if not my scalp, were Mr Marrack to find out.'

Even when he was absent, she was compelled to behave like an obedient wife. Although she did once provide lunch for a group of American officers, which neither Sid nor Hugh knew anything about. Charlie had been among them. They'd had a hard time of it keeping their glances apart, and when she'd placed a bowl of soup before him, his fingers had accidentally touched hers. Sara felt as if she'd been scalded.

The children found it a long, hard struggle up Battery Lane but they came out at last on to the grassy slopes of St Saviour's Point and then burst into a run, as children do. From here, the coastguard lookout could see for fifty miles or more, from Prawle Point in the east, past the Eddystone light off Plymouth to Black Head and The Manacles near the Lizard in the west.

Today the sea looked calm, almost benign, but Sara knew this to be false. There was no element more dangerous and somewhere, out on those cold, unfriendly waters, among that vast assortment of enemy and friendly shipping, was her husband.

Did his heart lift whenever he sighted the ruined buttress of St Saviour's ancient chapel, as sailors by the score must have done in years gone by? Did he think of her and long to rush to her side, as they must have done, eager to be with their sweethearts and wives?

She rather thought not. His kisses these days were more chaste and dutiful than passionate. Whatever had gone wrong between them, she didn't seem able to put right.

Sara sighed, and walked on, putting her romantic visions aside.

They followed the coastal path which would ultimately lead to Polperro, were they to have the time and energy to walk so far; the coves of Lantic Bay, Lantivet Bay and Lansallos Beach closed to them which made Drew shout out in his little boy voice how much he hated the war.

'It's so unfair,' he said, stamping his feet and making them all laugh. 'Those nasty Germans have spoiled my fishing.'

The walk was strenuous and they were ready to sit down and rest by the time they found a small sandy hollow far enough away from the hustle and bustle to set out their picnic. Deprived of the thrill of going down into one of the pretty little coves to build sand castles and paddle, or fish in rock pools, the children happily engrossed themselves with digging trenches.

'I'm going to shoot at all the German planes that go over, Mummy.'

'Are you, darling? How very brave of you. Well, make sure they're not ours before you do fire at them, won't you?'

'Course I will. What I really need is a telescope, like Daddy's, then I can spot what all these ships are, make sure I'm not being spied on, like Daddy does. Oh!' He stopped talking, suddenly going very red.

Sara laughed. 'I rather think Drew is hoping that this war will go on long enough for him to join up. Fortunately, at five, I reckon he's fairly safe, don't you? They say one last push and it will all be over. I wonder what will happen to us then? We'll be free to choose and make plans for a new beginning.'

Both sisters fell silent, trying to imagine how freedom would feel after all these years. Sara felt uncertain, even afraid of the future, which was stupid. She longed for the war to end, so that Hugh would never need to go to sea again. He would be home all the time and Charles Denham, along with the rest of the US marines, would return home.

Somehow this thought didn't bring her the cheer it should. Bette, she could see, was filled with a nervous energy, bursting to unburden herself even further. Sara wasn't sure she wanted to hear any more confessions. 'Tea?' She began to pour from the thermos while Bette handed out sandwiches.

Jenny screwed up her small nose. 'Ooh, not fish paste again.'

Drew made a vomiting sound in his throat. 'Why can't we have egg, or some of that peanut butter stuff Charlie brings us?'

'Charlie?' Bette raised her eyebrows.

'The children call him that. The peanut butter is for the fête, not for greedy little boys to gobble up,' and she tickled her small son, making him giggle.

Bette archly commented. 'Perhaps Mummy could ask Charlie to get you some to have all to yourself? I'm sure he would, if Mummy asked him.'

'Would he, Mummy? Ask him, ask him, ask him,' Drew yelled, Jenny chiming in.

'Now look what you've done. Calm down, children. I'll see what I can do. Yes, I promise, now run along and play but don't go anywhere near the edge. We don't want you falling down the cliffs.'

'We'd get blown up by a mine,' yelled Drew. '*Bang!* And you'd be in little bits, Jenny, like Little Black Mingo in the story book.'

'I wouldn't, would I Mummy?'

'For goodness' sake, play quietly for once the pair of you, and stop frightening her, Drew. Just be good and stay where I can see you.'

Bette's eyes were twinkling. 'What will they say when they hear they're going to have a little cousin? I do wonder how our children will turn out when they grow up, don't you? Will they make the same sort of mess of their lives as we have.'

'Speak for yourself.' Sara bit into a fish paste sandwich and, despite her earlier comment, wrinkled her own nose. She was as bored with it as the children, but it was cheap and plentiful in these parts, so they should consider themselves fortunate.

'You can't claim to be happy with bossy Hugh. He's so – so controlling! "You must do as I tell you, Sara. No, you may not serve in the bar, Sara. Good heavens, one of those dreadful men might take a shine to you, darling. Stay upstairs out of the way, and be a good, obedient little wife."' Bette gave a mocking salute, then fell about laughing. 'A bit of a little Hitler himself, in a way.'

Sara couldn't help but giggle. She always did find Bette's impersonations so life-like and funny. It could easily have been Hugh, the tone of voice absolutely right.

'And you let him. Yes, sir. No, sir. Three bags full, sir.'

'I don't all the time.'

'Yes, you do.'

Sara was frowning now. 'I suppose I married the first man who came along and thought him a real catch. Now, I'm not so sure. He's changed recently. Behaving even more oddly than he did after Valda died. His poor mother used to tell me how she'd failed him, not ever being able to love him as she should. How he was the sort of little boy who loved to pull wings off flies, and how she'd never known him to actually cry. He's impervious to pain, she'd say, his own and other people's. I paid not the slightest attention, yet I'm beginning to wonder if perhaps she wasn't trying to warn me, in her gentle way.

'Now he's told me I must resign from the War Weapons committee. I'm not to do any more war work, would you believe? I'm to stay at home and be a proper wife and mother.'

Bette had been listening sympathetically as her sister poured out her heart, now she was outraged. 'What? And to hell with the fact that you enjoy the work and want to carry on.'

'It would seem my wishes are of no account.'

Bette made a growling noise deep in her throat. 'I assume this is because he doesn't approve of the contact it gives you with the Americans.'

'That's about the size of it.'

'And you've been seeing quite a lot of this Lieutenant Denham. Do you perhaps fancy him just the tiniest bit? Ah, you're blushing again, so I'll take that as a yes.'

'It's impossible.'

'Why?'

'You know why. He's married. I'm married.'

'You could get unmarried. It's been done before, I believe.'

'Don't be flippant, Bette. This is so awful. Dreadful! I can't believe I feel this way, like a young girl again. A silly young girl. And there are the children to consider. Even if Hugh ever agreed to the unthinkable disgrace of a divorce, he'd never let me have the children. Never! Oh, God, Bette, what a mess! Why ever did these men have to come here, to our town?'

'Oh, and aren't we glad that they did. Does he feel the same way?'

Sara gave the barest inclination of her head.

'So what are you going to do about it?'

'What can I do?'

'I could make one or two suggestions, though as you never take my advice, I shan't waste my breath. Let's just say that when I love someone, as I do Barney, I don't give up easily. It isn't going to be easy getting official permission to marry, but we're quite determined to get it. You'll see, any moment now, I'll be Mrs Barney Willert. And, even more exciting, I've persuaded him to wangle transport to ship me out to the States.'

There was a long, strained silence while Sara's eyes widened in shock. 'America? You're going to America? When did you decide this?'

'Oh, lord, I forgot to mention that, didn't I? I can't stay here, can I, when my husband is American with a good business back in the States? And what is the point with the war almost over? I could be getting things ready for him back in his home town, getting to know his folks. Don't look at me like that, Sara, I have to get out of this place. I couldn't face the reproachful glances, the whispering behind hands that would be bound to go on here if I stayed.'

'You don't care what people think. You never have. You want to go because you've always yearned to travel.'

Looking shame-faced, Bette patted her golden curls with slender, pink tipped fingers. 'Well, that's true. I can't deny it.' Her eyes were shining now, a brilliance to them more gold than green. 'There's a whole world out there, away from this small town. Don't you just ache to explore it?'

'Not really.'

'Oh, I do. I can't wait, I'm so excited.'

'I'll miss you.'

Bette's face suddenly fell and all the happiness vanished from it. 'Oh, and I'll miss you too. I was so thrilled, so wrapped up in my own happiness, I never thought about the fact I'd be leaving you. How could I be so dim? What will I do without you?' And the two sisters fell into each other's arms, tears rolling down their cheeks.

'You'll cope fine. Everyone will fall in love with you, as they always do and be putty in your hands,' Sara said, drying both their tears with one soggy hanky.

'And you, what about you? Can you cope on your own, without me? With only Mam to share your troubles with?'

'Oh goodness, don't you worry about me. I can look after myself.'

'I'm not so sure. When does Hugh get back from this latest trip?'

'I don't know. I'm never sure how long these expeditions might last. Soon, I should think. I hope. I do worry about him.'

'And will you tell him, about Charles Denham – Charlie?'

'Lord no, far too dangerous. Anyway, there's nothing to tell. I've no intention of ever seeing Charlie again, not alone anyway. It has to stop now, before it goes any further.'

'I wish you would tell him. I wish you'd have a mad, passionate affair and then confront Hugh with it. And I wish you'd do it before I leave so that I can see you happy at last. Oh, and I'd just love to see Hugh's arrogance pricked.'

'That's a horrible thing to say.'

Bette giggled. 'OK, but I really would. Anyway, you know that we've always looked after each other, so if I were still here, I could console you and pick up the pieces when he explodes like a big, fat balloon.'

'Or like a land-mine. *Bang!*' And for some reason neither girl could have explained, they both found this terribly funny and began to shriek with laughter, even as tears again began to fall.

21

Hugh and Iris were out at sea, not in driving rain this time but in considerable danger nonetheless. They'd been waiting nearly twenty-four hours for a rendezvous and still there was no sign of it taking place. He was beginning to sweat with fear, despite the chill night. The pick-up was the crew of two American bombers who were shot down over Paris three months ago. Half a dozen men had survived the attack and been evading capture ever since, protected by the French underground movement, hidden in cellars and lofts, barns and haystacks, wherever the Bosch might not think to look, or have already searched.

One attempt to rescue the men, now known as the evaders, had already been made, only to end in failure when a break-down in communication had resulted in the wrong pick-up point and the men left stranded. Yet again they'd been rescued by the French resistance, dependent upon them for survival.

Now, a couple of weeks later, Hugh had been alerted that another attempt was to be made at picking them up. Iris listened in each evening to the BBC, and had recognised the prearranged signal. So here they were, putting their lives at risk for a bunch of Yanks. Hugh would much rather have been rescuing 'our boys' but was compelled to follow orders.

They should have made contact hours ago but a second dawn was breaking and the fear of discovery was growing in his mind. Surely someone would spot them lurking here in the channel, pretending to fish. This part of the Brittany coastline was plagued with strong currents and hidden reefs, not easy to navigate without lights. It always seemed a miracle to Hugh when they arrived in one piece, not having encountered any mines or foundered on the rocks.

This was, in fact, his second trip across to Brittany in less than a fortnight. The first time had been to bring Iris and drop her off on a small island where she'd been collected by some stranger in a canoe.

The last he'd seen of her on that occasion had been a wave of her hand as the man had paddled it away. It was with some relief that he'd collected her again just eight nights later. Again she'd been transported by canoe, a different man this time and he'd watched, heart in mouth, as it made slow progress between the rocks, frequently swamped by waves.

Once on board, she'd stripped off her wet clothes and gratefully drunk the hot soup Hugh had prepared for her, then related her adventures in a breathless, exhausted rush.

All about how she'd located her contact without too many difficulties, although she'd had to keep a wary eye out for German soldiers who seemed to stroll about the town with consummate ease, staking their claim as conquerors. She finished by explaining that she'd given him the information he'd needed and they'd had time for some productive debate. Hugh knew better than to ask what kind of information or debate that might be. You didn't ask questions. Not in this business. The less you knew, the better.

'Then he took me to meet the evaders. They've had to be frequently moved, of course, just in case the enemy should return a second time and find them. I was moved three times, in just five days. It must have been a nightmare for them. They've been living in fear of their lives for months while false papers were drawn up and arrangements made to get them out.'

As she talked, Hugh kept his eye on the shore, partly

blanketed in sea mist, praying for sight of them. They couldn't stay here much longer, not without arousing suspicion. One never knew what hidden eyes were watching you. Iris maintained they were well hidden behind this bluff of rock but Hugh felt as if they must stick out like a sore thumb, visible for miles around.

Tension was so high in him that he couldn't even find the energy to pass the time with Iris in the usual way. He had no interest in sex right now. His eyes were darting everywhere, alert, watchful, deeply afraid that out of a pearl grey sky would come death.

God knows what would happen when the air crew finally did appear. Would they be ferried across by boat or come by canoe, as was often the case? Whichever, he hoped and prayed they kept an eye open for mines. The last thing he needed was an explosion announcing to all and sundry that they were present in these waters. It was his own skin he cared about the most, of course, not theirs.

'How I loathe Americans, always creating problems and putting other lives at stake because of their own incompetence. Where the hell are they? They should be here by now.'

'I'm sure they will be, at any moment.' Iris appeared unperturbed by the delay, as cool as ever. She even managed a chuckle. 'Your prejudice is showing, Hugh, although I notice your wife doesn't share your views.'

'My wife has no contact with the Yanks. I made certain of that.'

The chuckle turned into a burst of laughter, rich and loud, so that Hugh hissed at her, reminding her how easily sound travels over water. Iris apologised, briefly, but then dropped a bombshell of her own. 'Not quite certain enough. You realise that she and the charming Lieutenant Denham are virtually inseparable, working together on all these war-weapons, fund-raising projects. Dear Nora spotted them only the other day bowling happily along in his jeep towards Lostwithiel. Cosy!'

Rage boiled up inside him, filling his head with a burst of heat that seemed as if that too might explode. Hugh couldn't ever remember being so angry in all his life. 'Are you saying that Sara has disobeyed me? Knowing that I have forbidden her to fraternise with these men, she's done it anyway and gone behind my back.'

Iris smirked. 'It would seem so. Hey, there they are. Look, I saw a brief flash of red. That's the signal we've been waiting for.' She grabbed a pair of binoculars, and stared out across the rocks. 'Yes, it must be them. I can see a couple of specks which might be canoes, and there's another. They're on their way but the sea looks rough, great big waves slapping up against those rocks. They'll have their work cut out, and they must keep a beady eye open for mines. Lord, I hope they get through the channel safely.'

But Hugh wasn't listening. While she was thus engaged, he'd been busy about the boat. Before Iris realised what he was doing, he'd shipped anchor but instead of heading in the direction of the evaders to make the pick-up, he began to quietly slip away.

'Hey, you're going in the wrong direction. What the hell are you playing at?'

'I'm heading home, Iris. I'm the captain of this ship and I've decided it's too dangerous to wait any longer.'

'But they're coming. Didn't you hear me say so? Don't you see them?'

'I didn't see a soul. Somehow I've gone deaf, dumb and blind where Yanks are concerned. They deserve all they get, in my opinion.'

Iris was screaming at him now, heedless of how the sound might carry, although the rising wind was whipping most of her words away. '*But there are six men out on that cold sea who will die if you abandon them*! You're condemning them to bloody death!'

'Then at least there will be six fewer marriages ruined. Six British soldiers' wives left in peace, and a bloody good thing too.'

'You won't get away with this. I'll have to report you.'

'You'll do no such thing.' The blow was unexpected and sent her sprawling, although not for long. Iris, being Iris, instantly struggled to right herself and flew at him like a tigress. 'Turn this boat around!'

Even with a bloodied nose she was still screaming at him, something about how he would mess everything up. 'You'll ruin all my plans. They trust me, rely on me. I'm considered dependable because I've worked bloody hard for years. I'll not have you spoil everything.'

She struck out at him and within seconds they were grappling together, one minute rolling about in the bottom of the boat, the next hanging over the sides.

Hugh considered tossing her overboard. That would ensure her silence. He could eliminate her quite easily, as she had once threatened would be done to him, if he talked and became a problem. But he instantly thought better of it and, grabbing hold of her by the collar, flung her like a whipped dog back into the tiny cabin, where he shut fast and locked the door.

She yelled and screamed and hammered on the panel, but he ignored her. He'd spared her life because Iris was useful to him in more ways than one.

Besides, he didn't want too many questions asked and was arrogant enough to believe that he could control her. A sense of power surged through his veins, making him feel strong, invincible. Iris would realise that he was not a man to cross, and his wife needed to be reminded of that fact, too.

*   *   *

Drew was waiting for him, curled up at the top of the stairs, as usual, when he got back and Hugh was at first irritated and scolded the boy, saying that he should be in bed, fast asleep. He grabbed the child and marched him back to his room, berating him all the while. Hugh felt as if his nerves were shot to ribbons and the last thing he needed right now was to deal with a disobedient child.

'But I want to hear about your mission, Daddy. Tell me, tell me.'

'Hush! You'll wake Jenny.' But the adoration in his son's eyes had a calming effect upon him. Hugh tucked the child back into bed, and keeping his voice low so that he wouldn't wake Jenny, began to talk. He didn't seem able to prevent himself. He made no mention of Iris, or their fierce scrap, or that he had abandoned the aircrew and deliberately left them to die. He simply said that men had died that night, and, in a moment of weakness, of need, admitted that he felt responsible, without quite saying why.

'Did the enemy shoot them? If you got me a telescope, I could help, couldn't I, Daddy? I could go out on to the headland and watch for you. Then I could send you a signal if I spotted an enemy plane.'

Hugh wasn't listening, paying no attention to his son's fantasies. 'I had to do it for you, son, to keep you safe. And for your mother.'

Even before he'd finished pouring out all his hatred of Americans, Drew was fast asleep, no doubt dreaming of flying a little plane like Rupert Bear. Hugh went to his own bed feeling cleansed, and quite free of guilt.

To Hugh's enormous satisfaction, and no small sense of relief, Iris kept her mouth shut about the incident of the abandoned aircrew. They learned later that two of the canoes had capsized and four young men were drowned. The remaining two crew members were still in France, awaiting rescue. Hugh had been given a grilling by the commanding officer in charge of operations, who seemed convinced by his story and accepted that he hadn't seen them. Hugh maintained the canoes must have been shrouded in the mist and twenty-seven hours was quite long enough to wait, any longer would have begun to arouse suspicion.

Iris too had been questioned, in private, while Hugh sat outside, chewing on his nails and praying that the warnings he'd given her before she went in, had fully sunk in. She still bore the bruises from their undignified tussle, he noticed, thickly covered in make-up.

Finally, the office door swung open. For a moment she stood framed in the doorway, the curve of her breasts up-tilted and enticing, making him salivate just to think of their cushiony softness beneath his hands. He steadied himself. Concentrate. What was she saying in these few final words to her commander?

Hugh wasn't even sure who he was, or what unit he was attached to, as this was the first time he'd met him. He wore no uniform and what his surname was, or his rank, Hugh had no idea, being instructed to address him simply as 'Sir'. At one point they both glanced across at him and Hugh began, very slightly, to sweat. But then she smiled at him, and strolled over.

'We are agreed that it was a terrible tragedy, all too common in war,' she said. 'We can go now. The investigation is closed.'

He felt sick suddenly, as if he'd looked death in the face and been granted a reprieve. Stepping outside, the sun seemed suddenly brighter and his heart lifted with gratification. How clever he was and, he imagined, untouchable. Invincible even. He could do as he pleased and get away with it. The buzz this notion gave him was intoxicating. He'd made a stand for England; proved he wouldn't waste his time on know-it-all, incompetent Yanks.

'You did well,' he told Iris, condescension strong in his tone.

'Thank you,' she dryly remarked. 'You realise I could have had you shot.'

Hugh snorted with laughter. 'Now why would you do that when you and I are having such a good time?'

She stopped walking to gaze steadily at him. 'I hope you realise that you owe me a huge debt.'

He pulled her towards him, his greedy fingers reaching for her breasts even as he nuzzled into her neck. 'And how would you like it to be repaid?'

She pushed him away. 'That's what we need to talk about. Oh, your secret is safe with me, Hugh old boy. Reasonably safe, shall we say. But that safety comes at a price.'

22

By the time she was done explaining, Hugh's eyes were nearly popping out of his head. 'You want me to carry information to the enemy, to the Germans? Good God, are you mad? What sort of information?'

'The Germans are desperate to learn as much as possible about the activity along the coastline here, about Operation Overlord, and from which direction the invasion might come. They aren't nearly so confident and well prepared as you might imagine so need all the help they can get. You and I are in a position to supply at least some of what they require. We need to keep our ears and eyes open at all times, so that we can feed them what they need.'

'I can't believe what I'm hearing. You don't seriously expect me to turn traitor?' Hugh's face was crimson and he was blustering now, outraged by her suggestion.

Iris smiled. 'Oh yes, Hugh, that is exactly what I expect you to do. Think of yourself as a double agent, so much sexier, don't you think? I will supply the material and you will deliver it, personally. I've been doing the whole task myself up till now, but I really don't see why I should continue to take all the risks. It's time they were more fairly distributed.'

'You mean . . .?'

Iris smiled. 'That you haven't simply been working for the British, but for the enemy, too? Absolutely. True, we've rescued a great many British airmen, and even Americans, despite your objections to them. Why not? That part of the exercise is excellent cover for my more important activities. It means that I can build up trust in the right places. Vital in this game. My husband is German, you see. I met him in Spain during the civil war. We were both fighting for the fascists. Klaus is a typically Aryan male, very self-opinionated. Rather like yourself.'

'And you're married?'

'Yes.'

'But I thought you were going out with a sailor?'

'That was just cover. I ditched him anyway, when you and I started – you know. Klaus and I married in Madrid in 1938 when we realised war between Britain and Germany was imminent and unavoidable. He returned home, to fight for his country, and so did I. It was my husband's idea that I use my English background to infiltrate Secret Operations here, and it seems to have worked out rather well.'

'But how come the Special Operations Executive haven't realised? You're married to a German, for God's sake!'

'Because I've been careful. Very careful. Anyway, why should they know? I still have my passport in my maiden name. Klaus is still in Germany, naturally, working with the Nazis. He finds me the necessary contacts in France but when I expressed a need for more reliable transport from someone who wouldn't ask too many questions, he agreed that I should involve you, using any methods at my disposal. We have that kind of marriage. And you haven't found the work or the rewards too objectionable, have you, Hugh?'

'I absolutely refuse to be involved any further. I'm a loyal British subject and will do no such thing.'

'Oh, I think you will. Whatever we do, you and I, will have little effect on the long-term outcome of this war. We are very small fry indeed. The war is almost over and, sadly, I'm not entirely sure that my darling Klaus will be on the winning side. However, as a good and loyal wife I will continue to do my best for him and what we both believe in, and, if we're clever, might even make ourselves a buck or two along the way. Isn't that what our American friends would call it? So that Klaus and I can disappear some place together, when it's all over. You aren't against earning a little extra, are you, Hugh? The Germans will pay good money for what we know.'

'But men could get killed. *Our* men!'

Iris shrugged. 'Such is war. Everyone must look out for themselves. Surely you, of all people would agree with such a philosophy? Think of it. If what we give them is not entirely accurate, does it matter at this stage in the game? Take the money and run.'

His temper was cooling slightly but still he hesitated. Hugh still didn't entirely trust her. Knowing how tough she was, what a fighter she'd been, he couldn't quite get to grips with this sudden turn of events. 'Everyone but me sees you as an empty-headed young barmaid, but you're neither as young nor as stupid as people imagine.'

Iris burst out laughing. 'You're absolutely right on both counts. I'm twenty-nine. I was just turned twenty-one when I met Klaus in Barcelona in 1936.'

'All right, so you've been working for the other side all along but why me? Why risk involving me? What makes you trust me?'

'Because you aren't in a position to cause me any problems. Why should I go on taking unnecessary risks when I can send you instead? The perfect solution,' and she tweaked his nose while Hugh's face flushed a dark, angry red.

'That's why you didn't spill the beans about that American bomber crew I left stranded. You saw that you could take advantage of what I'd done.'

'Got it in one.'

'Well, you've mistaken your man this time. I may rage against my stupid wife, who seems hell-bent on turning into a flighty tart just like her sister. I may hate Americans and be perfectly willing to do whatever I deem necessary to undermine their sanctimonious self-importance, but I'm no traitor, and never will be. I'll not do it.'

Iris smiled, and it was not an invitation. It was a smile every bit as cold and calculating as his own. 'Yes, you will do it, because otherwise you might find yourself looking down the collective barrels of a firing squad. I don't think you really have much choice, do you?'

Hugh was still reeling with shock when he climbed into the marital bed some time before dawn, turning over in his mind this startling turn of events with Iris, and not a little fearful for the future. What sort of a mess was she getting him into? This wasn't at all what he'd intended, although he seemed to be stuck with it, could see no way out. The very prospect of a firing squad made him shake, feel sick to his stomach. He fully believed her when she'd threatened to talk if he didn't do as she said. Iris Logan seemed to be one woman he was quite unable to control.

Sara was asleep, curled up as innocent as a babe. But she wasn't innocent, was she? Iris had seen her with that Yank, that young lieutenant. It was bad enough to have Iris ordering him about, proving far more difficult to manage than he'd expected. Having his wife disobey him as well, was too much.

He prodded her awake. 'Sara, wake up. What have you been up to while I've been away?'

'What . . .? Hugh?' She was unfurling like a cat, warm and languid, her silver fair hair spread out on the pillow.

'Who else would it be? Your soldier lover?'

She gave a soft chuckle, as if he were making some sort of joke, but he recognised its falseness, the fragility of her nerves in the way her eyes blinked wide open, the tell-tale colour flooding in and then draining from her cheeks.

'I've been worrying about you, Hugh. I'm so glad you're safe home again.'

She reached for him, her arms sliding about his neck, but he pushed her away. 'Have you resigned from that damned committee yet?'

'Goodness, no, why should I?'

'Because you know I don't want you involved. You've more than enough to do caring for me and the children.'

She seemed to sigh with relief, as if this were a far safer topic to argue over. 'Do stop fretting about me, darling. I don't have half so much work to do now that I'm no longer needed in the pub, so it's only right that I do my bit. We've had this out a dozen times and I am determined not to give up my war work. It's important and they badly need my help. Besides, I really quite enjoy it, irritating as Nora Snell is at times. I need to feel useful. Please try to understand.'

She gave him a peck on the cheek as if her words, and this tender action should satisfy him, and then snuggled back down into the pillows. 'Do go to sleep, darling. You must be worn out. I certainly am.'

If she'd hoped to fob him off with excuses, she'd mistaken her man. Hugh pulled her onto her back, lifted her nightdress and pushed his fingers inside her.

Sara let out a startled cry. 'Hugh, for heaven's sake, what are you doing? Don't do that!'

'Why not? You're my wife.'

'Yes, but you could at least kiss and cuddle me a little first.'

'Kiss and cuddle, that's all you ever ask for. You shouldn't need all of that nonsense. If you really loved me, you should be ready and waiting for me any time I want you.'

'Don't be ridiculous.' She was drawing up her legs, trying to get away from him. He pulled them back down again and she let out a tiny whimper. 'If this is all because of some stupid jealousy over the GIs again, then you're being very silly. Now leave me alone and go to sleep, you must be worn out after your trip.'

She tried to push him away as if he were a naughty child but the gesture so infuriated him that he grabbed his pyjama chord, wrapped it swiftly about her wrists and had her tied to the bed-head in seconds, before she'd even realised what he meant to do.

'Hugh, what on earth are you doing? Stop it! I don't like this, please stop.'

She was gasping, pleading with him but he ignored her. He didn't stop. He shoved open her legs and took her quite brutally, making her cry out in pain, although she soon stifled her cries, no doubt fearful that the children might hear. Instead, she bit down so hard on her lower lip that she made it bleed. The trickle of blood somehow excited him to a greater frenzy, that and the vision in his head of three canoes frantically paddling through the mist, the cries of men calling desperately for help.

He thought of railway lines blowing up, of Iris telling him she was going to make him act as some sort of spy. And while he was facing such danger, his wife was cavorting with her American lover.

Rage came hot and tight in his chest, blurring her face to nothing more than an unidentifiable blob on the pillow, her mouth an oval of silent agony. He tried to take her again but she bucked beneath him, desperately struggling to fight him off, to kick at him with her feet. Ferocious as a tiger she spat at him.

'Stop it, stop it! That's enough, Hugh. Let me go, for pity's sake. Untie me at once, please. Please, I beg you!'

He liked it better now that she was sobbing and begging, all her quiet dignity gone, far more satisfying than outright resistance. It always irritated him that even in love-making he could never entirely possess her. Sara had rarely responded to his love-making as he would have wished, or needed her to respond. She was forever fussing about kisses and cuddles, always a part of her that he couldn't quite reach. So it was good to see her usual calm self-possession in ribbons. It felt good.

He tied her feet to the bottom rail, her body spread-eagled on the bed, open and inviting for him to take or use as he wished, her eyes wide and frightened, proving her vulnerability. So enticingly seductive.

'You know you love this really,' he told her. 'Is this what he does to you?'

He saw her pale lips curve around the word *who*, but it remained unspoken, no sound came out.

'Your lover. The lieutenant. Don't think I don't know what's going on, why you insist on remaining on this damned committee, so that you can work closely with him. It has to stop. Is that clear? I've asked you to resign but since you've refused, I can only think the worst. But you need to remember, Sara, that you are still my wife, and I would like confirmation of that fact right now.'

'I – I don't know what you're talking about. I've done nothing. Ch-Charlie is just a friend, nothing more. Let me go.'

'Charlie, is it now? Very cosy. Prove to me that you still love me. Do for me what you no doubt do for him. Take me in your mouth. Go on. Do as I say.'

She was frantic to get away from him, wriggling and bucking so hard, the cords and straps making deep indentations into her wrists and ankles. But what did it matter? She was utterly helpless.

The sensation of power soared through his veins like wine, for in that moment she was entirely his to command and do with as he willed, and he made the most of it. Nobody, least of all a Yank, would ever be allowed to take her away from him.

Afterwards, when he'd taken his fill and finally released her, he generously bathed the weals in warm, soapy water, smoothed Vaseline over the red, raw sores. Sara sat unmoving, letting him do it, a shrivelled wreck of her former, sophisticated self.

'You would do well to remember this night, darling, so that you can make the right decisions in future. All right, my love?'

She said nothing, her defiance crushed at last. He could hear her weeping quietly into her pillow, but Hugh paid not the slightest attention. He simply turned over and went to sleep. He felt so much better now.

23

The moment Sara had taken the children to school she went straight to the salon. She could hardly walk she was so sore, but gave no sign of this as she entered. Bette was washing Ethel Penhale's hair so could only give half her attention to Sara. She was surprised by her sister's sudden appearance at such an early hour.

'Is there something wrong? You look like you've seen a ghost.'

'No, no, I was wondering if I could just have a quick word.'

Bette pulled a face, indicating Ethel's head covered with soap suds which she was holding in the sink. 'Bit tied up at present. Not too hot, is it, Ethel?' A bad-tempered mumble came by way of response. 'Sorry!'

'Later then,' Sara said. 'Where's Mam?'

'Having the morning off, would you believe?' Then glancing down at her customer, with much rolling of eyes and pulling of her face, indicated that Sara should lean closer while she whispered in her ear. 'Barney is asking the major's permission today about – you know. Getting wed. Ooh, I can't wait to see him tonight.'

'Do you think he'll get it?'

'Course he will. Barney has the sort of charm no one can resist.'

Sara couldn't help but smile. 'You certainly couldn't.'

A screech rose from the sink. 'Ooh sorry, Ethel, did I get

soap in your eyes?' Bette pulled a face at Sara who shook her head in despair.

'I might pop in and see Mam. Bye, Ethel.'

Sadie had her slippered feet up on a stool and was enjoying a mug of tea and a slice of toast and dripping while listening to *Workers' Playtime* on the wireless. 'Hello, what ill wind blows you in? Short of something to do now you've been sacked, are you?'

Not quite the response Sara had hoped for but she reached for the kettle, determined not to rise to the sarcasm. Settled with a cup of steaming tea cradled between her frozen hands, which for some reason she couldn't seem to get warm this morning, Sara prepared to put her question to her mother. There was never any point in beating about the bush with Sadie who could spot any attempt at clever manipulation a mile off. Certainly whenever Sara tried it. 'Can I move in with you for a while? Hugh and I are having a few – difficulties – at present, so I need somewhere to go.'

'What, to lick your wounds?'

'I suppose you could say that, yes. I'd be bringing the children.'

'Had a row have you? Been quarrelling with that lovely man? You don't know when you're well off, girl.'

'Not exactly quarrelling, no, but I just need . . .'

'You need your head seeing to, that's what you need. And why would I want a houseful of children? Haven't I enough with your sister's men friends, and her coming and going, getting under me feet the whole time. I shall be glad when she's finally wed and I can get a bit of peace around here. If you're short of something to do, you could come and help out at the salon. You could wash customers' hair at least, even if you're not capable of doing anything else. Though I expect you think yourself above such menial labour.'

Sara closed the door softly as she left. What on earth had possessed her to imagine that her own mother would help?

The very next time Hugh went out with Iris in the boat, he felt as nervous as a young boy. Why had he agreed to this madness? Because he really didn't have any choice, not if he was to live to see the end of the war.

They picked up two young airmen and the operation passed off quite smoothly, as usual. He breathed a sigh of relief.

Acting as carrier pigeon was a far more hazardous exercise. His first experience came later in the week. Never had he experienced such fear. He was dropped somewhere close to the same area around the Brittany coast where he'd abandoned the aircrew, except that this time there was no canoe waiting. Wearing a rubber waterproof suit he swam ashore without too much difficulty. He carried false papers comprising a work permit and ration cards, all with official-looking German stamps which Iris assured him would pass scrutiny were he ever to be challenged.

Hugh didn't care to even consider such a possibility. Placing a parcel by a railway line under cover of darkness was one thing, actually walking into town in broad daylight, into the enemy camp as it were, was quite another.

Yet he did what was required of him. He secreted the suit behind a rock, then took the package to the address he'd been given, collecting some papers in exchange from the woman behind the counter of the little *patisserie*, and in a blessedly short time was hurrying back out of town in great haste.

Never had he felt more relieved to be safely back on board his own boat. And to find Iris waiting for him.

They enjoyed a bottle of French wine together on the journey back, which helped to ease relations between them but there was apparently to be no rekindling of their passion. When he made an approach, placed his hands on her breasts, she laughingly pushed them aside. 'I don't need to suffer your clumsy advances any longer.'

'Clumsy? I didn't hear you complaining of that at the time.'

'OK, so some of it was fun, but I have a much stronger hold on you now.'

He hated her for that, could easily have strangled her with his bare hands there and then, were it not for his stronger need for his own survival. 'So where's my share of the loot?' he asked, greedy to at least get his hands on the cash.

What loot?'

'The money you promised me for doing this courier business for you.'

'Be patient. You'll get your reward, all in good time.'

Following the rejection by her mother, Sara moved her things out of their bedroom, into the guest room. Hugh moved them back, remonstrating with her, pointing out that she couldn't escape her responsibilities by hiding away in there.

'I'm not hiding away, but I will not tolerate such love-making, if you can call it that. I won't have it, Hugh.'

He stared at her as if he'd never realised before that she had a voice, let alone the courage to use it.

'Are you saying we are going to sleep apart in future, that you are leaving the marital bed?' His eyes were hard and angry.

'For the moment, yes. Until you're out of this dreadful mood or depression, that you're in.'

She could only think that his behaviour was influenced by these ops he was involved with, whatever they were. Somehow they seemed to have hardened and toughened him in a way that was really quite alarming. 'If I didn't firmly believe that marriage should never be abandoned lightly, I'd leave now, this minute.'

She wouldn't of course, because of the children. She already regretted involving Sadie because, like it or not, her mother was right in a way. Hugh was still her husband and clearly in need of care to help him deal with whatever devils were troubling him. Sara had made up her mind that this current difficulty was a phase which would hopefully pass.

'You will not leave, Sara. You are my wife and will ever remain so. You can stay in the guest room, if you insist, but when I want you, I shall come for you. I have my rights.'

Sara locked the guest-room door and sank onto the bed to find that she was trembling.

He was right, she couldn't ever leave him. But if she couldn't escape, then she must help to make him better. And if she couldn't do that either, then she would simply have to endure. At least she had her darling children.

She did her best to be understanding, to behave like the good, obedient wife she'd always been, the one Hugh expected and demanded. She was as compliant as butter, anxious to prove her loyalty and innocence, and to keep his unpredictable temper sweet. She made him tasty meals, kept the children out of his way, made no mention of her war work and never asked to borrow the car.

She privately resolved never again to accept a lift from Charlie, or Lieutenant Charles Denham as she must now think of him. Any feelings she held in that direction must be resisted and ignored at all cost, on the grounds that she was still a respectable, married woman and would ever remain so.

Night after night she would lie in the guest bed and hear him shuffle to her door and knock gently. 'Sara, can I come in? I'm so sorry for what I did. I'm ashamed of myself. I don't know what came over me. Come back to bed, let's try again. I need you beside me. Let's stop quarrelling.'

She lay with tears sliding down her cheeks, dampening her pillow, remembering the Hugh she had once loved.

*   *   *

One bright spring morning, Sara was washing up after breakfast when Bette burst into the kitchen all noise and energy, gabbling out her news at record speed since she never did anything quietly. 'He's done it. Barney has fixed me up with transport. There's a freight carrier leaving for the States on the first tide on Monday. It's going to cost me thirty-seven pounds, ten shillings, plus money for rail fare and meals in the States, but I'm off. It's going to happen. Isn't that wonderful? Oh, and that means I've got three days to prepare for my wedding.'

Sara nearly dropped the plates she was stacking. 'You can't be serious. You don't even have the major's permission to marry, do you?'

'So what? Barney has wangled a special licence, thanks to Sadie and Cory giving their permission, and lending me the money, so by the time the major finds out, it'll be too late. The deed will have been done.'

'You can't leave, just like that, so suddenly.' Sara's grey-green eyes had quite lost their habitual calm, as they grew round with panic.

Bette ran to put her arms about her sister and the pair hugged and wept.

Hugh sat at the dining table with the newspaper spread out before him, covertly watching the two girls. From Sara's behaviour, chatting to the children, making toast for their breakfast, you'd have thought that she didn't have a care in the world. Just as if the events of the other night had never taken place. Now here she was in floods of tears over a wedding.

'But when will I see you again?' Sara said. 'Maybe not for years. How will I manage without you?'

'Oh, don't say such things.'

'Hugh, tell her she mustn't leave, that we need her here, with us. Tell her to wait till the war is over when they can go together. Tell her, Hugh.'

'She must do as she wishes.'

Personally, he'd be glad to see the back of the stupid girl, interfering busybody that she was. Not that he approved of her decision to marry a Yank and run off to America. Craziest thing he ever heard of, except that Sara might behave better without her sister's troubling influence around. As an only child, he'd had no such soul-mate, had no one to take his side, so he couldn't understand the fuss Sara was making.

The maroon went up at precisely that moment. 'That's the lifeboat. I have to go.' He folded his paper with some relief, and quickly left. He really couldn't bear to witness their sickening closeness a moment longer.

The call-out involved a rescue mission on a burning ship. It was a Dutch cargo boat with a sizeable crew, all in something of a panic, running here, there and everywhere. This, he thought, was the very opportunity he'd been seeking to improve his situation. Being hailed as a hero after some of these missions was all very flattering, but did little to fatten his wallet, and acting as a secret agent for the enemy could prove to be even less profitable, since he had little faith in the promises Iris had made to him.

Hugh had therefore resolved to use his wits and take advantage of whatever hazardous situation he found himself in, otherwise where was the point in it all?

If the war really was to be over soon, he needed to secure his future, make certain that he was in the best possible position to look after his family. A fine house on the esplanade perhaps, a new car. He deserved these things for the risks he'd taken. A few spoils of war.

He managed somehow to be among those who went on board, and in the chaos, while his colleagues were searching cabins, ensuring the ship had been properly evacuated before it was sunk, he carried out a swift search on his own account.

It proved to be most profitable, yielding three gold watches, several sets of fine cuff-links, tie-pins and, from the captain's cabin, a selection of silk ties. He also found a stamp collection, which surely must be worth a bob or two. Serve the captain right for being foolish enough to bring it with him.

Pleased with his hoard, he rapidly stuffed them in his jacket pockets and was back shouting 'clear the decks' in no time.

The fire had a tenacious hold by this time but no lives were lost, and for Hugh at least, the exercise had been a lucrative one as he was able to cash in his hoard, taking care to sell only one item at a time, and to different second-hand dealers in various localities so as not to arouse suspicion.

The two sisters spent a frantic day rifling through wardrobes, choosing and altering dresses, finding something borrowed, something blue. Barney popped into the pub that evening and was informed that he certainly could not see what she would be wearing. Sara smiled as Bette ran to kiss him, the pair seeming to be in a happy daze, at least Bette was. Barney looked more stunned than anything, as if events had over-whelmed him and he couldn't quite take it all in.

But then who could blame him, poor boy? One minute he'd been fooling around with a pretty girl, the next he was about to put a wedding ring on her finger and become a father. Probably not at all what he'd expected.

Sara hoped and prayed that Bette was making a wise choice, that he would make her happy.

Watching them together, she couldn't help feeling a pang of envy for her sister's newfound joy, even if it was clouded by a slight apprehension for her. What wedding didn't have doubts and anxiety attached? This was a new chapter in her life, a new beginning, but Sara was pleased for her, she really was. Bette was bubbling over with happiness, as if she'd been drinking pink champagne.

Even so, had her sister been capable of a single coherer
thought beyond her coming wedding, Sara would have gone t
her, even now, and begged her not to go. The thought of Bett
leaving on Monday morning brought a sick feeling to the pit o
her stomach. She would miss her so much. Sara couldn't begi
to imagine life without her. Particularly now when her own lif
seemed to have fallen into the realms of nightmare.

She longed to pour out her heart, to confide in Bette abou
what Hugh was doing to her, yet hesitated to do so. How coul
she spoil her sister's happiness? It would be too cruel. If the
must part, let it be with good, happy thoughts, not trouble
and worries.

Besides, what could Bette do? They were both helples
against Hugh. When he put his mind to it, he could b
unspeakably, heartlessly cruel. She'd never known him t
be quite as bad as this before, and didn't quite know hov
to deal with it.

Sara put her arms about her beloved sister. 'Darling Bette
you look so beautiful. I wish with all my heart, that you ar
granted a happier marriage than I.'

'Oh, please, Sara, don't. You'll make me cry all over again.
Bette's excitement was tangible, effervescent. Soon, she woul
be Mrs Barney Willert, off to a new life in America. She wa
quite unable to keep still, so when she heard the doorbell rin
she ran to answer it, her face a picture of bright hope an
happiness. It was Barney, as she'd expected, standing on th
doorstep, bearing an expression so solemn that fear douse
her joy in an instant.

'What is it, what's wrong? Oh, no, the major has found ou
about our plans and is threatening to court-martial you.'

'Nothing so simple.'

'Simple? You would call a court martial simple?'

Barney had reconciled himself to Bette's rush to the altar o
the grounds that she was a sexy little thing, and hell, he migh

ever live to see the kid born, anyway. The war might solve the problem for him. Even if he survived, as he hoped he would, it would be a whole new world by then and he could divorce her easy enough, if things didn't work out. Now something totally unexpected had happened and he didn't know whether to laugh or cry.

He drew in a deep, shuddering sigh, fidgeting with discomfort and glancing awkwardly about him to right and left. I'm not sure how to tell you this, Bette, but I was wrong. I got it all wrong.' He seemed to lose his voice, or else he was struggling to catch his breath.

'What is it? For God's sake, Barney, I can't bear it, I . . .'

He handed her a letter and when Bette looked at the handwriting, that was when she fainted.

24

The wedding was off. Chad's letter explained how he'd been shipped out of the war, too badly wounded to fight any more. He'd spent the last several weeks in hospital in a coma and had woken up to find he was missing an arm, and his face and body were pitted with burns and sores.

I don't know what hit me but it sure must have been a humdinger. Even poor old Mom didn't know where I was but the whole exercise seems to have been put under wraps. Can't say much right now but . . .

The next few lines had been scrubbed out with lines of black ink by the censor. The letter finished with his usual declaration of love for her.

I'm so grateful that you still love me, that you waited for me. It's great to be back Stateside but you must get transport out here just as soon as you can. I need you with me, hon, and can't wait to see you.

What could she say to that? Reading his loving words, just seeing his handwriting, made her heart flip over. Did that mean she still loved Chad, or was it simply guilt, or fear that she might be about to lose Barney?

'What can I do? What should I say to him?' she wept to Barney. 'We have to tell him the truth, that we are to be married. He doesn't know about the baby yet. Should I tell him that it might be his? Or should I say that it's yours? He doesn't know that . . . that we . . . Oh, hell! And the baby *could* be his. It most probably is, when you come to think about it, check dates and such. But if I go to him, as he wants me to, how could I bear to leave you? Oh, God, what a mess!' Tears were rolling down her cheeks and her chest felt as if it might explode. It was all so awful, so painful.

Barney silently gave her his handkerchief. 'It's hard, I know, sugar, but we have to do what's right.'

'Yes, but that's what I can't work out. What is right? I love you both in a way. I don't want to hurt either of you.'

Barney knew it was important that he choose his words with care. He could at least see a way out of his own dilemma and didn't want to screw up by saying the wrong thing. 'I should have told him how I felt about you from the start, instead of playing tricks on him and bragging what a great guy I was. That time we went to the pictures, we should have told him then how things were between us. It's too late now. He's sick, he's injured. He needs you.'

'But you need me too, don't you?'

'Sure I do, sugar. I always will.' *But not as a wife*, said the little voice at the back of his head.

Bette sobbed, 'How could we have told him? He was your best buddy.'

'Still is. He'd give his life for me, I know he would, and all I've ever done to him is pinch his girls, and play stupid practical jokes so that I could steal you off him too, the prettiest girl he ever did have. Then they transferred him and he got blown up. I should be the one to lose an arm, not poor old Chad. It's all my fault.'

'Oh, Barney, don't say that. You don't know it was because of those so-called accidents that they sent him to Devon, not for sure.'

'It sure does feel that way. God knows what the poor guy has suffered.' Barney let out a heavy sigh, and gathering her small face between his two hands, lifted her mouth to his for one last, chaste kiss. 'We have to do what's right, OK? You're carrying his child. Look after him, Bette. He needs you more than I do. No, not more than I do. How could he? Well he does, in a way. Aw hell, I don't know what I'm saying any more.'

Bette felt as if her heart were being torn in two. 'You're telling me to go to him, aren't you?'

'I don't think we have any choice, sugar.'

'Oh, Barney, how can I bear it? I love you so much. I love you both.'

'We'll just have to be strong, sugar. We'll just have to be strong.' And he put his arms about her, patting her gently as Bette sobbed out her misery on his shoulder.

'So you're still going?' Sara gazed sadly at her sister, unable to think beyond that, quite unable to offer any soothing words of comfort.

'I must. It's the right thing to do. Barney says so and I agree with him. Oh, but I feel so confused, I feel numb inside. I can't get my head around any of it. Do you think I should go, that I'm doing the right thing?'

Sara could only shake her head in despair and gently point out that this was one occasion when sibling advice was no use at all. 'I don't know what to advise, love, I really don't.' Sara had no solution to her sister's dilemma. Chad was alive and they were all delighted. The fact that his fiancée loved his best mate too and couldn't decide which of them she wanted to marry, was a problem only she could resolve.

'Poor Bette. What a pickle you've got yourself into this time. But you mustn't marry Chad simply out of a sense of duty. You have to think of your own happiness, too.'

Tears washed down Bette's face and she swept them away with the flat of both hands. 'But I am still fond of him, love him to bits, really. We had some good times together. He may not be so strong or as good-looking, or as dynamic as Barney, but he's a good, kind man. He deserves better than me as a wife, but I must go to him. You do see that? He needs me now more than ever. How can I let him down? How can I marry his best buddy, maybe live in the same town and let Barney bring up Chad's child. It doesn't bear thinking of.'

A small, farewell reception was held at The Ship Inn with a gathering of family and friends to see Bette off on her new life. Cory, and even Sadie to a degree, seemed unusually subdued, clearly not in a mood for a celebration although they put a brave face on things. At one point Cory took himself out for a walk to the quay, coming back with suspiciously red eyes. His youngest child was setting off to the far side of the world and he feared he might never see her again.

Sadie kept hissing at him under her breath to buck up and smile. 'At least the daft tart won't bring any more shame on us with her trouble, once she's over there and safely wed. It's worth handing over half our savings, just to be rid of the worry.'

'Don't you call my little bird those nasty names, girl. Mistakes do happen, even to the best of 'em.'

'Which she never has been, the no-good little madam.'

'That's enough! Do as I tell you for once, and shut your mouth.'

Sadie gasped, never having heard her pragmatic Cory speak so sharply to her before. She took one look at his tight face and for once, did indeed remain silent.

Barney did not attend, although he made all the necessary arrangements for Bette to be transported on the freight carrier. This all had to be kept very hush-hush as, strictly speaking, it was quite illegal, avoiding all that hanging around for the necessary permits and paperwork. Bette wouldn't be the only prospective war-bride on board, several more had apparently arrived and were hidden away in various parts of the town, quietly waiting for Monday's morning tide. Some of them already married, others engaged and going out to be reunited with demobilised men, as she was. Fowey seemed to be turning into the back door to America for war-brides.

'You will take care, won't you,' Sara told her. 'Write to me every week to let me know how you're getting on, or if you want me to send you anything.'

'Oh, Sara, you're the best sister a person could have. Why would I need you to send me anything? I'm not even taking many of my old clothes with me. Chad will buy me all new in this land of plenty he lives in. No war, no rations, no coupons, it will be marvellous. I certainly won't go without. Maybe I'll be able to send stuff back home to you and the children. Oh, I shall miss Jenny and Drew,' and she ran to envelope her nephew and niece in a suffocating hug.

The children got quite over-excited, not understanding the significance of this journey, Drew demanding details about the ship and the crossing and Jenny only interested in what America might be like.

Only Sara went with her sister to see her off, since Bette declared she couldn't bear goodbyes. They clung together in a quiet quarter of the docks on a chill morning in early April, before even it was light. They'd nothing left to say, yet were reluctant to let go, clinging to each other as if they hadn't heard the call from the ship, urging Bette to jump to it and get on board.

Long after all sight of her sister waving from the deck had vanished in the morning mist, Sara remained where she was, weeping as if her heart would break.

★   ★   ★

Sara felt quite alone. Utterly bereft. If it hadn't been for the children, she'd have gone mad. Even Sadie was going around with a face like a wet fortnight for all she might claim to be glad to have the house to herself at last. Cory was beside himself, grieving for his younger daughter as if she'd died.

'We'll see her again one day,' Sara said, hugging her father close, desperately trying to put some conviction into her voice.

'Not till this blasted war is over, at least, and when will that be? Even then, how will we ever find the money?'

Cory was right. America was the other side of the world, so how would any of them ever be able to afford to go and visit her? Or how would Bette find the fare to come home if things didn't work out between herself and Chad? Such a prospect didn't bear thinking about, and Sara set it firmly aside. They would be happy as Larry, of course they would.

She felt lost in a welter of emotion. It was as if a part of her had been physically ripped away. Sara also regretted that she wouldn't be there for her sister when the baby was born, although at least it would be an American citizen by birth, which seemed to please Bette as it would save such a lot of paperwork and ensure the baby's future in the new country.

'Who will keep us cheerful now our pretty little maid has gone?' Cory was saying, his small, pisky face mournful. 'Who will make us laugh? Who will bring light and mischief into our lives now?'

Not me, Sara thought bleakly. She'd always been the quiet one, the one in the background expected to offer support but never to actually instigate any humour or action on her own behalf.

Even her marriage had been engineered, she saw that now quite clearly. Sadie had selected a husband for her, pushing the gauche young girl she'd once been into accepting a date with a mature, handsome man with money enough to provide for her. Hugh had flattered and charmed her and she'd fallen for him, hook, line and sinker.

But if she could turn back the clock, would she do anything different? Sara instantly thought of Jenny and Drew, and knew in her heart that she loved her children far too much to wish any such thing. It would be like wishing they'd never been born. In any case, she really shouldn't put all the blame on to her mother just because things had gone wrong between them. She could have refused Hugh at any point during the courtship, had she felt the slightest doubt. Even now, in the depths of her unhappiness, she couldn't bring herself to leave him. Sara kept hoping that something would happen to make him stop treating her so badly, that the war would end, that he'd fall in love with her all over again. That she could love him as she'd used to, and put everything right.

Yet all she did was long for Charlie.

In the days following Bette's departure Sara was grateful, in a bleak sort of way that Hugh was away on one of his ops, thankful to have this time on her own to grieve for a much-loved, greatly missed, sister.

'Oh, Bette, I miss you so much. I hope you are safe and well.' She glanced at the calendar which she kept pinned up on the kitchen wall. She'd been four days at sea, almost halfway.

25

The only way Sara found to deal with her loss was to work harder than ever for the WVS, burying her sadness in activity. She'd thrown herself into helping to plan Salute the Soldier Week which was to be at the end of May, their target being to raise twenty-five thousand pounds to equip a medical unit. There was to be a parade, bands, a dance, flags and bunting everywhere, and a big opening ceremony up at Place, with Mrs Treffry herself doing the honours.

Meanwhile, there were other, smaller events, like the one this coming Saturday, when a small fête was to be held in Mrs Glynn's garden on the Esplanade, which might raise a contribution towards that huge sum.

There were stalls selling all manner of things from homemade cakes without fat, of course; jam with very little sugar; a good supply of plants and vegetables at least, and the usual supply of woollen sweaters, mitts, socks and even kettle-holders, knitted in rainbow colours of every hue under the sun.

Cory was selling great tubs of scallops and mackerel. Hamil Charke could be heard tunelessly sawing away at his fiddle while folk dropped pennies into his collecting box, more out of pity than appreciation. Isobel Wynne dressed as a gypsy and told fortunes, and Nora Snell stood at the gate and charged everyone a penny as they came in, collecting their praises as they left, just as if she'd organised the whole thing herself single-handed. The weather was kind to them; prizes were awarded to the children who had collected the most salvage and the event, on the whole, was a great success.

If it hadn't been for Nora Snell, it might have been fun as well.

She cornered Sara as she returned to the kitchen to refill a teapot. 'Were you looking for someone, dear?'

Sara assured her that she wasn't.

'I thought perhaps you were looking for that nice lieutenant. He isn't here.'

Sara didn't rise to the bait. 'I've been talking to Fred Pullen, as a matter of fact, admiring his vegetables and ordering some more for my pasties.'

'You should try growing your own dear, or at least some herbs. The government is advocating that we all do. Even POWs need them to augment a monotonous diet. Look at all these grown here in this lovely garden: mint, sage, thyme, parsley and what is that one?'

'Marjoram.'

'Well, there you are then. If Mrs Glynn can grow herbs, so can you.'

'Where? Among the gravestones in the churchyard?'

'No, dear, on a window sill. You have plenty of those even at The Ship, which you generally fill with geraniums I know, and very pretty they look too, but herbs are so much more *useful*, dear. Pity you don't have a garden, it would be so much better for the children. I was saying so to your dear husband only the other day. You should have a place like this. It would be lovely for them.'

Sara made her escape, promising she would give the subject of herbs her most serious attention. Could she never escape Nora and her endless organising?

The highlight of the afternoon was the raffle, the major prize being, to everyone's delight and amusement, a banana, generously donated by one of the GIs. Sara wondered if it had been Charlie. It was just his sort of humour.

It was after all the prizes were gone and Sara went off in search of a much-needed cup of tea herself when he suddenly appeared before her, conjured out of thin air, or her own thoughts.

They stood and stared at each other in silent delight for some seconds. 'There you are,' he said, thereby admitting that she'd been on his mind too. 'I've been hoping to run into you but you always seem to be dashing in the opposite direction.'

Sara sent up a silent prayer that Hugh wasn't here. He'd opted to open the pub in the hope of making a few bob from escapees who grew bored with the excitement of buying other folk's cast-offs. 'I think I probably should do so again now. I don't suppose it would be a good idea for us to be seen together. I'm sure Nora will notice, even if nobody else does.'

'Not even for a cup of tea? I know how you Brits do love your cuppa.'

She couldn't resist letting a small smile play at the corners of her mouth. 'Are you taking the mickey?'

'The what? Who's Mickey, another of your conquests?' And they both laughed. 'Come on, I'm just your regular Joe, no harm in me. And you look in need of sustenance. Look, let's skip the tea tent if you like and do a runner. Would they miss you, do you think? Have you done all that's required of you, madam organiser?'

'I – I think so, but . . .' She glanced nervously about her. The children were happily playing with Cory, but where was Nora? Did she have her binoculars trained on her quarry?

'Great, then I'm going to spirit you away for a little well-earned peace and quiet. I need you to myself for a while, is that possible?'

Possible or not, it was highly desirable.

Sara couldn't afterwards imagine what had possessed her to allow him to take charge of her in such a way, except of course that he did it so much more delicately, more charmingly than Hugh ever would.

They took the Bodinnick ferry and set off along Hall Walk, her favourite place as a girl, where she and Bette would follow the wooded footpath through the wood to walk the perimeter of the creek all the way to Polruan where they would take the ferry back to Fowey again. Sometimes Cory would row them up the creek in his clinker-built boat in search of a secret spot to enjoy a picnic, Sadie grumbling about the weather and mud on her clothes.

It had felt like fairyland, a magical kingdom and Sara and Bette had marvelled at the secret silence of the place, the sweep of green branches bowing over the river from where at any moment a Cornish pisky might appear. Not that they ever saw one, no matter how hard they looked, though they sometimes might see the blue flash of a kingfisher, or disturb a heron seeking its lunch.

Bette was now on the other side of the world and she was strolling along with a man who was not her husband.

'I'm not sure I have the energy to walk all the way to Polruan,' she told him. 'Not after all the work I've done today for the fête. Could we just sit on the bench at the end here and look out over Pont Pill?'

Sara never tired of watching the river, there was always something going on, the ferry tacking to and fro, shipping coming and going, and on the opposite shore the cluster of white cottages by Fowey harbour, topped off by the church tower.

The men who had been born and raised in this place claimed to have the sea running in their blood, whether they were pirates in the middle ages, pilchard fishermen, or, in more recent times, shipping minerals. They'd built the old-fashioned tall ships, and now turned their skills to the new. And the soldiers, sailors and marines who had come here to train and build their landing craft, depended upon their capable hands to help them survive.

'Perfect. I can't think of anything I'd like better.'

They sat side by side, not saying a word. Sara utterly tongue-tied, acutely aware of the fact that they were alone, that he was seated so close beside her she could sense the heat of his body, hear his every breath.

'I know you aren't happy. I can tell. Unhappiness emanates from you like a miasma. I wish I could make you smile, make you truly happy.'

'I think you've only made matters worse.'

He said nothing beyond a small sound of disgust at the back of his throat; ran his hands through his hair then leaned forward, elbows on knees, clasping them loosely together, then rubbing one against the other in a cycle of agitation. She longed to reach out and gather those hands between her own and carry them to her lips. They were strong and brave and yet clearly in need of a gentle touch to still them.

'I'm not blaming you, Charlie. Don't think that for one minute. My marriage was in a mess anyway. Hugh is – difficult. Moody. He expects life to be ordered to suit him, which isn't always possible. Certainly I don't seem able to provide whatever it is that he needs to make him happy.'

He turned to her then and those strong hands were grasping her own, their warmth seeming to envelope her and reach right down into her soul. 'What have we done? Nothing! I wish we had done something. I know that I could make you happy. You could make me the happiest man in the world.'

She smiled at him, all her love in her eyes, saying all she wasn't allowed to say.

'I can't help the way I feel. I never meant this to happen.'

'Neither did I.'

'I know it's impossible, that there are obstacles, huge obstacles between us. But don't we deserve a little happiness?

Come away with me, Sara, just for a weekend. If we can't have a lifetime together, let's have one night at least once.'

Sara blushed fiery red and snatched her hands away. 'I couldn't do that!'

'Yes, you could. You know this op is coming up. Operation Overlord. The invasion will be soon and I'll be amongst it, along with hundreds of other men. I'm not asking for your sympathy, Sara, and it's unfair of me, I know, to put this sort of pressure on you but it's a fact nonetheless, that some of us won't come back. I might be one of the lucky ones. I might not. Can't we have a little happiness before I go?'

She was gazing into his eyes, seeing the love he held for her shining out of them. Never had she known such a blissful certainly that this man was right for her, that they belonged together. It was as if she had been waiting for him all her life.

'Ask yourself one question: Do you love your husband? If you do, then I'll go away and never bother you again. If you don't, then I flatter myself that I might be able to give you the love that you deserve.'

An unwelcome picture of the violence that Hugh had brought into their marriage, flashed into her mind. How could she love such a man, a man who thought only of his own selfish needs, who didn't consider the effect of what he did to her? Had he ever been truly caring of her? Suffocating, cloying, domineering, dictatorial, overpowering at times, but had he ever asked her what she wanted? Did he ever unselfishly take her views or wishes into account? Not that she could recall, whether in their bed or in their life together.

His jealousy over the GIs was a result of a need to possess her, like an object, not out of love for her as an equal partner. Perhaps he was angry because he realised that he never could possess her, nor control her. Maybe that was the reason he was using brute force on her instead. Sara shuddered.

'Are you cold? Do you want my jacket?'

'No, no, I'm fine. It was just a goose walking over my grave.'

He laughed. 'You Brits have the oddest expressions. Sure sounds a gruesome thought.'

'Yes, that's just about what it is.'

He ran his hands up her arms. 'You know that I haven't even kissed you yet, and I sure do long to, but hey, you're a married lady, as you keep on reminding me, so I'll put my hands back in my pockets, shall I?'

'They never were in your pockets.'

She was laughing at him now, gently teasing him. Unaware of having made the decision to do so, Sara leaned forward and put her mouth on his. She felt the tremor run through his body then his arms were about her, crushing her to him, and she was wrapped closer to heaven than she had ever been in her life.

26

Bette had never felt more sick in her life. She'd expected the crossing to be rough but she was normally a good sailor, certainly whenever she'd gone out with Cory in the fishing boat she'd been fine. But then, the coastline of Cornwall wasn't anything like this great ocean, and being pregnant didn't help one little bit.

The food was plentiful but just the smell of it set her heaving. And despite it being April, the chill of the Atlantic was bone-numbingly cold. She realised almost at once that she hadn't brought nearly enough clothes with her, and those she had packed were wrong. She'd had the soft warmth of a southern climate in mind, which Chad had talked about with such fondness. In the teeth of a gale force wind she felt she might die of exposure. So bad was it that she gratefully accepted a pair of dungarees and warm sweater from one of the crew. They were a good bunch of men, some of them a bit rough around the edges but generally keeping their distance.

Her cabin-mate, a girl called Joyce who hailed from Birmingham, had become quite friendly with them, not wishing them to be distant at all, for all the captain had made it clear, the day they left Fowey docks, that fraternising with the crew was not allowed. She'd whispered something rude behind her hand and ignored that rule and most others, so far as Bette could see.

Joyce had a child, a toddler of about fifteen months who

slept between them in the bunk. Each morning Bette would wake to find herself soaked in urine and if she hadn't washed the sheet each day, Joyce certainly never would.

'I've enough problems trying to wash these dratted nappies in salt water, not to mention getting them dry. Bette didn't like to complain too much, as she would be in the same situation herself soon, with a baby to care for. The prospect excited and terrified her all at the same time.

Joyce didn't seem to feel the need to restrain herself in any way just because she wore a ring. Bette would often wake in the night to find herself alone with the baby, its mother elsewhere up to God knows what. After the third time that this happened, she decided to say something.

'Look, if anything happens to your baby while you're away, I won't be held responsible. You're his mother, you should stay with him.'

'For God's sake, a girl deserves a bit of fun. Don't be so prissy. There are some good-looking guys on this ship, too good to waste, and I've the rest of my life to be a good little wife.' She giggled at this. 'Not that it will be easy, mind. Not in my nature to be the faithful sort.'

Joyce hadn't seen or heard from her husband in over eighteen months yet was determined to find him. 'We got married soon as I fell pregnant and he never has seen little Barry here. Got himself wounded and conveniently shipped home to the US of A, but the bugger can't escape me that way. The child is his and he can bloody well take care of it, and me an' all. What else have I got to live on? I've no family of me own. I'm a bleedin orphan, me.'

'What if you can't find him?'

'I've got his address in Minnesota. I'll find him all right, and I have my marriage lines to prove we're his responsibility now. Stop crying, Barry, for God's sake. You'll see yer daddy soon. Oh, you hold him for me a minute, will ya. I have to go and pee.'

Bette was yet again left alone with the baby and sat staring at it, trying to decide how she would feel if this were her own child. Would she love it to bits, or be glad to leave it with strangers as Joyce did? She touched her stomach, prodded it here and there but could feel nothing. How would she feel when the baby was born? She was hurting so much inside over losing Barney, Bette couldn't find space in her heart to care about her child.

Two hours later when the baby's mother still hadn't re-appeared, he started to cry from hunger. Gingerly, Bette picked him up, holding him awkwardly aloft as the poor mite was dripping wet.

She changed him into a dry and less foul-smelling nappy, gave him his supper, although she couldn't face any herself, and put him down to sleep. Poor soul, it wasn't the baby's fault that he had a useless, uncaring mother. Bette felt sorry for the little chap. Perhaps he would be better off with this unknown GI father, but she'd give anything to be a fly on the wall when the couple met up again. Somehow she didn't think Joyce would be getting too warm a welcome.

Some of the other girls had children with them too, others were pregnant and going out to meet husbands who had been demobilised, as she was. Except that she and Chad hadn't actually tied the knot yet. Nor had he given her a ring. Nevertheless, Bette thought of herself as engaged and called him her fiancé, deliberately putting out of her mind the fact that she'd only recently been bragging to Sara that she was engaged to Barney, and that he was about to buy her a ring.

It seemed ironic in a way; two lovers and still no ring. But that was a small concern, compared to some of the women.

One had been told that her husband was dying and that she mustn't come as she wouldn't be allowed in and most likely sent to Ellis Island. She'd come anyway, desperate to see him one last time. Another girl, little more than twenty-one and heavily pregnant, admitted she'd been told by her husband that he'd gone back to his old girl friend but she'd convinced herself that once he saw her again, he'd come back to her.

'What will you do in a strange country if he doesn't?' Bette asked her, appalled.

The girl had no answer.

Lying beside the baby, rocked by the boat and drifting quietly into sleep, Bette thought that perhaps she was the lucky one, all things considered. At least she had the comfort of knowing that Chad loved and wanted her. She missed Barney, would always love him, but everything would turn out fine, she was quite sure of it. She resolved to be optimistic for hadn't this been her dream for so long? A new country, a new life, a new husband. Despite the difficulties of her situation, she couldn't help but feel excited.

At least Chad would be pleased to see her.

There was no welcome for the freight carrier as it berthed unnoticed among a dozen other similar vessels. It had travelled back to the US largely empty, save for the women, returning to its home port for its next load of munitions, basic supplies and food. They'd been instructed to stay below until after the ship had docked, crowded together with their pitifully few possessions and fretful children, in one stuffy room, so were deprived the pleasure of standing at the rails to take in their first sight of land as it approached. They were not allowed to marvel at New York's famous skyline or the Statue of Liberty, save for what they glimpsed out of a tiny porthole.

The women's first view of their new country was when a member of the crew came to let them out and ushered them secretly down a gangway set up at the stern of the ship. Some of the babies were crying, but there was no one to hear, it being night and with no one about. There was nothing in fact to see but stacks of boxes on the docks waiting to be loaded on board once the ship had been cleaned and checked ready for its return voyage.

The most amazing thing of all to these women was that despite it being night-time, there were lights everywhere.

'Christ, no blackout,' said Joyce. 'What a bloody treat.'

There'd been great excitement beforehand, hair washed and curled, best dresses dragged from suitcases and crumples smoothed out, lipstick applied. Every woman present wanted to look their best. Bette was no exception, even though she knew she wouldn't be meeting up with Chad until the following day.

Before that, she faced a long train journey south and her first task was to the find the railway station, and the right train, which suddenly seemed an overwhelmingly difficult task.

Fortunately there were one or two others in the same situation, which was a comfort since there were no Red Cross officials to help these war-brides who had entered the country illegally. But then nor would there be any medical check-ups, no interrogation about status, or paperwork to process, and no hot supper waiting for them either. For the first time since the journey began, Bette felt a pang of hunger, though that could have been purely a pang of nervousness.

Bette stood with the other women, blinking in the glare of lights, wondering what was to happen next, then noticed a group of men approaching out of the shadows. Fear stabbed in her, sharp and strong. Had they been discovered? Would she be put back on board and sent home, without even having seen Chad?

And then she heard the squeals and whoops of joy. Some of the girls' husbands had come to meet their wives, found their way to this quiet corner of the docks. They elbowed one another aside, seeking a familiar face, and when they found it, reunion in many cases was ecstatic. The women wept in their arms, babies were cuddled, there were tender hugs and passionate kisses. Bette looked on and marvelled with tears in her eyes. How could one not be moved by such a sight?

True, there were one or two who enjoyed a less than enthusiastic reunion and there were other women, like herself, and like Joyce, for whom there was no one. One girl just stood there crying and was eventually led away back to the ship, to be returned home like an unwanted parcel. The rest picked up their suitcases, gathered up straying children, and followed the crew member who had volunteered to take them to the station. Bette could only hope that when this long, unknown journey finally ended, there would be a welcome for her too.

The women had a long wait at the station before the train finally left, by which time Bette was exhausted. She'd had problems changing her money and buying a ticket, which cost five dollars, far more than she'd bargained for, plus some food for the journey which would apparently take an entire day.

She felt tired, dirty, hungry, exhilarated and afraid, all at the same time, emotionally unstable before even the train left the station. It was all so strange, so different.

The member of the crew who'd accompanied them to the station had given careful instructions on procedure, including that they make sure they got into the right car. This had puzzled Bette at first, until she realised he was referring to the rail carriage, or compartment. The ones at the back would be uncoupled and dropped off early in the journey, so you had to make sure you got into the right one. But clearly, even the language was going to present problems.

At least she wasn't alone. Several of the women had banded together and their little group began to attract some attention. Quite out of the blue, a flashbulb went off. Someone had taken a photograph and suddenly they were surrounded by the press, who'd apparently got wind of their arrival and started firing questions at them.

'Are you all war-brides?'

'Where are you meeting your husbands?'

'Do you reckon they'll be pleased to see you?'

'What do you say to folks who accuse war-brides of depriving the wounded of their rightful place on the transport that brought you here?'

'Is that kid your husband's?'

'Quick, let's get on board,' Bette cried, seeing one poor girl reduced to tears and another in danger of socking one journalist in the mouth if he didn't shut up. Pulling open the nearest 'car' door, they all rushed on board, falling over each other in their anxiety to escape the mêlée of reporters gathering on the platform, and find themselves a seat.

Their undignified arrival alerted the other passengers who craned their necks around to see what all the fuss was about, then started chatting to them.

'Are you folks from Canada?' was generally the opening remark.

Once they learned the women were from Britain, had come out to join their GI husbands, they took them and their precarious situation to heart. The warmth and welcome of the other passengers made the journey bearable, as they shared their food, bullied the train guard into warming babies' bottles and supplying them with beds or blankets, even if they hadn't paid for one, and helped to reunite the women with their baggage.

Even so, the journey seemed to go on forever, with frequent stops along the way when the train would stand at an empty platform in the middle of nowhere, waiting and waiting until finally one lone person might turn up and get on board, and then it would lurch into movement and go on its way again. Or the guard would grow bored with waiting and set off anyway, without anyone getting on. On a few occasions, passengers were allowed off to enjoy a breath of fresh air and a bit of exercise, but Bette was always anxious not to wander too far, in case the train should set off without her.

When hot meals were brought round, she would surreptitiously and repeatedly count her dollars and cents, trying to work out what the coins were worth and whether she could afford to buy herself anything. More often than not she contented herself with a cup of hot coffee. After all, a day's starvation wouldn't hurt and there'd be plenty of food once she reached North Carolina, her new home.

27

For the first time in her life, Sara told Hugh a bare-faced lie. She told him that she was going to visit her aunt Marjorie in Penzance. She did have an aunt of that name who lived in the town although Sara sincerely hoped the old lady would not be called upon to prove her recalcitrant niece's presence, as she was well past eighty, quite deaf and a strict Methodist.

'Aunt Marjorie hasn't been well and there's little point in Sadie going, she'd be hopeless, yet a member of the family should visit and check on her from time to time, see that she has the care and attention she needs.' Sara hated herself as she spun the web tighter.

If only Bette were here. It would be so much easier as they could have gone off on a jaunt together and Hugh would have been none the wiser. This was a much more dangerous plan, yet one she was determined to carry out, however much he might frown at her. She couldn't seem to help herself.

The prospect of one night alone with Charlie seemed too good to be true. Magical.

She went to St Austell, where nobody knew her, and bought herself a pretty new nightdress, not too frivolous or sexy, since she must wear it afterwards and needed to be careful not to make Hugh suspicious. But at least it would be something to remind her of their one, glorious night together.

She felt shivery, sick with anticipation. What would he think when he saw her in it, and in the flesh? Would he still find her attractive? She was no young girl coming to her lover with a firm young body. She was twenty-six, with two children for heaven's sake. Her stomach was no longer as flat as it might be, and these were surely wrinkles at the corners of her eyes, although Bette had always insisted on calling them laughter lines.

'Oh, Bette, what am I doing?'

The plan was for Sara to meet Charlie on the train on Friday evening. She would get on at Par, and he would join the train at St Austell and they would travel together to Penzance. That way she had the ticket to show Hugh. She might even call in briefly upon Aunt Marjorie, just to be on the safe side.

Before then, however, she had a whole week to get through, a week in which she must appear absolutely normal, as normal as life could be between them. Sara prayed for Hugh to be called out on one of his regular ops but, perversely, he was home every day, never going further than around Fowey itself.

Sara rushed about, as usual, taking the children to school each morning then dashing back home to cook breakfast for Hugh, spoiling him, anxious to keep him happy. 'You wouldn't believe how I had to bribe the butcher to get this bit of bacon for you. But you deserve it, a breakfast fit for a king, for my brave soldier,' and she placed it proudly before him.

He scowled down at the plate. 'No egg?'

'You know we are only allowed one each per week and I save them for the children.'

'You can give them yours, but I'll have mine fried tomorrow, thank you very much. I need the energy, Sara, you surely realise that.'

'Yes, of course, I'm sorry.'

'And don't take it into your head to stay on with this sick aunt of yours for any length of time. I need you back home by Sunday night at the latest. How I shall manage to cope with the children all weekend on my own, I cannot imagine. It really is most inconsiderate of you. And this toast is cold. Please make some fresh.'

Sara bit back the apology which came instantly to her lips and rushed off to make fresh toast, even though it would never have gone cold in the first place if he'd not left it standing while he berated her over the lack of an egg.

The following afternoon Sara attended yet another meeting of the War Weapons Week Fund-Raising Committee and Nora Snell, as usual, was pushing through various motions with no real protest from the rest of the members. Sara was paying very little attention, her mind elsewhere, worrying over what she should wear. Her clothes seemed so dowdy and she so wanted to look good for Charlie, yet she couldn't dress up too much, since she was only supposed to be going to visit her aunt. She was brought sharply back to the present when she heard her name spoken. 'Sorry?'

'You are the ideal person for the task, dear.'

'Am I? Oh, um, what, exactly, do you want me to do, I mean . . .?' Sara was reluctant to admit that she hadn't been paying the slightest attention and didn't have the first idea what job she had been selected for. Nora, however, was quick to notice her confusion.

'Do pay attention dear, we can't have people day-dreaming when we are discussing important business.'

'Sorry.' Nora always made her feel like a naughty schoolgirl.

'In any case, I'm sure there won't be any problem, since you and he are so very friendly. Come straight out with it. Take the bull by the horns, as it were. Just pop up to Windmill this very afternoon and ask that nice Lieutenant Denham if we can 'borrow' some of his men to help shift scenery for the concert in the Town Hall this summer.'

'Oh, oh I don't think I can do that. I wouldn't be the right person at all, not at all.' The last thing Sara wanted was to see Charlie. They'd agreed not to meet, not today, not at all this week. How could she possibly see him, speak to him and not reveal her feelings, their secret plans, just by the way she looked at him? Someone would be sure to notice her behaving like a love-struck schoolgirl, and tell Hugh. No, no, she must avoid that, at all cost.

'Stuff and nonsense, of course you are. Absolutely ideal! But do try not to be bullied into giving away any free tickets in return for the work, dear. Rather defeats the object, I always think, if we can't rely on people's generosity on these occasions. We'd never buy any battleships or torpedoes if everyone was given free admittance just because they've done us some small favour or other. And also mention that we need someone to put up lights too, would you, dear?'

'Couldn't someone else go? I'm rather busy at present.'

'Rubbish, what else have you got to do with your time since your dear husband has barred you from working in the pub?'

'He hasn't barred me. He just doesn't need me behind the bar now that he has Iris. But I have other work. I'm still fully involved making the pasties and so on, as you well know.' Why on earth did she feel the necessity to defend herself, or Hugh?

'Yes dear, of course you do, and it must be a great relief to be free of such an unseemly occupation as serving pints of beer to raucous, noisy GIs. Although, it's perfectly obvious that you were a favourite among them. Which is why you are the very best person for this job.'

And so the motion was carried and the meeting brought to a hasty and welcome conclusion, everyone hurrying away in case Nora should find something else for them to discuss, or a job for them to do.

It was a great relief to Sara too that it had ended, as she hated to have her personal and private business openly aired, in danger of practically being written about in the minutes.

It wouldn't surprise her if Isobel put 'Sara's Friends and Working Arrangements' or 'The doings of the Marracks' on the agenda.

Nora managed, however, by dint of being remarkably agile on her feet, despite her mature years, to catch up with her before she even reached the door. Perhaps to apologise, Sara thought, on a note of wild optimism. She should have known better.

'Now you will go and see that nice Lieutenant Denham this very afternoon, won't you, my dear. Do it right away, seeing as how busy you're going to be over the next few weeks with your packing and so on.'

'I beg your pardon? Packing? What packing?'

'For your move, dear. Of course, I won't breathe a word. As you know, I am the soul of discretion. Not a word will cross my lips until the deal is all signed and sealed,' and she gave a conspiratorial wink, as if she were in on some private secret.

'Um, I think you've made a mistake. We're not moving. Heavens, rumour runs riot in this town. Who on earth gave you the idea that we were?'

Nora gave a girlish titter behind her hand, which somehow didn't suit her tight-lipped, schoolmarm image. 'Oh dear, have I spoiled his surprise?'

'What surprise? Have you been talking to Hugh? What has he been saying?'

'Oh, dear me, no. He hasn't said a word, not to me. I may have got it all wrong but I spotted him coming out of Cyril Lanyon's house on the Esplanade, and everyone knows the poor man has been trying for years to sell that property. Far too big for a widower. I saw them shake hands in a very businesslike way, quite clearly having come to an agreement. Ah, I thought, so Mr Marrack is going to buy that fine house. How very splendid. And good for the town too, as he can probably afford to return it to its former glory. Poor Cyril has neglected it badly in recent years. Our local hero deserves the very best, I thought. You know, we really should suggest that Hugh try for the council. Exactly the sort of candidate we're looking for.'

Sara was listening to all of this waffle in something of a daze but this last comment was too much, and she very rudely marched away without even a goodbye.

Later, when she confronted Hugh in his den under the eaves, and challenged him on the subject, he quite calmly agreed that yes, he had indeed made an offer for Cyril Lanyon's house and so long as the bank were prepared to give him a mortgage, which he was quite sure they would, then they would be moving into it quite soon.

Sara was flabbergasted. 'And when were you planning on telling me this important piece of news? I mean, how could you make such a decision without even *thinking* to discuss the matter with me? Don't I have any say at all?'

He set down his pen with a frown of impatience. 'Had you been in my bed, where you ought to be, I might have thought to mention it. However, what useful contribution could you possibly have made? You know nothing about property and, as my wife, must live wherever I think is right for us, wherever I feel we can afford.'

Fury lashed through her, leaving her speechless for a good half minute. Even when Sara did finally find her voice, she spoke in a rush, breathless with anger. 'Even a *wife* has an *opinion*, or don't you grant me with sufficient intelligence to even be allowed any say over where we live?'

'Are you saying that you have no wish to reside in that lovely, regency house?' He waited patiently for her answer, a sardonic smile twisting the corner of his mouth.

'Oh, don't be so bloody pompous.'

'Sara!'

She'd shocked him, at last, and oh, she was so pleased. How she hated him in that moment. She could quite easily have knocked that self-satisfied smirk right off his face. 'No, of course I'm not saying any such thing. How could I? It's a lovely house. Beautiful. But I would've thought that, as man and wife, we should make joint decisions about such things, discuss the matter together.'

'I really don't see why. You can make no financial contribution so obviously the decision must be mine. Besides, a move might well assist us in our current difficulties, don't you think? It's not as if I'm asking you to live in a pig sty, so I don't quite see your objection.'

It was an utterly amazing house, so why was she objecting? Why wasn't she pleased that he was clearly doing well in the business and could afford such a move?

Because if they moved into a fine new house, she would feel obliged to live in it with him, perhaps even share a bedroom again, and in her heart she knew that was the last thing she wanted to do.

Yet she must give no indication of these feelings in case he investigated the reason.

Sara drew in a shuddering breath, desperately striving to steady herself. 'Did you mean it as a surprise, perhaps, to please me?'

He must have seen something of her misery in her face, for he set aside his papers and came to take her in his arms. 'Don't I only ever want what is best for you, for us both? Look, why don't you come and see it right now, this very afternoon. I'm sure Cyril won't mind. If you absolutely hate the house then I shall be disappointed, displeased even, after all the trouble I've taken, but I wouldn't dream of forcing you to live in it. When have I ever forced you to do anything that you have no wish to do?'

Sara stared at him transfixed, knowing with a dreadful certainty that he genuinely believed this to be true.

She dashed up to Windmill and left a note for Charlie, asking him for volunteers to help with the concert, then collected the children from school, ready to meet Hugh on the Esplanade.

The house was quite tall and grand, with four bedrooms on three floors and panoramic views over the river, admittedly slightly marred by the water tank on what had once been the croquet lawn of the Fowey hotel, but that would go eventually, when the war was over.

Hugh was pointing out the magnificence of the mouldings on the ceiling of the drawing room, the chandeliers and the stylish bedrooms and bathrooms. Sara instantly fell in love with the long, basement kitchen with its solid fuel stove, and knew that when Hugh was working at the pub, this would be where she would spend her time, in the warm heart of the house. That is, assuming their marriage survived. Yet how could it not? There were the children to think of. They were even now running all over it in excited anticipation.

'Can I have the big front bedroom, Daddy?' Drew yelled, jumping up and down with excitement. 'Then you could buy me a telescope and I could watch for enemy ships for you from my bedroom, instead of you having to go out on to the headland.'

'No, son, the largest bedroom is for Mummy and I,' Hugh quickly responded, fearful the boy might be about to say more. He smiled at Sara, a cool and calculating smile that made her shiver. 'But you can have the small one next to that, and if you're very, very good, I will buy you a telescope of your own, so that you can watch the ships coming and going.'

'Oh, t'rific! Just like William.'

The house, so far as the children were concerned, was perfect. There was a long garden at the back for them to play in, with plenty of room for a swing beneath the shade of a sheltering elm. Jenny was even now pestering her father to build them a little tree house within its branches. Hugh brushed her aside with a gesture of irritation.

'Are you sure we can afford it?' Sara asked, still bemused by this sudden change in their fortunes.

'If I say we can afford it, then we must be able to do, mustn't we? What stupid questions you ask, Sara.' He sounded deeply irritated and she hastened to placate him.

'I wasn't meaning to doubt you, Hugh. I'm simply amazed – stunned really. It must have cost a small fortune.'

'Not at all. It's been for sale for years and is quite run down. Besides which, property prices are depressed at the moment. It's definitely a good time to invest.'

'Yes, I suppose it is. And the bank are agreeable to lend us the money?'

His response was sharp and terse. 'I've already told you, Sara, you can safely leave all of the financial side of things to me.'

And then he pulled her to him and kissed her, stroking back her soft, fair hair and for the briefest of moments revealing the patient, caring husband he'd once been, before the war had changed everything.

Except that later came the betraying thought that it wasn't quite fair to blame the war. Perhaps Hugh always had been bossy and intimidating but she'd never really noticed, not until she had grown up a little more herself and wanted more say in her life, or until she'd met Charles Denham. Somehow, the thought made her feel more trapped than ever.

28

As the end of her journey approached, Bette's feeling of nervousness and unease increased. Would Chad be waiting for her at the station? Would he be pleased to see her? And most important of all, would he still love her?

Of course he would, she consoled herself, over and over, as the miles slipped by and there was nothing to do but think of the baby she carried, and of Barney who she'd left behind. Would she ever see Barney again?

Perhaps, in the circumstances, it would be for the best if she didn't.

Most of all she thought of Sara. She'd never really considered, until the decision had been made, how much she would miss her sister. Already she was longing for her, wishing she was sitting beside her, sharing this adventure, instead of this skinny stranger with a baby who'd done nothing but grizzle and cry the entire day.

The train was hot and uncomfortable, resonant with snores, and out of the window all she could see was a sun-baked landscape that seemed to stretch to the horizon, punctuated here and there by the thin ribbon of a river, an occasional swamp shimmering in the heat, or a rare and verdant patch of unfamiliar trees half clothed in moss, which she later learned were called live oaks. In the far distance she could see a range of blue mountains, though they never seemed to draw any closer. Barney had said that America was a big country but she'd had no real concept of what that meant in reality.

Would she ever get there, Bette wondered?

At the next station stop there was nothing to be seen but one guy standing on the platform in blue shirt and trousers and a wide brimmed hat, looking almost as if he'd stepped right out of *Gone With the Wind*. Behind him was a horse and cart. The girl sitting beside Bette began to cry.

'Oh, God, that can't be him, can it? Where's his uniform? He looks so different. Where are we? I can't even see a town. I'm not getting off here. I can't, I can't. I want to go home.' She sounded so anguished that the baby on her lap began to cry yet again, this time in sympathy with his young mother.

The guard came and attempted to oust her from her seat. 'Hurry along please, madam. We can't keep the train waiting all day,' which seemed a bit rich after all the delays en route. Still the poor girl made no move, and the other passengers began to watch this small side-show with open curiosity.

The guard tried a firmer line. 'He's your husband, honey, you gotta go to him.'

For a moment it looked as if he might be about to physically eject her from the seat and Bette quickly intervened. 'Come on, love, I'll hold the baby while you gather your things together. It'll be fine. Look, he's taken off his hat and he's smiling and waving.'

She didn't appear greatly reassured by this sight but somehow Bette managed to persuade the girl to get off the train. As it drew away, the pair were left standing on the empty platform, staring at each other.

Bette sank back into her seat, heart pounding. 'What in God's name have I got myself into?'

And then a couple of hours and three stops later, there he was, grinning from ear to ear, a whole crowd of people gathered about him, presumably all his family and friends. A great welcoming committee, in fact, who had turned up to view the war-bride. Bette could even see a man with a camera,

who must surely be a reporter from the local paper. She felt a
surge of relief and even excitement that her own welcome was
to be so different from that of her travelling companion. And
yet she experienced the same sense of panic and disorienta-
tion. A part of her wanted to turn the train around and rush
back home, just as her companion had.

This was not the Chad she remembered, all big and brawny
in his smart, US Marine uniform. This man was dressed in
brown trousers, or pants as Americans seemed to call them.
They were faded and stopped short of the ankle, and his shirt
was a strange mustard colour that had seen better days. He
had more hair than she remembered too, as muddy brown in
colour as the pants, and he seemed thinner and shorter, as if
there were much less of him than there used to be. He was
walking along the platform beside the train as it shunted into
the station, waving madly to her, limping slightly, with one
sleeve flapping empty in the wind.

Her heart gave an uncomfortable thump. She'd forgotten
about the missing arm. Bette took a deep breath, smiled and
waved back. Now all she had to do was get off the train, meet
his family and friends, tell him how much she loved him and
wanted this baby, then be a good wife to him and not think of
Barney at all. Quite simple really.

It was one whirl of activity and excitement from the moment
she set foot on the platform. Never in her wildest dreams had
Bette expected there to be so many people thronging the
station, waiting to greet her. Far too many to even catch
anyone's names.

Local dignitaries from the nearby town of Carreville were
there, worthy ladies in hats, businessmen in neatly pressed suits
with their hair slicked down. Shops had apparently been closed
so that the owners could introduce themselves and shake her by
the hand. Everyone seemed friendly enough but stared at her as

if she were some sort of oddity, a creature from another planet. They kept asking her to repeat things, saying how they just loved to hear her talk. Camera bulbs flashed and questions were fired at her by a local reporter who'd come especially to interview her as 'You're the first war-bride to arrive in our town.'

'How many more are you expecting?' Bette asked, casting Chad a hopeful glance of enquiry, since she'd be glad of some English friends to help stave off the first stirrings of home-sickness. He only shrugged his shoulders and looked perplexed.

Bette felt a wave of sympathy for him, and for herself. They hadn't so much as shaken hands, let alone kissed, since the moment she'd arrived. Barely exchanged even a word of greeting.

Chad was feeling completely tongue-tied, unable to do little more than stand and stare at her. He'd forgotten how very pretty she was with her small nose, pointed chin and elfin face. Even with her hair all mussed up from the long journey, the golden brown curls straying free from their battery of pins, she looked so lovely he wondered what on earth had possessed her to travel halfway across the world to marry a great, gawking, one-armed lump like himself. There must have been any number of guys ready to snap her up the minute he'd left Fowey. Barney for one.

He'd need to talk to her about Barney, make sure his old buddy really had behaved himself. But not now. He should make her welcome, take her home, show her to his mom who had refused to come and 'goggle like a fishwife.'

He thought that perhaps Bette too was a bit overwhelmed by all the shindig. The moment of reunion was difficult enough, without having an audience.

He'd so wanted them to be alone when they first met, all quiet and civilised, with no hassle. He wanted to take her in his arms and kiss her, except that he only had one arm now, so perhaps that wouldn't work any more. She might not even want him to hold her till she'd got used to the idea of him being a cripple. Anyway, it was imperative he make her feel welcome but she seemed different, sort of distant and remote, like a girl in a magazine, somehow untouchable, beyond his reach.

Bette was flattered by all the interest, that everyone should consider her so important and give her such a royal reception. She rather hoped that someone would think to offer her some form of refreshment after her long journey over land and sea. Apart from the heaviness of the heat, she was faint with hunger. Her body felt as if it had been shaken to bits, and as the heat and humidity hit her, she came over all giddy.

As she wavered slightly, would have slid to the ground had he not caught her, she heard Chad cry, 'Hey, give her some air,' pushing everyone aside as he called for a glass of water.

Moments later she was sitting on the station bench thankfully sipping from a chipped mug, though still with her faithful bevy of onlookers. 'Thanks, but could I perhaps have a cup of tea and a biscuit?'

Chad was quick to point out her mistake. 'We only have cold tea here in the south, and what you call a biscuit is a cookie to us. A biscuit to we Americans is what you Brits would call a scone. OK?'

'I think so.' He'd found his voice at least, she was glad to note, instead of standing there dumbstruck, but her brain seemed to be in even more of a whirl. What did a name matter? Not a soul moved to fetch either biscuit, cookie or scone, and there was no sign of a cuppa, hot or cold.

Chad wiped the sweat from his one sticky hand down the back of his pants, took a steadying breath and was about to ask if she was ready to get on home when the town mayor launched into a speech of welcome, so they were forced to stand patiently listening, sweltering in the heat, swatting away flies and trying to look interested in his views on the American role in the war.

Thankfully, the speech soon drew to a close, promising a more formal reception later in the week, but then the band struck up the National Anthem, adding to the din and Bette felt as if she was slowly being cooked alive with no hope of escape.

Then someone rushed up, elbowing Chad out of the way, dragging her some distance from him so they could snap her with their Box Brownie. It was utter pandemonium and Bette offered him a tremulous smile of apology, for which he appeared pathetically grateful.

'You must be plum tuckered out,' he shouted above the rumpus, and she nodded, those green eyes so entrancingly flecked with gold, laughing impishly up at him.

'I never guessed I would prove so popular.'

'What?'

'I said . . . oh, never mind.' She was laughing now as it was quite impossible to hear a word either of them said as people milled about, but her laughter eased the tension in him and he grinned, finally summoning up the courage to reach forward into the mêlée, grab her by the arm and start to shoulder his way through the throng, dragging her behind him. The trouble was that the more he tugged and pushed, the more the crowds surged them back on to the platform, and the press were not done with her yet.

Bette was whisked off next to the local radio station to be interviewed, where she told all about how she'd met Chad, what her home town of Fowey was like, and agreed that the Americans had arrived in the nick of time to save the British from a fate worse than death: invasion by the Nazis.

Finally satisfied that everything possible had been done to welcome their newcomer, people wandered away and Bette was left to climb into the pick-up truck and be driven to her new home. She could hardly wait to see it.

29

He found her carriage easily enough and slipped in beside her onto the seat without a word. Sara could hear her heart beating, even above the banging of doors, the hiss of steam and sound of porters' whistles. Perhaps he could hear it, too. If she was going to change her mind, this was the moment to do so, before the train left St Austell station. She could make a break for it and just run back to Hugh, to her life, and pretend she'd never met Charles Denham.

But how could she go home, less than an hour after she'd left, supposedly visiting a sick aunt? And it was only a week-end, she reminded herself. She'd be back in Fowey by Sunday, after all. It wasn't as if she was leaving Hugh, or anything so dramatic.

No, simply intending to commit adultery.

She could sense a tension in Charlie too, which was com-forting. She didn't want him to be the sort of man who was accustomed to running away with other men's wives. What they were doing was wrong, she knew that, yet here she was in her best navy blue coat and hat, a fetching new nightgown in the suitcase on the rack above their heads, and every muscle, every bone in her body, aching for him to touch her.

It was just as well that they were not alone in the carriage. The old woman, busily knitting opposite, sent her several sly glances. Sara had the awful feeling that she knew exactly what was going on, which was quite impossible. How could she know? Yet there was something in the way she covertly considered Sara, and then turned her attention to Charles, almost as if she were pairing them up.

Sara was on her feet the moment the train pulled into Penzance station and left the compartment without so much as a backward glance, not at Charlie, nor even at the woman folding away her knitting and surely deliberately hanging back to check if he followed her.

They met up again in the station buffet where they sat sipping tea as if they were strangers who had met quite by chance.

Charlie finally cleared his throat. 'Is it safe to talk now, or will we need to keep this up for the entire weekend, do you think?'

Sara giggled. 'I suppose it is rather ridiculous. I was just a bit anxious, in case there was someone on the train who knew me.'

'I realised that. Maybe I should have gone into a different compartment, or worn a disguise, a fake beard maybe. Would that help?'

'Now you're teasing me, and it isn't fair.'

'I just love to see you smile.'

'We shouldn't even be doing this.'

'Yes, we should. It may be all we're going to have, things are hotting up on the military front, but we sure as hell are going to enjoy these two precious days together. Come on, let's get out of here. I've had enough of the stink of soot and sulphur.'

They walked along the wide expanse of sandy beach hand in hand, breathing in the soft spring air, the sun warming them and making the sea shimmer to a clear and sparkling blue. Out in the bay stood St Michael's Mount, its grandeur proclaiming that life would go on, war or no war; that nothing could destroy true beauty.

Sara said, 'It started out as a Benedictine priory, and has a twin in France, I believe.'

'Yep, Mont St Michel in Normandy.'

Sara glanced at him quickly, noting a change in his tone of voice, realising that for some reason she'd made him think of something unpleasant. Guessing it was connected with the coming invasion, she slipped her arm through his and lightened her tone. 'We used to come to Penzance for day trips when I was a child, visit Aunt Marjorie where we'd suffer one of those unendurably lengthy Sunday lunches in her stuffy house, and then be let loose to play on the beach. I thought this must be a fairy palace, and I would dig and dig, hoping to find treasure buried in the golden sands.' She laughed. 'I was a fanciful child.'

'I imagine you were real cute.'

'Cory always says this is the first safe harbour for anyone crossing the Atlantic Ocean. Isn't that a lovely thought, that when a ship comes in here, they are confronted with all this beauty, this wide sweep of land and sea all the way from the Lizard to Land's End. I can't think of a better place to first discover Cornwall, can you? I hope Bette gets as a good welcome in the States.'

'I hope so, too.'

'And in Newlyn, just down the coast, where all the artists go, because of the light, you know?'

'First you won't talk to me at all, now you're talking too much. Sara, if you're not happy about this, if you want to change your mind, it's OK.'

'Oh, I am happy, really I am. I'm just a little nervous. Kiss me please, that will make me feel so much better.'

Laughing, he pulled her into his arms, then paused to lean away from her, a teasing look coming into his gentle brown eyes. 'I can't kiss you. You're not wearing a kiss-me-quick-hat. This hat is very pretty but it's also a very serious, proper sort of hat, not at all in keeping with this wild and wonderful setting. I'm sure it would object if I were to kiss you.'

Sara burst out laughing and pulling out the hat pin,

whipped it off, shaking out a cloud of silver fair hair. She saw his eyes darken with desire but still he didn't kiss her. Instead, he grabbed her by the hand and marched her very smartly along the sands.

'Where are we going?'

'Somewhere I can kiss you without a dozen kids and their grandmothers watching. Somewhere I can take off more than that damned hat.'

'Sorry to hear that Aunt Marjorie is ill,' Hugh said to Sadie, a note of commiseration in his voice. He'd noticed Sara's mother standing in a queue outside the butcher's as he'd happened by, so took advantage of the meeting to stop for a short chat. Nothing to be lost by checking a few facts.

'Aunt Marjorie?'

'I've been abandoned for the weekened, while Sara goes to offer succour and comfort. I've been left holding the baby, as it were.

He laughed as he indicated the two children whom he had firmly in his grasp, one to each hand, in case they should take it into their silly heads to dash off somewhere, as children do. They looked very much as if they wanted to and Sadie said something to them, giving them both a kiss, while Hugh carefully watched her expression to see if she looked surprised or puzzled by this piece of information.

'Sara always was very close to Marj,' Sadie agreed, after a moment's consideration, her eyes bland, carefully noncommittal.

Hugh was deeply disappointed. He was highly suspicious of his wife's sudden decision to head west, but couldn't quite put his finger on why. He nodded and smiled again at Sadie, who seemed to be watching him closely. 'Nothing serious, I trust,' he continued, still fishing for information.

Sadie said, 'She's an old woman, bound to have her off

days. Would you like me to come and cook something for you, Hugh, if you're on your own?'

Panic hit him like a cold douche. 'No, no, I can manage perfectly well. Sara has left food ready prepared, and Iris can always cook me something.'

'Course she can,' Sadie agreed. 'Very handy at cooking things up, is Iris Logan.'

Sadie was beginning to get the picture now, to understand why her daughter had come begging for a bed. But whose bed was she in tonight, that was the interesting question?

Hugh came to an instant decision that it was time to move on, make his excuses and leave. The conversation had not gone quite as he would have wished, and he'd elicited no further information from Sadie at all. It was only later that he realised he'd missed an opportunity to ask her to mind the children. If Sadie would have them, then he could follow Sara, surprise her by turning up at Aunt Marjorie's with an offer to help, or claim that he missed her. Maybe he should give that serious consideration.

The hotel was small and tucked away in a quiet corner of Marazion, the bedroom painted in an unprepossessing brown and cream and smelling faintly of fish.

'Will you be wanting an evening meal?' enquired the landlady, looking down her long nose as Charlie signed them in as Mr and Mrs Smith. 'I could do you a bit of haddock.'

'No, thank you. We'll get something in town.'

'There won't be anything open late, save for the chippy, so you'd best get yourself a high tea. No one will be serving lunch now.' Making it sound as if they'd planned the entire day wrong. 'Were you wanting to see your room right away?'

Charlie smiled, using all his charm. 'If that wouldn't be too much trouble.'

Sara didn't know how she managed to keep her face straight.

'Here you are then,' she said, flinging open the door. 'The bathroom is just down the hall. I'll be downstairs if you want anything, though I don't suppose you will.'

'I didn't expect it to be quite this dreadful,' Charlie mourned, the minute she'd gone, chin held high and her disapproval made plain in the rigid line of her backbone. 'Not particularly romantic, is it? I though it might be more discreet to stay in a small place but I wish I'd found something more grand for you.'

'It doesn't matter. I don't care. We're together, that's all that counts. Anyway, how could it be other than awful, there is a war on you know,' laughingly mimicking Nora Snell.

'God, if I hear that phrase one more time . . .' He took off his jacket and slung it over a chair. 'Come here, I'm going to kiss you as you've never been kissed before.'

He kept his word. Sara was dazed by his kisses, by his sweet loving, yet he was making no move to rush her into something more, sensing she wasn't quite ready. They lay together on the bed, content to be at last in each other's arms, to kiss and caress and talk the kind of nonsense that lovers do.

Later, after they'd freshened up, they took a stroll around the town, enjoying exploring the narrow streets, the quaint little shops and cottages, and seemingly around every corner could be glimpsed the vista of that wide bay and St Michael's Mount. They found a small café which served them a delicious meal of ham and eggs, followed by Cornish splits, home-made jam and real clotted cream. It was the most delicious meal Sara had ever tasted, all washed down by endless cups of scalding tea.

'Perhaps there isn't a war on, after all.'

'For tonight there isn't, not here in Marazion, not for us.'

Arms wrapped about each other, they walked until darkness

fell, talking and talking, mainly about the war and how they prayed it would soon come to an end. Charles thought Hitler's biggest mistake was in not invading England, perhaps out of the misguided illusion that the British would sue for peace.

'Anyone with any sense would know that you Brits never roll over and play dead. But back in forty-two he had the chance to make his move. Victory had seemed to be in the Führer's grasp. Now he's facing the reality that an Allied invasion will be the final battle.'

'And we will win, won't we? And you will stay safe?'

'We will win, my darling, and then I shall come home for you.'

They didn't talk about Hugh, or how this miracle might be achieved. Nor did they speak of the future. Much easier to deal with the practical, the here and now, to remain positive and not give in to gloom.

And then as the cool of night set in, it was time to go back to the hotel. The moment that Sara had longed for so much, and yet feared because of the irrevocable step she was about to take, had finally arrived.

30

The truck drew to a halt in a cloud of dust and Bette looked around her, bewildered. 'Are we here?'

'Yep.'

She climbed down from the truck, rather stiff after all her travelling, and gazed upon the house. This was not at all how she'd imagined it would be. It was certainly large; a long, low building, built of wood, clapboard Chad called it. It was clean but shabby and looked in dire need of a lick of paint but big enough to hold goodness knows how many rooms to accommodate Chad's family. All along one side ran an open porch that held a couple of rocking chairs and a sagging sofa, and off the end a huddle of outbuildings that looked about to fall down.

There were screen doors, to keep out the flies, he explained, which opened straight into the family kitchen. A young boy ran out, fourteen or fifteen years old, with a shock of sandy red hair and a wide grin on his face. He didn't speak to her but grabbed her bags and hurried back indoors with them, almost falling over his own feet as he kept his eyes fixed on her the entire time.

Bette heard a woman's voice within start fussing about a wood-burning stove having gone out, issuing orders to the boy, apparently called Jake, who turned out to be Chad's younger brother, to 'fetch some chips from the wood store real quick'.

Nobody emerged to welcome her, a telling omission which seemed to embarrass Chad more than her.

Bette hovered on the porch, hot and sticky in the heat, while he went inside to exchange a few, hasty words with the woman, his mother, she presumed. She felt thoroughly bemused, not knowing quite what she should do. What on earth had made her imagine that she was coming to a grand mansion, but that was surely how Chad had described his home to her, back in Fowey?

'Is this one of those ante-bellum houses you talked of, with servants and fine furniture?' she asked, when he came back out again.

He laughed, and she saw that he was embarrassed, denying ever having said that he lived in such a place, that she must have misunderstood, then offered to show her round while his mother got the place tidy. 'We ain't used to visitors and Mom has been busy with outdoor chores all morning, too busy to come into town but she sure can't wait to meet you.'

'Likewise,' said Bette, without too much conviction. Her heart was sinking deeper by the minute and she was beginning to feel quite sick with hunger.

When he'd told her that he owned land, she'd imagined a great sprawling estate, surrounded by similar houses, either in or quite close to a town. As he walked her around to the back of the house, Chad now told her that the family owned a hundred acres or so, nowhere near as much as she'd expected. Nor was it apparently of the rich, agricultural variety owned by those folk who lived in the valleys lower down the mountain. From what she could see, she would agree. This was nothing more than a dusty, dry farm with a few ramshackle outbuildings and an old barn, mainly open to the weather, in which stood an ancient, broken-down tractor.

'Does it work?' she asked, scraping off a patch of rust with her fingernail.

'Sure, she goes fine, on a good day. Sometimes though, nothin' will get her going, jest like a woman.'

Bette made no comment to this. 'You told me that you owned so much land you couldn't even see the end of it, that it stretched right to the horizon and was as big as Fowey and Golant and Lostwithiel put together.'

'Naw, you got that wrong, hon. I said some folks in the States owned that much land. I didn't say we did.'

She bit back an instinctive reaction to argue. Where was the point? Either she'd misunderstood, or he'd misled her. What did it matter now? It was all far too late. Bette set the issue aside with a sigh. 'So what do you do with it? Do you grow potatoes, cabbages and such like?' Half her mind was still on food, which someone would surely bring out soon. She couldn't remember the last time she'd eaten.

'We grow corn mostly, some vegetables and tomatoes. The major crop in this state is peaches, of course. Carolina is the nation's biggest producer of peaches but we don't do so well with them this high up. We keep a few chickens and turkeys, dairy cows, hogs and calves mostly.'

Bette thought that if she'd had to own a farm, she would much rather have grown peaches than suffer all the fuss and mess of animals. Her mouth was watering at the thought.

But this wasn't at all how she'd imagined her life in America would be, living on a small, decrepit farm. She could have done that perfectly well in Cornwall. She began to understand what he'd meant now by a two-bit town. The one where she'd been interviewed on the wireless had possessed little more than a general store and a petrol station. Though small as it might be, at least there were people there, and Chad had somehow failed to mention just how many miles it was from his home. As they'd driven here in the pick-up, she'd seen no sign of another dwelling, save for the odd wooden shack. Where on earth had he brought her?

'Does the farm make a good living?'

'We get by.' Which didn't sound particularly encouraging.

'I thought all you grew down south was sugar.'

'Heck no, that's on the big plantations way down in the deep south. They grow cotton too, of course. Up here in the Blue Ridge Mountains, it can get mighty cold in winter and spring is often slow in coming.'

So she would have to suffer severe cold as well as intense heat. Looking around her, Bette felt as if she'd been set down in the middle of a wilderness. It was certainly beautiful with its rolling hills and deep forests, rich with the green of late spring but the stillness and remoteness of the area, the whole vastness of it, filled her with a strange sense of trepidation. She certainly wouldn't care to be alone up here, miles from anywhere.

'Wouldn't you rather live somewhere more exciting, like New York or Washington?'

'Heck no, I love this old place. It's my home. Yours too, now.'

'Yes,' Bette said. 'I suppose it is.'

And now they were alone together in a room they were, apparently, to share. Chad cupped her face with his hand and kissed her, then slipped his arm about her shoulders and kissed her again, with more enthusiasm this time.

It was a warm, loving kiss, not unpleasant in any way but she felt oddly shy with him after all this time, and her heart plummeted with dismay. Even his kisses weren't quite as she remembered them. Where was the excitement, the thrill that she'd once experienced? All she felt was a deep sadness. Was that because he could only hold her in an awkward, one-armed embrace, or had all her love for him quite gone, leaving only pity in its wake.

'It sure is good to have you here. You don't mind sharing a bed right from the start, do you?' he quietly asked her, and the glitter in his eyes spoke of his need and excitement at the prospect.

'No, I don't mind.'

'Even though we're not wed? Only we don't have no spare rooms for guests. Packed to the rafters we are. Won't trouble you none, will it? I swear I won't touch you, hon, not till you feel ready. You must be plum tuckered out, for one thing. And Mom and Pop have no objection to our sleeping together, so I reckon it'll be OK.' Just as if their opinion mattered more than hers.

'That's good,' Bette agreed, for want of something better to say.

She was surprised that his family were so broad-minded on the subject, and also on her own account, not sure that she was quite ready to sleep with him yet. But how could she say as much now that she was here, and about to confess to carrying his child. What possible excuse could she give?

Bette assured him that since they were soon to be man and wife, and since there was no alternative accommodation available, sharing a bed didn't trouble her in the slightest. She kissed him soundly, to prove the sincerity of her words, striving to pretend that she was as keen as he was.

She wished he would go and leave her in peace for a while, give her time to adjust to all that had happened to her this day but he just stood there, smiling shyly, not quite knowing what to say.

'We thought you were dead, Barney and I. We were told you were missing, believed killed in action.'

A shadow seemed to darken his face and Bette wished instantly that she'd not reminded him of that painful time. Then the words seemed to gush out of him, as if she'd tapped a spring.

'Many men *were* killed at Slapton Sands, I know it. I feel sure of it. Not that anyone's admitting to it, ya know. They're pretending the training was all a great success, that nothing went wrong, but we survivors know that it went badly wrong.

They messed up good and proper. I remember we set off at the right time, first light, as we'd been ordered to, but the other units didn't join us. There were delays, something to do with the landing craft not arriving when expected and everyone was held back till later. Unfortunately, the message didn't get to us in time, so we went anyway. The navy were there, I remember we spotted them, and then all hell broke loose. I don't remember a damned thing after that, not till I woke up in that hospital bed weeks later.'

She wanted to stop the memories now, put a lid on them and lock them away so she wouldn't again see his face twist with pain. 'Well, you're safe home now, that's all that matters. Best to forget it.'

'No, it isn't. I can't forget. I mustn't. They shouldn't have done it, shouldn't have bungled it as they did.' His tone was harsh, bitter with regret. 'All my mates – all those young lives. I was lucky, I only lost an arm, broke a leg that mended pretty good, barring a bit of a limp when it aches. Many guys lost much more, were burned, blinded, killed. God knows!'

'Don't!' Bette thought about Barney, still back there fighting.

He seemed to realise he'd gone too far. 'Sorry, I get a bit carried away.' He pushed back his shoulders, and drawing in a steadying breath took her to the window to show off the view: a magnificent panorama of mountains spread out before them. Bette tried to give the expected response, say the right things. She wanted to reach out to him, to bring the smile back to his face but couldn't quite seem able to manage it.

If she didn't love Chad quite as much as she'd hoped, he was still a lovely man and she ought to feel herself fortunate that he still wanted her, was proving to be so considerate and kind, his family so obliging.

In her heart of hearts she knew why she'd come, because Barney had been keen for her to do so, almost relieved to be rid of the responsibility of marrying her. She'd felt it at the time, though had tried to shut her eyes to it. Hadn't she been the one to do all the planning, done most of the organising for the wedding?

He was only going through the motions to please her, perhaps thinking he'd be called off to war before ever they got around to the ceremony. Maybe he'd have dumped her at the altar. Oh, lord, don't think about Barney, not right now. It was too late to blame him, to blame anyone. Too late for regrets.

She smiled brightly up at Chad. 'It's a lovely spot, but we won't be living with your family after we're married, will we? Won't we find a place of our own?'

'There'll be plenty of time to talk about such things later. You've only just got here.'

'Oh, yes, of course. Sorry, I'm always so impatient, wanting to make things happen right away.' She had to tell him, and now was as good a time as any. 'Look, there's something you should know, something I haven't had the chance to tell you, what with you being transferred. I'm pregnant. I'm having your baby.'

He stared at her for a long moment, seemingly uncomprehending, then his face lit up into an expression of amazement and delight. 'A *baby*? You're having my baby?'

He would have swung her up off her feet, but then thought better of it, sat her down on the edge of the bed instead, and finally, at last, offered her a cup of tea.

Bette had to laugh. 'Later. I've waited this long for a cuppa, I can wait till supper. You are pleased, then?'

'Cock-a-hoop!'

'And you still want to marry me?'

'Sure I do, the sooner the better,' and then as quickly as it had appeared, the smile faded. 'Only, let's not tell Mom tonight, huh? Give her time to get to know you first.'

'All right, if you think that's best.'

'You don't mind?'

'Of course not. Now I'd really like to freshen up and rest, if that's OK.'

'Sure thing, hon. Take just as long as you like.'

Bette thought there was a new spring in his step as he left her, and she was glad of it. He deserved some happiness. But she certainly intended to take advantage of his offer of restraint for tonight, at least, and claim over-tiredness; postponing the intimacy they'd once enjoyed until a time when it would feel less daunting.

Bette enjoyed the first bath she'd had in nearly two weeks and it was glorious. At last she could relax a little before facing the ordeal of putting on her best frock and bravely facing a group of strangers who were to become her new family: Chad's parents, his brother Jake, his sister and her husband, and goodness knows how many of their children. What could she possibly have in common with these people?

Bette quite understood Chad's reluctance to tell his mother about the baby right away. It could wait for another day, but she worried about her possible reaction. She'd been here hours and hadn't even met a single member of his family yet.

She lay back in the deliciously cool water and suddenly burst into tears, overcome by emotion and a great reluctance to get out of it. She longed to climb into bed this very minute, to curl up and slip into a deep, dreamless sleep and not see anyone. Why hadn't she believed Sara when she'd insisted that Chad was spinning her a yarn?

Barney too, with his talk of a string of restaurants, not to mention undying love. He'd probably made up the whole thing, bragging he was rich just to get inside her knickers.

She began to wonder which of them she could believe, whether both men hadn't in fact told her a pack of lies. Bette felt stung by her own naivety and foolishness. She saw herself now for what she was, a silly, empty-headed girl with a passion for fun and a longing to see the world. What a gullible fool she'd been, drinking in every word they told her as if it were gospel. Well, this is where that stupidity had led her. She was seeing the world now right enough, from the back of beyond, and it was nothing like so glamorous and exciting as she'd imagined it would be.

If she'd possessed any money at all, she would have got back on that train and returned home to England at once. But since she scarcely had a penny or a cent to her name, nowhere enough to buy a passage home, she must grit her teeth and make the best of things. Here she was, in America, the land of the free, and here she must stay.

She wiped away her tears with the flat of both hands, ducked her head under the water and washed herself clean all over.

Once she was dry and dressed in her prettiest frock, she began to feel better. It was bound to feel strange at first, as if she didn't belong, but there was no reason to suppose things wouldn't improve. And hadn't she always longed for an adventure? Well this was her big chance, so she'd best make the most of it.

Despite such brave thoughts, Bette took a long time getting ready, drying and brushing out her hair before coiling it tidily in loops on top of her head, putting on her brightest lipstick. She was so nervous she might have skipped supper altogether, had she not been so ravenously hungry. She'd had precious little to eat yesterday on the train, owing to her reluctance to spend her last few dimes, and even less today. But tempting as it might be to hide in the bedroom out of pure cowardice, such behaviour would not endear her to her future in-laws, nor would it fill an empty stomach.

Bette was also wise enough to realise that as a newcomer she was a novelty, but that would soon wear off. Once all the fuss had died down, the articles read and tossed aside, she'd be looked upon as a stranger here, an immigrant who would need to quickly learn a new way of life, different customs, manners and ways of doing things.

Sara had warned her of that too, had reminded her that she would be many thousands of miles from her own family and all the people who loved her. Only now did Bette truly understand what her sister had been trying to tell her.

Never had she felt more alone in all her life. She'd come to this unknown country to marry a man she hardly knew. What had she been thinking of?

31

The boiler gave a funny sort of clank as Sara ran the hot tap and she took rather a longer time than usual to wash herself and comb her hair, and slip into the new nightgown; shy suddenly, now that the moment had come. And then she was lying beside him in the bed, as nervous as a young girl on her wedding night, except that she wasn't a bride, and they weren't married, at least not to each other. The sheets smelled slightly musty, as if they hadn't been properly aired, and Sara worried that the bed might be damp and they'd both catch a chill.

'Are you cold?' Charlie put his arm about her, stroked her face, her bare arms, put his mouth to hers in the sweetest kiss. He admired her new nightdress, the pretty lace, the ribbon as he untied it and slid a hand over her breast. She wanted, oh how she wanted him. Her whole body cried out for surrender. The touch of his hands on her flesh was blissful, as if she had waited for this moment all her life.

'I can't do it.'

'Sara . . .'

She was out of the bed in a flash, standing shivering in the darkness, tears stinging the backs of her eyes. 'It's no good, I do want you, I really do, but I can't go through with this. It's not that I love Hugh, it's just that he's my husband and . . .'

'And I'm not.'

'Yes. I'm sorry. Oh, God, I'm so desperately sorry.' She was crying openly now and he was holding her, cradling her in his arms.

'Don't be. We've had a lovely day together. Let's not spoil it with regrets. Get back into bed, love, you're shivering. I'll manage on the chair in the corner.'

'Oh, Charlie, are you sure? I'm so s . . .'

He put one finger to her lips to stop the words. 'I shall be fine with a pillow and a blanket. Tomorrow, I'm going to buy you a slap-up lunch in the best hotel I can find, then I'll take you home. I love you, Sara, and always will. Perhaps we were wrong to try this but I don't regret it, not for a moment, and nor must you. You are as you are, and I love you for it, for your sweetness and your integrity. Maybe one day things will be different for us. Our day will come, I'm sure of it.'

They travelled in separate compartments on the train journey home in case someone she knew was on the train. Unfortunately this gave her far too much time to think, depression descending upon her like a great black cloud.

Yet would she feel any better if she'd actually gone through with it, if she really had betrayed her husband? Poor Charlie had spent an uncomfortable night on that awful chair, though neither of them had slept much, just talked and talked until exhaustion had overcome them. But he'd made not one word of complaint and at breakfast they'd been forced to endure the disapproving sniffs and cold glances of their landlady, who'd counted them as guilty even when they weren't.

A part of her felt as if she'd lost him, as if she might never see him again.

Sara was surprised to see Hugh waiting for her at the station. Somehow it made her feel strangely edgy. Almost before he kissed her, he'd asked the first question.

'So how was Aunt Marjorie? Was she grateful for your care?'

'Oh, indeed, I'm sure she was very pleased to see me.'

'Your mother didn't even know she was poorly.'

In the end, it had proved impractical to follow Sara to Aunt Marjorie's, much as he would have liked to do so. He'd been kept far too busy at the pub. But Hugh couldn't help noticing how her eyes widened at this simple statment, like a startled fawn. For some reason, he loved her best when she was frightened and revealed her vulnerability.

'Mam? You've been talking to Mam about Aunt Marjorie?'

'I saw her in the butcher's queue and happened to mention where you'd gone. She offered to cook for me, though I told her you'd left everything ready prepared.'

He decided not to mention the fact that he'd deliberately made the approach, tackled Sadie on the subject straight out. He went on with his interrogation, noticing how flustered she was becoming. Why was that? Surely Sara didn't have it in her to lie? He would need to watch her every move, and, should he discover that she was indeed playing him false, he would make her sorry, very sorry indeed.

'So what was wrong with the old dear that you had to run to her side?'

'Oh, it was all a lot of fuss over nothing. Aunt Marjorie is a bit of a hypochondriac. She'll outlive us all in the end, as I'm sure Mam told you. Still, she is over eighty, so of course I had to go and check.'

'So how could you possibly help? What good did it do, for you to waste an entire weekend with her? I hope this isn't going to become a habit, Sara.'

'Don't start an argument now, Hugh. I'm tired and cold. Come on, let's hurry home. It looks like rain.'

Hugh made no further comment as they set off to walk briskly back to the inn, but he watched carefully as the other passengers streamed out of the station, keeping a sharp look-out for anyone suspicious, such as that American officer who was always hanging round The Ship. But he saw no one, which was almost a disappointment. If his suspicions were correct and the pair had spent the weekend together, then he must have got off at an earlier station and hitched a lift back to base, as these Yanks often did. Hugh hadn't expected her to be half so cunning yet something was going on, he was convinced of it.

When they got back home, Sara carried her bag upstairs only to find that he'd moved all her belongings back into the marital bedroom. He'd moved Drew into the spare bedroom, including his toy cupboard and little desk, and a very excited little boy was proudly waiting to show off his new bedroom.

'Daddy says I'm old enough to have a room to myself now, Mummy, instead of sharing with Jenny. And if I look after it properly and keep it very tidy, when we move to the new house he'll let me have the room at the front, and buy me a telescope to look at the ships out at sea. Isn't that exciting?'

Sara caught him to her breast in a tight hug. 'Yes, darling, it certainly is.'

She considered sleeping in one of the inn's guest bedrooms but dismissed the idea. Not only did they need the income from letting them, but also she wouldn't be able to hear if Drew or Jenny woke in the night and needed her. Consequently, there was nowhere left for her to sleep but with her husband.

Sara came to dread the moment when Hugh joined her in bed, feeling herself grow stiff and rigid as he stroked and caressed her. After years of indifference and lack of interest on his part, suddenly now, when she wanted him least, he'd decided to reclaim what he termed as his rights.

He'd never been a particularly unselfish lover, but any tenderness that had once existed between them had quite gone, replaced by something far more dark and troubling.

Thankfully he didn't ever repeat quite the display of aggression he'd used when he'd tied her up, but the memory of that night was strong in her. It hummed below the surface between them and Sara was aware that his mood could change in an instant. Resistance was not only futile but dangerous. If she turned away or told him she didn't feel like it tonight, he would be irritated and impatient and take her anyway with a brutal heartlessness. She became simply grateful that he at least no longer used the pyjama cord, allowed him to have his fill of her, on the grounds that the sooner it was done the better.

She'd hear him chuckle to himself in the darkness, as if it amused him to know she no longer wanted him, but that he could take her at any time he wished. He seemed to enjoy toying with her as a cat would with a mouse. Some nights he would make no approach, do nothing, on others he would start to kiss and fondle her and then abruptly turn away and ignore her, as if needing to make clear that the moment would be of his choosing.

She knew only too well that at some point during the night, although not every night by any means, or perhaps in the early hours of the morning, or even when she was about to rise and make breakfast, he would pull her to him and take her without any warning whatsoever.

All of this meant that Sara was quite unable to sleep. She would doze a little then wake in a panic, wondering if he'd touched her, or when he might reach for her.

She hated it most when he talked to her, which dragged out the agony.

'I knew you enjoy this every bit as much as I do, for all you refuse to respond. I shall possess you, Sara. You are my wife and it's been too long, far too long. We've let life and this dratted war get in the way of our love. We mustn't shut each other out ever again. As you once said yourself, we need to put some romance and excitement back into our marriage.'

When he was done with her, she would thankfully turn from

him to sleep on the furthest side of the bed, or get up and creep to the bathroom to eradicate every trace of him.

'I ask only loyalty and obedience,' he would carefully explain, in those falsely patient tones she'd come to hate.

And what of love? the voice inside her head would cry, hotly rebelling, longing to declare that she was innocent of all charges, except of trying to live a useful and worthwhile life.

Yet in her heart Sara knew that wasn't strictly true. Try as she might, she couldn't stop wishing she'd slept with Charlie after all.

32

They were all seated at the table waiting for her, when Bette finally plucked up the courage to go downstairs. Aware that she'd spent far more time than was strictly necessary fussing over her hair, putting on lipstick and making herself presentable, yet she'd needed to do all of that in order to bolster her flagging confidence. Bette addressed her apology directly to his mother, who was presiding over events from the end of the table. 'I'm so sorry I'm late, Mrs Jackson. The bath was lovely and I was so desperately tired after all the excitement, I nearly fell asleep in it.'

The response was more informative than warm, but forgiveness was implicit in the words. 'It's your first day, so you're allowed to be late, but we never do start eating till all the family is present.'

Chad chipped in. 'Come sit by me, hon, and I'll remind you of everyone's names. This here is Jake, my rascal younger brother, over there is Mary-Lou and her husband Harry, and these whipper-snappers are their offspring: Laurie, Mel, and Billy-Jo.'

Bette swiftly offered a polite smile of apology all round, including the three little girls, then sat quickly down in the chair he'd pulled out for her. 'I'll remember to be on time in future, Mrs Jackson.'

Chad gave a shout of laughter as if she'd made some sort of joke. 'Her name is Peggy but you must learn to call her Mom. We all do.'

Bette smiled and nodded, privately wondering how she would ever manage to think of her in such terms. The woman was reed thin, the bone structure of her gaunt face sharply defined into a broad forehead, high cheekbones and blunt jaw line. No one could call her beautiful yet there was a handsome, regal quality to her, almost formidable, if only in the erectness of her posture as she sat like a queen before her family. Her very stature seemed to imply that she had been beautiful once. The grey hair had been dragged up into a tight bun at the nape of her neck, which somehow made the clear blue eyes seem overlarge and Bette shifted uncomfortably in her seat beneath the woman's scrutiny.

As she set dishes and plates on the table, Bette noticed the work-worn hands, ingrained with the kind of dirt that no amount of cream or lemon juice could dissolve. The scrubbed, pale complexion that might once have been porcelain-like was now marred by pink threads of broken veins from being out in all weathers, and Bette thought with almost nostalgic longing of Sadie's more flamboyant, colourful looks, scarlet lipstick and the flowing, pink floral gown she wore at the salon.

Glancing about her, Bette realised how very overdressed she was in this, her favourite green crêpe de Chine dress, and suddenly regretted the swirl of auburn curls she'd so carefully arranged on top of her head, the rouge and bright lipstick, as she took in the tidy but undoubtedly shabby appearance of her future mother-in-law's print cotton frock and apron. Even Mary Lou, at little more than thirty, looked plain and homely in faded blue cotton.

Where was the style she'd expected to find in America, the elegance, the prosperity? Bette tucked her short skirt over her knees and prayed they would at least eat soon, before she passed out from hunger. Right beside her was a dish of mashed potato which smelt heavenly and, unable to resist any longer, Bette picked it up and started to dole some out onto her plate. Everyone suddenly stopped talking to stare at her.

'We ain't said grace yet,' Chad gently reprimanded her, taking the spoon from her hand.

Bette hung her head in shame, though grace was not something she was used to at home. Her own family rarely even bothered going to church these days.

When that task had been properly carried out, bowls of food were passed from hand to hand, which she found strange. Back home, Sadie would divide their meagre rations equally between them, allowing Cory an extra sausage or spoonful of potato, him being a man and head of the household, and that's what you got, neither more nor less.

Here, there appeared to be no such restrictions and Bette set to with gusto. She was young, after all, with a healthy appetite, and the journey had been long which she'd spent largely being sick. Perhaps this desperate hunger drove her to indulge a little too freely, for after watching her scoop out spoonful after spoonful of potato, mashed swede and carrot, and help herself to two huge slices of meat loaf, Chad whispered in her ear.

'You're making a pig of yourself, Bette. There are other folk who need feeding here.' Only then did she notice that the amount of food in each bowl was not as plentiful as might at first have appeared. The yellow corn she'd ignored altogether as something hens ate, not people. But if she'd consumed all that she'd piled on her plate, then some around the table would have gone without.

Bette hastily and apologetically returned some of the untouched food back into their bowls beneath the condemnatory gaze of the entire Jackson family, recognising what a terrible mistake she'd made, in more ways than one. Food was not plentiful in America, at least, not here in this town, with this family. These people were not rich. They couldn't possibly own a string of restaurants, or anything else for that matter.

'Didn't they feed you back in England?' his mother enquired, in quietly, critical tones.

'It's been a long time since my last meal. Sorry!' There she went again, yet another apology.

Chad attempted to intervene on her behalf. 'I did explain about the rationing, Mom.'

'Rationing is good for the soul. Greed is not.' Bette was about to put a forkful of food into her mouth when she continued, 'Will you cut my Chad's food for him, since the poor boy has lost half his arm fighting for the British, or shall I do that myself, as usual?'

'Oh, lord, sorry, I didn't think.' Not more apologies! It was starting to become a bad habit. And what was that snide remark about fighting for the British? Bette bit down hard on her lip, reminding herself she was a guest in this house, a stranger in this country.

After helping Chad with his food, she remained silent for the rest of the meal, leaving the chatter to family members, thankful to fade into the background and be ignored at last.

Though for some reason, Bette's ravenous hunger had quite vanished, leaving her sick at heart, aching for home and her own family. How she longed to hear Cory call her his little maid, have Sara give her a loving hug, or even for Sadie to scold her for being no better than she ought to be.

Which brought her to the very reason of why she was here, at the other side of the world. Her unborn child. It was too late to want to go home now. She'd burned her boats good and proper this time.

When supper was over, the men went outside on the porch to smoke and drink beer. Mary-Lou took the children upstairs to bed and Bette offered to help wash and dry the dishes in an effort to make up for her various blunders. But the taps were called faucets and didn't work quite like they did at home.

Water had to be boiled on the mysterious wood-burning stove, and even when everything was finally washed in the big brown-stone sink, she didn't know where anything went in the myriad of kitchen cupboards.

Mrs Jackson was clearly exceptionally house-proud and although she declared that it really didn't matter a hoot where Bette put things, if she set a salt pot or mug back on the wrong shelf, the cupboard door would be quietly opened again for her to retrieve it and place it on the shelf above, or wherever it should properly reside.

Bette tried various opening gambits to get a conversation going but it was like trying to draw the proverbial blood from a stone. She was having none of it, making only occasional, noncommittal grunts. Bette was almost dropping with fatigue by the time they were done, beginning to wonder if this day would ever end. At last she put the sopping dish towel to dry on the rack by the stove and declared her intention to retire.

'I'll say goodnight then, Mrs Jackson, or would you mind if I called you Peggy? Mom does feel a little – er – um – too familiar at this stage.'

'Peggy will do fine!' The woman kept her back steadfastly turned towards Bette as she wiped down the sink, even on this homely task remaining stiff and unbending.

'Thank you. Oh, and thank you also for an excellent supper. It was wonderful.'

There was no immediate response to this and it was not until Bette reached the door that the comment which fully explained the coolness of the woman's attitude, finally came.

'If you thought you'd hooked yourself a fine GI with a pocketful of dollars, I hope you've realised different now, girl. Goodnight!'

Bette could see that she had a long, hard hill to climb so far as her future mother-in-law was concerned.

Lying in the big bed waiting for Chad to join her, was nerve-racking. Bette's mind turned back to those times spent hidden in the rocks on the beach at Whitehouse. It hadn't seemed to occur to them then that there were ships just yards away in the river, the pillbox on the rocks behind, a war going on out at sea. They'd been in love, desperate to touch and kiss and be together, hardly able to keep their hands off each other. Why had it all changed when he went away?

Because of Barney.

For some reason Bette couldn't begin to explain, she'd fallen in love with him, too. But was it possible to love two men, or had she simply been infatuated with Chad, charmed by his quiet Southern charm? But if she didn't truly love him, then why was she here, willing to become his wife? Because she'd no choice. Barney had let her down, in the end. He was ready enough to make love to her, but not to shoulder the responsibility of a child; willing to fight the enemy but not his buddy, not for her anyway.

She could see Chad's awkwardness as he undressed some distance from the bed, his back turned towards her as he struggled with the buttons on his pyjama jacket. Bette's heart went out to him. He deserved a better wife than she could ever make him. She'd no right to love two men, particularly one as dangerous and heartless as Barney had turned out to be. It wasn't decent. Hadn't Sara told her so a million times? Oh, why did her big sister always have to be right? No wonder Peggy had made that barbed remark. She'd looked like a tart in her fancy frock and mouth plastered with lipstick.

Bette didn't care to think how her future mother-in-law would react when she learned the truth, that she'd behaved like one too by getting herself pregnant at just twenty years old.

She must never let it slip that she wasn't even sure that Chad was the father.

She slid out of bed and went to help him but Chad was quick to protest that he could manage very well on his own, thank you very much.

'I'm sure you can, but I want to help. That's what wives do.'

'You're not my wife.'

'Not yet, but I soon will be.'

He made no further comment, pulled back the sheets and lay down in the bed. Bette did the same. They were lying side by side, stiff and awkward and, true to his word, he didn't touch her, didn't even speak to her. They might as well have been planks of wood for all the romance there was between them. She could have been sleeping with a complete stranger.

Exhausted as she was, Bette would have welcomed a little cuddle, to feel his arms about her and hear again how pleased he was that she had come. But he made no move, so she lay silent beside him as tears slid down her cheeks.

She was woken shortly after five-thirty by a raucous din coming from the next room, which Bette took to be Mary-Lou's children having a fight. After about ten minutes of shouting and thumping, when she was on the point of going in and sorting the little brats out herself, she heard their father's voice bawl something at them, followed by a few more thumps and bumps, before blissful silence fell.

She drifted back to sleep but then Chad was shaking her, telling her to get up and get dressed, quick as possible as breakfast would be in ten minutes. Since Bette had no wish to disgrace herself by being late again, she did as she told and by the stroke of six was seated at the table, along with the rest of the clan. She couldn't ever remember having been up so early before, could barely keep her eyes open long enough to see what was happening.

Breakfast proved to be as much of a nightmare as supper the night before, with something called grits that tasted revolting, together with scrambled eggs, and biscuits which were soft, doughy scones and tasted delicious. Bette made the mistake of reaching for a second but a warning look from Chad, stopped her just in time.

Unfortunately, Mary-Lou noticed. She looked down her long nose and made some pointed remark about foreigners who reckoned they could walk right in and take food from her children's mouths. 'You know the kids aren't done yet. Do you ever do anything but eat?'

Peggy said, 'Mary-Lou, we been through all this. The girl is hungering for home, as well as food. Leave her be.'

Bette was grateful for Peggy's intervention so rewarded her with a beaming smile. 'Don't worry, I mean to earn my keep. I shall get myself a job just as quickly as possible. I know it's some distance into town from here but when we get a place of our own, we could maybe move closer, or into the town itself, so I can get work.'

They were all looking at her as if she'd lost the use of her senses. Bette glanced at Chad, hoping he'd back her up but he'd turned away to talk to Jake, paying her no attention at all.

Mary-Lou said. 'What sort of job you reckon you could do, exactly?'

'I don't mind. I could be a shop assistant perhaps, or a secretary. I'm really much more organised than you might think. I used to help my mother run a hairdressing salon.'

Several pairs of eyes swivelled to her hennaed curls. Peggy sniffed, and her disapproval was all too plain. 'Women in these parts generally find they have enough to do keeping house and looking after their men-folk.'

'That's right,' echoed Mary-Lou, in that whining voice of hers which Bette had already come to hate. 'Shucks, why would you want to, anyway? I wouldn't dream of going out to work when my children need me. Besides, Harry would never approve, would you, sugar?'

'Ain't normal. Ain't a woman's place,' was the grumpy response, spoken through a mouthful of grits.

Bette looked from one to other of them, her jaw slack with shock. 'How can you say such a thing? Of course it's normal for women to work. They're working hard and fighting to win the war back home in England.'

Chad's father, who, so far as Bette could recall, had not yet even acknowledged her existence, suddenly decided to enter the conversation by bellowing out in a big loud voice, 'Then your Englishmen should hang their heads in shame. I wouldn't let no woman do my dirty work. I can fight my own battles.'

'No, no, not fighting in the physical sense. I mean working in factories, on the buses, on the land. All kinds of jobs that used to be done by the men till they had to join up and fight Hitler.' She turned to Chad. 'Tell them, Chad. Explain to them how it is in England.'

Before he could open his mouth, Peggy had answered for him. 'This ain't England. And I don't reckon you'll have time to go gallivanting off to town, even if we could afford the petrol to take you. There's more'n enough work to do here on the farm. And why would you need a place of your own, when Chad has a perfectly good home here with us, his family? Don't make no sense. It'd be jest throwing good money away.'

That was the moment when Bette saw the true reality of her situation, and the closest she came to despair. The prospect of spending each and every day of her entire life, shut up in this house with her mother-in-law, with moaning Mary-Lou and her three brats was unthinkable, more than she could bear to even contemplate. But now was definitely not the moment to argue the point. She merely smiled and sipped her coffee, making a mental note to tackle Chad on the subject at the very first opportunity.

33

In the two weeks or so since their stolen weekend together, there had been so much work to be done, Charlie had scarcely had time to think. Along with the other officers, he'd been ordered to make the final preparations for Operation Overlord. They'd been given details of the number of boats, which units were to be deployed, plus a comprehensive outline of the landing beaches, codenamed Utah and Omaha, with the help of maps and aerial photographs.

The men were to be briefed, provided with French currency, and morale kept high by a more relaxed approach; good food and great movies provided every evening. The last supper of the condemned, Charlie thought with wry, dark humour.

The time left to see Sara was becoming frighteningly tight. He was well aware that once all the men, equipment and supplies were in position, security would be tightened up considerably. Orders were that no one would then be allowed out of camp.

Movement of civilians would also be strictly curtailed, passes needing to be shown wherever they went. But Charlie was desperate to risk one last meeting. The question was, how to achieve it?

Late one afternoon he hung around the kitchen door at The Ship but didn't see her and couldn't stay too long. He tried again the next day, still with no success. If only he had the time to wait, to look around town or dash up to the school in case she was there, but he only ever had a brief half hour before having to dash back to base. And she could be on one of her WVS collection trips, out with the children. She could be anywhere.

The Charlie who loved Sara was desperate to escape duties for just a day, half a day, to be with her for one last time; to hold her in his arms and tell her again how much he loved her.

Lieutenant Charles Denham was forced to set this longing aside and concentrate on the task in hand. Lives depended on his doing so.

He was quite certain they were as ready as they would ever be for the invasion. Hidden away in the forests, fields and green English valleys, in old mills and agricultural buildings, in docks and warehouses, was an arsenal of weapons and artillery.

Tanks, jeeps, Bren-gun carriers, trucks, armoured cars and ambulances by the thousand. There was food and medical supplies, howitzers and anti-aircraft guns, bulldozers and excavators, and rolling stock which would be taken over to replace the shattered French railway equipment. In addition, two huge man-made harbours, called 'Mulberries', made up of steel floats, were to be towed to the Normandy beaches so they could be used for Allied shipping.

Last, but by no means least, there were the strange landing craft: The LCTs or Landing Craft Tanks, designed to carry up to nine tanks or twelve lorries, and the LSTs, Landing Ship Tanks, the bows of which opened to allow tanks and trucks to be driven straight on to the shore.

Loading was to be started by the end of May as it would take time to get everything in place. More and more soldiers and equipment were pouring in every day. Nissen huts were overcrowded, tents sprang up everywhere as make-shift accommodation, and it could take what seemed like hours to collect your chow.

Despite his need to see Sara, Charlie, like the rest of the men, was filled with impatience for the operation to get underway. There had been any number of delays over recent months while preparations were put into place, and although the troops gave every appearance of calm, the strain was tangible. Tension was high, men spending a lot of time sitting in quiet corners writing to their loved ones.

Charlie wrote a note to Sara, several in fact, and then threw them all away. How could he write to her? Hugh might open her mail.

Every now and then a shout would go up. 'Let's go finish him off.'

'Sure thing. Put an end to this goddamned war.'

'Put an end to Hitler.'

It was like a baseball chant, only much more deadly. They were buoyed up, excited, sick with fear, for not a man amongst them underestimated the dangers they faced.

They were itching to get the job done; keen to drive back the great armies of Wehrmacht and declare this damned war over. Hitler might claim to have built an impregnable fortress around Europe yet he couldn't be entirely certain from which direction the attack would come. The hope was that the Germans would expect it at Pas-de-Calais. The bombing in that region was meant to keep his armies fully occupied with hopefully insufficient men to guard the entire coastline.

Charlie wanted to come home safe not just for his own sake, but for Sara's. He knew that she needed him, if only to get away from that dreadful husband of hers. How was he treating her? Was she coping? Had Hugh found out about their tryst? He sure did hope not.

He knew that she loved him, as he loved her. He made a silent vow to come home and save her. Wrote it in a letter and again tore it up. It might make it worse for her, if he wrote.

But he knew it wouldn't be easy to stay alive. There'd been

other, earlier raids on Europe, some quite bloody. The brave Canadians had, in one battle alone, suffered over 3,000 casualties including 900 dead. In the cold early hours, alone in one's bunk, Charlie, along with his comrades, found it difficult not to feel he was facing almost certain death.

It was Cory who brought the news, almost running into The Ship to announce to all present that Falmouth had been hit. 'We'll be next,' he cried, creating uproar in seconds.

'What rubbish are you talking now, Cory? There've been no enemy planes in Cornwall for months.'

'You won't read it in the papers, all being kept hush-hush but 'tis right, I tell you! They came two nights ago.'

Everyone was aware that the time of the invasion was drawing near. The roads and narrow winding lanes of Cornwall, like the rest of southern England, seemed to be constantly blocked with military transport at all hours of the day and night. The sound of them rumbling through villages woke people up, putting an end to secrecy at last. Buses had stopped running, many roads were closed to civilians and no one was in any doubt that at long last, a mighty armada was gathering. Among them came thousands of men from Falmouth and Plymouth, some by sea, some by land.

Even patients had been sent home to free up hospital beds.

Queues to reach embarkation points stretched for miles and some men had set up stoves to cook food while they waited. But this time as they arrived at their destination, it was in complete silence. There was no rejoicing, no cheering, no flag-waving or days off work to welcome them.

All people felt was fear.

Cory was well on with his tale. 'Thirty planes came in fast over Carrick Roads and the docks, dropping flares to mark the bomb path and then their pay-loads after. The place was packed with American servicemen. They're not sure how many lives have been lost yet, but hotels on the front got hit and there was a terrible fire at a fuel supply depot no one was supposed to know was even there. Sent a river of fire into the village, apparently, which the National Fire Service men are still fighting. That's all they could tell me, but they're saying someone squeaked, someone has been talking to the enemy. There must have been spies. Mebbe there's spies here amongst us in Fowey, this very minute who could scupper the whole operation.'

A strange stillness fell over the pub and eyes swivelled to left and right as people surreptitiously eyed up their neighbours.

Hugh said, 'Drinks all round, Iris. Fill up everyone's glass, on the house. Let's drink to the courage of the Falmouth fire fighters, and hope to God it doesn't happen here.'

Hugh was growing nervous. Could he have been instrumental in taking information about fuel depots to the enemy? He'd no idea what had been in any of the documents he'd delivered for Iris. The money she had promised him had never materialised, not so far, yet he'd found it impossible to extricate himself. How could he, when she threatened to blow the whistle on him over that American aircrew he'd left to drown.

If fingers started pointing in his direction he didn't care to imagine what sort of trouble he'd be in. They wouldn't see him as the town hero then, but as a traitor. Not that Hugh saw himself in that role. In his mind he was a victim, a man fighting a war of survival on the home front, protecting a way of life from invaders of a different sort, trying to save his marriage.

It was all Sara's fault. If she hadn't let those Yanks fawn all over her, he wouldn't have been so anti-American, and then he might not be in this mess.

He'd been highly suspicious over her weekend away, the answers to his questions evasive, and at night, in their bed, even more distant than usual. He deeply regretted not following her to Penzance.

Even his efforts to win Iris back had failed miserably, which deepened his black mood all the more. His temper was strung out like a high tensile wire that could snap at any moment. Where better to expel that fury, than on his wife? All he had to do was choose his moment with care and he'd get the truth out of her, one way or another.

Charlie did write her a letter, in the end. He called at the back kitchen door and again finding it locked, scribbled a hasty note and stuck it through the gap at the bottom. It was simple enough, suitably discreet, saying only '*Monday – 7pm.*' He wrote it in block capitals so that should Hugh chance upon it, he'd assume it was a note from the dreadful Nora Snell about another committee meeting.

But as things turned out, it was ill judged.

Hugh was indeed the first to go into the kitchen that lunchtime to turn on the oven to warm the pasties. Sara was at her mother's and Iris had volunteered to do lunches but was late, as she increasingly was these days. He picked up the note, read the single, pointed instruction and stuffed it in his pocket, a thoughtful frown on his face.

Sid Penhale later told his best mate, Cory, that he'd never known his boss to be in such a foul mood.

'Must have lost a shilling and found a halfpenny, he were that crotchety today. Near snapped my head off just for not tightening the screw lid on a sarsaparilla bottle. Then Iris comes in, half hour late and he yells blue murder at her too. Heard him shout at his missus often enough, but not at Iris. Favours her, he do. Don't know how your little maid puts up with it.'

When Cory arrived back home, Sara was still with her mother with whom words had clearly been exchanged, not for the first time during these last weeks. Relations seemed to be at an all-time low. Yet again Sadie was tight-lipped and Sara's eyes all red and blotchy.

He went over to her. 'And how's my little maid? Not working too hard?'

Sara hugged her father. 'I've been showing Mam a letter from Bette, well, a postcard really, saying the ship has landed safely and she was waiting to catch a train. Nothing much else, except that it's hot and she promises to write more later. I'm missing her something dreadful.'

Cory patted her shoulder, looking suddenly old and haggard, for he too missed his younger daughter sorely. He sighed and moved away, not wanting to share his grief since no one could offer him any comfort. She was at the other side of the world and he really didn't expect ever to see her again.

He blew his nose loudly before returning to the other matter on his mind. 'I've been hearing that Hugh is a bit hot and bothered at present. Quite lost his rag with Sid this morning, all over something and nothing. Why is that? Can't he cope with you not helping out in the bar any more? Is he regretting that daft jealousy of his?' No one was under any illusion of the reason behind the decision.

'Who knows what he thinks, I certainly don't. But you're right, he is tense. He doesn't just run the pub, remember, he's out all hours of the night on exercise and ops. He says little about it, but I do know he's involved in pretty dangerous work.'

Sadie said, 'All the more reason for his wife to stay home and look after him properly, not go gallivanting off on unnecessary trips to see Aunt Marjorie.'

Sara did not take up the challenge. She'd heard the same accusation times without number since that fateful weekend. Her mother had dismissed the Aunt Marjorie story as nonsense, on the grounds that the old lady had never enjoyed a day's illness in her life and certainly would not send for Sara if she did.

'Wouldn't even let a doctor in the house, let alone a useless niece.'

The questioning started up every time she called. Even today Sadie had called her all manner of dreadful names, the sort you use on women of ill repute, not on your own daughter. So far, Sara had managed to hold fast to her tale, though there were times when she nearly cracked under the strain. Her mother was nothing if not persistent, gnawing away at the subject like a dog with a bone.

What had she made Aunt Marjorie for tea? Had the old lady taken to her bed? How had she contacted Sara in the first place? And why hadn't Sara thought to mention the fact that she was ailing?

Now Sara was anxious to be off before it all started up again. 'Bye Mam, bye Dad. I must go and join the queue at the butcher's in the hope of finding something decent for tea, and then pick up the children.'

But Sadie must have the last word. 'Next time you go to see Aunt Marjorie, I'll come with you.'

34

Would it never end? Now she would have to go and see Aunt Marjorie, certainly before her mother did, and try to find some way out of this web of lies she'd created. And it was so difficult to keep track, to maintain the fiction. Every now and then Hugh too, would ask her a question. Innocent enough but fraught with hidden traps, unless she kept her wits about her at all times.

Having made the mistake of trying to fend off his curiosity by foolishly telling Hugh that her aunt was a hypochondriac, when really the opposite was the case, Sara now found her tale tied up in all manner of dreadful knots. She could hardly remember what she'd said from one minute to the next and really hadn't appreciated how necessary a good memory was when helplessly embroiled in lies.

How spies managed to fabricate stories, she really couldn't imagine, but then they didn't have to be questioned by her mother.

And she was so worried about Charlie, so desperate to see him again, so fearful for his safety, and yet terrified of Hugh finding out where she'd really spent that weekend.

Sara sat on her bed and cried as if her heart would break. Sadie's persistence had unnerved her. She really would need to be careful; hope and pray that Hugh would stop fussing and asking so many questions.

Despite Hugh's very obvious suspicions, she didn't regret her decision, either to spend that precious time with Charlie, or to baulk at the final hurdle. It was just one of those things. She wasn't the cheating sort and simply longed for things to be normal.

But they weren't normal, not in the least. Nevertheless, she must stay with Hugh, for now, even though every instinct was to pack a suitcase and leave, for good this time. Yet there was nowhere to run to. She certainly couldn't go to Charlie, not yet.

Most important of all, the last thing she wanted was to risk losing her children.

She wiped away the tears, washed her face and put on fresh lipstick.

The invasion was imminent, everyone was aware of it. After that, who knew what fate awaited them? They would just have to be patient, wait and pray that he came home safe and well. As he'd said, their time would come. Right now there was a war to be won.

And he'd promised her faithfully that even if he got tied up with all the preparations, they'd meet up for one last time on the headland beyond St Catherine's Castle. All she had to do was wait for him to name the day and time.

He would contact her soon, she was sure of it.

Sara had given the children some bread and jam to eat on the kitchen doorstep in the sunshine when Hugh came in, and something in his expression told her that all her efforts at secrecy had been in vain.

'Sara, I wish to see you upstairs. At once, if you please,' and he turned and walked away, clearly expecting her to follow.

'Don't wander off, stay there,' she instructed the children before going to answer his peremptory summons. She found him in their bedroom, sitting quietly on the bed with his head in his hands. For a moment, Sara felt a stab of pity for him. He looked so lost and alone, so deeply depressed.

Yet her mind was racing. What had he found out? Had Sadie bluntly informed him that Aunt Marjorie never was and never would be ill? She took a steadying breath, warning herself to be strong, to maintain her innocence. But would he believe that? No sooner had she closed the bedroom door than he went on the attack.

'I know what you've been up to.'

Sara felt a bolt of shock but she mustn't weaken. She must hold her nerve. 'I'm s-sorry? I don't understand. What are you talking about?'

'You know perfectly well. You and that officer, what's his name, Lieutenant Denham. You spent that weekend with him, didn't you? Don't lie to me, Sara. I have his note here in my hand giving details, presumably, of your next assignation.' He held it out to her but when she would have taken it from him, he slipped it back into his pocket. 'This confirms what I've suspected all along, that this Aunt Marjorie story was all a complete fabrication. Well, what have you to say? What excuse are you going to offer me this time?'

Her knees had gone weak and Sara longed to sit down but there was no chair handy and she had no wish to sit next to him on the bed, so she stood before him like a recalcitrant school-girl, hands clenched tight, trying not to reveal that she was trembling.

'Are you going to own up and be honest about your sordid little affair?'

The words seemed to burst out of her. 'We aren't having an affair. Nothing happened. Nothing at all.' Too late, Sara realised that the very form of her denial was an admission. She saw it in the way his cruel lips twisted into a sardonic smile. But then she should have known from the outset that she was quite incapable of prevaricating or maintaining a lie, any more than she was capable of committing adultery. Oh, but that was no excuse. What had she done? She'd betrayed him in her heart, if not with her body, and having largely admitted her transgression, there seemed no alternative but to continue.

She took a deep breath. 'All right, I'll confess the whole story, which isn't in the least bit sordid. Tell the truth and shame the devil, isn't that how the saying goes? There have been times recently, Hugh, when you've seemed very much as a devil to me, so is it any wonder if I found another man more appealing?

'Charlie is attractive, of course, but also kind and caring, while you have been hard and cruel, criticising me the whole time, finding fault, treating me as an object for your own pleasure, even jealously stopping me from working behind the bar.' Sara could hardly believe she was finding the courage to say these things. She daren't begin to imagine what his reaction would be.

His response, as always, was calm, at least on the surface. 'Oh, so it's my fault, is that what you're saying?'

Sara let out a weary sigh. 'No, of course I'm not. We never meant this to happen, but it did, so there we are.'

'And where are we exactly, Sara? What precisely did happen? You slept with a Yank, like hundreds of other silly young girls?'

'No, I've already told you. It wasn't like that at all. Nothing happened. Nothing at all. I couldn't do it. I wanted to, but I couldn't.'

'Perhaps he didn't want you, when it came to it.' His sarcasm taunted her, yet she smiled at that.

'Oh, he wanted me all right but he spent the night on a chair, because he loves me and had no wish to take advantage. So unlike you, Hugh, who only ever think of yourself and your own needs. That is what's wrong with our marriage. Your utter selfishness, and your determination to treat my needs and wishes with contempt. Is it any wonder I fell in love with another man?'

'You're making yourself appear innocent so you can shift your guilt on to me.'

Sara had the grace to flush. Was there an element of truth in this? She sincerely hoped not. 'We couldn't help it. Something just grew between us. I'm not some sort of puppet whose strings you can pull to suit the tune you happen to be playing, Hugh. I'm a living, breathing person with thoughts and opinions, dreams and ambitions of my own. I'm sorry if I've hurt you but perhaps later, when you've got over the shock and calmed down a little, we can talk about the future. Obviously I would like my freedom, but there's the children to think of and . . .'

She thought for a moment that he was going to strike her but she should have known better. Hugh was far too controlled for anything so reckless and demeaning. Instead he strode to the door, turning with his hand on the knob to face her. 'I've heard enough. Your freedom indeed. You are my *wife*, in case you've forgotten. You'll stay here, in our bedroom, till you've got this silly romantic nonsense out of your head.'

'What? I don't understand.'

'Then let me make it crystal clear. You will not be getting your freedom, or taking the children away, and you certainly won't ever be running off again with your *Yank*. You are *my* wife and will remain so, even if I have to keep you under lock and key. Which is where you will stay for the foreseeable future, until you've repented of this foolishness. Is that clear enough for you? You are going nowhere, Sara. You are mine!'

The last thing she heard was the key turning in the lock.

Charlie waited for two hours just beyond St Catherine's Castle, but finally gave up and went back to base. She surely must have got his note. She spent half her life in that kitchen. But then, as she had so often told him, she was a respectable married lady and it was, after all, a woman's prerogative to change her mind.

They were almost ready to depart. Ships filled the River Fowey, so many that you could have walked from one shore to the other without getting your feet wet. A living mass of men and machines, seething with activity and noise: a throbbing, whining, whirring and rattling; a clattering of gas masks, canteens and weapons, and the endless chatter of hundreds, packed tightly into every corner, waiting for the order to leave.

Hour upon hour they waited, cold and damp, sick to their stomachs with apprehension and fear, in full combat gear, weighed down with equipment.

The loading had been done chiefly at night, scores of vehicles driving straight onto the LSTs; thousands of foot soldiers directed up the gangway and counted on board.

It was June 4 and they left later that night but by the following day were driven back by the weather to spend yet another night in harbour. After all these months of preparation, all the careful planning and organising, the fate of Operation Overlord appeared to be at the mercy of the elements. There was a storm brewing and if the weather did not improve, there would be further delays.

Twenty-four hours later the decision finally came. This time for real. On the night of June 5 they left the safe waters of Fowey, Falmouth and the Helford River, and all the other ports along the south coast for the last time and headed out to sea. Operation Overlord was underway at last.

Hugh released Sara from her bedroom the first time they left. Compelled to go along with his tale, she explained her absence to the children by saying that she'd been suffering from flu and had not wished to infect them.

But now she was free and when she was quite certain that he was asleep, Sara slid from their bed, hastily pulled on some clothes, then ran pell-mell up through the churchyard, along the Esplanade, past Point Neptune, skirting the coils of barbed wire on Readymoney beach, slipping and sliding up the coastal path, tripping over stones, nearly falling headlong over the edge into the sea at one stage in her breathless dash to reach the headland beyond the camouflaged castle, and watch them leave.

Gasping for breath, she wrapped her arms about herself and shivered, straining her eyes in the darkness, waiting for the short June night to end so that she could catch a last glimpse of him.

The sea broiled with ships, ensigns snapping in the wind. An armada so massive it was still visible when dawn broke on that longest of all days. Far out to sea the minesweepers led the way, like a great inverted vee, each one trailing a long, saw-toothed wire to cut through the moorings and detonate floating mines. Behind these came the dark, intimidating throng of destroyers and cruisers, protected above by a barrage balloon attached to each ship. To the rear of these came the landing craft, carrying thousands of men, tanks, gun vehicles and ammunition. The convoy stretched for miles and would surely frighten any army destined to be the one to meet and fight it.

But what state would those poor boys be in when they finally landed? Soaking wet through, cold and seasick, she would imagine, expected to climb down some scramble-net, fully loaded with equipment, and fight their way across a beach in the face of enemy fire. What hope could there be for survival against such odds?

Sara could almost hear them praying. She clasped her hands together and prayed with them.

And overhead came the aircraft. The sky seemed to be filled with hundreds of planes. That heart-stopping drone of engines making the hairs stand up at the back of her neck. She'd heard the first wave of bombers go out the night before, yet still they came, like a flock of giant blackbirds, an armada of the skies, as well as the sea.

And somewhere, among all this mass of ships and activity, was Charlie, yet she couldn't see him, couldn't reach him. He was lost to her, perhaps for ever. Thanks to Hugh, she hadn't even been allowed to say goodbye. All she could do was stand and watch, dry-eyed, till the last dark speck had vanished from the horizon. Only then did she turn and walk back into a town swamped by an eerie silence; back home to her husband and a life without Charlie.

35

When Bette had arrived at the farm she'd been barely three months gone. Now, nearly two months later, still no mention had been made of a date for their wedding, let alone a place of their own. Relations with his family remained difficult and, so far as she could tell, Chad still hadn't told them about the baby. Yet it couldn't be hidden for much longer. She was beginning to show and this troubled Bette deeply.

What if Chad refused to marry her in the end, then what would she do, where could she go? She'd be alone in a foreign land with no money and a child to keep. It didn't bear thinking of.

Once, in those early weeks, she'd tried tackling the subject head on. 'Your mom seems awfully protective, maybe a bit reluctant to let go.'

'We're a very close family.'

'Mine were glad to see the back of me, I should think.' Bette had laughed, trying to make light of it. 'But we should have our own place. I don't honestly think it will work, us all living here together. You mother is – lovely, but she has enough with your brother and sister and her family, without us as well.'

Chad frowned, which didn't exactly fill her with confidence. 'Trouble is, there ain't that many empty houses round these parts. Haven't you heard of the housing shortage? Goes right back to the lean twenties.'

Bette began to feel distinctly uneasy. 'But with all this land you own, couldn't we build a house on it somewhere?'

'Building a house takes a whole heap of money. You'll jest have to be patient awhile. Besides, I can't work, let alone build us a house with one arm, now can I?'

And once again Bette was left feeling she'd said the wrong thing.

Chad resisted every effort she made to help him, whether it was fastening the buttons of his shirt, tying his shoe laces, or cutting up his meat. Peggy was allowed to help, but not Bette, for some reason.

And still he'd made no effort to touch her.

'You are glad I came, aren't you?' she asked him one night as he again refused her assistance in undressing for bed.

'Course I am.'

'I was wondering . . . I mean . . . isn't it time we fixed a date for the wedding?' She put out a hand and stroked the stub of his arm, feeling him instantly flinch away from her. 'You'd perhaps feel more comfortable with me then, if we were man and wife, and we do need to think of the baby.'

His response was uncharacteristically sharp. 'I've already told you, we can't get married yet awhile.'

'You haven't told her yet, have you?'

Bette was surprised to see his neck and jaw suffuse with crimson. 'I'll tell her when the time seems right.'

Bette could hardly believe what she was hearing. 'When the time is right, and when will that be? You're saying that I've left my home, my family and friends, to travel thousands of miles to marry you and you can't bring yourself to tell your family that I'm carrying your child?' A shard of ice stabbed between her shoulder blades and she turned away from him. 'You don't mean to marry me at all, do you, Chad Jackson? Is this all some sort of cruel joke? Have you realised that you've made a bad mistake in asking me to come here?'

'No, no, I want you to stay, Bette. 'S'matter of fact, I'm

surprised that you came. I reckoned mebbe you'd stay with Barney.'

'Why would I do that?' Bette could hear the slow beat of her heart. Had he guessed? Surely he didn't suspect the truth?

'Barney allus was sweet on you. Told me time and again how you was too fancy for a country-boy like me.'

'That's silly. I'm just a small-town girl myself, a two-bit hairdresser.' She tried to make a joke of it but Chad wasn't laughing. He was lying on his back staring at the ceiling.

'He took you out some, I expect. Dancing and suchlike.'

Bette steadied her breathing, desperate to sound casual. 'We went to the Armoury from time to time, just as friends you understand.' She could tell that he'd turned his head to look at her, and was grateful for the semi-darkness yet felt it necessary to defend him. 'He was the perfect Southern gent. You'd have been proud of him.' She felt, rather than heard, his sigh of relief.

'He wrote me to say he wouldn't be returning to North Carolina. He'd be going some place else when the war was over an'all. I reckon he doesn't fancy the idea of seeing you dangling on my arm, 'stead of his. Though since I've only the one, I ain't such a good bet as a husband no more. Must sicken you to the stomach jest to have to lie beside me in this big ol' bed.'

He wasn't looking at her as he said all of this but Bette would have been a fool not to recognise the heartrending vulnerability in these words.

She pulled him round to face her, grasped his face between her two hands. 'Look at me, Chad Jackson. You're my man, right? I've travelled half round the world to be with you. Maybe we both feel a bit insecure, me having left my home and family, you with your injuries, but don't for one minute imagine that you aren't important to me, arm or no arm.'

'Barney is generally the one who gets the girl.'

'Well, he didn't this time. So when are you going to make an honest woman of me?'

Now his sigh was heavily regretful. 'She can be real ornery, my mom. I would have told her by now, about the baby, only . . . It's jest that she's a Christian, church-going woman. Don't do to offend her none. She done preach that bible at me more times than I care to recall, if I'm honest.'

Bette couldn't help but chuckle, relieved that in the matter of religion at least, they were in total agreement. It had come as quite a shock being obliged to attend church every Sunday in her best frock, hat and gloves, with her face scrubbed all clean and not a touch of pan-stick. 'So what about offending me? Don't you care about my reputation?'

He reached across the chasm of the great bed and stroked her hand, lingering a little before he withdrew it. 'Sure I care, hon. How can you think such a thing? I can hardly wait for us to be wed. Don't you know that I worship the ground you walk on. You and me is gonna be real cosy together. I'll be a good husband to you, Bette, I swear it.'

She wriggled closer, curling up beside him to whisper softly in his ear, not wishing to quarrel but anxious to make her point. 'But you're not, are you, love? You're not my husband at all, not even my lover, but folk don't know that, do they? If people knew that we still weren't married, they'd take me for some sort of tart, living here, sleeping with you and still unwed. If your mother is as bible-loving as you say, how come she puts up with it?'

'Because she thinks you'll up and leave any day.'

Bette was shocked to the core. 'What? Is that what all this is about? You won't name the day because your mom thinks I might leave? Where would I go? I can't even get to town unless someone drives me in the pick-up. I'm stuck here. Trapped.'

'That ain't no way to look at things. You are happy, aren't you, hon?'

He sounded so intense and worried that Bette took pity on him, as she always did, put her arms around his too-thin shoulders and hugged him tight. 'Of course I am, at least, I'm sure I could be. Big and empty as this country is, I think I might get to quite like America. I might even come to like your sassy, difficult family, if they'll let me. Come on, let's snuggle up so's I can kiss you. It's long past time we were lovers again, as we once used to be, don't you think?'

'Aw, hon, I'm not sure I can, not yet.'

'We could try. Nothing ventured, nothing gained, isn't that what they say?' She wanted to show him that she cared, that he was truly important to her.

Bette began to kiss him, to stroke the rough brown hair, smooth a hand over his broad shoulders and down his chest, feeling the tension in him as her fingers grazed his skin, a quiver of longing run through him. She didn't touch the stub, the place where the strong muscles ended leaving the flap of empty flesh which for some reason shamed him.

He began to relax a little, to respond to her kisses, even cupped her breast in a sweet caress but then took his hand away, slid it awkwardly around her waist and then on her thigh, as if not quite knowing how to hold her and love her at the same time.

Bette longed to love him in her heart, truly and deeply as she once had, not just go through the physical motions, but her mind was filled with Barney. Even though he'd rejected her in the end, it was Barney's kisses she longed for, his hands she wanted to caress her. Chad was holding back, she could sense it. Was he too waiting for that thrill which had once pulsated between them like an electric storm. Where had all that emotion gone? Had the war destroyed that too? And then suddenly, without warning, he turned abruptly away, to lie with his back to her.

'It ain't gonna work, not tonight. I'm too tired and we don't want to hurt the baby none. We'll leave it for now, till we're wed, or the baby's born.'

Bette blinked back a blur of tears. She knew it was her fault. She'd been thinking too much of Barney and he'd sensed her lack of interest. How difficult it was to put the past behind her, to love two men after all.

At length, when she was more in control of her emotions, she snuggled closer and whispered to his unyielding back. 'Would you like me to tell Peggy about the baby? I don't mind. She has to be told some time, then we can get on with planning the wedding. I'll choose the right moment and be very gentle, I promise. Maybe then things will get better for us. Shall I try?'

She took his silence as assent but was quite certain that neither of them slept much that night.

36

The skies were still filled with bombers but the streets of the town were strangely quiet now that the Yanks had gone; ominously so. People walked about in silence, hardly speaking, their eyes constantly glancing out to sea as if willing the armada to appear on the horizon, to come home safe.

Sara felt empty and alone and Hugh had scarcely spoken a word to her since they'd left. The subject of her betrayal had, apparently, been swept under the carpet and the illusion that they were a devoted couple continued as before.

The thought of Charlie waiting for her in vain at St Catherine's Castle, as she guessed he would have been, filled her with anguish. Did he think that she'd abandoned him in his hour of need? Perhaps he went off to war believing that she no longer loved him. Oh, she did hope not. That was far too terrible a prospect to contemplate. Surely he would realise that she'd tried but that something had occurred to prevent her.

Underneath this awesome silence, there was an air of anticipation, a bubble of excitement, the whole town waiting for news, glued to the wireless, listening for John Snagge's voice to give them some hint of what was happening on the front line.

Confirmation came at nine-thirty on the morning of the sixth when the familiar voice announced that D-Day had come. 'Early this morning the Allies began the assault on the north-western face of Hitler's European fortress.'

The town seemed to erupt in jubilant cheers. People threw

impromptu parties in the street, danced and kissed and hugged perfect strangers who passed by.

Even Nora Snell popped into The Ship for a port and lemon to drink a toast to Montgomery. Sadie brought round a game pie that she'd made specially, and family and friends ate together that night to celebrate, Cory declaring he was itching to be out there on the sea with them, that he'd knock the spots off those blooming Germans if he got the chance.

Later they all listened to the king together as he told them that 'After nearly five years of toil and suffering we must renew that crusading impulse on which we entered the war and met its darkest hours.' He exhorted them all to pray as the great crusade got underway, and they did, Sara amongst them. There was little else left for them to do now.

More than 11,000 aircraft, 4,000 ships and nearly 200,000 men were out there fighting the last battle. If they didn't win this one, the war would indeed be over and they would be the losers.

News spread around Fowey's streets like wildfire over the next few days: that France had been liberated, that General de Gaulle was encouraging his compatriots to fight on and win, that the Americans were fighting tough opposition on the road to Cherbourg, hampered by floods.

Then, just as news filtered through that enemy E-boats sheltering in Le Havre had been attacked by Bomber Command, Hamil Charke came dashing into the pub one evening to announce that his cousin in London, together with his entire family, had been killed by a new sort of flying bomb, called a V1.

'It's raining with the damn things all over London.' This terrible news silenced everyone. The war wasn't over yet.

Iris was growing increasingly uneasy and hastily reminded Hugh on the vital importance of keeping his mouth shut about their clandestine activities, speaking in whispers under her breath as she smiled at the customers and pulled pints. 'I've checked with the SOE and there might be the odd mission left to do, bringing agents out, I should think. After that we're on our own, and your silence is still a requirement, understood? The French Resistance are working harder than ever against the occupying forces, while our collaborators are fleeing for their lives, so that side of our work is over and done with, unfortunately.'

Hugh became very still. 'Are you saying that we too are in danger?'

'Not if we keep our mouths shut!'

'It's your fault that I'm in this situation. You were the one who got me involved in this.'

'You got yourself involved when you left those men to die,' she snapped at him. 'I did what I had to do, for my husband, for what I believe in. What's your excuse?'

Hugh had no answer. He'd never really thought the matter through to its logical conclusion. His one object had always been to survive, to save his own skin. He quickly changed the subject, casting about for someone else to blame, as was his wont. 'What about the money you promised me? I've not seen a penny of that yet.'

Iris frowned, clearly irritated. 'We can talk about that later,' and chose this moment to tell Hugh that once their last mission had been accomplished, she'd be leaving, going to live with her mother in Truro. 'Better if we're not seen to communicate in future. You can have Sara back behind the bar now the Yanks have gone for good, can't you? It's nearly over.'

Hugh felt a surge of disappointment, suffering a sense almost of anti-climax. Despite the danger and the terrors he'd had to endure, there'd been some exciting, thrilling times that he'd thoroughly enjoyed, particularly with Iris. At least until she'd put a stop to their fun and games.

He smoothed a hand over her backside and gave it a little squeeze as she stood sipping a celebratory sherry. 'We've had some fun, you and me. Couldn't we have one more, for the road?'

She smiled up at him then, that lazy, seductive smile that always turned him on. 'I'll think about it.'

Watching them from where she sat with her mother and Cory, Sara felt her heart sink. Some things wouldn't be solved by the end of the war. Some problems had no solution.

What would she do when it was all over? Would Hugh allow her to take the children with her if she left him? Sara rather thought not. She was tied to him as firmly as ever.

And where was Charlie? What was happening to the boys on the ships? If only she could be certain that he was safe, that would be some consolation at least.

Charlie, along with his comrades was enduring the unendurable. The noise was deafening as the bombardment continued, the roar of guns, tanks and ships' engines; the screams of the dying in some macabre contest of sound, each trying to outdo the other. The dead floated in a churning mass of green, stinking water, quickly turning red with their blood, the living sheltering amongst them as they struggled to reach shore. Soldiers still waiting to disembark from their landing craft checked and re-checked their weapons, touched their rosaries, kissed pictures of their girl friends and thought of their mothers.

Barney too, sat patiently waiting beside his buddies, oblivious of the water washing around his knees until they heard a cry ring out.

'We're sinking, we're sinking. Start bailing. Unload.'

They were too far from shore to wade in, and too loaded down with equipment to swim far. Barney took off his helmet and began to bail. In desperation they tossed overboard all unnecessary equipment, entrenching tools, gas masks, and with it, by accident, went Barney's lucky charm and his picture of Bette which he'd fixed to his first-aid box for safe-keeping. He watched in misery as it sank, although this indulgence lasted only a matter of seconds before his buddy was pushing him over the side too.

'We're done for. Start swimming!'

They floundered in the water, sitting ducks under a blistering fuselage, some men sinking instantly under the weight of equipment, others screaming for help, praying they'd be spotted by rescue craft. The lucky ones were quickly picked up but when the rescue boat was full, the rest were resolutely left behind. 'We'll come back for you, if we can.'

Barney and his buddy were two of the unlucky ones and he didn't hold out much hope of rescue. Only a blind fool would willingly venture into these seas a second or third time.

Minutes after the boat had gone, he watched in horror as his buddy slipped down below the waves, his last words, 'Help me, Barney, I'm drowning. Help me for God's sake!'

Knowing he hadn't a hope in hell of saving him, not weighted down with equipment as they both were, Barney was in despair. He managed to catch hold of a piece of flotsam and swim over to a twisted piece of wreckage, or perhaps it was some obstacle placed there by the enemy. He didn't greatly care but hung on and took cover behind it, desperately trying to keep out of sight. It was the hardest thing he'd ever done but, as he saw it, it was every man for himself in this war.

Charlie was about to disembark, the ramp was let down and his captain and comrades instantly swarmed into four or five feet of water, wading through heavy surf with weapons held high, strafed by machine-gun fire with many men mowed down before ever they'd had a chance to retaliate. Death could come in seconds for some, while others reached shore easily and crossed the beach with a sense of spurious safety.

'Keep moving! Keep moving!' Charlie roared. 'Don't look back.'

Artillery roared, rockets whooshed overhead and mortar shells rained down all along the four miles of Omaha, yet still the German gun fire pummelled the Allies with uncompromising ferocity.

But that didn't stop them. The beach was barely visible, swathed in a haze of fire and smoke. Filthy, cold and miserable, some vomiting from sea sickness and terror, the men slogged bravely on, calling upon every ounce of courage and experience they possessed. Many had crossed beaches before: North Africa, Sicily and Salerno. For them this was just another bloody beach, another bloody battle.

For Charlie, this was his first experience of frontline action, though he resolved to do his utmost, to give his life for freedom if necessary, he could only marvel at the fortitude and courage he saw all around him. Prayed he could emulate their bravery.

'Come out and fight, you bastards!' yelled one young soldier, while another began to sing 'Roll out the Barrel', as they valiantly clung on to their morale. He was sickened to see that poor boy go down, but his mates took up the song and kept on singing, and from some distance away came the wail of bagpipes.

All along the crescent-shaped beach were littered boxes of ammo, gas masks, field telephones and radios, steel helmets and life preservers. As he turned to check that his captain was beside him, Charles saw him fall backwards into the water, a look of complete surprise on his face. He might have gone back to try and save him but the next two LCTs to come ramming through the surf took direct hits, bursting into flame, instantly killing everyone on board.

'Lucky buggers,' said one marine, slowly being swamped by the incoming tide, unable to escape because half his leg had been blown off and no medics were around to come to his rescue.

Witnessing all of this horror, seeing their captain fall, some of the men lay frozen in a state of paralysis. They'd lost all their equipment and were huddled together, too terrified to move either forward or back, the stink of gasoline and burning flesh strong in their nostrils, paralysing their limbs as explosions went off all around them, set off by snipers firing at mines. Lieutenant Charles Denham didn't hesitate, he simply took charge, yelling at them to move, move! Jolting them out of their shock.

'Head for the sea wall. We can't stay here. Run! Run! Run! And when you get there, put up the flag so our own troops won't shell us.'

'You mean *if* we get there, sir, don't you?'

'We've no time for jokes, soldier. Get the hell out of here!' By this time Charlie too was running as fast as he could up the beach, swerving from side to side, yelling at his men to follow. And they did.

'OK, let's get the son-of-a-bitch,' they roared, anger now taking the place of fear.

He reached the wall and fell on his belly, then something smacked him in the back of the leg and Charlie looked up to see three Germans half hidden in their gun nest, their grinning faces peeping at him over the dune. Before he had time to lift his tommy-gun, his jokey comrade had shot them all dead.

It was small comfort, for Charles knew he'd been injured. Worryingly, he couldn't feel a thing, though guessed he was bleeding badly. If he was lucky, he'd catch sight of a medic but, injured or no, he had to fight on, for as long as life remained in his body. If only because he had a damned good reason for wanting to survive.

Hugh and Iris were heading out to sea too, on their last and final mission. Members of the Secret Intelligence Service had reconnoitred the situation at Juno Beach, preparing the way for bringing returning agents home. Hugh's boat had joined up with the rest of the group off the Isle of Wight and received their orders: to liaise with the motor gun boats who were also engaged in the task. Fishing boats too were involved in the manoeuvre, some of them taking out fresh supplies of munitions for the Allied forces. Unfortunately the weather was not good. Gales were blowing up fast and looking to settle in for days.

Men were still being taken ashore by the thousand as the invasion continued, and the terrible weather could well have led to disaster on the beaches were it not for the Mulberry harbours, some of them the size of a five-storey building, and the artificial breakwaters known as 'Gooseberries'.

Hugh was simply thankful he didn't have to go that far and anchored well off-shore, as instructed. He was well equipped with flares and life-jackets, and as usual Iris had stowed the radio on board, just in case someone needed to contact her. Now all that was expected of them was to wait for the signal.

He was well accustomed to the routine by this time but was concerned about the weather. Waves were smashing against the side of his boat, threatening to snap it in two, washing over the decks and the pair of them were soon soaked through, despite the waterproofs they wore. Hugh could hardly see a hand in front of his face for the sweeping rain, let alone a red flare on shore, and he swore that he'd wait only until the storm abated, 'and then I'm going home for the last time, with or without the dratted agents.'

'Have patience and for once in your life, Hugh Marrack, give some thought to others, to those poor lads who want to get home too after the hazardous lives they've led.'

'Why the hell should you care?'

Iris shrugged. 'I have feelings. I'm not inhuman, like you.'

'When we do get back, you can pay me what you owe me for

all the risks I've taken. Meanwhile, we'll have that farewell romp you promised me, just for old times' sake, eh?'

'I promised you nothing.'

'You bloody did. In your eyes, in the way you tease me by flaunting that luscious body of yours.' He reached for her, grabbing her by the wrist and pinning her down in the bottom of the boat while he shoved his hands under her windcheater and all over her breasts.

She struggled to fight him off as the boat rocked and bucked on the rough seas. 'For God's sake, Hugh, this isn't the moment for any of that. Let go of me. Stop it!' She slapped his hands away, giving him a hefty shove to release herself from his grip. He might well have proceeded regardless, despite her refusal, as his blood was up and the lust hot in him, but something she said next halted him, her words ringing out above the noise of the storm.

'Anyway, there isn't any bloody money! I said that just to keep you sweet. Why would the Germans pay me when I'll work for them willingly, for my Klaus? You only did it to save your own skin, because you're a coward.'

'No money?' Fury rose into his throat like bile as he thought of the risks he'd taken, the dangers he'd been exposed to. 'You mean I've done all this for bloody nothing? You'd never any intention of paying me?'

'Not a cent. Not a dime, as the Yanks would say. Not even any more how's yer father.' Iris laughed as she got to her feet, catching hold of the side of the boat to steady herself, shouting to him over the sound of the crashing waves. 'I'd never any intention of paying you a penny.

'You did all of this so that the Americans wouldn't string you up for leaving their men to drown, or to stop the British from putting you before a firing squad for being the traitor you undoubtedly are. You're no better than me, Hugh Marrack, so don't pretend otherwise. You're not the town hero everybody imagines you to be. You're a bastard of the first order. I know that, and so will they if you don't shut up and be thankful that at least you're still alive to relish this dratted storm.'

He hit her. His hand came out and he slapped her full across the face, sending her sprawling across the deck, as he had done once before. This time as she started to scream, he did what he should have done then. He picked her up and tossed her backwards into the broiling seas. 'You relish it,' he roared. 'See how you like it?' Then he calmly shipped anchor and turned for home.

37

Had it not been for Chad's sweetness and good nature, Bette might well have left, just as they all expected her to. There was no further talk of her getting a job, not that she could have done it for long in any case, with the baby coming. And with no offer of a lift into Carreville, few trips anywhere in fact, except to the Episcopal church every Sunday, rain or shine, there was little hope of one in the future either. She'd be stuck at home baby-minding, and Bette wasn't sure how she felt about that.

Peggy had soon made it clear to her, that she was expected to concentrate on homemaking. 'You have to learn the American way,' she would say whenever Bette attempted to protest over some skill or other she was being forced to learn. Peggy even attempted to teach her how to make grits, which Bette loathed.

'You take coarse stone ground grits, chicken paste, a pat of butter and mix it all together with half water, half milk and stir it on the stove till it's cooked. Takes a while. Do it the night before, then you can finish it off in the morning.'

Bette did her best but her own efforts were solid and quite uneatable. 'I suppose these are like oats. In England we make porridge a bit like this, only without the chicken paste stuff,' she added, wrinkling her nose, 'and serve it with sugar or golden treacle, if we can get it.'

'This ain't England,' commented Peggy, predictably.

Strangely, once through those first difficult few days, more and more food began to appear on the table, mounds of freshly cooked vegetables, home-baked chicken pie, huge steaks and other good things. Far more than anyone could eat and much of it wasted. It was as if Peggy had deliberately starved her in order to make a point: that the family wasn't wealthy.

As she'd told Bette on that very first night, '*If you thought you'd hooked yourself a fine GI with a pocketful of dollars, I hope you've realised different now, girl.*'

But now she seemed to want to show off her culinary skills, presumably out of a sense of pride. An abundance of food on the table was meant to indicate that the farm was doing well, and Bette was expected to be suitably impressed, and grateful.

In truth, quite the opposite was the case. Bette found it hard to reconcile herself to this casual attitude towards food when she thought of her own family back in England. She would watch in dismay as mounds of vegetables, huge portions of steak, even fruit, which had been so precious in England, were thrown away or given to the animals. More food was wasted in the Jackson household than the Tredinnicks were allowed in rations for an entire week. Bette knew better than to make any comment, however. It would only be taken the wrong way.

Peggy was a difficult, perverse woman who snatched any opportunity to show American superiority to the British. Even now, despite her best efforts, Bette was no closer to her future mother-in-law than on first acquaintance.

And she still hadn't managed to talk to her about the coming baby.

If ever she should try to start a conversation, Peggy would protest that she was too busy to stand about 'jawing', or scold her for wasting time and not concentrating on the task in hand. Or she would simply pretend that she didn't understand her accent.

'I can't think what she's trying to say, Chad, you talk to her.'

Chad would simply grin and agree that they'd rid her of

'that darned English accent' in no time. For that reason alone, if no other, Bette clung on to her Englishness more fiercely than ever.

One never to be forgotten morning as Bette was pounding shirts in the tub and wondering why on earth the Jackson family didn't invest in a proper wash boiler, quite out of the blue, Peggy said, 'Weren't you sweet on Barney Willert once over?'

Bette felt as if she'd been slapped in the face, but somehow managed to keep her composure as she scrubbed at the stubborn dirt on the collars, hoping the flushed cheeks would be put down to exertion and steam from the tub.

'Whatever gave you that idea? Barney was a good friend and Chad's best buddy, a great support to me after we heard he was missing. Everyone needs a friend at such a time, wouldn't you say? I'm sure you found your family a tower of strength.'

As Bette glanced up, needing to judge the effect of her words, Peggy picked up the laundry basket and left the room.

There were other family tensions to contend with. Apart from Jake who clearly adored her and followed her about everywhere like a pet lamb, always anxious to help her carry the logs, or the washing basket, there were times when Bette felt as if she'd fallen into a nightmare.

Mary-Lou became increasingly peevish and jealous, taking every opportunity to make some snide remark or humiliate her by pointing out her failures and inadequacies. Harry, Mary-Lou's husband, rarely spoke at all, although he would watch her walk by with the kind of gaze that made Bette's skin crawl.

Pop Jackson, when he wasn't out working the land, drank a good deal, mainly some stuff he brewed himself in one of the barns. He was sarcastic to both his sons, who were expected to work alongside himself and Harry, most of all he was hard on Chad who he continually yelled at, calling him 'boy' and telling him he always had been useless and now with only

one arm, he might as well stay home and learn to do women's
chores.

It broke Bette's heart to see Chad shrink in upon himself,
like a whipped dog.

All in all, it was perfectly clear to Bette that, try as she might,
she never could think of North Carolina as home, and she
really had nothing at all in common with these people.

Bette's one trip out each week was every Wednesday afternoon when she attended a sewing bee, held generally at a
neighbour's house some miles away. Harry would take them in
the pick-up, one week accompanied by Peggy, the next Mary-
Lou, while the other stayed home to mind the children. Bette
was not so foolish as to offer to take a turn at this task. The
three girls seemed, in her opinion, to be wild, disobedient
creatures, heedless of discipline or parental control, only ever
being quiet when Peggy set them some bible verses to learn or
write out.

They didn't even seem to attend school, Peggy insisting
there would be time enough for that later when the eldest
turned seven. Bette had offered to learn to drive, so that she
could perhaps borrow the pick-up and drive the children to
school in town each day. This helpful suggestion had been
greeted with complete silence.

So for now, she depended for her social entertainment upon
the sewing bee. If there was one thing Bette hated, it was
sewing, but she dutifully went along, at first in the hope of
perhaps making herself a new dress, regretting now all the
lovely clothes she'd scorned to bring with her.

But no, the ladies' main task was quilting, which was
inestimably dull, sewing endless scraps into squares and
triangles.

Bette endured it because she must, and because she was
desperate to find the right moment to speak to Peggy, hoping

that one of these trips might offer her the opportunity to do so. Unfortunately, and despite the cosiness of the sewing circle and the undoubted friendliness of the other ladies, which was welcome, things never quite worked out that way.

On the drive there and back, Peggy would studiously ignore her while she talked to Harry, or she would sit in tight-lipped silence, often with her eyes closed, which none of them dare broach. At the meeting itself, she always sat with her friends, across the room from Bette.

The youngest of the group of rather elderly ladies was called Esther, who made a point of trying to be helpful. She would sit beside Bette and talk quietly to her under cover of their sewing, gently asking if she was settling in, offer some quiet advice, perhaps on the climate, or how to grow or use certain vegetables.

Esther once asked when she and Chad had got married and Bette muttered something about back in rainy old England, surprised, and really rather relieved that she believed they already were.

Bette let fall a few hints over how she worried about Chad a good deal. 'He was very badly injured and isn't coping too well working the land. I don't think he ever really enjoyed it and was glad to escape to join the marines. But he can't seem to find any alternative now, because of his arm.'

'I'm sure he'll think of something. He's a resourceful young man, arm or no arm. And you're a fine young woman. I hope you'll both be very happy together.'

'His family don't seem to understand his frustration, his loneliness. And his father is pretty tough on him.'

'That's the mark of the Jacksons,' said Esther. 'Comes with the territory.'

Bette felt she'd found a friend, longed to open up and share more problems with her. She wanted to talk about how isolated she felt stuck up here on the mountain, her need to work, to have a place of their own, and about how cold his mother was to her but was far too aware of Peggy seated opposite, and her condemning, all-seeing gaze.

But Esther seemed to instinctively understand these concerns and tactfully asked how things were up at the farm, if she was getting along with her in-laws. 'It isn't always easy, don't I know it. I lived with my Henry's family for near two years before we escaped to our own place. Be firm, child. Put your foot down and make Chad build you a cabin, if nothing else. And I hope you're putting your feet up and getting plenty of rest, you're far too thin and quiet. What you need is to get out and about more, meet girls your own age.'

'Where would I find any?' Bette almost laughed out loud, thinking what Sadie would say to hear her younger daughter accused of being *too quiet*!

'Well, you could join the war-brides club for a start. Wouldn't that be a fine thing to share problems with your compatriots? You all got the same troubles, after all. Homesick for your own families and good old Blighty?' Esther's kind face creased into a smile.

Bette gazed at her in astonishment. 'Are you saying that I'm not the only one? That there are others like me? More war-brides living around here?'

'Of course, dear, and many, like yourself, are pregnant. When is your baby due?'

For some unaccountable reason, that was the moment when all the other ladies in the group chose to stop talking, and not one amongst them, Peggy included, missed hearing the remark. Esther's words rang out clear as a bell and, realising this, she flushed deep crimson.

It was the moment that was to change Bette's life. Realising there was no way she could deny it, and that she'd tried and failed in every previous attempt to talk to Peggy, Bette simply laughed.

'Well, our little secret is out. Yes, Chad and I are expecting a baby in the autumn, sorry, the fall. And I must say, we're thrilled to pieces.'

As one, the ladies burst forth in a chorus of congratulations, oohs and ahs, gasps and sighs, all begging for details and wanting to know whether she hoped for a boy or girl, and if they'd chosen a name yet.

Bette laughingly did her best to answer all their questions, while looking straight into Peggy's eyes, challenging her to deny her this moment of triumph.

38

Later, when the cost was counted, an estimated 2,500 men were declared killed, wounded or missing on Omaha Beach alone, not counting Utah and Gold, and the rest. Among them was Sid and Ethel Penhale's son, John. And Dan Roskelly, who'd really wanted to stay on at the docks but had reluctantly answered his call-up, was blown up at sea and there wasn't even anything of him left for his family to bury.

Even so, despite the pain and human suffering, even in the midst of it all, people were proud to have a son or husband 'out there', the invasion greeted with a mix of relief and pride, even a feeling of jubilation, which helped to offset the underlying fears and anxiety.

In August came the V2s, which caused even greater havoc, but the Germans failed to halt the Allied advance though the battle continued to rage. The communist wing of the French Resistance paralysed the capital, posters appearing everywhere, calling their citizens to arms against the Nazis. Even the Paris police joined in the strike.

'Rommel has abandoned his men and gone on the run, and Churchill has visited France,' Sid Penhale announced, having got this snippet of information from a reliable source among his mates in the fire service, 'which must mean the end is in sight.' No one was entirely convinced. The end seemed to be taking an unconscionably long time to arrive.

It seemed as if each and every day, a ship arrived in Fowey, some damaged and needing repair, others with wounded on board. The cottage hospital was full to bursting, as was the Navy Hospital, Carnethick House and the beds requisitioned at Fowey Hotel. The ships themselves were so filthy and stinking that hundreds of soiled mattresses were loaded into railway wagons and taken away for burning.

Sara watched the unloading of every one, dreading seeing Charlie, always breathing a sigh of heartfelt relief when he wasn't on board. But what if he'd been brought in during the night, and she'd missed him?

Unable to just sit back and do nothing, she volunteered her services.

'I've no nursing experience,' she told them up at the hospital. 'I've been helping the WVS but I can wash bed pans, make beds, serve tea, whatever you need an extra pair of hands for.'

They'd handed her an overall and she'd started that very day, spending the next several weeks working harder than ever. But then keeping busy helped her to cope.

The walking wounded, and survivors from ships lost, were located up at Windmill to recover. Movies and dances were arranged to entertain them, ATS girls brought in as dancing partners. This made Sara think of Bette, as she did a hundred times a day. How she missed her sister. She would have given anything to have her here with her now, helping her through all of this.

She did what she could to help here too, organising whist drives, parties and picnics, finding books for the men to read, writing or posting letters to their sweethearts and mothers, and then enduring the heartbreaking task of seeing them off again when they were returned to duty.

And always, as a new batch of survivors arrived, she would anxiously scan each and every one, seeking one familiar face.

★   ★   ★

By September, Montgomery was promoted to field marshal, which surprised no one and there was talk that the Home Guard would soon be stood down.

'If that includes the river patrol, then that'll be good for my rheumatics,' Cory admitted. 'Although I'll have no excuse to escape the missus then, will I?'

'There's always the fishing,' Hamil reminded him. 'We all do know how good you are at catching fish.'

'That's true, m'boy. Very true.'

Summer was fading into autumn and Hugh and Sara had moved into their new home, all their furniture and possessions transported along the Esplanade in Scobey Snell's old van, boxes unpacked and beds made up, even a swing put up in the garden for the children. Cory had helped her to dig over the vegetable patch, plant some leeks and potatoes, still industriously digging for victory.

The house on the Esplanade was lovely, there was no doubt about that, even though a fresh coat of paint was needed here and there to brighten the place up, and perhaps the odd new piece of furniture once such things became generally available again. Although every time she thought about the end of the war, her mind went into a sort of paralysis. Everything depended on whether Charlie came home safe.

Fortunately, Hugh didn't trouble her much in bed these days, his mood of aggression passing as swiftly and mysteriously as it had come, for which she was grateful. Perhaps he was tired from working hard at the pub. Iris had left weeks ago, some time in late June. Hugh said she'd gone back to her mother's in Truro which Sara didn't question.

'I shall need you back in the bar,' he'd informed her at the time, rather like an imperious summons. Sara had declined.

She'd always known that she would miss living at The Ship, the hustle and bustle of locals coming and going, the chatter and the gossip around the fire of an evening, being at the centre of things, sharing with these people she loved their celebrations and joys, their fears and their grief. But she'd filled her life with other things now and was as content as she could be, in the circumstances.

'I'm so sorry, Hugh, but I'm much too busy to spare you the time. I'm needed at the hospital every day, which is far more important work, as I'm sure you'll agree. You and Sid can surely cope on your own, now that all the servicemen have gone.'

'It isn't my job to spend every waking moment behind the bar. There are other tasks to be done, the accounts and so on. And who will change the beds for guests if you aren't there?'

'I'm afraid you'll have to manage that yourself, too. It isn't difficult. You can send the sheets to the laundry. You insisted on moving us into this new house after all, which has a created a great deal more work for me, and I do still make the pasties. Quite enough to do in addition to my hospital work and working with the WVS up at Windmill. And of course I cook delicious meals for you and the children, and dig the garden. I try very hard to be a proper wife and mother. Isn't that what you wanted?' Sara gave a sweet little smile.

He hadn't liked it, not one little bit, but nor had he been able to think of any way to force her to do his bidding, not on this occasion. A small triumph perhaps, but sweet.

Consequently, he sank into one of his gloomy, black moods, rarely speaking to her, let alone touching her.

The very fact that their lack of intimacy brought Sara nothing but relief seemed to indicate that their life could never return to normal. She still hadn't heard from Charles, had no idea whether he was alive or dead, so for now she had no alternative but to go on with the charade of being a happily married woman, if only for the sake of her children. Above everything, they were the most important factor in her life.

She would go along with this difficult situation for now, because in her heart Sara knew that it couldn't last for ever.

Doodlebugs might still be doing their worst in London but there was a cautious optimism in the air. Folk were wary of tempting fate and yet quite certain that success was only weeks away.

And then one evening Sid Penhale dashed into the pub to say that our boys had reached the Rhine and a cheer went up loud enough to raise the roof, with fresh drinks called all round. Victory in Europe was in sight.

When the letter, postmarked Truro, arrived with the afternoon post, Hugh knew at once that it came from Iris's mother. Not troubling to read it, he tore it into small scraps and threw it away in the waste-paper basket, then emptied the basket into the dustbin, just to be on the safe side. He'd told all the regulars that she'd gone home and no one else had troubled to enquire about Iris's whereabouts, not even the SOE, who were presumably winding up operations and no longer interested.

But he hadn't considered the mother. Half an hour later he regretted the action. Perhaps he should have read it after all, so that at least he knew what Mrs Logan was doing about her missing daughter. He could have written back to the woman, made some excuse, told her that Iris had changed her mind and had, in fact, decided to go to Germany and find her husband. He could still do that, just to make sure she didn't start asking awkward questions, except that he didn't have Mrs Logan's address.

Come to think of it, he didn't even know if Logan was Iris's genuine maiden name, or simply one she'd made up. After all, most people in Fowey didn't even know that she was married. Drat! Hugh went back outside and began to root through the dustbin, searching for the pieces so that he could put them back together again and find it. It wouldn't do to make a careless mistake, not at this stage.

'What on earth are you doing?'

He looked up, startled, to face his wife's amused frown. Hugh could think of no excuse, no explanation for digging in the dustbin.

'Have you lost something?'

'No, er, yes. It doesn't matter. It's not important. I thought you were on your way to The Ship to deliver the pasties. Oh, and Sara, I noticed you'd forgotten to clean out the beer pumps yesterday.'

'No, I hadn't forgotten. I've decided that I haven't time for that job any more, either. In any case, you never were satisfied with my efforts so you're much better off doing it yourself in future. Once I've delivered the pasties, I shall be occupied all afternoon, helping out at the hospital.'

Hugh grunted. 'Why the hell you've got yourself involved with all of that, I really cannot imagine. How am I supposed to manage on my own at the pub, with you up there all the damned time?'

Sara sighed. She should have known that he wouldn't simply let the matter drop. 'You aren't on your own. You have Sid.'

'That's not quite the same.' He marched into the kitchen to wash his hands. 'It really is too much. You're getting very full of yourself, Sara, always dashing about here, there and every-where. You never seem to be in this lovely house for more than five minutes. Where was the point in my buying it for you. It's really quite infuriating.'

'I didn't ask you to buy it for me, you bought it for yourself. But it's true that I am very busy.' She smiled, taking his criticism as a compliment.

Hugh tossed the used towel on to the floor and glowered at her, 'I don't remember your asking me if I minded you working at the hospital?'

Sara stared at the crumpled towel, considered picking it up but then changed her mind and turned to make herself a sandwich instead. She hadn't even had time for breakfast this morning as she'd dashed straight up to the base at Windmill after taking the children to school, and she was hungry.

'That's because I didn't ask you. I didn't see any reason to. Ham sandwich do you for lunch?'

'No reason? Have you quite lost your mind? I'm your husband, and no, I will not have a ham sandwich. I'll have a cooked lunch, as usual, if you don't mind.'

'Ah, but I do mind. I don't have time to cook, not right now. I've promised to take some library books round the wards. Those poor boys get so bored, and no doubt Sister will have other jobs lined up for me. In any case, you're my husband, not my keeper, so I really don't have to ask your permission, do I? I can do whatever I please. It's time I grew up and made some decisions of my own, don't you think? That's perhaps what I've learned most from this war, that there are all kinds of things I can do. And it's really a rather wonderful feeling.'

Hugh was staring at her as if she'd gone mad, as if the world had turned on its axis and was going in the wrong direction. His whole life seemed to be falling apart, first Iris, and now Sara. He grasped her by the wrist and gave her a little shake. It was clearly time he knocked some sense into her. 'Stuff and nonsense. You are my *wife*, and you will do as I say!'

Sara had the temerity to laugh as she wrenched her hand free. 'Dear me, how very cross you sound, like a bad-tempered school teacher with a wayward pupil. Is that how you've always seen me, Hugh, as a child to scold and punish if I don't do as I'm told?'

'I see you as an obedient, loving wife.'

Following the débâcle of her illicit weekend away, it had given him enormous satisfaction to watch his chastened wife feed and nurture her children, because those very same children were his greatest weapon in keeping her. Sara would never risk losing them, no matter how much she might yearn for independence or want to indulge her romantic dreams. Her greatest charm, also perhaps her greatest weakness in a way, had been her quiet compliance, her readiness to do whatever he asked. But since that fateful weekend something had changed in her. His control over her seemed to be slipping away.

Even now she was tilting up her chin in a most defiant manner.

'Let me tell you that I am not a child, that I'm a woman with needs you've largely ignored. All right, so I'm your wife, and because of my darling children I will agree to stay married to you, for the time being at least, but things have changed between us, you know they have. I'll tolerate no more bullying, Hugh. I will not allow you to lock me in my room like some recalcitrant adolescent, or take your pleasure of me whether I wish you to or not. In fact, since we are now living in such a large house and have all this lovely space, I think it would be best if you moved into the guest room at the back. Yes, I think that would be an excellent idea, don't you?'

'What the hell are you suggesting?'

'That we can maintain the fiction of a happy marriage, for the sake of appearances, without having to endure each other's constant presence. Or would you prefer it if I moved into the spare room? I really don't mind.'

'I thought I'd made my position clear. You'll stay in *my* bed and do as *I* say.'

'No, Hugh, I will not.' And smiling coolly at him, she picked up her sandwich and walked away, leaving him to make his own lunch.

39

The triumph didn't last long. Peggy took her revenge for what she deemed a public humiliation by checking all Bette's papers and quizzing her on her home background, on when she'd met Chad and how she'd managed to get transport to the States. When Bette explained about Barney finding her a billet on a transport ship, she was instantly suspicious.

'That don't sound legal to me.'

'Nobody queried it when we arrived so I shouldn't think anyone is going to bother about that now.' Bette tried to sound unconcerned, but could have kicked herself for this carelessness. She wouldn't put it past the woman to try to have her thrown out of the country.

'And why would Barney help?'

'I've told you, he was a friend.'

Peggy considered her with a shrewd, calculating gaze, lips pressed firmly together. 'You and he must've got mighty cosy around that time.'

More chillingly, on another occasion, Peggy suddenly, and quite casually remarked, 'They do say that a child most resembles its father at the moment of its birth.'

Bette's heart skipped a beat but even as she struggled to find some sort of answer to this weighted comment, Peggy blithely changed the subject and began talking about bottling peaches and stocking up the wood store before winter set in. Bette said that it was still only July so there was plenty of time for such things, but Peggy insisted that winter came early in these parts, and in any case she'd be wanting the house warm for the baby, wouldn't she, and food to eat? 'We all do know how you like your grits.'

Nothing Bette said seemed to be right.

A wedding was hastily arranged the very next week, the parson coming up to the farm specially to conduct the ceremony in peace and quiet. No friends or neighbours were invited, as Peggy insisted that Bette was too far gone in her pregnancy to display herself as an object for folk to gawp at, just as if she'd been the one putting off the wedding all this time.

Chad, while being thankful that he'd been relieved of the task of breaking this difficult news to his mother, apologised to his young bride for the paucity of the ceremony. 'I meant for us to have a fine, grand affair with you in a fancy frock and a big cake an' all.'

'It doesn't matter,' Bette insisted. 'We're married at last, man and wife. That's all I care about.'

Bette wore her one good dress, the green crêpe de Chine and carried a posy of marguerites which Chad picked for her. The entire family took a day off from working the land, drank a good deal and ate mounds of food, laughing and shouting and being generally raucous and loud. Only Bette sat at the table feeling like a stranger at her own wedding.

Never had she missed her own family more than she did at this moment. What she wouldn't give to have Sara act as bridesmaid, Cory to give her away and even Sadie around to tell her how things should be done. She felt so alone without them.

That night, she tried again to persuade her new husband to make love to her, but he patted her shoulder kindly and set her away from him. 'Wait till the baby is born, hon, maybe I'll feel more comfortable then. We don't want no problems.'

Bette turned over, curled up in a ball and by sheer will

power, managed not to cry. What would happen when the baby was born, she dreaded to think. She didn't even know where the nearest hospital was, should anything go wrong. She felt so lonely and afraid, so desperate for affection, for her mam and dad, for Sara, it was a wonder she wasn't howling into her pillow. And how could she ever love this baby, when it had got her into this mess?

Bette went into labour on the thirteenth of October. The pains were shocking but thankfully short-lived and a golden dawn was breaking over the Appalachian Mountains when Jackson Junior slipped quietly into the world, making no fuss and crying on cue when his new grandmother picked him up by the heels and smacked his bottom.

Bette, in a daze of exhaustion and relief, was simply thankful that the birth had been relatively straightforward, and that it was all over.

'Is he all right? Let me see him. I want to hold him.'

Peggy seemed to be examining the child with a scrupulous intensity, holding the squirming infant close to the light while she studied its features. Once she was done, she plonked the child unceremoniously into its mother's arms. 'That ain't no Jackson. That's a Willert, as I live and breathe. You married my son under false pretences, girl, just as I always suspected.'

Bette could hear voices at the other side of the bedroom door: a mix of Chad's, Mary-Lou's and Peggy's, and every now and then the resonant notes of Pop Jackson, but she caught only the odd word. Willert being the one which most rang in her head, hammered in it like a drum beat. In her worst nightmares, she had never imagined such a moment. But no matter how carefully she studied the baby's features, she could see no obvious evidence of Barney in his features.

Admittedly the fuzz of hair on his head was darker than

Chad's, and slightly curly, but then they said a baby's hair rubbed off in the first few weeks and came back a different colour, so how could she be certain? His eyes were dark, neither grey nor brown, which surely proved nothing. They too might change. Barney's eyes had been clear grey with a rim of violet around the iris, nothing like this child's, and Chad's were a deep, warm brown. What could Peggy possibly have seen which so convinced her that the child was not Chad's? Or had she simply made up her mind from the start that she had no wish to accept the child as a Jackson.

All seemed to have gone strangely quiet beyond the door, perhaps because they had moved downstairs to the kitchen to continue their frantic chatter, and still Chad had made no appearance to welcome his son into the world. Bette felt bitterly disappointed, cheated of his presence and desperately close to tears. Why didn't he come?

The baby began to cry and not knowing what else to do, she put it to her breast. At first he refused to suck and Bette was nearly in tears. 'Oh please, someone help me. How do I feed this baby? Why won't he suckle?' As the baby became increasingly distressed, Bette began to sob. 'Hello, is anyone there? Can someone help me, please!'

Nobody can have heard her because nobody responded to her cries and her chest felt tight with fear, sheer panic overwhelming her. Had they all gone out and left her alone? How would she manage? The baby would starve and fade away. So would she? Oh, why had she come to this wild place in the middle of nowhere; why had she stayed? She could have been home in Cornwall with her family around her, and Barney, oh Barney, whose child is this?

She stared at the baby in her arms as if he were a stranger, his tiny, wrinkled face red with fury, his small mouth open wide in desperate, heartrending cries.

The child was hers, that's who he was. What was she

thinking of, giving way to panic? Slapping away the tears, Bette steadied her nerves and began to massage and tug at her breasts, trying to encourage the milk to flow, to demonstrate to the baby what he must do. Thankfully, a tiny drop of clear liquid emerged and he suddenly got the idea, gripping the teat with his tiny, birdlike mouth and holding fast with single-minded tenacity.

Bette felt a surge of love flood through her, a huge swell of emotion and she knew it was going to be all right. Everything would be fine. She lay back on a sigh of relief and actually laughed, smoothing a hand gently over her child's head, seeing the pulse of life beating on his crown and it suddenly no longer mattered whether Barney or Chad was the father. He was her child, a part of her that she'd created. He was sucking stronger and stronger, a fine, healthy baby. She was so very lucky.

All she needed now was for Chad to come and see him. Once he clapped eyes on this tiny scrap of humanity, this fine little boy who was his son, Bette felt quite certain that he would fall in love with him, just as surely as she had done.

All day she waited but Chad did not come. Sometime around noon, Mary-Lou brought her a bowl of tomato soup and a crust of bread. She peered closely at the baby, now asleep in the crib they'd prepared for him. 'What you going to call him? Barnaby?'

'Your sarcasm won't work today, Mary-Lou. I'm far too happy. Isn't he wonderful? Where is Chad? Is he out? When will he be back? I'm longing to show him his son.'

'Mom says he isn't Chad's, that he's not a Jackson.'

'Well, your mom is wrong. Tell her I want to see Chad, please.'

But still he did not come. As the day wore on, Bette's newly bolstered courage began to fail. Not even Peggy came in to see her again. Mary-Lou brought her more food, around supper-time, barely glancing in the baby's direction this time. When Bette asked where Chad was, if someone had told him that the baby had arrived, she merely shrugged her shoulders and left.

Bette called after her. 'You will tell him, Mary-Lou. I'm counting on you.'

No reply.

Getting herself to the bathroom when she needed to go, took all her effort. Bette managed to get out of bed and pull on her dressing gown, gingerly making her way to the bedroom door she called for help, but there was no response. She felt so sore, and worried about leaving the baby unattended. What if he smothered himself, or stopped breathing when she wasn't looking?

'Mary-Lou, Peggy, can you mind the baby while I go and use the john.' Taking care to use an expression they would understand.

She could hear a distant buzz of voices downstairs in the kitchen but nobody heard her, or if they did, paid her no heed. There was nothing else for it but to take Matthew, as she now called her son, with her. She'd chosen the name partly because she felt sure Chad and his family would want a biblical name, and because she'd always liked it.

Gathering him gently in her arms, Bette made her way slowly along the landing to the bathroom, lay Matthew carefully on his blanket on the floor and did what she had to do, taking the opportunity to wash herself all over while she was there, since her mother-in-law had barely done more than wipe her with a damp flannel after the birth. She felt much refreshed afterwards.

Back in her room she put Matthew in his crib and, realising he was wet, took a clean nappy from the cupboard where she'd stored them and struggled to pin it on him. It took her a long time because he was so very tiny and she was terrified of sticking the pin into him. After all of that, she climbed back into bed, exhausted, and was asleep in seconds. When she woke, it was quite dark and the baby was crying to be fed again.

So began the longest night Bette could ever recollect.

Matthew would wake at regular, and all too frequent, intervals for his feed, take a little milk from her and generally fall asleep in the middle of it, only to wake again two hours later, crying for more.

Bette was in despair, at the end of her tether. She'd never been so tired in her life. Could there be something wrong? Had she run out of milk? Wasn't it coming through as it should? Could that be because she was so fearful of the future, so afraid, quite certain that even now the family were plotting against her, planning a way to rid themselves of this interloper who was trying to foist another man's child on their son.

It was around mid-afternoon of the following day when the door creaked open and instead of a sour-faced Mary-Lou bearing fresh food or more cold tea, Chad himself walked into the room. Bette sat up quickly in the bed, wishing she'd had warning so that she could have tidied her hair or put on some lipstick, but what did it matter, he was here, at last.

'Chad, I'm so glad to see you. I thought you'd never come. Didn't they tell you that he'd been born? Just look at him. Isn't he marvellous?'

Chad made no move to approach the baby. He stood at the bottom of the big bed, grasping the iron rail tightly with his one hand as he stared down at her. 'Mom told me everything. You lied to me, Bette. I can see now why you were in such a hurry to marry a one-armed, clapped out marine. He's Barney's child, isn't he? Did Barney turn you down? He would, of course. Barney doesn't go in for commitment. He takes a girl and leaves her, that's his style.'

'Oh, Chad, it wasn't like that, really it wasn't. It's you I love.

I don't want Barney.' Bette was kneeling on the bed now, putting her hands out, trying to reach him.

'Are you telling me that you never slept with him?'

He waited in silence for her denial, and when it didn't come, when he saw the rising tide of colour in her pale cheeks, he knew the answer to his question. He blinked as if she'd struck him, then clenched his fist into a tight ball of fury and on a sharp, indrawn breath, walked away.

'Chad, don't go. Don't leave me like this. I need to explain. I want to talk about this.'

His last words were like a knife through her heart. 'There's nothing left to say. You've got what you wanted, much good may it do you.'

Bette's lying-in lasted no longer than six days and throughout that time, Chad never came again. She spent it largely alone and unattended, and by the end of the week she was near screaming with frustration and boredom, wanting to get up and go out. Bette felt desperate to find him so they could talk it all through and she could attempt to make reparation.

She needed to explain that she and Barney had both believed Chad to be dead, that they'd been overwhelmed by emotion, a moment of weakness, partly brought on by grief. She told herself this story so often that she almost began to believe it; resolutely putting from her mind the passion she'd felt for Barney, how much fun they'd had together, how she'd wanted to marry him only a short while ago.

That was a fact Chad must never discover: that the wedding had been called off only because they'd heard he was still alive. He'd been hurt enough. Besides, he was right in a way. Barney had taken advantage of her, and been eager enough to escape the penalty of marrying her.

Having issued her judgement on the father of the child, Peggy hadn't set foot through the bedroom door again.

Throughout the six days, Mary-Lou had been the one to take away soiled sheets and bring fresh linen, carry in trays of food and drinks, and even she had been resolutely uncommunicative.

It was quite plain to Bette what kind of future she could expect with the Jackson family. Bad as it had been before, it would be ten times worse now.

She didn't even know where her husband could be sleeping in a house that was supposed to be bursting to the rafters with not an inch of alternative sleeping accommodation to spare.

It was Peggy, in fact, who told her, on the seventh morning when Bette walked into the kitchen, Matthew in her arms, unable to stay in bed another minute. 'If you're looking for Chad, he ain't here.'

'Where is he then?'

'Took himself off to the cabin.'

'You have a cabin?' Bette was astonished. Why had she never heard about this before? All these months they'd been living cooped up with his family, and yet there'd been an alternative. 'What sort of cabin? Where is it?'

'T'aint no palace. But I reckon you'd best join him there.'

'Does he want me to?'

'Don't make no difference whether he do or not. You're man and wife in the eyes of God, so you'll just have to knuckle on down and make the best of things, like the rest of us. Mary-Lou will help you pack your things.'

So she was to be banished from the house, after all. Bette felt a surge of relief. She was delighted, although fearful of the reception that awaited her in this so-called cabin. She didn't, not for one minute, expect Chad to be putting out a welcome mat. He saw her as a cheat and a liar, and probably he was right. She had cheated on him, let him down, flirted with and loved both himself and Barney, and this was the result. It served her right if she was now to pay the price for such foolishness. Hadn't Sara warned her that it would all end in tears?

In a strange way, the six days of isolation had given her renewed strength, perhaps because of this tiny scrap of life which depended upon her entirely. Matthew deserved a better mother, that was certain, but he also needed a father, and Chad would make a good one. Bette knew this instinctively.

Not only that but through all those long, lonely hours she'd had ample time to realise that she did still care for Chad. Perhaps now the baby was safely delivered they could start again, begin afresh and learn to love each other as they once had. She just needed him to give her a second chance.

40

As it turned out, cabin was a somewhat grand word for what turned out to be little more than an unpainted, wooden shack. It's four walls were made of unsawn logs resting on a few piles of stones. It bore a crooked, tin-can chimney, that smoked fitfully, on a corrugated iron roof. Bette stared at it, appalled, unable to believe that anyone could actually live in it.

Harry had taken her there in the pick-up, not saying a word the entire journey, although his little piggy eyes constantly raked over her, so that she had to keep checking that her knees were well covered with the baby's blanket.

He deposited her bags, boxes, the crib and the baby's things on the shabby old porch, got back into the truck and roared away in a cloud of dust without even a goodbye.

Bette cradled the baby in her arms while she stood and watched the truck depart until every speck of dust had settled again and all that remained was a shimmer of latent heat glazing the surface of the unmade road.

The door of the cabin remained firmly closed. No one had come out to greet her. Not only was there no welcome mat but there was a disturbing, unlived-in feel to the place, yet Peggy had said quite clearly that Chad was here.

He must be waiting inside, sulking perhaps, unwilling to apologise for his harsh words. Bette knew it would be up to her to take the first step and make amends. All she had to do was to pluck up the courage to go inside and ask his forgiveness. He loved her, surely she could make it right between them?

Bette wished he would come out now, quickly. Then she could sit down and rest and he could hold the baby, see what a handsome little fellow he was.

Left standing out here, all alone, she was beginning to feel nervous, and desperately alone.

There was no sound, other than that of the wind soughing in the branches, a timely warning that summer was passing and autumn, fall, was upon them. A shiver ran down her spine and hoisting Matthew to a more comfortable position in her arms, she turned the handle and went inside.

The shack was empty and it took no time at all for Bette to explore it. It comprised one single room with a table and a few stools down the centre and a large cupboard against the end wall. The floors were rough wood planks with the ground beneath visible between the cracks. The windows too were cracked, cardboard blocking the worst holes, presumably to stop winter winds from whistling through. The only sop to comfort were a couple of battered rocking chairs set before a wood-burning stove, and at the top of a ladder which led up into the loft, she found a mattress. No sign of a bed, but at least the pillows, sheets and blankets looked clean. But then Peggy would have seen to that.

The rest of the cabin too, had been cleaned and swept by someone, a pegged rug on the floor and a bible picture on one wall, though with precious little else to cheer its starkness.

She discovered that the kitchen was a tiny outhouse built at the back of the cabin, in typically southern style. It looked as if a breath of wind might blow it down and contained nothing more than a sink and a rusty old wood-fired cooker which looked at least fifty years old.

There appeared to be no running water or bathroom in the place, and further exploration revealed a well and a bucket behind the cabin in what the Jacksons would call the yard, but was actually a stretch of garden leading on to woodland.

Still carrying the baby in her arms, not yet having found the courage to put him down anywhere, Bette brought in her things, bit by bit. Then she changed Matthew and lay him down in his crib before sinking thankfully on to a stool, giving the cradle a little push with her toe to make it rock.

Jake had made it for her, for which she was immensely grateful. It was beautifully if plainly carved, though he'd promised to inscribe the baby's name on the foot, once she'd chosen one. Now, he probably wouldn't be allowed to do even that.

Bette was resolutely keeping her mind away from the fact that Chad was not here. It didn't bode well for their future together, but she would think about the implications of that later. When her husband returned from wherever he was, he would certainly need feeding.

When she felt rested and had caught her breath a little, Bette examined the contents of the cupboard which was, quite literally, bare, save for a few bits of crockery and a couple of pans. In the out-kitchen there wasn't any sign of food either, not even any washing-up left in the sink which surprised her. Bette hadn't realised that Chad could be so tidy.

At least Peggy had packed some food for her, which would do for now. Once Chad got back, he could drive them to the store.

First, she fetched water and gave the shelves a thorough wipe down, just to be on the safe side, then spread out some clean newspapers she'd found stacked in a corner.

They were a few months old, one having a report of the coming invasion. *Bogus army and false landings invented by Allied chiefs to confuse the Germans*, shouted the headline. Bette sank to her knees, reduced to tears by the rush of memories.

She thought of Fowey and all the excitement of the GIs arriving, the fun the dances and going to the flicks, the thrill of all that flattering attention, the whispers and secrets surrounding the planned invasion. She thought of Sara and her young niece and nephew, of Cory and Sadie, the explosion of fish that had led to her meeting Chad, and last but not least, of Barney.

Never in her wildest dreams and hopes of coming to America, had she imagined that she would end up living in a wooden shack that Cory wouldn't even consider good enough to house his boat.

Matthew gave a little hiccup and Bette ran to the crib to check that he was all right. His bright eyes seemed to smile up at her, and she put down her finger for him to grasp with a fierce grip. He was so wonderful. How she adored him.

This was no time for self-pity and nostalgia, things were as they were and she must make the best of it. Like it or not, she somehow had to cope because now she had a child to consider. She must eat properly to make sure she kept producing milk so that he would thrive. She must get the old cooker going, come what may, and cook supper for her husband.

And at least she would no longer have to sit and eat with the Jacksons. She would make a good place for them here, a place of their own as she had dreamed of having.

Bette turned to the boxes, surprised by Peggy's generosity, and began to unpack them, setting the dry goods in the cupboard, the vegetables in a rack under the sink in the out-kitchen, but where to put the fresh food was a problem. There was no big refrigerator here, such as Peggy owned up at the farm. In the end, once she'd filled the large wooden water barrel that stood in the corner of the yard by the back door, she put the cheese, eggs and milk in the water bucket and hung it in the well. There didn't seem to be any alternative.

Now there was the matter of supper to be addressed. After an hour battling with the rusty old cooker in the out-kitchen, she abandoned it in favour of the wood-burning stove in the cabin itself. Even that took a while to get going but finally, after several failed attempts and a fit of coughing when the room filled up with smoke, she got it burning nicely.

Bette opened a tin of soup, adding a few potatoes, peas and other vegetables to make it more substantial, thinking that would surely do for their first night, then set it on top of the stove to warm through. She'd do better tomorrow, when she was less tired, assuming she was still here and Chad hadn't moved them to a better place.

The first opportunity she got, Bette intended to ask around for a decent house which might be to let, and a job so that she could earn some money. She certainly had no intention of spending her life in this old shack. She felt as if she'd stepped back in time to the last century when the pioneers were settling.

Content that she'd done everything possible to make the cabin feel homely and welcoming and feeling not a little proud of her efforts, with even Matthew fed and changed and put down for the night and the vegetable soup warming nicely, Bette turned her attention to her own appearance.

She washed herself all over so that she was fresh and clean, smelling of soap at least, and not of dust and cobwebs; then combed her hair, letting it fall loose about her shoulders as Chad liked it, and applied a dazzling pink lipstick. All right, it was too soon after the birth of the baby for anything physical between them, but she could at least look pretty for him. If she looked good, he might find it easier to forgive her.

When she was ready, she sat in the rocking chair and waited for her husband to come home.

The wind had risen, making her jump as doors rattled and shutters banged, and there were strange whistles and bumps. The black bear roamed these forests and Bette certainly had no wish for one to come calling. It wasn't until well after midnight that it dawned upon her that Chad wasn't coming at all, and it was then that the awful truth hit home. The Jackson family had packed her off to this shack with all her belongings and a few boxes of food, and washed their hands of her.

He didn't come the next day either, or the one after that. Bette had stepped out into a magnificent arena of colour, although the glory of the trees was not the most important factor on her mind right now.

She'd done a lot of hard thinking as she lay alone on the lumpy mattress, snuggled beneath the blankets in an effort to keep warm, and had worked it all out. She couldn't simply catch a bus out of here, or even pick up her bags and walk to the farm. They'd driven miles to reach the cabin, and there was no hope of her finding her way back.

Neither could she stay here all alone with a new-born baby. Matthew might need medical attention, so might she for that matter. She was still bleeding badly and there was a constant, dragging ache in her groin. In addition, she felt bone-weary and kept bursting into tears all the time.

Each day she would walk a little further along the lane, just to make sure that there wasn't a house around the next bend, or the one after that. She'd look rather foolish if she imagined herself stuck here, alone and abandoned, when all the time she had neighbours.

She'd strap a length of cotton cloth around her back like a sling to hold the baby, papoose fashion, and having satisfied herself that Matthew was safe, contentedly cradled against her breast, she would set off along the road.

Bette refused to believe that Chad would totally desert her. He would come for her eventually, she was sure of it.

She would gaze hopefully along the road, narrowing her eyes against the early morning sun as she willed the pick-up to appear in a whirl of dust and Chad to come for her. But no matter how far she walked, she found no sign of either a dwelling or the truck.

The track twisted and turned round boulders and fallen trees, the view stunning: distant mountains glazed with purple and blue shadows, jagged peaks and the occasional glimpse of a waterfall. And mile upon mile of trees.

Bette had learned some of their names in the months she'd spent in North Carolina, and she amused herself by describing the ones she recognised to her child.

'See, Matthew, that bright yellow is hickory, oh and just look at the vivid orange of the sassafras tree, the deep red of the dogwoods. And there's a kestrel, probably with an eye on its breakfast.'

Huckleberries grew in profusion on the banks above the track, prettily bordered with golden rod and late aster. Yet the dirt road itself presumably stretched for miles all along the ridge, to the farm in one direction, and to town in the other.

But how many miles, that was the question?

Too many for her to walk, even without a baby. She knew that the Blue Ridge mountains traversed ridge upon ridge for 500 miles from Georgia in the south through to Virginia in the north, and Bette didn't care to think how far of that length she would need to walk before she even found another living creature.

For all it was late October, the day was warm, the sun high in the sky and she couldn't even be sure how long she'd been walking. Matthew was starting to grizzle, she was exhausted and Bette knew she had no alternative but to turn around, yet again, and go back to the cabin.

Sara was beginning to seriously consider nursing as a career. Although she wasn't allowed to change dressings, give injections or anything of that nature, she was finding great satisfaction in helping the nurses with the more basic chores. She didn't mind washing bedpans or changing beds, had even helped to give blanket baths when the nurses were overstretched, as they certainly were these days.

Now she was beginning to wonder if she was capable of coping with exams and training, once the war was won. Hugh had always drummed into her how stupid she was. But then he'd said and done a great many things that weren't right, had used her badly, as if it had been in his interest to keep her down. Sara had decided he was wrong. She was beginning to think herself capable of anything, and the prospect of becoming a nurse excited her.

Sister had promised to get details for her, and the necessary papers for her to fill in and apply. She'd quite made up her mind that it would be something really worthwhile to do.

There was a US Hospital Training School in Fowey, but that was for military personnel, simulating battle conditions. She would need to go off to Truro or Plymouth every day to do her training, which would require Hugh's support. He'd have to get Iris back in the bar, or some other girl to take her place. And what about the children? Arrangements would need to be made for Sadie, or even Hugh himself, to pick them up after school and take care of them until she got home.

Was that possible? Would he agree to do that? Or was she only laying herself open to fresh disappointment by even considering the idea?

'How I wish you were here, Bette, then I could talk this through with you. But I am at least taking heed of your advice to think for myself.'

They brought in more wounded that afternoon. Each LST had gone out to France carrying eighteen tanks or a couple of dozen vehicles, plus troops. They were returning with hundreds of wounded, an endless stream, day after day.

How the surgeons kept up the number of operations, removing shrapnel, amputating damaged and diseased limbs, dealing with burns, was quite beyond her.

Some operations were actually carried out on board, with others postponed until the patient reached specialist care at Plymouth or Truro. But scores remained to be treated here in Fowey, and Sara was filled with admiration for the medical staff's stamina and skills.

As she wheeled the tea trolley and newspapers around to those boys who were slowly recovering from their ordeal, she took the time to offer a few comforting words to those still facing theirs. She stopped at each bed in turn to ask their name, how they were feeling, if there was anyone she could contact for them.

'Would you like tea and biscuits, or can I post any mail for you? Write a letter to your mum perhaps?' she would say.

A young nurse came over and gently tapped her shoulder. 'Sara, there's a young man over there who says he has a letter for you.'

'Oh, God!' Sara felt as if the blood had drained from every limb, leaving her limp and useless. Charlie. She knew at once that it must be about Charlie.

The nurse sounded brisk and businesslike, but her eyes were filled with compassion. 'I hope it isn't bad news.'

Sara couldn't speak, could make no reply to this. She half

ran over to the young patient, little older than herself, yet who knew what horrors he'd encountered out there to make him old before his time. He was in a bad way, his stomach half ripped open from the shelling, a scattering of shrapnel punctures in a young face racked with pain, yet his expression brightened when he saw her.

'You have a letter for me?'

'You're Sara Marrack?'

Sara had to bend down to hear what he had to say, his voice little more than a hoarse whisper. 'It's in my bag, in the locker. I was told to put it into your hands only. Nobody else's.'

'Who told you this? Who is the letter from?' She was searching the locker even as she spoke, then she had it in her hands and relief flooded through her, making her gasp. The handwriting was his, she would have known it anywhere. 'He's alive?'

The young sailor was grinning now, even though it made him wince to stretch the muscles of his face. 'He was the last time he shouted at me for not getting out of the way of that dratted shell. Said I was a lucky son-of-a-bitch, begging your pardon ma'am, to be shipped home, and the only reason he'd let me come back to Fowey was if I brought this letter to you.'

Sara kissed him. 'I think I love you.' Then tucked the letter into her pocket and patted it.

'Aren't you going to read it?'

'Later, there's work to be done.'

The nurse was back at her side, smiling widely at seeing the news wasn't too bad after all. 'Let's get you ready for your op, young man. This is your lucky day. We have the best surgeon on duty and he's going to make you whole again. Come on, Sara, you can start doing a bit more to help, since you're going to enter the profession.'

It was late in the afternoon before she found a moment alone to read the letter, while she was on her own tea break. It began with an expression of his love for her, his longing to see her again, but as Sara read on, her brow began to crease with worry.

They wanted to send me back with young Tim, (my post-boy here) but I refused. There's limited space available on these home-bound ships and he is a far more deserving case than me. My leg is a bit knocked up but not serious enough to allow me the excuse to take time out, at least I hope not! This damned war has to be finished, once and for all, then I can come home and claim you. I've written to Yvonne asking for a divorce. Is it permitted for me to beg you to do the same with Hugh, and marry me? I waited for you, as we agreed. When you didn't come I thought maybe you'd changed your mind, that you didn't want me any more. But I've had time to think about it since, and I'm wondering if something happened to prevent your getting there. Did he stop you from coming, Sara? If I'm wrong, if you've decided that you love him best after all, I'll have to accept that. I'm hoping that I'm not wrong, that when all this is over, and if I'm fortunate enough to survive, you'll come over Stateside with me to a new life. The children too, of course, if Hugh will allow it. Will you think about it at least? Write me at this address when you decide. I love you, Sara, whatever.

Tears were rolling down her cheeks by the time she'd finished reading the letter. Oh, if only life could be that simple and straightforward. If only she could go to Hugh and tell him that she loved Charlie, that she wanted a divorce and could she please have the children, too?

She knew what his answer would be, without even needing to ask. He would never agree, never.

She could walk away, of course, if she so wished; go off to America with Charlie without Hugh's permission. Except that Hugh could claim that having enjoyed an affair with her lover she was an unfit mother, and since they had spent a weekend together how could she prove her innocence, that nothing at all had happened between them?

Sara might well win her divorce, but lose her children, which didn't bear thinking about. She folded the letter and put it back in her pocket.

Making the children their tea, giving them their baths, washing their hair and doing all the ordinary, everyday things with them, brought home to her how very important it was for her to keep them safe and a part of her life. Not for a moment would Sara contemplate losing them. They were far too precious.

They sat in their plaid dressing gowns, drinking their cocoa while they played Ludo, then a rowdy game of Snakes and Ladders. Drew cheated a few times, as he loved to do, pretending he'd forgotten that you couldn't go up snakes and hoping no one would notice.

Jenny kept shouting, 'He's done it again, Mummy, tell him!'

Laughing, Sara rumpled his hair. 'He's a cheeky monkey but it's time for bed now, so come on both of you, clean your teeth then I'll come and read you some more of Rupert Bear.'

A chorus of moans had already started up but mention of their favourite story-book character changed these swiftly to oohs of delight and the two children scampered off eager to hear if the dragon would catch Rupert, and how Bill Badger, Algy Pug and Edward Trunk would help. Perhaps he might even take to the air in his little plane.

Sara sat by Jenny's bed with Drew on her knee and read quietly to them, always a favourite part of her day. She couldn't ever remember Hugh putting them to bed, not in all their married life. He claimed it was her job, part of the role of a mother, as if he were somehow not involved in his children's welfare.

When their eyes were drooping closed, she quietly closed the book, kissed Jenny's sleep-flushed cheeks before carrying Drew, already limp with sleep, to his own room where she sat and looked at him for a long time before going back downstairs. No indeed, whatever the sacrifice, her children must come first but it was worth one last stab at happiness before she quite abandoned all hope.

She damned well would ask him. He could only say no.

'I'd like to talk to you Hugh, if you don't mind.' He was sitting reading the paper, as he seemed to do a great deal these days, now that he wasn't constantly out on his missions. His temper had grown ever more irascible, his moods blacker and more morose of late and as Sara took the chair opposite she tried to appear calm, even though her heart was pounding and her hands were trembling. She clasped them tightly in her lap,

'I don't think we can go on like this for much longer, hardly speaking to each other, do you? We lead largely separate lives, sleep in separate beds and . . .'

'If you are complaining again about our sex lives, Sara, that is entirely your fault, not mine. I never wanted us to sleep apart, that was your choice. I can't say I enjoy it in the least.'

Sara momentarily closed her eyes in a gesture of despair. 'Let's not go over all of that again. The fact is, even in our love-making, if you can call it that, we are no longer compatible. We seem to have different needs, a completely different way of looking at things. You constantly criticise and disapprove of everything I do, while I want to go my own way, do things outside of the home now that the children are older. I'm afraid I haven't been happy for some time, Hugh. I'm not blaming you entirely but . . .'

'I should think not, since you were the one who had the affair, not me.'

Sara was taken aback by the venom in his tone, had to force herself not to lose her nerve. After all, she suspected him of having an affair himself, with Iris, although it seemed fruitless to argue that point now that the girl had gone back home. She steadied her breath, tried again.

'Charlie and I didn't actually have an affair, not in the way you imagine. But it is true that I love him. He loves me too, very much, and . . . well, what I'm trying to say is that if you would be good enough to grant me my freedom, we intend to marry.'

'I beg your pardon?' Hugh tossed aside his paper and stared at Sara, eyes wide with disbelief, brows climbing right up into that shock of fair hair which still fell over his brow. 'Grant you your freedom? My dear girl, what are you saying? Can you be serious?'

'Very. We need to be together.'

'You *need* to be together?'

'Do please stop repeating everything I say. It can't come as any great surprise to you. You've known for some time that I'm not happy. Our marriage isn't working, Hugh, and it's time we accepted that fact.'

'I accept nothing of the sort. The problem lies with the war, with women taking on roles that don't in the least suit them, like driving buses, joining the armed services, and other such jobs that they were never meant to do. The problem lies with GIs who steal our wives and sweethearts, not with hard-working husbands who are trying to do their bit.

'I also blame Nora Snell and her damned committee. On top of all of that, you've now got yourself embroiled in this nursing nonsense up at the hospital.' He got up, carefully folded his paper and slapped it down on the polished mahogany coffee table.

'The trouble with you, Sara, is that you're never satisfied. You are always imagining that the grass is greener on the other side of the fence.'

Sara gasped. 'I don't think that's quite fair.'

'Fair? Fair? You have a lovely home, children, even a husband who loves you, and a business we used to happily run together, but that apparently is not enough. You want fun and excitement, romance and illicit sex. Now you apparently also want your freedom. To do what? Run off to America with a Yank, like your stupid sister? I don't think so, Sara. I don't think that would be a very good idea at all.'

At this point in his unstoppable lecture, he leaned so close to Sara that flecks of spittle from his mouth cascaded over her as he spat his next words at her. 'Let's put it nice and plain, so that even you, dim as you are, can understand. If you leave me, Sara, I shall never, ever, allow you to take the children. Got that? Have you hammered that simple fact into your thick skull?'

Sara stared at the notice as she had done a dozen, a score of times over the last few weeks, with unseeing eyes. *The public may use and bathe from this part of the beach but at their own risk. Beware of barbed wire and other obstructions. Do not touch any suspicious objects.*

It was dated 25th July, 1944, by the garrison commander.

Readymoney beach was being returned, at least in part, to the people of Fowey. Did this mean that life too could now return to normal? Somehow she didn't think so. Sara couldn't imagine ever feeling as carefree as she once had, before the war, when she had been young and full of hope and optimism.

She turned over the conversation she'd had with Hugh the previous night and knew, in her heart, that the result had been entirely expected. In a way the decision had been made for her long since. She'd no choice but to stay, because of the children. Nothing, not even her love for Charlie, would induce her to risk losing them. She was trapped, with no way out.

But living with Hugh once the war was finally over would be very far from easy. It was going to be every bit as dangerous as crossing the wrong part of this beach. An absolute minefield.

42

Chad was spending a couple of weeks out in the forest, sleeping under the stars, hunting the odd turkey or the white, red-eyed quail, and licking his wounds. The peace and quiet gave him much needed time to think and recover from the shock of Bette's betrayal, and he'd come to the decision that perhaps he'd been a bit hard on her.

Both Bette and Barney must have believed that he was dead. No information to the contrary could possibly have come through because he'd been in that coma for weeks, and the army had been at great pains to keep everything hush-hush, under wraps.

Besides which, Barney could charm the birds from the trees, if he set his mind to it. Was it fair to blame Bette if she fell for his flattery while beside herself with grief? The poor girl probably didn't know what the heck she was doing, what with the baby coming an' all.

And it still *could* be his. He'd made love to her first. How could Mom be so sure that it wasn't? Didn't all new babies look alike? He hadn't so much as glanced at the poor creature, or made any attempt to form his own opinion on the matter. Bette must think him entirely heartless. It wasn't the baby's fault, after all, and the poor thing would need a pappy.

The question he had to ask himself was, did he still love Bette? Did he want her to stay or should he assume that this whole marriage was a sham and call an end to it? What would happen then? Divorce? It didn't bear thinking about.

The answer came back to him clear and strong. He did still love her and although he felt badly hurt and let down, by his best buddy as much as his wife, he supposed Bette at least deserved the opportunity to explain. Maybe even a second chance, if he thought she still cared for him some.

Harry and his father were out on the land somewhere and only his mother and Mary-Lou were sitting at the kitchen table, peeling vegetables when he walked back in, carrying his bag. Peggy half glanced up, nodded at the bag and asked, 'Turkey?'

'Sure is.'

'Just in time for Thanksgiving. You feeling hungry, son?' She wiped her hands on a cloth and got up to slice a loaf of bread, fresh baked that morning.

'No, I'm fine. Had me some beans. I need to see Bette right away.' Dropping his bags he pulled open the door and was halfway up the stairs when Peggy called up to him.

'She ain't there.'

'Why not? Where is she?'

'She packed her bags, took the baby and left. Harry ran her to the station, like she asked. Gone back to where she came from, I imagine, and good riddance.'

How long had she been here? Bette couldn't quite remember. That had been her first mistake then, not to start a calendar and keep a track of the days. Her second, and far more serious, was to believe that the loaded boxes of food were the result of generosity on Peggy's part. Now she understood that they weren't anything of the sort. The food had been meant to last her for weeks because she was stuck in this cabin, miles from civilisation with a new baby and no transport. Once that food was used up, Bette hadn't the first idea how she would survive.

Surely the woman wasn't so heartless and unfeeling as to leave her to starve?

Yet despite all appearances to the contrary, Bette remained steadfastly optimistic, clinging to the hope that Chad had perhaps been away from home, down in Carreville on business for his father. She felt quite unable to believe that he would abandon her completely.

'He will come today, Matthew,' she would say to the baby whenever she woke to yet another empty day.

She'd given up walking down the lane. There was no point, nowhere to go.

Bette busied herself cleaning the cabin, giving it a good bottoming as Sadie would call it, making it as comfortable and homely as possible. She even picked some of the golden rod and aster to make the place look loved and cared for.

She found an axe and split some of the logs from the wood-pile. By dinner time she had quite a stack.

Next, she set about trying to make the cabin weatherproof. With the weather likely to worsen, every hole and possible source of draft must be stopped up. She used rags, cardboard, some of the newspapers she'd found, anything to make the place cosy and sound.

The roof rattled ominously in the wind and the chimney seemed to howl and whistle, as if in pain. The stove was always difficult to light and get going and sometimes she would be blinded by smoke, her eyes stinging, nostrils filled with the stink of it. She must take such care. Once it was burning well though, her cheeks would glow from the heat and the fire would smoulder happily on very little wood for hours. The smell of the pinewood was soporific and in the evening she would find that it had warmed the loft above, which helped her to sleep.

After that she scrubbed the old cooker in the out-kitchen and was so pleased when she got it working again. Now she could cook and each day she would make something good and tasty, once boiled ham and mashed potatoes, another day a

delicious roast chicken which she and Chad could enjoy
together just the moment he arrived. She even baked an apple
pie.

One afternoon she set a dish of spicy chicken legs to bake in
the oven, then went out into the garden to enjoy the late
sunshine, rocking Matthew's crib gently as she passed by.

'Now you sleep well and be a good baby. This could be the
day that your daddy comes. I feel sure of it.'

Leaving Matthew asleep in his crib just by the back door,
she wandered idly down the length of the back garden, curious
to see what grew there, to explore the woodland of oak, beech
and birch which ran along the bottom of it. The day was
pleasantly mild and warm, and in any other circumstances she
would enjoy a walk in the woods.

When she reached it, some thirty or forty feet from the
cabin, the blaze of colour from the autumn leaves faded into
shadow, growing ever darker as she cautiously edged her way
further into the forest.

Bette glanced back at Matthew. She mustn't go too far,
must keep him in sight. A red squirrel leapt in front of her,
making her jump, and then laugh, as it suddenly scampered
pell-mell up the trunk of the nearest tree along a branch and
seemed to fly over on to the next one, like an aerial acrobat.

'How clever you are, Mr Squirrel. I wish I could do that.'

Bette listened. Surely that was water she could hear somewhere in the distance, a spring perhaps.

If only Chad would come, then she might feel brave enough
to explore further.

She adored that lovely tang which reminded her of autumn
at home, of the bonfire they would build every Guy Fawkes
night up at Windmill, treacle toffee and roast chestnuts. Why,
here was a chestnut tree, laden with nuts.

Delighted to have found something which reminded her of
home, Bette stepped further into the undergrowth to pull some

from the tree, greedily picking as many as she could reach, gathering up her skirt to hold them. The forest smelled so fresh and moist, sharp with the tang of pine as if someone really were having a bonfire with that tantalising aroma of wood-smoke.

She whirled about, eyes growing wide with horror as she saw smoke pouring from the window of the out-kitchen, mere feet from where Matthew was sleeping.

Bette was running, scattering the chestnuts, falling over her own feet in her frantic anxiety to reach her baby. The garden seemed to have lengthened to fifty feet, seventy, eighty, twice its actual length and Bette felt as if she were running in slow motion, making no progress at all.

She heard a loud crack as something inside the kitchen exploded. The old cooker perhaps, and she flung herself the last few feet.

She had him, swept up tight in her arms, crib and all, but the fire was getting worse, would quickly spread. She ran back down the garden and set the crib down some distance from the cabin, where he would be safe.

Snatching up the water bucket Bette ran to the big water barrel by the door, refilling it over and over again to dowse the flames now licking the edge of the kitchen roof. When that was almost empty, she tossed the eggs and cheese aside, dipped the bucket in the well and used that water too. She beat at the fire with the broom, gasping and choking with the smoke, feeling her cheeks and hands blister with the heat till at last there was nothing left but a charred ruin where once had been the kitchen.

She collapsed on to the grass, black with her efforts and weak with exhaustion, the baby's cries ringing in her ears. But at least she'd saved the cabin, and also the forest. She'd managed to contain the fire and not let it spread.

Bette spent much of the next week curled on her bed in shock, the baby beside her, either in a welter of tears or snatching what sleep she could between feeds. From time to time, because it was important to keep up her flow of milk, she would climb down the ladder to find food, which she ate without appetite, standing up, before creeping back up the ladder again.

There was very little of it left, and she'd lost all the eggs, milk and vegetables in the fire.

Sleep remained her preferable occupation, although, exhausted as she was, she never woke refreshed. Deep in the pit of her stomach was this huge knot of fear, burning her up, paralysing her limbs. What was going to happen to her? Would she die? Would the baby die? What if there was another fire and she couldn't put it out next time? What if she never saw Chad again?

However foolish and stupid she'd been, and Bette freely admitted now that she had been very silly indeed, she really didn't deserve to be treated like this.

One morning, late in the second week following the fire, or was it early in the third, Bette got up from the bed and looked out of the grimy window across to the distant mountains. They seemed to be further and further away every time she looked, the distances beyond comprehension. Was that snow on the highest peaks? Could winter be coming already?

The knot of fear tightened. How would she survive? The silence was awesome, her sense of isolation complete. She was alone, utterly and completely, save for her child.

Her clothes were crumpled and dirty. She smelled of sour milk, wood-smoke and sweat. The bleeding had stopped, at least, but the sheets remained soiled because she hadn't troubled to wash them. The blisters on her hands and face were healing but still dreadfully painful to the touch. What was happening to her? She couldn't just lie here weeping, feeling sorry for herself. Yet what else could she do? Bette wasn't sure. She couldn't even begin to think.

In the end, before her store of food quite ran out and the snows came, she would have to walk the ten miles or whatever it was to the nearest habitation. What alternative did she have?

Except that she daren't take the risk until she felt certain that Matthew, and herself for that matter, were fit enough for the journey. It could be twenty miles, or fifty, for all she knew.

Her small son was lying on the bed, cooing happily at her, since his belly was full, and she sat cuddling and kissing him for quite some time, tickling his toes and making his little mouth open in delight. He seemed so perfect, and yet so fragile. Was that a smile, or simply wind? Thank God he seemed to be healthy and thriving. Not for a moment dare she risk anything else going wrong.

But she couldn't go on like this, crying her eyes out hour upon hour, sleeping and sleeping, doing nothing, day after day. What if Chad did come, after all? Although she'd largely given up hope now. It would do her no good at all to be caught looking a sight and Bette was far too vain and proud of her good looks to allow that to happen. And with winter coming on, she couldn't, in any case, just sit here and die of cold and starvation. She had to *do* something.

Driven by a sudden surge of anger, and an instinctive need to survive, she pulled on fresh warm clothes over her night-dress, a pair of stout boots, then set baby Matthew's crib in a pool of sunshine, where he would be safe and she could clearly see him. Bette found herself checking him every five minutes, so jumpy was she.

But there was work to be done and no one else to do it but herself.

She scoured the garden for whatever she could find to eat. Found a few onions which she strung up and hung from the beamed ceiling; potatoes, turnips and carrots which she earthed up, remembering they must be kept dark if they weren't to go green. There was an apple tree, although the fruit was small and green, gooseberry and currant bushes.

On the edge of the woods she found wild strawberries and plums, but all of this fruit could be stewed. If only she could bottle or store them in some way? How had Sadie done that? If only she'd paid more attention. If only she had some jars. She must search every corner of the cabin to check there wasn't something, anything she could use.

Bette wished there was a lake nearby, wondering if she could remember all Cory had tried to teach her about fishing; how to make a line and fix bait.

Still restless, Bette hitched the baby up in her arms and wandered along the road a little way, just as she had done before, hoping against hope she might find something, a track to some hidden house in the forest, a tribe of Indians maybe. Unlikely since they all lived on reservations, or in Cherokee and drove big pick-ups. She saw no one, no house, no farm, not even a lake.

The days became a blur, blending one into the other but Bette gritted her teeth and went relentlessly on with her preparations, trying not to think too much about the reality of a winter alone in this cabin. She was afraid now to lie down on the bed during the day, terrified the weeping might start up all over again and she would lose the will to go on.

She was afraid to leave the stove unattended, fearful of straying too far from the house in case she got bitten by a snake or something equally dreadful. Where would she be then? What would happen to Matthew if she gave up, or if something terrible happened to her?

One night, sometime towards morning, she woke up with a start, aware that something, some sound had disturbed her. Her first thought was for Matthew but he was sleeping soundly, doing well now and going longer between feeds. Dear Lord, don't let it be a bear!

And then she heard it, the unmistakable sound of an engine. Bette was out of bed in a flash, scrambling down the ladder without even bothering to find her dressing gown or slippers, despite the severe cold.

She ran barefoot out on to the road into the grey light of dawn and was just in time to see a cloud of dust where the vehicle had vanished. The pain was so bad she doubled up with the agony of it, fell to her knees in despair.

Someone had gone by and she had missed them!

When she saw the boxes by the door, it came to her that it must have been the pick-up, driven by Harry no doubt, and he'd left her fresh supplies.

43

Bette sat in the rocker, still in her nightie and bare feet, and felt as cold and empty inside as the dead ash in the stove. She felt dazed and numb, desperately trying to fight her way through the mists of shock and view her situation rationally. The Jacksons clearly weren't going to let her starve. Well, that was something. At least they weren't so cruel and heartless as to want her death on their hands. But neither were they prepared to have any contact with her.

Could it have been Chad driving the truck? Surely not. More likely Harry, since he was the one who'd brought her here in the first place.

Then why hadn't Chad come to see her? Why didn't he care what happened to her? Why didn't anyone?

What was Peggy telling the ladies at the sewing bee? What explanation had she given to Esther for her daughter-in-law not coming along to show off her new baby? Why was no one looking for her?

And then it hit her. *Because they didn't know she was even missing!*

Peggy had told them some sort of lie. But what? That she was dead, had died in childbirth perhaps? Surely, even here in the back of beyond, there would need to be evidence of a death. There'd have to be a body, a funeral. More likely she'd told them that Bette had left the farm of her own free will, and gone where?

Home, of course, back to England. Was that what she'd told Chad, too?

The blood seemed to soar in her veins, filling her with fresh hope. That was the reason he hadn't come to see her, not because he hated her or refused to forgive her and try again.

But because he had no idea where she was!

Peggy had no doubt tricked her son just as cleverly as she'd tricked her all too trusting daughter-in-law.

Bette was on her feet in a second, bursting with a rush of energy that pulsated through her like wine. There was still hope. Chad might still want her. She didn't have to allow that woman to get away with it.

And then common sense returned and she sank back down again.

Chad had come to see her only once since the baby was born and didn't even glance in his direction. He didn't want her, didn't love her any more. He believed that the baby wasn't his, and she couldn't deny that she and Barney had been lovers, so how could she be sure who the father was? Was it any wonder if neither man wanted her? Chad had rejected her, and so had Barney.

So where did that leave her? Reaping the reward of her foolishness, that's where.

But one thing was certain, she couldn't stay here, living off Jackson charity grudgingly given, all alone on the side of a mountain with a young baby throughout what would un-doubtedly be a long, freezing winter. Therefore she must take the risk and leave. She must somehow find the town and try to make a new future for herself and Matthew.

The next minute she was climbing back up the ladder, pulling open her bags to find warm, clean clothes for herself and the baby.

It took longer than she'd expected to prepare for the journey, choosing what to take, how to carry everything she needed but in the end Bette decided to wear as many clothes as she could to save carrying them, and leave the rest behind. She dressed Matthew too, as warmly as she could in leggings, two vests, jumper, jacket, warm helmet and mitts.

Even so, the bag carrying his things simply couldn't be made any smaller, for all it weighed her down. He would need several clean diapers, an extra matinée jacket and a couple of pairs of spare leggings for when he needed a change of those too, plus a shawl in case it got really cold.

Then there was the food. Bette knew she should take as much as she could carry. There were eggs in the new box of supplies, which she hard boiled. There was fresh bread and a chunk of cheese. She also packed the stewed apple and put a few of the tiny wild strawberries and plums in her pocket to nibble as she walked along.

By late morning she was ready and with Matthew in his papoose sling across her chest, and the bag over the other shoulder, Bette closed the door of the cabin for the last time and set out once more on the road in what she judged to be the direction of town.

This time she had no intention of coming back. She meant to escape this desolate place once and for all, even if she died in the attempt.

Bette walked and walked until she felt she could walk no more, till her heels were blistered and she could feel the blood squelching between her toes. She'd heard the whippoorwill, seen the blue flash of a jay, watched a woodpecker hammer away at the bark of a tree, as if trying to gain entry. She'd even spotted a Carolina wren who came to sit cheekily beside her on a log when she'd stopped to feed Matthew around noon. Other than these creatures, who helped to cheer her along the way, she'd seen no one.

She must have been walking for seven or eight hours, with still no sign of a house or farm, let alone Carreville. Worse than that, the light was beginning to fade and as the autumn sun slipped down the sky, a chill was settling over the land.

She walked on for another hour or so, and finding a patch of bushes, with dry bracken beneath, crawled inside, thankful to be at least relieved of her burden and be able to lie down and rest.

It was reasonably sheltered under the trees, protected from the wind. Bette fed the baby one more time, almost falling asleep herself in the middle of it. Yet that was the last thing she must do. Aware of the risk of snakes, or bears, Bette knew there'd be little sleep for her that night.

She wrapped Matthew in both shawls, then propped herself against a tree right beside him. She felt so dreadfully tired, her eyes so dusty and scratchy, but Bette had no intention of closing them, not even for a moment. Within seconds she was asleep.

She woke a couple of hours later in a blind panic. But all was well, the baby snuffling gently beside her. It was so hard to stay awake, her exhaustion too much to bear. Bette rubbed her eyes, shook herself awake and sat up, determined not to make the same mistake again.

Surely it shouldn't be too difficult, she was growing used to long, lonely, cold nights. This would simply be another. The only difference being that she wasn't in her warm, unkempt bed at the cabin, she was out in the open, under the stars and the temperature was dropping fast.

The first pearl grey of dawn was coming into the sky when she must have fallen asleep again to be woken by Matthew's frantic cries.

'What is it? What is it, my precious?' But he was only hungry.

She fed and changed him, nibbled on a hard-boiled egg by way of breakfast and got wearily to her feet. There was a definite chill in the air this morning, that sharpness which betokened the threat of rain, or even snow.

Bette tucked baby Matthew inside her sweater, where he could share the warmth of her body, then shouldering the bag of provisions, continued on her way.

It felt more difficult today, somehow, to keep up any sensible pace. Her thighs and calves were aching, her feet felt as if they were on fire, and the bag seemed twice as heavy as yesterday. Bette was forced to keep stopping to rest every twenty minutes or so. It would take forever to reach town at this rate.

Matthew seemed more fractious, crying a good deal, and yet refusing to take his feed when she stopped to rest in the middle of the day.

The sun did finally break through the bleak grey clouds and, overcome by exhaustion, Bette took the risk of getting some sleep, hoping she'd be safe in broad daylight, otherwise she never would reach the end of this blasted road.

When she woke again, darkness was falling, and with fingers clumsy with cold, Bette changed and fed the baby. Like her, he seemed too sleepy to bother, again showing little interest in food, which deeply troubled her.

Could he be sickening for something? Fear rose in her throat like bile. They must surely be nearly in Carreville by now and she set off again almost at a run.

'We'll find the town any minute, my darling,' she told him, kissing his head. It felt clammy and hot. Had he got mountain fever? She'd heard Peggy speak of it, but hadn't the first idea what it was, or even if it existed.

As night drew in and it grew dark, it became harder to keep track of where exactly she was. Bette felt light-headed and bone weary.

The dirt road wandered and twisted, dipped and climbed and she very soon became disorientated. She fell over tree stumps which really shouldn't have been there at all, and then to her horror the ground gave way beneath her and she found herself slipping and sliding down a bank, tumbling and rolling amongst stones and earth, frantically trying to hold on tight to the baby and protect his head as he lay cuddled within her sweater. She must have reached the bottom because she sprawled on to gravel, grazing her knees and cracking her head on a rock, whereupon blackness descended.

44

As that long, last winter of the war progressed, Sara went through the motions of being a good wife, putting food on the table, washing Hugh's clothes and cleaning his shoes, even running his bath for him which had always been a requirement, but relations between them were at an all-time low.

She continued to occupy the spare room, not able to consider ever returning to her husband's bed, despite his frequently bitter and snide remarks that she was neglecting her wifely duties, that it would serve her right if he took a leaf out of her book and had an affair himself.

'Please do. I really wouldn't care in the slightest what you do, or with whom.'

'Oh, dear me no, Sara. I am giving you no grounds to divorce me. I intend to remain very much in control.'

Normally, the most he ever said to her was to frostily demand that she pass the salt. More often than not he communicated by leaving notes on the dresser.

Will you please have the evening meal ready by six, on the dot. I am going out. He rarely troubled to tell her where.

Or a more peremptory demand. *Take my suit to the cleaners. Go to the Post Office and get me some stamps.* Or even, *Haven't you noticed that we're running out of soap? You really don't try, Sara.* Ever ready to criticise.

She would leave him a note in return. *Sorry, been rather busy and forgot to put a fresh piece out. There's plenty more soap in the cupboard, if you took the trouble to look.*

Sara had written a long letter recently to Bette, opening up her heart and telling her everything, as she could only do with her sister. It was at times like these that she missed her most.

'Oh, Bette, write to me. I need to know you're OK, at least, even if I'm not.'

Her one triumph and joy was her new career in nursing. Sara was well on with her training now, and enjoying it enormously. For all Hugh's lengthy list of parental requirements that he demanded of her, he never seemed to apply them to himself. He could hardly be classed as a loving, caring father and largely ignored his children, except when he wanted to show them off, or scold them for some supposed misdemeanour, or display of bad manners. He'd certainly made no effort to help Sara cope with the new demands upon her time.

Sadie, however, had turned up trumps, taking the children to school every day and collecting them afterwards, happily minding them until Sara got home. She would often give them their tea, to save Sara the trouble, and very occasionally insist on feeding her daughter too, if she thought she was looking a bit run-down and peaky.

'About time you did something useful with your life,' was her surprising comment. 'No need to run round after a man all the time.'

'Thanks, Mum. You don't know how much I appreciate your help.'

'Did you sleep with him, that Yank?'

'No.'

Sadie nodded as she set a dish of macaroni cheese before her. 'Didn't reckon you would.'

'I wanted to.'

Her mother smiled. 'Don't blame you. He's a tasty number. I might have been wrong about Hugh Marrack. He's a cold fish, that one, likes things all his own way. I thought he'd look after you, make you happy, but mebbe I was wrong.'

This was rare for Sadie to own up to a mistake and Sara felt moved by her admission, and by her effort to make reparation. 'Yes,' Sara said. 'He is cold, towards me and the children, anyway.'

'I'll not ask if you're going to leave him. None of my business, but if you do, I wouldn't blame you. Your dad, neither. I know we don't always see eye to eye, but we want you to be happy.'

Sara swallowed a lump in her throat. She made no attempt to hug Sadie, knowing any display of affection would be rebuffed but simply nodded, then said more brightly. 'I have the children, and my work. I'm particularly interested in midwifery and thinking of specialising in that.'

'That would be a good way to spend your life, helping other women.' For the briefest of seconds she rested a hand on Sara's shoulder. 'Once you're properly qualified, you'll be less dependent on your husband, more able to earn your own living.'

'I suppose I will.'

It wasn't exactly the kind of freedom she had dreamed of, but it was better than nothing.

Cory and his chums were missing their work on the River Patrol. Their much-loved routine had vanished. No longer did they have to row up and down the river watching out for marauding Germans, who fortunately had never materialised. And since the Home Guard too had been stood down, all their cheerful rivalry had gone, the little competitions they'd used to hold to see who could shoot best were over and done with. They didn't even hold their regular football matches up at Squire's Field any more. Cory found himself quite at a loose end, with far too much time on his hands.

He could find himself a bit of work here and there, doing a few odd jobs to help folk get back to normal. Guest houses and small hotels such as the Penlee that had been requisitioned for US navy use, were being handed back, but all were in need of major repairs and Cory was a handy man to have around. He would never go short of work but he missed the excitement of the River Patrol, the feeling of importance and easy comradeship with his mates.

And he badly missed his precious younger daughter who had sailed across the Atlantic Ocean never to be seen again. Several others had followed her, in a constant stream of ships which seemed to be taking vast numbers of young Cornish women overseas to America.

Cory did not approve, but then, he was worried.

He wasn't a great letter writer himself, and nobody could claim that Sadie and her younger daughter were close, yet there was usually the odd postcard arriving with a few loving words from Bette at least once or twice a month. He'd heard nothing now for weeks and it troubled him.

Of course, it may be that she was settling at last, no longer homesick for her old dad, and now that he didn't have the River Patrol and with the war as good as over, time passed more slowly so it probably seemed longer since he'd last heard from her, than was in fact the case.

He had his other lovely girl, of course, but even Sara was looking a bit peaky. Working too hard at this nursing lark, he shouldn't wonder.

Stuck for something to do today, he'd made up his mind to do a bit of fishing. Never again had he made a catch as abundant as the one shortly after the Americans had arrived when Scobey had set off that shell. Go down in history, that would, and a right royal welcome of a fish supper it had given them all. Cory was proud to have been involved in it. But a few plaice or monkfish wouldn't go amiss and it would please Sadie. Nothing she liked better than a nice bit of fish.

He called on his mate Hamil, who was more than agreeable to

while away a few pleasant hours on the river, and the pair set off with rods and nets and bait. It was as they were preparing Cory's own little clinker-built boat, somewhat battered after years of wear, that he spotted his son-in-law's much larger craft.

'Haven't seen him out in this 'ere boat in months.'

'Pity,' said Hamil. 'Cos tis a fine vessel and no mistake. Wouldn't mind one such meself. I dare say as how it be finely appointed inside?' Cocking a quizzical eye at Cory by way of enquiry.

Cory shook his head. 'Don't ask me, I wouldn't know. Hugh Marrack and I are not on such chummy terms. I've never been invited to make an inspection.'

'What, you've never been on board your own son-in-law's yacht?'

'Dare say he thought I'd mess things up by putting my oily fingers all over the fancy panelling.'

'But you say he doesn't use it much now, and he's working in The Ship today.'

'He is indeed.'

The two men regarded each other with boyish complicity.

'Wouldn't hurt to take one little peek. My hands aren't oily, are yours?'

Cory rubbed his grubby palms down the seat of his trousers. 'Clean as a whistle, come on, let's have a decko.'

The yacht was indeed very finely appointed with the kind of polished cherry-wood panelling that had Cory keeping his hands very firmly in his pockets. The saloon had plank seating which, with the addition of bunk cushions, could double as beds and would, the two men decided, be reasonably comfortable as well as functional. At the starboard end was fitted the galley with a small gas cooker and basin, and there were cupboards and lockers fitted into every corner.

Both men were equally impressed with the equipment in the

cockpit, content to investigate every device, discuss mainsail and jib, winches, compass and fenders, and likely handling of the vessel in bad weather.

'Fine workmanship,' Hamil observed, once they had explored every gadget on board. 'And the stern locker is spacious and waterproof.' He pulled it open and both men peered inside. 'You could keep anything dry in here. See this bag, no doubt where he stows his wet-weather gear. It's probably been here for months and not a drop of sea water, not a mark on it.'

Cory peered inside it. 'Seems to be a bag of stuff for emergencies. Torch, bandages, iodine, flares, oh and what's this?' He pulled out a metal implement of some sort.

Hamil examined it closely. 'Looks like wire-cutters to me. Now why would your son-in-law have call for a pair of wire-cutters on board?'

'Well, you never know, I s'pose, and here's a couple of maps, one showing the coastline right down to the Scillys, and the other is of France.'

They both looked at the maps, a red circle marking one particular spot off the Brittany coastline, then at each other. Cory said, 'Well, he was in the coastguard service I s'pose.'

'Not in France he wasn't.'

Cory put everything carefully back in the bag and stowed them away in the locker. 'Like I say, he'm not a man to cross, ain't my son-in-law. What he do is his business, not mine.'

Hamil wandered back into the saloon while Cory kept continually glancing over to the harbour, beginning to grow nervous of seeing a dinghy coming this way. 'We should be going. What if he were to come? Hugh is not the mildest of men, he do have a sharp temper on him.'

'This is clever,' Hamil said, continuing to inspect the boat regardless. 'Removable panels to gain access to the underside of the cabin and the wiring.' He began to pull one or two aside and Cory became really alarmed.

'Here, don't you go messing about with none of that.'

'Don't fret, m'boy, I'll put it all back, d'rectly. Now what be this? There's something in here, pushed right to the back under the benches.' Hamil reached into the shadowed recesses of the locker and dragged out a small battered, leather attaché case. 'Looks like he was planning to make some sort of a trip.'

Cory looked at the case blankly for a long moment. 'Hold on, if that's what I think it is . . .' He flicked up the two catches and both men stared in open-jawed disbelief at the contents thus revealed. 'Jumping catfish. Who would've believed it? Now what would old Hugh need with one of these?'

'And what in tarnation do we do about this little catch, now that we've found it?'

45

Chad had never been so unhappy in his life. Here he was pacing the floor of the room they'd once shared, wishing he could turn back the clock and do everything different. How could he have made such a mess of things?

Even when he'd been stuck in the hospital, slowly recovering from his wounds, he'd comforted himself with the thought that Bette loved him, that she surely wouldn't desert him just because he'd lost an arm. He'd been so certain of her. Though apparently he'd been wrong about that.

All the time he lay there, wounded, she was fooling around with his best buddy.

Yet as soon as she'd discovered that he was still alive, she'd written back to him, claiming to still want to marry him and had got the first transport to come out. OK, those first weeks hadn't exactly been easy, but she'd stuck it out, hadn't she? Mom hadn't helped much either, nor Mary-Lou with her miserable complaining.

Let's face it, his whole darned family had been a problem from the word go. They would keep interfering, telling him that she'd up and leave any minute, so why bother to wed her? That she wasn't to be trusted, was only after a rich husband like most war-brides. If that were true, was it any wonder if she'd got the wrong idea?

Back in England, he'd boasted far too much, made out they had thousands of acres of land as well as a fancy house in town. He'd certainly given her the impression that he was loaded. Barney had made it worse with his own embellishments about catering establishments.

Chad admitted to himself that he'd given her no hint that the Jackson family merely rented a holding high in the mountains, and a small one at that, by local standards.

Was it any wonder if she'd been disappointed by what he had to offer? He'd seen it in her face, heard it in her tone of voice, much as she'd tried to disguise it. What must she have thought of him?

That he was a liar and had got her here under false pretences.

Because of that, and his reluctance to stand up to his family and marry her in spite of their dire forecasts of disaster, he'd been filled with guilt, couldn't bring himself to even have sex with her, when really he was desperate for her love.

Even so she'd stuck it out, had shown no inclination to go back to England. On the contrary, over and over she'd asked him to look for a place of their own, begged him to name the date for the wedding and he'd done nothing.

He couldn't get it into his head that Bette would come all this way, suffer all of those problems with his family, even struggling to learn to cook and sew and wash his shirts. Where was the point in enduring all of that if she didn't really care for him? Why hadn't she left right away, the minute she'd discovered he wasn't what he said he was?

It didn't add up.

Did she decide to hang on until he'd at least made an honest woman of her? Was that all he represented to her, a marriage licence? Bette might have been naïve and foolish but she was also sweet and kind and romantic. She liked to have fun and was a bit naïve perhaps but he'd never seen her as the scheming sort.

And he found it hard to believe that any woman who could be so calculating, would up and leave when she did. Why take such a risk as to run off the minute the baby was born, before it was barely a week old, and with winter coming on. A new-born baby might not survive such a journey. It didn't make sense.

Or was he simply clinging on to false hope?

Exhausted from going over and over the same old questions with no easy answers, he flung himself out of the room and headed for town. He needed a beer. It might help him think.

'Folk generally get in my truck the normal way, I niver did have none come bouncing in the back of it before. Let alone one carrying a young 'un.'

'Where am I?' Bette could feel movement, the world seemed to be spinning around her, as if she were on a whirligig. 'I've a head on me like I've drunk two bottles of whisky and then been hit by a frying pan.'

Her rescuer let out a gale of laughter. 'At least you haven't lost your sense of humour. Don't panic, child. You's safe with old Joe. I ain't gonna hurt you none, nor this little whippers-napper here, though he seems mighty hungry, by the rumpus he's making. Time mamma's milk bar be open pretty damn quick, I'd say.'

Matthew was screaming. Bette felt like doing the same herself her head hurt so badly, except that she was too delighted to hear another human voice to care a scrap about her headache. Even though she could see nothing but a blaze of light flashing in her eyes in the darkness, the driver of this vehicle, which she now realised was the cause of the movement as it jolted along, was male but sounded friendly enough.

'Where are you taking me?' Despite her confusion and the pain, she thought she'd better ask.

'Kitson Point, that's the one-horse, two-bit town where old Joe, that's me child, case you hadn't cottoned on to that fact, have the misfortune to reside. Once we get you there, we'll have us some good hot coffee and you can tell old Joe your troubles. For such a skinny guy, I got the biggest, broadest shoulders you ever did see. My sister Josie now, she got these iddy-biddy shoulders and the rest of her is *huge*!' Whereupon he put back his head and roared with laughter.

Bette laughed too, largely out of relief that he sounded so friendly, and she'd almost forgotten what another human voice sounded like. She'd never heard of Kitson Point, nor did she care. But she understood now all about two-bit towns and if this one possessed nothing but a dry-goods store and a petrol station, she loved it already. Anything would be better than that lonely mountain cabin. Even this bumpy old truck was better than the cold isolation of that place.

She beamed at him. 'Sounds good to me,' then pulling open her blouse, put the baby to her breast without embarrassment.

Their journey seemed to be coming to an end by the time Matthew was satisfied, a pearl drop of milk on his upper lip as he lay replete and fast asleep in her lap, and Bette could see lights ahead.

'Here we be child, and you's can get right in that big old bath jest the minute I park up.'

Bette had told the old man enough of her situation by this time to make old Joe frown and scratch his head, and mutter something not very polite under his breath.

He supplied her with hot coffee and a doughnut, which were delicious, then she was wallowing in sweetly scented hot water, tucked into a big feather bed, with fervent promises that Joe himself would be only too happy to mind the babby.

'Don't you fret none. Joe will take good care of you, girl. Where you want to go? The train station? Home to England?'

Bette shook her head. She didn't have the fare for one thing, and she really had no wish to go home with her tail between her legs. 'You don't know a place called Savannah, do you? I heard, from a friend once, that it was quite pretty, and rather big.'

Joe beamed at her. 'It sure is bigger than Kitson Point and that's a fact. Well, you's in luck, child. That's where my sister Josie lives – in Savannah, way over in Georgia. She owns a store jest like the one I have here. She'll do right by you, will Big Fat Josie. Take us a while but we'll set out first thing. Pretty girl like you shouldn't be living in the back of beyond with an old sod like me. You gotta get out there, gal, and live your life.'

Bette would certainly have agreed with him, had she not already fallen fast asleep.

Chad was drowning his sorrows in a second beer in the town bar. He'd asked around but nobody had seen a girl fitting Bette's description, not here in Carreville nor in any of the small villages and hamlets he'd driven through on the way. Maybe what his mom said had been right after all. She had left and gone back to England.

He didn't think to go to Kitson Point, way over to the east.

Joe kept his word, though it was a long tiring drive in his old truck. Bette didn't care. It was the most beautiful town she'd ever set eyes on. There were tall Regency houses built of wood and painted in bright colours, set in a series of squares. Some were more fanciful with ornamental iron work forming balustrades, staircases, porches and waterspouts. There were trees and wooded parks, walkways and quiet corners where folk stood and chatted together as if they had all the time in the world.

'We got us some mighty fine ante-bellum houses here in Savannah,' said Joe. 'That means they was built before the war, our war that is.'

'I know,' said Bette with a small smile, remembering Chad's boasting.

Joe took her to a pretty wooden house painted bright blue

with paler blue shutters at each sash window. It had the usual porch running down the length of it, 'Sideways to the sea to catch the breeze,' he explained to her.

Bette was enchanted. What she wouldn't give to live in such a house with Chad and Matthew. A real family house. Her family.

Big Fat Josie was indeed exactly as her brother, and her nickname, described, except that she saw herself as being more shapely and better looking than he. She certainly laughed a good deal and swept them inside as if she'd been looking forward to their arrival all her life.

Next door to the little house stood the kind of general store in which you could buy anything from a pair of jeans and a cowboy hat, to a bag of nails or loaf of bread, from needle and thread to a bolt of fabric or tin of paint. There was a long wooden counter behind which were shelves stacked high with goods; tins, jars and boxes of every description. And in the centre stood a pot-bellied stove beside which sat two old men engaged in a game of checkers. They glanced up briefly from their game to touch their caps at Bette then got back to business.

Big Fat Josie addressed one of them as she gathered up an armful of Bette's possessions. 'Mind the store for me Jake, will ya, while I show this child upstairs. This is where I used to live, honey, before I bought me that fine house next door. You'll be nice and cosy living over my store.'

In the days following, the old woman cared for Bette without asking too many questions, or expecting any recompense. Bette was expected only to sleep and eat, 'or set a spell on that old porch and watch the world go by.'

And that's just what she did, filled with gratitude for the kindness of Big Fat Josie's hospitality. She put on weight, the colour came back into her cheeks and her sores healed, the physical ones at least. After a while she began to take short strolls about the town, carrying Matthew in her arms or wheeling him in a big black perambulator that Josie had spirited out of nowhere.

Bette explored the many fine squares and parks, marvelling at the pretty clapboard houses and gardens, then she would walk down to the bluff where the early sailing ships used to come in loaded with cotton, or along Bay Street to Factor's Row with its range of red-brick buildings named after the cotton factors who first brought prosperity to the town.

There was always something happening, people going about their business, ever ready to give her a cheery good morning. This was the America she'd dreamed of, back home in Fowey.

One morning, Bette told Big Fat Josie that she was ready to work. 'I'm feeling much better now and I've no wish to be a liability to anyone. Besides, I have a child to bring up.'

Big Fat Josie set her hands on her substantial hips and frowned. 'You could help me right here in the store and welcome. I sure am getting mighty tired of working this hard. But I did reckon as mebbe you'd be anxious to get on home to Cornwall.'

Bette shook her head. What did she have to go home to? The shame and disgrace of a failed marriage before ever it got started, and her mother saying 'I told you so'? 'No, I'm in no hurry to go back home and yes, I'd love to work for you, Josie. Just tell me what to do, and I'll do it.'

It seemed a small miracle to Bette that the woman could put her hands on the right size of screw or knitting needles in an instant, although she would sometimes hunt for a good half hour, muttering 'I know I've got one here some place. Saw it jest the other day.'

The coffee bar, or diner as she called it, was situated at one end with a couple of tables and check cloths and the constantly appetising aroma of freshly made coffee. Big Fat Josie would grind the beans herself. Ladies with baskets, or old timers with an hour to kill, would sit awhile and pass the time of day. Nobody seemed to be in a hurry when they came by Big Fat Josie's place.

Josie said, 'There was a time when I had the energy to do everything myself. Did all my own baking and folk'd come from miles around jest to taste my apple pie. But I'm dead beat by closing time these days. Time I retired and went to rock out my days on that old porch o' mine, so you's right. I need me some help.'

'I'd love to help,' Bette agreed. 'I've never worked in a shop. I was a hairdresser with my mum in Fowey but I'm quick to learn.'

Josie's big brown eyes opened wide. 'You telling me you can do hair? Well, ain't that somethin'. Hey, could you do mine, child? Cut it all short and sassy?'

Bette gazed at the glossy, ebony mass tied back from the fat, honey-brown face with a twist of string, and reaching halfway down her back, and said, 'Why would you want to? It's beautiful as it is.'

Big Fat Josie chuckled. 'You sure got a way with words, girl. I like that about you. You'll do fine.'

'But will everyone else accept me? I'm a stranger here.'

Big Fat Josie put back her head and laughed again, making her several chins bounce and shake and wobble with mirth. 'If they'll accept me, they sure will take a shine to you, child. I was left this place by my pappy. He was a Spanish sailor who came to Savannah on the boats, met and fell in love with my momma, and stayed. She died when I was just a young 'un.'

'Oh, I'm sorry. That must've been hard.'

'I got by, but folk didn't take too kindly to me at first; had a whole heap of problems when I was a gal. But my pappy, he done think I was the best thing on two legs, so I stuck on in here after he passed on, and here I still am, forty years later.

'Why would they object to you, just because your father was Spanish?'

'Bit more to it than that, child. My folks have lived in Savannah since way back. My great, great grandpappy on my momma's side, now he was English, from Yorkshire. He married an Indian girl, one of the Yamacraws. Always were mighty friendly were the Indians in these parts. All thanks to James Edward Oglethorpe, leader of this here colony in the early days, 'cause he treated them with proper respect. Always does pay to treat folk with respect. Don't you reckon, gal?'

'Oh, yes,' agreed Bette, thinking of Peggy.

Big Fat Josie marched Bette over to the counter, behind which hung a large framed portrait. 'There she is, my great, great grandmaw, still minding the place. Pretty little thing, jest like you. So ya see, I'se got all kinds of blood running in my veins but it never did me no harm. This is who I am, right? My folks believed in doing what they'd a mind to, and hang the consequences. You gotta do the same, gal. You makes up your mind you gonna do somethin', you dang well gotta do it. Don't let nobody tell you different. That's how this whole darned country got built.'

Bette could feel energy flowing back into her, just listening to this lovely woman talk. Already she adored Big Fat Josie and would have done anything for her. 'I mean to make a good future for my son, and love him as your pappy did you. He's all I've got now. I might have made some mistakes in the past but I'm learning, and I mean to take good care of him. I just need to earn some money.'

'Sure you do. Well, I been thinking about that some while we've been jawing, and not all folks have hair like mine that don't need nothin'. Plenty'd be glad of a make-over. There ain't no hairdresser in this part of town. You could open up a salon right here in my store, and help me between clients, when you is quiet. How 'bout that, gal?'

Bette was bewildered, taken aback by Josie's generosity and belief in her. 'That sounds wonderful, but do you think I could do it?'

'Sure you could do it. Bright, pretty thing like you.'

'But I don't have any money to set it all up.'

'Don't need none. Jake'll fix you up a sink in the back store room. You can give it a good clean out and we'll have you in business faster'n you can swat a horse fly.'

46

Largely due to Big Fat Josie's power in the community, within twenty-four hours, not one, but two sinks, had been duly installed, which Jake just happened to have lying about in his lock-up. And by the end of the week, assisted and generally bossed and bullied by Josie puffing and blowing alongside her, Bette had cleared out all the rubbish and shifted such items as were to be kept into one of the other store rooms.

She'd swept and mopped the floor, found a couple of chairs for the clients to sit on, and some old tablecloths to drape around their necks to protect their clothes while the cutting and shampooing was done. They looked more like a barber's cloth than a gown generally found in a ladies' hair salon, but would serve the purpose well enough. Big Fat Josie was certainly well pleased with their efforts.

'There you is, child, you's in business.'

Whereupon Josie stuck a large notice on the window. *Ladies Hair Salon Now Open. Cut and Shampoo for less than a Dollar.*

'It won't work,' Bette said, suddenly overcome with nervousness at the prospect of becoming a businesswoman. She'd been carried along by her benefactor's plan on a wave of relief and excitement, now she asked herself what the hell she was doing, setting up a hairdressing salon in this fine town with a woman who was part English, part Spanish and part native American? Had she gone completely out of her mind?

And then the door opened and her first customer appeared. A young girl of eighteen or nineteen, a shy smile on her pretty face. 'Is this the hairdresser's? Could you make me blonde, like Betty Grable?'

'Of course I can, er . . . certainly, madam.'

'Hey, are you from Canada?'

Here we go again, thought Bette, reaching for her comb.

Chad found the letter Sara had written to Bette stuffed at the back of a drawer in the old kitchen dresser. He'd been looking for a writing pad and pen, meaning to write to her himself, believing her to be back in Fowey. He was missing her so badly that he still nursed a hope he could persuade her to return.

He couldn't remember a winter that had lasted as long as this one. When he'd been a boy, he hadn't minded the cold blasts of wind that roared over the mountains, the weeks of snow, the lack of entertainment, things to do or people to talk to. But he must have changed because this one had driven him near demented with loneliness. He needed Bette, he wanted her. She was his wife and he loved her. He could understand now how lonely she must have felt, being in this strange place, this foreign land, and with a family who weren't exactly welcoming. Maybe, he should go back to Fowey and live with her there, if that's what she'd prefer.

Yet how could she have gone home, if Sara was writing to her here?

The letter was postmarked only a few weeks ago, yet according to his mother, Bette had walked out and gone back to England in the fall, just a week after the baby was born.

Something was wrong.

'Mom, what did Bette say exactly, when she left?'

Peggy looked up from her darning and stared blankly at her son. 'You've asked me that a million and one times, boy and I've answered best I can on every occasion. She didn't say nothin'. She just up and left.'

'But she must have said *something*. She wouldn't just walk

out of a door with a new baby and all her worldly possessions without a word. Besides, she needed a lift to the station. What did she say to Harry?'

'Have you ever found Harry talkative, 'cause I ain't.'

'Mom! Tell me the truth.' His tone had an edge to it now, and Peggy, sensing that he was losing patience, judged it wise to add a little more.

'Don't you go sounding off at me, boy. I've only ever tried to do my level best to make you happy. She said as how she didn't like it here. Too quiet for a city gal, she says. How it had all been a big mistake her coming here to marry you. Complained about missing her mom and wanting to show her the baby.'

Chad listened to all of this with an increasing sense of disbelief. 'She isn't no city girl, and she doesn't really get on with her mother. Never met the woman myself but she and Bette always seemed to be at daggers drawn. Are you sure that's what she said? She didn't mention her sister, Sara?'

Peggy turned away, looking slightly flustered and confused. 'Heck, she might've done. How would I know what family the girl has, or where she comes from. Anyways, they're all back together now, and good riddance.'

He was flapping the letter in her face now. 'How can they be? Her *sister* wouldn't have written this darned letter if she was back home with her in England, would she? What's happened to her? Where is my *wife*?'

'Don't make no difference to me where she is. She's not the right wife for you, that I do know, and that child ain't a Jackson.'

'How do you know that? How can you be so certain? What colour was his hair, his eyes?'

'Middling brown, I s'pose.'

'Like mine.'

'He didn't have the Jackson chin, that's what fixed it for me.

We all has this square jaw, as you know well enough. Minute I set eyes on that infant, I didn't see no square jaw.'

Chad couldn't believe what he was hearing and stared at his mother almost open-mouthed. 'You decided he couldn't possibly be my son because of the shape of his *chin*! Didn't it cross your mind that he might have inherited his mother's, which is small and pointed.' Like an elfin's, he thought, or a Cornish pisky. God, he missed that chin. He missed her.

His mother was putting away her darning, even though she hadn't finished it, fussing about, doing nothing in particular and managing to avoid eye contact, as she tended to do when shown to be in the wrong. 'You jest be thankful you're well shot of her and that's all I have to say on the subject. Wouldn't do no good at all for you to be tied to that little strumpet for the rest of your cotton-picking life. She's no better'n a whore.'

'Don't call her that.' He grasped Peggy by the arm and jerked her round to face him. 'You made her go! You told her that she wasn't wanted here, or some such tale. Didn't you?'

Her silence, and the suffuse of colour in his mother's face answered his question more eloquently than words ever could.

'No wonder she went off so suddenly with a new-born baby in her arms. Bette didn't go of her own free will at all. You sent her away. Damnation Mother, why the hell don't you keep your blasted nose out of my business.'

As Chad slammed out of the house, Peggy yelled after him, shaking a fist in fury. 'All the darned British have ever done for you, is to rob you of a good arm and the ability to work the land. And taught you to swear!'

Chad didn't pause to answer. He stormed across the yard to the barn where Harry was storing turnips, grabbed him by the collar, spun him nimbly round with his one good hand and then smashed his fist plumb centre into his brother-in-law's face, sending him sprawling backwards into the muck and straw.

'Next time you fancy poking that dirty nose of yours into my affairs, I'll bust it for you, OK? Think yourself damned lucky I don't break it right this minute. Where is she, damn you? Where did you take her? Was it to the station? Which train did she catch?'

Harry was struggling to sit up, holding his nose and whimpering, quite certain that it already must be broken, judging by the pain. He mumbled something which Chad didn't quite catch and got kicked in the ankle for his trouble, making him scream with fresh anguish.

'No, I didn't!' He was spluttering through spittle, snot and blood, pouring through his fingers. 'I took her to the cabin, like I was told. She won't starve. Take her provisions regular, jest like Mom tells me to, though she didn't take in the last lot. Still there out on the porch.'

This little confession very nearly earned him another kick as Chad became incandescent with rage at the thought of his family conspiring to keep his wife away from him. He grasped Harry by the collar and shook him, like the rat he was. 'I'd like to snap your damned thick neck in two.' Then he seemed to collect himself and flung Harry aside in a gesture of contempt. 'If I find you've hurt her . . . Man, you'd best high-tail it out of here quicker than a buzz fly, before I come looking for you with a loaded shotgun.'

Harry was shaking now, cowering in a quivering mass of fear on the dirt floor. 'Never laid a finger on her, though she's a tasty looking gal. Too soon after the birth for any fooling around, and she had the baby with her.'

Chad gave a sound of disgust and minutes later he was racing down the road in the pick-up. He'd always avoided driving, leaving it to Harry because only having the one arm made gear changing a bit dicey, but he'd darned well cope somehow, or die in the attempt.

A couple of hours later he discovered, to his despair, that the cabin was deserted. And by the look of it, it'd been empty for weeks. The ash in the stove was stone cold and a film of green had formed on the water butt. To his horror he saw that there'd been a fire in the back kitchen.

'Dear God, don't let Bette be dead.'

Boxes of stale groceries stood about on the porch. Chad kicked at one in frustrated rage, making the eggs shatter and flour spill everywhere. How could Mom do such a thing? What had possessed her? Jealousy perhaps? Over-possessiveness because of his injury? Or a foolish, out-dated hatred of the British maybe.

Chad addressed the silence, the empty, freezing cold landscape and the mountains he loved. 'The Boston tea party took place a helluva long time ago. This is World War Two, another war altogether. And I want my wife back.'

She couldn't have just vanished off the face of the earth. Nor would she risk going off into the forest, not with a young baby. God, he hoped not. There were any number of hazards waiting for her there. Snakes, bears, he didn't care to think.

He got back in the truck and headed east. Bette may not be a city girl, but she sure did like towns and shops and such like, so that was the most likely direction she'd take. He'd stop at every town he could find, every petrol station, every general store. He'd ask every person he saw. Search the entire damn country till he found her.

A cold winter had passed by, spring was here, trade was good, and Bette was content. Christmas had helped, with everyone wanting to look nice for parties and dances. Bit Fat Josie was the easiest person in the world to get along with and they were, in Josie's parlance, happy as two bugs in a rug.

Bette was delighted to be making money and paying her way at last. She was making a success of her life. Better still, she was able to mind Matthew while she worked. He could sit up now, safely harnessed in the old black perambulator, smiling cheerfully at all the lady customers, getting thoroughly spoiled.

Each afternoon, Bette would walk him around town, as she so loved to do, passing the time of day, should she spot a customer, or stop and chat for a while. It felt good to be part of a community again, and word was spreading. Her engagement book was filling up as more and more ladies ventured into this part of town for a new hair-do. Bette was considering offering facials and manicures as well, which surely couldn't be too difficult and would bring in even more trade.

In the evenings, while she and Josie ate supper together, Matthew would lie on his blanket on the hearth rug so he could kick without being encumbered with his diaper. Then Bette would bath him and put him to bed.

Only then, as night approached would she feel a twinge of loneliness and regret.

She missed Chad badly, more than she'd expected to and often wondered how he was coping, and if he'd managed to find work himself. It wasn't too bad during the day while she was kept fully occupied working. At night, it was different.

There were times when she couldn't get him out of her mind. She would lie in her narrow little bed up in the loft and the memory of his face would haunt her dreams to the extent that she would sometimes wake up in a lather of sweat, sure that she'd heard his voice calling her.

Of Barney she thought not at all. She couldn't even remember what he looked like. She wondered about him from time to time, if he was safe and well, if he'd survived the war. But no more than that.

Over in Europe, peace had been declared, or so all the papers proclaimed.

She missed her family, of course, Sara and Cory in particular. She'd sent them a card giving them her new address, without offering any further details. For some reason she didn't feel ready to tell them that she and Chad had separated, that his family had turned her out. Far too humiliating. She wanted to make a success of her life before she told the whole sordid tale of her failed marriage. Now that she had a thriving business, she meant to write again soon, a proper letter this time, maybe by the end of the month.

She just had to find the right words to explain why it had all gone wrong.

Her heart still ached for Chad. If only his family had given them the chance to be on their own and properly get to know each other. Bette was quite sure things would have turned out entirely differently then. She really didn't care if she never clapped eyes on any of the Jackson brood ever again. But she longed to see Chad again. She loved him still.

And then one day the door opened and there he was.

47

Ships' sirens and hooters sounded, every light and searchlight in the harbour, and in Fowey town itself, was switched on; a blazing celebration of peace. The town band played, church bells rang, special services were held. The narrow streets were bright with flags and bunting as the Flora Dance made its lively, happy journey through town led by the Carnival Queen, pausing every now and then for the dancers to hug and kiss friends and loved ones. The parade involved everyone, the men of the Coastguard and Lifeboat service, Hugh amongst them; Cory and his fellow crew members from the River Patrol; the WVS with Nora prominently to the fore. The Red Cross, British Legion, Girl Guides and Boy Scouts, members of the armed forces and, bringing up the rear, a happy band of nurses. Sara walked along with these, smiling broadly in her new uniform, and there was a great deal to smile about.

It was over. The war was won.

There was a pause in celebrations long enough for people to gather about their wireless sets and listen to the voice of Winston Churchill telling them that at last, the war in Europe was at an end.

'Long live the cause of freedom. God save the King.'

Later that same evening in early May, Sara sat alone in her bedroom and wept, her happiness pricked like a burst balloon. Somehow the day had been too emotional, too exhausting. Glad as she was of the end to hostilities, she ached for Charlie.

Had he survived that last, long, hard winter of battle? Would he ever come home? And if he did, it wouldn't be to her.

Having given up all hope of divorce, she'd written back to him to explain the situation, to say how very important her children were and how she could never risk their happiness. She'd known that he would be upset and bitterly disappointed, but that he would understand. Of course she didn't really know if he'd ever got the letter, Sara just hoped that it had been forwarded to him by now.

The invasion of Normandy last summer had taken longer than hoped and just before Christmas, when everyone was beginning to congratulate themselves on success, the enemy thrust forward again into Belgium right into Allied lines and it had taken well into January before the Battle of the Bulge had been won.

And now, at last, peace had been declared.

But where was Charlie now? Sara couldn't bear to think that she might never find out what had happened to him. Was he safe, back home in America perhaps, with Yvonne? Or in a hospital somewhere undergoing surgery on an injured knee? She didn't have the courage to write again, to discover the answers to these agonising questions, to find out if he was alive or dead. She must try to shut him from her mind. Oh, so much easier said than done.

Sara hadn't heard from Bette in ages, not since the baby had been born, which was causing her some concern. Then just the other day she'd got a postcard to say that she was now living in Savannah. No explanation, no details of any sort about her new life in America. She'd been deeply disappointed, and not a little concerned.

But then Bette had always been a bit scatterbrained. Perhaps her little sister was simply busy learning to be a new mother, growing up at last.

Sara had to admit that she too had slipped out of the habit of regular correspondence, allowing herself to sink into depression because of her difficult situation. Now that she'd brought herself to put pen to paper she would write again to Bette each and every week from now on, starting by giving her cheerful news about the parade and peace celebrations. It was no good feeling sorry for herself. She'd made her decision and must live with it, even if it broke her heart to see the joy of other couples starting life afresh.

Men were returning home, every day bringing happy reunions. Prisoners of war were being released, some men turning up on the doorstep of a wife or mother who had believed them to be dead. Happiness was everywhere, permeating the entire town, except here, in Sara's new home on the Esplanade.

Not for one moment had she expected such a reunion for herself, but then it happened, right out of the blue. She came home one afternoon from the hospital, collected the children from her mother as usual, and the three of them were having tea in the garden in the lovely May sunshine when a voice quietly remarked: 'I think what I've missed most have been your Cornish pasties.'

Drew squealed, '*Charlie*,' and leapt from his seat, sending his glass flying, spilling orange juice everywhere as he flung himself into his friend's arms. Sara simply stared, quite unable to believe her eyes, heartily wishing she could do exactly the same.

Jenny laughed with delight and ran to hug Charlie fiercely about the waist. 'Oh, I'm so glad to see you back safe, Charlie. We've been so worried about you.'

Sara blinked back tears, thinking that it had never crossed her mind to imagine that her children would be worried too.

'Have you any gum, chum?' Drew cheekily asked.

'I certainly have, old buddy.' Charlie fished a couple of

packets out of his pocket, then stood grinning from ear to ear as the children ripped off the paper, stuffing the gum into their mouths and jiggling up and down with coos of delight. But his gaze remained fixed on Sara.

She tried his name, just to make sure she wasn't dreaming all of this. 'Charlie?' Then went over to put out a tentative hand, to touch his face, his cheek, his strong jaw, trace the outline of his mouth. He grasped hold of her exploring hand and pressed it quickly to his lips.

'It's me. A bit battered but still all in one piece.'

Sara longed to fall into his arms, to kiss him for all she was worth, but the children were watching with wide, innocent eyes. Relief washed through her in a warm tide of love. Charlie was here. He was safe, and that was all that mattered.

'We've missed you,' Jenny said, her little face suddenly serious. 'Mummy has 'specially. She's cried for you, I heard her.'

Charlie's gaze locked with Sara's again. This was dangerous territory which must be traversed with care. Children were vulnerable creatures and had a happy knack of bluntly coming out with the absolute truth, sharing secrets you'd much rather keep quiet. He gently ruffled the children's hair, one hand on each small head, making them giggle and squirm. 'I dare say your mom has only been crying when she gets tired, like after spending hours picking up the mess that you terrible twosome make, or when you won't go to bed on time.'

'That's not true, is it Mummy?' Jenny said, outraged. 'I'm very tidy. Daddy inspects our rooms every morning and if they're messy we're not allowed to play out. Or he puts us on what he calls fatigues, which means we have to scrub the kitchen floor or wash his car or something. Daddy is horrid sometimes, like a sergeant major inspecting the troops. Drew's room is always a mess though and Daddy lets *him* off, 'cept that he says if he doesn't clear it up this time, he'll take the telescope away.'

Drew tried to stick out his tongue and Jenny giggled because the rude gesture turned into a chewing gum bubble.

Sara knew she should scold them, try to sound stern and tell them not to be naughty but she couldn't seem able to do so.

'Did you fight many battles, kill loads and loads of Germans?' Drew wanted to know and Sara hushed the excited little boy, finally finding her voice to remind him that Charlie must be tired and wouldn't want to talk about all of that right now.

'I'll tell you another time,' Charlie agreed. 'Maybe one day when you come out to the States to visit me.'

The two children gasped, then looked at each in delight. 'Wow, is that a promise?'

Once again Charlie's eyes were on Sara. 'If your mom will bring you.'

Sara swallowed. It was unfair of him to use the children to try and reach her. Yet somehow she couldn't bring herself to blame him. She saw that he longed for her as much as she longed for him, and what did she owe Hugh after all he'd done to her? The thought of going to America with Charlie was delicious, wonderful, although quite impossible. She simply couldn't do it. Mustn't even think of such a thing.

'Drew, Jenny, go and play on the swing for a little while. Lieutenant Denham and I need to talk about war business for a moment.'

'Don't be silly, Mummy. The war is over.'

'Yes, I know, darling, but there are still things to . . . . sort out. Please, do as I say.'

'Here, I brought you some comics too,' and Charlie handed them a brown paper packet.

'Gosh thanks, I mean, aw gee, thanks,' said Drew, trying to copy Charlie's American accent and sound big and important.

When her children had skipped away, arguing robustly over who was to read *Superman* and who *Batman* comic first, Sara turned to Charlie with anxious eyes. 'You should go! What if Hugh were to suddenly arrive home. What excuse could we possibly give for your being here? Oh, but it's so wonderful to see you.'

'I wish I could touch you again, hold you, kiss you.'

'We'd best sit down before you do.'

'I just might, kids or no kids.'

They sat together on the garden seat, not quite touching, not speaking and yet Sara's head was bursting with words, her arms aching to hold him.

He'd taken off his forage cap and now he ran his fingers through brown hair even shorter than before, and Sara wondered if a part of it had been shaved off and was just starting to grow again. She could make out a few scars here and there, patches of raw, red skin that might once have been burns or blisters, although nothing too serious. His face was pale and gaunt, lines etched at the corners of those lovely, warm, brown eyes. He looked like a man who had known pain, a soldier who had suffered.

Unseen by the children she slid her hand into his. Instantly, his fingers curled about hers. 'You still don't look well. Are you truly recovered? How is the leg?'

'My leg is fine, got a few dents and cracks in it but nothing that won't heal in time. My heart, however, is another matter. I doubt that will ever heal, not if I have to live the rest of my life without you.'

A tear slid down her cheek, fell on their joined hands, ran over her thumb. Neither of them wiped it away.

'You know that I can't leave him. I must stay. I have to, because . . .'

'Of the children, I know. It's OK, I understand. At least, it's not really OK. I don't like it one bit, but I do understand.' Another small silence and then, 'Yvonne wrote me. She's found someone, another guy. She's happy to agree to a divorce. There won't be any difficulties. Would it help if I talked to Hugh, promised to look after the kids as if they were my own. Because I would, you know.'

'I know you would, Charlie, but no, that wouldn't help at all. He'd be furious. It's not that Hugh is particularly interested in the children. He's never spent much time with them but they belong to him, do you see? They are his children, just as I am his wife, and he intends to keep us, like possessions. Trophies on his wall.'

'Hell's teeth, the man's a creep.'

'Perhaps one day, when the children are older . . . but no, that's not fair. You must find someone else, not hang around waiting for me.'

'I don't want anyone else, Sara, I want only you.'

'Don't be silly, you didn't survive this terrible war to spend the rest of your life alone. I want you to marry, to be happy, to have children of your own.' Emotion caught in her throat and she gave a little hiccupping sob.

'Don't ask me to do that. I couldn't begin to even think of looking. You're the woman for me, and always will be, Sara. I love you.'

'Don't . . . When do you leave?' As if it mattered.

'Day after tomorrow.'

Not much time then to change her mind. Sara was openly crying now, tears rolling unchecked down her cheeks, her emotion quite beyond her control, and he was gripping both her hands now, so hard that she felt sure her fingers might snap in two. She dragged her hands away, slapped at the tears, aware of the children not too far away. 'You must go. Now, this minute, before Hugh comes home. Before I beg you never, ever, to leave me.'

'Sara, please come with me. It's not too late and . . .'

She stood up quickly, half turned away while she fished for a handkerchief up her sleeve. 'No, please don't touch me again,

Charlie. I love you so much, too much. I'm going to call the children in a moment so they can say bye-bye, and then I want you to go, as if you and I were simply friends wishing each other well for a peaceful future. Will you do that for me?'

'You think they'll be fooled? You have sharp kids.'

She pushed back her hair, resolutely turned up her mouth into a parody of a smile. She looked so brave in that moment, Charlie's heart clenched with love for her.

'Drew, Jenny, come and say goodbye. Lieutenant Denham has to go now.'

'Can I write to you?'

He was standing beside her, so close she could sense the warmth from his body. Sara kept her eyes on her children as they came bounding over. They would reach her any second. She glanced at the kitchen door. Hugh had still not appeared. If she was going to change her mind, it must be done quickly, *now*, before he walked out of her life for good. 'No, please don't write.'

He hugged both children, went through the motions of urging them to come visit him in America, promising that he'd be sure to call in on them, next time he was in Blighty. But their little faces were sad, knowing that he lied.

When he turned to Sara she had herself back under control again. She held out a hand for him to formally shake, a polite smile of dismissal carefully in place. 'Thank you for taking the time to call and see us and let us know that you've fully recovered. I wish you every happiness for the future.'

He ignored her outstretched hand completely. 'Kids, shut your eyes for a moment. I'm going to kiss your mom.' And he did. He gathered Sara close in his arms and he kissed her, long and hard. Seconds later, he was striding away across the lawn. A door banged, and then he was gone.

48

'Chad? I don't believe it.'

'I can't quite believe it myself. Can I come in?' He stood in the doorway, shuffling his feet, his awkwardness all too plain to see.

Bette's first instinct was to run to him, to fling her arms around his neck and kiss him. It quite alarmed her how badly she wanted to do that, but she stiffened her resolve. He'd let her down. His family had turned her out. He'd rejected her, and his son. Walked away without so much as a backward glance. 'If you like.'

Fortunately she had no one in at present, so she went and put the closed sign on the door. Glancing across at Big Fat Josie serving coffee behind the counter, she jerked her head in the direction of the salon, indicating her unexpected visitor. Josie got the message all right and nodded.

Back in the salon, Chad was standing by the pram, peeping in at Matthew. Bette's heart gave a little jump. Why hadn't he shown an interest earlier? The baby was six months old and growing into a fine little chap, no thanks to his father. She felt suddenly possessive of him, as if she somehow didn't want Chad poking his nose in. It was far too late.

'I'd best move him, so we don't wake him.' She opened the back door and wheeled the pram outside, parking it in a dry, sunny spot where she could easily see it, then turned to face her husband, chin high and her expression cool.

Chad looked different. All tidy and smart, for one thing,

instead of the rough working clothes she'd grown used to seeing him in. But there was something more, something different. At first she couldn't make out what it was, and then it came to her. Both sleeves of his jacket were filled, and from one protruded a piece of metal apparatus she couldn't quite make out clearly. He was wearing a false arm. A rush of sympathy came instinctively to her but she tried to harden her heart against it. Pity had always been the last thing he'd wanted.

Nothing the direction of her gaze he gave a small grimace. 'It's new. Not got used to the darned thing yet.'

She offered him one of the chairs she used to cut clients' hair. Made tea, and Chad tried to hold the cup with the metal clamp that served as a false hand.

Bette quietly watched him struggle, didn't rush in to offer either assistance or sympathy. Then with a sigh of exasperation, he used his good hand instead.

'Sorry about the pot arm. I'm supposed to spend hours each day learning to use the darned thing, getting my balance, trying to hold a cup or some such, breaking most of'em. It's OK for the doctors to tell me it'll be fine, they don't have to try and operate it.'

'I dare say it'll take a bit of practice,' Bette coolly remarked and saw him push back his shoulders, seeming to welcome her brisk acceptance.

'Sure! I'll get the hang of it in the end. Anyway, these last months have been mightly lonely without you, Bette, arm or no arm.' He set the cup and saucer aside, the tea largely untouched. But then Bette had forgotten that he preferred it iced, as all southerners did.

She had to ask him. It was the one question that had haunted her from the day of Matthew's birth. Even so, a part of her didn't expect, or even want an answer. Bette had no wish to hear his excuses. But then another part was desperate to know, and to understand.

'Why didn't you come?'

There it was, out in the open. She had said it. Striving to keep her expression neutral as their eyes locked, Bette was shocked to discover that she did still have feelings for him, and nothing to do with pity at all. 'I waited and waited for you, but you never came. Did you hate me so much?'

'We've both made mistakes.'

'Is that meant to be some sort of apology, or an excuse?'

Chad drew in a deep breath. 'Neither, it's a fact, that's all. We messed up, both of us. I thought you'd gone back home, Bette. Mom said you had. Only recently did I discover that she'd lied. I found a letter from Sara, so realised you couldn't have gone home.' He handed it to her. 'I'm sorry about that.'

Bette stared at the envelope in her hand, then set it down on a table, to open later.

'I searched the cabin, Carreville, every place I could think of. Been looking for weeks. Finally chanced upon a little place called Kitson Point, talked to a general store keeper called Joe. Said he rescued you one dark night and took you to his sister's in Savannah. So here I am.'

'Yes, here you are.' Bette didn't know what else to say, didn't know if she could forgive him for rejecting her child.

As if reading her thoughts, he cleared his throat and went on: 'I don't know why Mom got it into her head that the baby wasn't mine, that he wasn't a Jackson, and all because of the shape of his chin. Hell, I would never have given it a thought if she hadn't planted the doubt in my mind, but then you confessed about Barney and I went off in a huff to do me some hunting and think on things for a spell. By the time I got back, you'd gone, and I believed her when she said you'd returned to England.'

He was leaning both elbows on his knees, rather awkwardly, admittedly, but he looked good. She'd forgotten how attractive he was, how kind his eyes. 'She lied to me too, said you were waiting for me in the cabin.'

'God, how you must have suffered all alone out there, and you had a fire? I saw the mess.'

'We were unhurt, Matthew and I, even if the kitchen wasn't.'

'Matthew. That's a fine name. If only I'd known . . .' A small silence fell between them. Bette was the one who ended it, softening a little as she recognised the genuineness of his emotions.

'You're right, we did both mess things up. I'm sorry about Barney. It was never meant, it just happened. He's an attractive bloke, quite the charmer, but we behaved badly and I'm sorry about that. You deserved better from me. But however unwilling, he was prepared to stand by me, when we both thought you were dead. That says something for him I suppose, though he was glad enough to be relieved of the responsibility once we found out you were alive, after all.'

Chad gave a wry smile. 'That's Barney all right. Real pain in the ass but stands by you when the going gets tough.' And then, after a long moment. 'I made mistakes back then, too.'

'Yes, you did.'

'I lied too, Bette.'

'Seems to be a family trait.'

'I made out I was this well-set-up guy, with land and plenty of dollars in my pocket. When I said all of that stuff, trying to impress you, I never thought it'd come to this. But then I fell for you real bad, and by the time you got out here I realised that I'd nothing to offer you at all, not any of the things I'd promised, not even a whole man. I was half a man, not able to cut my own steak, or tie my own shoes. I hated that, to be beholden, needing you to help me with everything.'

She met his gaze and saw the pain in it, and her heart went out to him. 'I really didn't mind. I loved you.'

'Past tense, I notice?'

Bette made no reply to this, merely continued to regard him in silence, her mind whirling.

She'd come a long way since the day she'd stepped off that train as a green girl, a young war-bride paraded about town like a trophy. Yet far from welcoming her, the Jackson family had trapped her, first at the farm and then in the cabin, and all because they didn't trust her, perhaps with some cause. Nevertheless, their behaviour was cruel all the same. They'd used a young girl's foolishness as a weapon against her.

But she wasn't a green girl any longer. The Germans might be on the run but Bette meant to stay put in this fine country, was building herself a good reputation here in lovely Savannah. She'd grown up a great deal in recent months, and was proud of her success. She'd been running her hairdressing salon for nearly five months now and knew that she could survive. On her own, if need be.

It was lonely at times but she was content.

She could afford to pay Josie rent now, and still have enough left over to get by comfortably enough, so she wasn't complaining. She'd painted and done it up real smart, bought herself a few bits of second-hand furniture, sewn curtains for the windows, even made some new friends. Big Fat Josie insisted she could stay on and live above the store for as long as she liked, but Bette was saving hard, hoping one day to buy a pretty little house in the square, just like Josie's. That was her goal. Independence, for herself and Matthew. And she meant to achieve it.

No matter what happened with Chad, she wasn't going to put her child's future at risk.

He got up from the hairdresser's chair and walked over to the window to gaze out upon the street, looking decidedly uncomfortable. 'I hoped that if ever I found you again, you might find it in your heart to forgive and forget; to give us a second chance. If I can accept what happened between you and Barney as a mistake, in view of the circumstances, then maybe you could forgive me all those stupid lies I told.'

He turned to look back at her then, his heart in his eyes. 'I never meant to cheat you. Could we try again, do you reckon, Bette?'

For some long minutes she still said nothing, her mind a turmoil of emotion, whirling round and round, asking herself what did she feel, what did she want? Bette felt so confused, she couldn't even begin to think.

He wasn't calling her any pet names now, she noticed. He was cautious and entirely respectful, nervous, as she was, of saying the wrong thing. But could it all be put to rights between them, or was it too late?

'Your family abandoned me, left me alone in a mountain shack in the middle of nowhere, with a new baby. That's just about as heartless as you can get. I'm not sure I can ever forgive them that, let alone you for allowing it to happen.'

He looked as if he were about to protest but Bette held up a hand to silence him and kept right on going.

'OK, so you were licking your wounds some place over my affair with Barney, but while you were doing that and ignoring your son, anything could've happened to us. Matthew might have caught a chill, got pneumonia and died, been bitten by a snake or something, let alone burnt to death in the back kitchen. We could've both been killed and who would have known, or cared?'

He looked stricken. 'Oh God, Bette, don't say that. *I* would. You know I would.' Instinctively he stepped forward, his good arm outstretched as if he wanted to hold her, but when she made no move towards him, dropped it by his side again, uncertain and fearful of rejection.

'I wish I could believe you.'

'I still love you, hon.' He offered her a sheepish grin, gazing at her then with all the love he felt for her brimming in his warm, brown eyes. 'The minute I found out where you were, I hightailed it over here, like some half-wit, love-sick fool come courting his gal. Will you take me back, Bette? Can we try again, do you reckon? I'm not asking you to come back to the farm, to my family. We can stay here, if you like, have our own place like we should've done from the start. You could carry on with your little business. I'll mebbe get lucky and find me a job, now I have the pot arm an' all.'

She tried to interrupt but he put up a hand to stop her, edged closer to touch her hair tenderly with his fingers, and kept right on talking.

'I don't want to spoil things for you and I know you prefer town life to the backwoods. I never was much of a farmer myself, 's'matter of fact. Joined the marines like a shot when I got the chance, and I don't regret it. Met you, didn't I? Heck, and you sure do look pretty. Don't know how I'm managing to keep my hands off you. Hey, did ya hear that? I said, hands! Hell, that's pushing it a bit, huh? Should I say hand and hook, do you reckon?'

And suddenly Bette got a fit of the giggles. He seemed so much more relaxed, just like the Chad she'd fallen in love with, always ready for a laugh and not so troubled by his infirmity, not any more. Happiness washed over her and she knew it was going to be all right between them.

'Nothing's been settled yet,' she cautioned. 'I've agreed to nothing, except that we've been silly young fools. We'd need to take things slowly. Give ourselves time to get to know each other again, and used to the idea of being married.'

'Right!' He nodded, very seriously, his eyes roving over her face.

'Is it too late, do you think, to put things right?'

'Not by my book. But I sure would like to kiss you before I bust a gut.'

Letting out a spurt of laughter, Bette reached up, put her arms about his neck and kissed him, long and hard, full on the mouth.

A chorus of cheering came from the door. 'Thank heaven for that,' boomed Big Fat Josie, a few of her favourite customers gathered about her, clearly enjoying the moment along with her. 'I thought you two would niver git together, and we ain't got all day, you've got clients waiting.'

'Nothing is settled yet. I've agreed to nothing,' Bette repeated, laughing nonetheless.

'Course you ain't. A gal should play hard to get. But after you've done Dolly-May's hair, we can all set awhile on my porch and talk over how you two is gonna let me have that retirement I allus dreamed of, and run this ol' store for me.'

49

Later, when Hugh did eventually come home, he didn't seem to notice that his wife was even quieter than usual. He was, as usual, in a rush to eat and get back to The Ship in time for evening opening, so demanded to know why his meal wasn't ready.

Sara apologised and ran about shaking and banging pans as if that would make things cook any quicker, acutely aware of Jenny's eyes upon her, as if her eight-year-old brain were trying to weigh up the situation.

'You are completely incompetent, Sara. I believe I shall have to insist upon you giving up this nursing nonsense unless you get much better organised. And the place is filthy, look at that sink, full of dirty pots and pans.'

'I prepared the meal in rather a rush. I shall clear it up now, don't worry. Of course, you could always fill the sink with hot water and wash them for me.'

'Have you even made the beds? I'm sure you do them perfectly well at the hospital every day, but are the children's made up, I wonder? They weren't the other morning.'

'I overslept. I was tired. It won't happen again.'

'I should hope it won't. Have the children seen you at all today? You're turning into a slut, Sara, and I will not have it.'

'Mummy has been playing with us in the garden and we forgot the time, Daddy,' Jenny chimed up, and Sara met her daughter's gaze with the uncomfortable feeling that, child or not, she seemed to understand what was going on better than was good for her.

Hugh turned on the child and told her sharply to go to bed this very minute.

'It's barely six o'clock, Hugh. Far too soon for bed. Please don't take your temper out on the children.'

'I'm not in a temper. I'm in despair over your hopelessness.'

'Perhaps if I had a cleaner, that would help. Or if you got someone else to make the pasties for you, and clean the pub at least. I really don't think I can go on like this, coping with two jobs, not now that my training is so advanced. I'm exhausted, Hugh. I need help, not criticism.'

'You are my *wife*! It is your duty to help me in the business. If you can't cope, you have only yourself to blame for taking too much on. This sudden passion to become a nurse is really quite pathetic. You aren't capable of completing the training, let alone passing the exams. Now that you've had your little rebellion, I shall expect you to hand in your resignation forthwith, or I will personally go and see your matron and tell her this simply will not do, that I am removing you from the course.'

'You will do no such thing.'

'Oh, but I will, Sara. Do not attempt to defy me in this. You are depriving your children of their mother, and *me* the proper care and attention a husband has the right to expect from a wife. I won't have it. You'll give up this nursing nonsense or I may be forced to deprive *you* of your children.'

Sara said nothing. She had no intention whatsoever of handing in her resignation, and surely, deep down, Hugh must be aware of that fact. She'd stood her ground and won over the committees, hadn't she? She'd stuck with Nora Snell till the bitter end, and would have her way in this too, with or without his assistance.

But she really didn't have the energy to fight him right now, not today, when she had to cope with losing Charlie all over again.

He sat drumming his fingers impatiently on the table while Sara calmly washed the dirty pans and dishes piled up in the sink, served up the meal and supervised the children. He made no attempt to help her, or pay them the slightest attention.

Jenny and Drew seemed to withdraw into themselves, huddled together in a corner reading the *Batman* and *Superman* comics that Charlie had brought for them. Before Hugh noticed, Sara quietly instructed them to go upstairs and get ready for bed.

If Drew were to blurt out that Charlie had called and given him some new comics, in his usual, enthusiastic, little boy way, all hell would break loose.

Thankfully the children said nothing. Perhaps sensing their father would be angry, for once they obeyed meekly and crept away.

Hugh didn't glance up from his meal, not even to say goodnight.

Sara couldn't help but compare his stern demeanour and casual dismissal of his children to that of Charlie, who had hugged and cuddled them quite naturally. Perhaps he always had been this distant, so wrapped up in himself. What kind of an upbringing was that for a child, if their father never openly demonstrated any affection for them? Sadie had been bad enough, always a little distant from her two daughters. Her attitude might have been foolish, but never malicious, as Hugh's generally was, and she'd improved somewhat lately.

He ate his meal in silence, reading the paper at the same time, saying not a word to Sara. When finally he left, without a word of thanks or appreciation, she breathed a long-held sigh of relief.

Much later, Sara was sitting on the sofa with the children cuddled on her lap, reading *William Does His Bit*, when there came a knock on the door. Her heart leapt and then steadied as she reminded herself that Charlie had gone. He wouldn't be coming back.

She opened the door to Cory, who came bouncing into the room, clearly the bearer of some important news or other. Hamil Charke was close behind him, carrying a box.

'We've something to show you,' Hamil said, and laid the small attaché case on the table before her.

Sara had badly wanted it to be Charlie, except where was the point? It was all too late. She couldn't quite remember when he'd said his train was leaving but perhaps even now he was on his way to the station. Even if he wasn't, she still couldn't go with him. Hugh might continue to be grumpy and morose, as bad-tempered and difficult as ever, but nothing had changed.

He would take immense pleasure in depriving her of the children, should she be reckless enough as to make a bid for freedom, or disobey him in any way. This was a weapon he was clearly going to make more and more use of in the future.

She struggled to pay attention to what Cory was saying. 'What is it? Some flotsam and jetsam you've picked up on one of your fishing trips?'

'You could say so,' Cory agreed, looking unusually solemn. 'But this ain't no flotsam that you've ever clapped eyes on, at least I hope you haven't. We've been sitting on it for weeks, in a manner of speaking, but it's like sitting on a stick of dynamite. Now that peace has been declared, we thought you should see it afore we contact the authorities.'

'Authorities, what are you talking about?'

'Send them nippers off to bed, this don't concern them.'

Drew was pushing himself through the huddle of adults so as not to miss anything. 'Is that the wireless set Iris used to use?' The little boy nodded sagely. 'Yes, that's the one.'

Sara looked down at her son, and then at the small case, in surprise and bewilderment. 'What are you talking about?'

Drew looked up at her with all the wisdom of his six years. 'Didn't you know, Mummy? Iris used to talk into it sometimes when nobody was watching.' He put his hand to his mouth to cover a spurt of laughter. 'At least, she thought no one was watching. She never saw me crouching but I saw her once in the stock room, and another time in Daddy's office.'

Cory nodded. 'I thought as much. It could be that Hugh knows nothing about this, although we did find it in his boat.'

Hamil Charke cut in, his face sympathetic. 'He could have held on to it simply to protect Iris, Cory m'boy.'

'Daddy knew about the wireless,' interrupted Drew, full of self-importance at knowing something the adults didn't. 'He was in the office with Iris when she used it.'

Sara sank onto the sofa, not able to take in the implications. 'What are you suggesting, Dad, that Hugh was some sort of . . .? No, no, he couldn't possibly be.'

'Mummy . . .'

'Hush Drew, that's enough for now. Let Mummy think.' Her mind was spinning, crazily searching for clues, for a solution. 'It's true that he was always off on some mission or other, that he kept hinting to me about what a hero he was but that he wasn't allowed to tell me anything. I know the work he did was often risky, dangerous even, but I still believed that he exaggerated, that he loved to boast and make much more of what he did than was actually the case.'

'Mummy! Mummy!' Drew was jumping up and down with frustration, desperate to gain her attention. 'You don't under-stand, Mummy. Daddy was a *spy*.'

'Don't be silly, darling. Look, you really should go to bed. You too, Jenny.'

Drew ignored the instruction. 'He let me look through his telescope sometimes, though he would never take me up on the headland. That's where he used to watch for enemy ships and submarines, and the French navy, no, no the French fishing fleet. Boats that caught men instead of fish. Would they use nets, do you think, Mummy? And he used to come and tell me all about his "ops" when he came home. He told me once that he could get shot for what he'd done. Did he do something really nasty, do you think, Mummy?'

A small silence stretched out for several long seconds after this somewhat garbled explanation, then Hamil Charke calmly remarked, 'Watch what you say, son.'

'But the war's over now,' Drew said in his piping, innocent voice, 'so I don't have to keep it a secret any longer, do I? It doesn't matter any more.'

'It does if you tell porkies, darling. I'm sure Daddy didn't do any such thing. Spy indeed! You've been reading too many adventure comics.'

The little boy was appalled that no one believed him. 'But it's true. It is, it is. He said that he went over to France lots of times on trips in his boat. Dozens and dozens. Rupert Bear flies to France in his little plane. I like listening to stories about Rupert Bear. Does Charlie fly a plane, Mummy? Did Daddy do a bad thing? He wasn't a traitor, was he? I read about traitors in my William books.'

Sara hunkered down. 'Hush Drew, darling. You're getting overtired and rather excited. The French were on our side during the war, so how could Daddy be a traitor? And it would be much too far for him to go over in his boat to France, not as often as you say. I think you must've misunderstood.'

'No, I didn't!' Drew gave a weary sigh as if in despair over the stupidity of adults. 'He saved lots and lots of lives. British pilots escaping from the Nazis. He told me.'

Cory said, 'The boy might be right but this radio transmitter does seem to indicate something much more serious than saving British pilots. Somebody should p'rhaps talk to Iris. Where is she? I haven't seen her around for a while.'

'Gone home to Truro to live with her mother.'

'Or so we've been told,' said Hamil darkly.

Drew piped up again, determined to be heard. 'He used to get cross with me when I asked why I couldn't go with him instead of Iris, but once he brought me back a French flag, for my collection. I've still got it in my room, so I *know* he went to France, all the time. He helped agents escape the Nazis. He called them evaders. Except one time he must've done something wrong, 'cos they all died. The only good thing, he said, was that they weren't British, they were only Americans. He didn't like Americans. He told me, Mummy, he did, he did. He said he was glad he'd killed them. Pow! Pow! Do you think he used a gun? He made me swear to keep it a secret. And I have Mummy, I have.'

Sara was staring at her son in dismay, struggling to understand the full implication of what he was saying, but something was buzzing in her head, like an angry bee, and she couldn't seem to take in a single word.

Cory instructed Jenny to be a good girl and go and fetch her mummy a small glass of sherry. 'She's had a bit of a nasty shock.' Then he patted the boy's head kindly. 'Don't worry, we believe you, son. Your dad is a very brave man, and no, I don't think for one minute he shot anyone with a gun, not even a Yank. Now look at what Grandpa has fetched for you, a nice sherbet dab from the corner shop, one each for you and Jenny. Now do you take that up to bed with you, for a treat.'

'Ooh, thanks Grandpa, can I, Mummy?'

Sara nodded, too numbed to speak. The only rational thought in her head was a question, quite a silly one in the circumstances.

Had it all been innocent then, all those hours he'd spent with Iris? Perhaps they hadn't been having an affair at all, but working together as British agents?

If that was so then she was the one entirely in the wrong, the one who had betrayed and ruined their marriage, just as Hugh had accused her of doing. And her husband was a hero, after all. But what was all this about dead Americans? Sara didn't seem able to take any of that in, not properly. She just felt sick, dreadfully, dreadfully sick.

'Goody, goody, come on Jenny.' Drew was saying, then just as he turned to run off upstairs, he delivered his final bomb-shell. 'I don't know what Iris was saying on the wireless, Grandad, 'cos she was using funny words.'

Cory softly enquired, 'Do you mean funny French words, like the fishermen who come up the river, son?'

'No, course not,' said Drew with weary impatience, already unpeeling the paper off his sherbet dab. 'She talked to the wireless transmitter thingy in German, like that man on the proper wireless does sometimes. Iris was a *German* spy, Grandpa, not a French one. Come on, Jenny, don't take all day.'

50

'Where are you staying tonight?' Bette asked Chad, quite casually, as she shut up the salon.

Chad cleared his throat. 'I was thinking mebbe I'd find me a room at some hotel or other in town. Where do you suggest?'

'You gotta be joking. You couldn't afford the charge. This ain't some two-bit, one-horse town, ya know?' Her mock American accent was strong and he glanced at her in pleased surprise.

'Hey, you got that real good.'

'Maybe I'll make a Yankee war-bride after all, 'cepting that, strictly speaking, we aren't man and wife yet, not so's you'd notice.'

'We been through the ceremony.'

'There's a bit more to being married than that, wouldn't you say?'

'Uh-huh! What do you reckon we ought to do about that? Don't want to scare you off.'

She was leading him up the stairs. 'Who said I would be? I don't scare easy.'

Big Fat Josie had insisted on minding Matthew for the evening. 'It'll give you young 'uns time to talk,' she'd said. 'Without all that fussing and wailing from the nipper. I'm only next door, so I'll bring him over later. Much later.' And she'd given a huge, roguish wink.

Chad was following her into the tiny living room. 'I was worried you might prefer to go back to England and marry Barney instead.'

'If I'd wanted Barney, I'd have stayed and married him when I had the chance. Probably would have been a big mistake but I wasn't quite so stupid as to make it. Anyway, we've been through all of that. Why bring Barney into it all over again?'

'He's a real man. He's got two arms.'

Bette drew the blind and the room was bathed in a cool, green glow. Chad wasn't looking at her but she would have been a fool not to recognise the heartrending vulnerability in those words. This was obviously still an issue for him, still creating a block. 'When did it take two arms to make love to a woman?'

'Aw, Bette. Don't make fun of me.'

She pulled him round to face her, grasped his face between her two hands. 'Look at me, Chad Jackson. You're my man, right? I've travelled half round the world to be with you, borne your child, survived your family's maltreatment of me, and I'm still here. I've stuck around. Does that convince you that I'm not leaving? Not now, not ever.'

As she talked, she was unbuttoning his shirt, sliding it down his arms.

'Hasn't it occurred to you that maybe I hung around because I was still hoping that you'd come calling one day? So don't for one minute imagine that you aren't the handsomest man in the whole world to me, and the number of arms you happen to possess, doesn't matter a damn.'

She was tugging off the vest he wore underneath the shirt, before turning her attention to the buckle of his trouser belt. It wouldn't come loose and he had to help her. And all the while she was kissing him, sliding her mouth over his, pressing herself close against him.

'Barney Willert still doesn't get a look in, however charming he might be. Maybe when we first got together, you and me, we were both a bit insecure, me having left home and family, you with your injuries.'

She pushed him down on the bed and he gave a low moan. But she didn't lie down next to him. Not yet. It was a warm, sunny day in June, the semi-tropical heat turning their bodies slick with sweat in seconds whenever they moved. She slid out of her cotton frock in seconds and sat astride him clad only in her French knickers. 'But that's all in the past. Now we have a second chance, an opportunity to get it right this time, and, thanks to Big Fat Josie, pretty good employment in the form of a business to run. What could be better?'

She chuckled as she said this. 'OK, I can think of one or two other things which might be a bit more exciting that we could be doing right now.' Bette wasn't even wearing a brassière in the heat, and lifting his hand she smoothed it over her firm young body, hearing the low groan deep in his throat as he did so.

'So can I.' He reached for her and she leaned away from him, making him wait.

'I should have said, rather than serving behind the counter in a general store, but I'm sure we can make something of it, if we work together, don't you reckon?'

'Aw, Bette, I'd do anything for you. It sounds great.'

She sank on to him now, rubbing her breasts against his bare chest. 'And we can always find something more interesting to do to pass the time when we're not working.'

She helped him to take off the false limb, unstrapping it above the elbow, and when the purple-scarred, floppy, loose section of boneless flesh which had embarrassed him so deeply was finally revealed, she kissed it. She stroked the severed stump, the scarred flesh, heard his small sob as she did so. She knew that it pained him still, for all the arm no longer existed. She remembered how she would often wake to find him crying in his sleep, or jerking and sweating and fighting the bed-clothes as if he was batting out a fire. She'd calm and quieten him, hold him close and even sing softly to him as she would a child, until he slept peacefully again.

She didn't try to soothe him now but deliberately set out to excite and captivate him. Bette kissed and fondled him, took his penis in her hand, savouring the velvety feel of it even as it hardened to her touch.

She stood up above him, slid down the satin knickers, then tossed them to one side. 'Can't you see anything about me that might interest you? Nothing at all worth touching, even after all this time? Don't you know what you did to me, Chad, sleeping beside me night after night and not laying a finger on me? I began to despair that you ever would touch me. It'd drive any girl wild.'

She dropped her voice to a seductive purr. 'And like I say, you're still a handsome bugger, arm or no bloody arm.'

He reached for her then, pulling her hard against him so that he slid inside her as sweetly as she remembered. She rocked and pushed and felt him throb inside her, his hand still roving over her, caressing her breasts, her neck, her throat, his eyes greedily taking in every detail of her lovely body, marvelling at her beauty, at the satin smoothness of her milk-white skin, the pinkness of her flickering tongue as he kissed her over and over again.

Chad didn't know how he'd resisted her all those long and lonely nights, so fearful of her revulsion and rejection he'd put all hope of love-making from his mind. Now he couldn't seem to get enough of her, wanting, needing her more than seemed right and proper.

He pulled her beneath him, taking her with such force that Bette gasped with shock and the sheer pleasure of it.

That afternoon, they reached heights of passion she'd only ever dreamed of. Afterwards, replete and entwined, they slept a little until the cool of evening woke them. Then Bette sat up, her expression thoughtful.

'There's just one thing left for you to do. Don't move, don't get dressed, just wait for me here.'

She pulled on her cotton frock and skipped down the steps. Within minutes, she was back. In her arms was Matthew. Chad made to get out of the bed but she ordered him to stay put. And he did, his eyes fixed on the baby as Bette placed the infant on his knee.

'There you are, Chad Jackson. Meet Matthew, your son. That's what we are after all, your family.'

He gazed upon the child, ran a finger over the soft curve of his cheek, gazed into the wide brown eyes, alert with curiosity, and so like his own. 'Aw Bette, did a guy ever have as sweet a gal as you, and as fine a son as could be found anywhere in the country, in the whole damn world. Have you any idea how much I love you both?'

Bette chuckled as she pulled off the dress once more and snuggled in beside him. 'I hope I'm going to have many years in which to discover the answer to that question.'

51

It was the longest night Sara could ever remember. She'd talked to her father about these revelations for some hours before, finally, he and Hamil had gone off to inform the authorities. In any other circumstances none of them would have paid any credence to the ramblings of one small boy, but the wireless transmitter was a physical presence before their very eyes, providing evidence for the child's words.

Not that Drew understood the significance of what, exactly, he'd accused his own father of doing: that if Iris was a German spy, then Hugh might be too. Like all other small boys who had grown up during war-time, it had all been exciting fun, and fiction and reality had become rather mixed up.

And where was Iris? If she'd gone back to her mother's in Truro, why hadn't she taken the wireless set with her? What was it doing in Hugh's boat?

Sara sat in her bedroom with the door locked and listened to him come in after closing time, as he usually did. She heard him noisily making himself a drink in the kitchen, clearly irritated that she hadn't waited up to make him some supper as he demanded.

It took some time but at last she heard him climb the stairs and go to bed. Even then she couldn't sleep, tossing and turning as she went over and over the conversation, trying to remember everything Drew had said.

Could it possibly be true? Sometimes she convinced herself that they'd got hold of completely the wrong end of the stick, or that Drew had. He was only a child, after all. How could he possibly understand what his father was up to?

But then she would come back to the puzzling, and indisputable existence of the wireless. One that was clearly not British, as Cory had been at pains to point out to her, and Sara could think of no possible reason for a German radio transmitter to be on Hugh's boat.

Would the authorities come right away? Would they wish to interview him or just walk in and arrest him? Or would they simply dismiss the whole thing as a small boy's fantasy?

Perhaps that's all it was. Drew must have got it wrong. Hugh had always seen himself as the town hero, and perhaps that's what he was, after all. Sailing out to France to save stranded British pilots.

Or was that simply a cover for something much more sinister?

So here she was again, right back where she started. Going round and round and very slightly mad.

They came for him just before dawn, their presence heralded by a loud banging on the door and then a crash as they burst it open. Sara was out of bed in a flash, her heart pounding almost as loud as the noise the soldiers were making.

Grabbing her cotton dressing gown, she stood out on the landing and watched in horror at what seemed to be a veritable throng of military police filling her house. They marched up her stairs, crowded in the small hall, and while some were clearly searching the room downstairs, others were already in Hugh's room yelling at him to get dressed, to jump to it.

What seemed to be only moments later they were leading him out, still in his pyjamas though with a raincoat over the top, hands held in a restraint behind his back.

For the briefest second his eyes met hers. 'You've got what you always wanted, Sara, your freedom. Apparently at the expense of mine. I hope you're satisfied.'

She could think of no response. Her teeth seemed to be chattering and Sara felt nothing but an intense cold and a very real desire to vomit.

'Move it!' said the officer in charge.

She clasped hold of the banister rail, as if fearful of falling. Hugh said nothing more as he was ushered out of the house with surprisingly little fuss.

Only when he was gone, and all the guards with him, did the officer turn to address her. 'I'm sorry to have disturbed you, Mrs Marrack.' Then he too was gone and the house echoed with silence.

Sara found she could no longer sustain any strength in her limbs and sank to her knees. Two small pairs of arms came about her neck. 'Mummy, don't cry, Mummy. We're here to help you. We love you, Mummy!'

'What you doing here, girl?' Sadie stood, arms akimbo, filling the doorway with her ample presence.

'They've taken Hugh away. Arrested him. God knows what will happen to him.'

'I think we can guess.'

Would the shaking never stop? When had morning come? She could remember little of the last several hours, since the soldiers had left. Some vomiting, Jenny putting a glass of sherry into her hands. That seemed to be all her children did for her these days. The children. Where were they? Had she sat here all night on the stairs, wrapped in her dressing gown, in shock? She couldn't remember.

How had it come to this? When had Hugh turned traitor, and why? Was his jealousy such that he would let innocent men die simply because they were American?

Sadie had the children. She could hear her mother talking to them downstairs, saying something about how they must be quiet and good for Mummy. Something about Daddy not being well and having to go away for a bit. She could hear Drew's piping voice asking if Grandma would read him some more of Rupert Bear.

Could they forget so easily? Could she hide the reality from them? Dear God, she hoped so.

Cory explained to her later what would happen. Hugh would be tried as a traitor and, if he was found guilty of treason . . . She'd stopped him at that point, didn't wish to consider what would follow such a verdict.

Jealous, unfeeling husband though he might have been, she wouldn't wish such a fate on him, not in a million years.

Drew's childlike confession of his father's secrets were later backed up when connected with a tale told by two surviving American aircrew of a rescue attempt that had gone badly wrong for them. The boat had apparently not spotted them, or at least had turned to leave at the crucial moment, resulting in the drowning of several of their comrades.

Evidence was also found among Hugh's belongings of petty pilfering. Officers returned to search his room, and The Ship, and several items were found in his possession which had clearly been 'lifted' from ships where he was present to supposedly rescue the crew. Looting, wasn't that what they called it?

Nor was Iris with her mother. She hadn't been seen since earlier in the summer when she'd been spotted heading out to sea in Hugh's boat. It could only be surmised that something dreadful had happened to her and, when challenged, Hugh had apparently admitted it. He agreed that they had indeed been lovers, and confessed to having 'tossed her in the water', declaring that she'd got what she deserved, since she'd not kept her word over the money.

What a terrible death, to be drowned by your lover.

It was the final, damning evidence. Within hours he'd been

transported out of Fowey to Exeter jail where he would be tried, and no doubt convicted of murder and treason. His final words to Sara that she had gained her freedom at the expense of his, rang in her head, proving to be cruelly accurate.

But what kind of freedom could it be without Charlie? He'd caught his train and left, knowing nothing of this, hadn't he?

What was worse, Sara hadn't the first idea where he lived, or how she could contact him. Somewhere in Boston, that was all she knew.

Another morning, another day to get through. Sadie again, hovering in the kitchen, making beans on toast for the children. Trying to do something to help and getting under her feet. Sara wished her mother would go home and leave her to cry in peace, to wallow in her misery. Instead, she kept asking stupid questions. 'Aren't you going to do something?'

'What can I do?'

'You could go and find him?'

'Find who?'

'Don't play dumb with me, girl, I'm yer mam. You know who I'm talking about. Your Yank. Aren't you going to find him and tell him what's happened?'

'Charlie's gone. Caught his train last night, yesterday afternoon, I don't remember, but he's gone back to the US.'

'No, he ain't, none of 'em have. They're all still up at Windmill having a knees up.'

'What?'

'I heard they weren't leaving till tomorrow night.'

'Oh, my God. Mind the children, will you?' Sara was out of the door without waiting for her mother's response, running along the Esplanade, up Daglands Road, slowing to a walk up the steep incline as she ran out of breath.

She reached what was left of the camp, but he wasn't there. She asked everyone she could find but nobody had seen him.

Most of the marines had gone home and only a few remained, clearing up the mess, taking down tents and some of the Nissen huts, although many were being kept, temporarily, local housing being in short supply.

Sara walked back down the hill much slower than she'd run up it, more despondent than ever. She should've known that Sadie would get it wrong. When had her mother ever got anything right in her entire life?

She must simply accept that she'd lost him. He'd given her the chance to go with him and she'd refused, wouldn't even exchange addresses so that they could write. So there wasn't the slightest possibility of her being able to contact him. He was lost to her forever, and serve her right.

In despair, and unable to face her mother, or even her children feeling so low, Sara instinctively turned right when she reached the Esplanade, and headed towards Readymoney beach. She walked past the sign declaring parts of the beach open but still warning about mines, up the coastal path through the woods and out onto the headland.

St Catherine's Castle, or fort as some liked to call it, was still shrouded in camouflage, just as it had been throughout the war. She remembered how ghostly it had appeared on that fateful dawn when she'd watched the huge armada of ships leave. She'd felt such pride in that moment, and such fear. If only she'd come to him that night, been able to see him off properly.

Now she felt a great sense of loss.

Sara stood on the headland, the breeze lifting her silver hair and looked out to sea. It made her think of the Atlantic Ocean, when they'd been in Marazion, and of Bette. She prayed that she was safe, and happy with Chad, that one day they would all be together again, reunited as a family.

'It seems that all the people I love are now in America.'

'I'm not, I'm still here, in Fowey. And I'd stay, if you wanted me to. If they'd let me.'

Sara whirled about and there he was, emerging out of the woods before her very eyes. She could scarcely find voice to say his name but he was smiling at her, taking her hands in his, warming them, making her heart soar with love for him.

'I hoped you might come here, as you once promised you would.'

'Oh, Charlie, I was just wishing that I had. Hugh . . .'

'I know, I've heard about Hugh. I'm sorry. Not particularly surprised, but sorry for you, that it should come to this.'

'I'm not sorry for me. It's a terrible thing to say but I'm free, Charlie. I'm free. Do you realise? He's set me free by his own hand, by his cruel jealousy and greed. He can't control me any more. I'm free to be with you now, if you still want me.'

She didn't hear his reply. His mouth had found something far more important to do than speak. But then, there'd be plenty of time to talk later.